Corporate Cthulhu

Lovecraftian Tales of Bureaucratic Nightmare

Edited by Edward Stasheff

with stories by

Charlie Allison
Justin Bailey
John M. Campbell
L Chan
Jeff Deck
Evan Dicken
Todd H.C. Fischer
Ethan Gibney

Marcus Johnston
Gordon Linzner
Adrian Ludens
Marie Michaels
Adam Millard
Harry Pauff
Pete Rawlik
Sam Rent

Andrew Scott
Max D. Stanton
Josh Storey
David Tallerman
John Taloni
Darren Todd
DJ Tyrer
Wile E. Young

eBook available at:

Amazon Kindle Store: http://tinyurl.com/CorpCthulhu-kindle

Barnes & Noble Nook: http://tinyurl.com/CorpCthulhu-nook

Google Play: http://tinyurl.com/CorpCthulhu-google

Apple iBooks: http://tinyurl.com/CorpCthulhu-apple

Kobo eBookstore: http://tinyurl.com/CorpCthulhu-kobo

TRIGGER WARNING

This is a collection of horror stories. They are intended to shock, disturb, and offend.

This book contains profanity and descriptions of monsters, insanity, elder abuse, violence (including against women), suicide, human sacrifice, cannibalism, nudity, and—although there are no graphic descriptions—there are references to sex.

Young and/or sensitive readers are advised to proceed with caution, or to avoid this book altogether.

Consider yourself warned.

ACKNOWLEDGEMENTS

Special thanks to Gordon Linzner, who organized the Corporate Cthulhu Reading fundraiser at the Lovecraft Bar in Manhattan, to Faith L. Justice who presented the event, and to Charlie Allison, Justin Bailey, and Max D. Stanton who read their stories before a live audience.

Thanks also to Darren Hughes, Christopher Lee Spencer, J.L. Benet, Cedar Sanderson, and Michales Joy, who promoted our Kickstarter on their blogs and social media. It made a difference.

But most of all, thanks to all our backers who donated hard-earned cash to bring this anthology to life:

Achab
Alex & Lisa Way
Alex Thaler
Alice Berkson
Allison Oleynik
Andy Donald
Anna Truwe
Ashley Cser
Ao-Hui Lin
Benjamin Rees
Benjamin & Tiffany Moore
Bernard Cooper
Bob L. Shirley
Bob Q. Rublic
Brandon Carter
Caitlin Campbell
Cal Kotz
Cameron Pryde
Eric Knudsen

Carlos Alberto Morote Bernal
Catherine Falconwing
Charlotte Kenyon
Cheri Harlan
Chris Basler
Christopher L. Spencer
Christopher "Vulpine" Kalley
Christopher Yarwood
CJ Zehmeister
Cornelis Holtkamp
Dakota Klaes & Adam Everist
David Bowerman
David Cantrell
David Starner
Debora Lustgarten
Donald Saxman
Dreaming Cthulhu
Eleanore Stasheff
le4ne

Eric Nadeau
Eric Priehs
Eva García Molina
Evalyn Warden Yanna
Felix
Gideon Kalve Jarvis
GMarkC
Hank Roberts
Hannah Rothman
Henri Desbois
Hugh Thompson
Isaac Chappell
James McKelvey
James Nelson
Janet McGowan
Jared Foley
Jason Technocrat Wilkes
Jeannette Ng
Jeffrey A. Johnson
Jim Stasheff
Joe Kontor
Joerg Sterner
John Bowen
John Davidson
John Matzavrakos
John Teehan
John Young
Jonathan Boles
Jonathan Ensor
Jowell Super Nurse
Kari Keller
Kevin Leib
Kevin "Wolf" Patti
King Heiple
Lauren Holmes
Laurie Reid

Linda D Addison
Linda Daives
LMF Yates
Lou Collobert
M. Becker
Madelyn Carey
Marc Margelli
Margaret Miller
Mark Froom
Mark Lukens
Mark Thompson
Martin Hohner
Martin Nørskov Jensen
Martin Tomasek
Matt Kohls
Matthew Carpenter
Maybelline A.
Melanie Fischer
Michael Cieslak and Dragon's Roost Press
Michael Douglas
Michael Vermilye
Miguel Leon
Mike & Andrea Coleman
Mike Rael
Mitch Harding
Moses Lambert
Nathan Campbell
Nathaniel Sickler
Nina O'Loughlin
Olivia Wong
Paul A. Maconi, Jr.
Paul y cod asyn Jarman
Pedro Alfaro
Robert Lusteck
Stephen A Hertz

Rob Voss
Roger Strahl
Russel Dalenberg
Samuel Lamb
Sarah Gesell
Scott Dicken
Scott Kuban
Scott Maynard
Sean Venning
Sébastien Derivaux
Shane McCammon
Shanna Magnuson
Shannon Beaty
Shari Mahon
Shawn Polka
Stephanie Gagnon
Stephen Mouring

Steven Mentzel
Steven Saus
Syndi & Rowyn Lovell
Thavron Solutions
Thea Flurry
Thomas Scott
Tim Lonegan
T'om Cth'irby (Thomas Kirby)
Tom Edwards
Tonja Condray Klein
Tristan Clapp
Ursula the Sea Witch
Valerie Robertson
Will Linden
Wingate Steitz
Xander Drax

To Ben Monroe
and the folks at Chaosium,
who reignited my love for Lovecraft

and

To the Memory of Alan Fulton Barksdale

TABLE OF CONTENTS

Introduction:

THE INVISIBLE TENTACLE

by Nicholas Nacario

"Corporations are people, my friend!" – Willard Mitt Romney

Corporations were originally created as chartered entities of a state to carry out a single task such as creating trade abroad, building infrastructure, or providing a service for the public. Their original intentions could be seen as good, trying to better humanity instead of harming it. Over time, however, they have deformed into the monstrosities that we are doomed to coexist with. They are strange entities; they have the same rights as we do but, they do not live and breathe or act as we do.

You are not one of them. They are not one of us. Tax breaks, bailouts, they seem to be part of an exclusive powerful group, right? You, meanwhile, are merely a tendril of a gigantic entity that only cares about its continuous growth and influence. A single unit of a cult(ure) that is uncaring about its members or its environment. You may be sacrificed so that the gods can continue to grow. You may be driven to madness while trying to complete a task for your overseer. But, you also may be promised the ability to rise to the rank of high priest, if you are devoted enough.

Starvation wages, environmental pollution, dangerous de-fective products … do they really have the world's best interest at heart? Could this evil be the work of just mankind? Possibly. What is a given is that it has been built on the backs of humanity. People just like you, day in and day out. This monster doesn't run just on money, but on your sweat, anxiety, and those restless mornings at the job where the only thing keeping you going is caffeine and looking forward to that precious time off. Where you can relax. Escape.

But you cannot escape. You need a paycheck in order to pay your bills and keep a roof over your head. We need their products and services to maintain our lifestyles. We need the entertainment that they create in order to de-stress at the end of the day. "The Invisible Hand" that Adam Smith proclaimed would control the markets through supply and demand has grown to squeeze the entire world into its fist. Or … is it a tentacle? Does this sound a little familiar?

The Great Old Ones of H.P. Lovecraft's Cthulhu Mythos are a group of uncaring beasts that have traveled from unseen planes of existence to influence our world and its denizens. They have lain hidden for millennia until the Stars Are Right and their restraints become unbound. Once they are free, they are prophesied to destroy the world to make it suitable for themselves. How often have we heard horror stories about corrupt Banana Republics where entire countries were beholden to companies' interests? What will the Citizens United v. FEC decision and the subsequent creation of Super PACs mean for America in the long-term?

Cultists worship these "deities" with such fervor that they are willing to go to extreme lengths to display their devotion: insanity, death, and destruction. How often have we heard about riots over some limited edition item? Or how the early Black Friday years were mired with reports of injuries and violence? How often does brand devotion play into the shopping trends of the American consumer?

Capitalist greed, corporate culture, and the Cthulhu Mythos have many commonalities between them. The existential dread that comes with every Monday morning could be comparable to the terror one faces when confronted by cosmic horror: one is totally insignificant and helpless. You've picked up this anthology because you agree with this assertion; perhaps your own job is so mind-numbingly dull that you feel like your mind is trapped in a Mi-Go braincase, or maybe the Board of Directors of your employer are the unseen beings that determine your fate. Nevertheless, these stories are sure to entertain, enlighten, and possibly empathize with your situation.

Follow an auditor in *Shadow Charts* to determine if the discrepancies in a private hospital's records are a clerical error or something more sinister. See the extent that a company will go to in order to find the perfect brand logo in *Boedromion Noumenia*. Learn why the turnover rate for temp work is so high in *Casual Friday*. Find out what happens to Innsmouth when it becomes a company town in *Esoteric Insurance, Inc.* What does the *Facilities Management at Dagocorp HQ* do to keep the employees comfortable and happy? Discover the dark trade secret to keeping employees from leaving for greener pastures in *Career Zombie*. Investigate the reason why the employees of Delapore Chemical have been disappearing in *Forced Labor*. Discover the dire consequences of artificially recreating the Shining Trapezohedron in *It Came from I.T.* Imagine how a statue of a Great Old One can change the corporate culture of an office in *Like a Good Neighbor*. What are *Maryanne's Equations* and why are they concerning her coworker?

Find out what depths a whistleblower will go through to unearth company secrets in *No Doves Comes from Raven Eggs*. Experience a ship crew's *Refusal* to their employer's wishes to travel across cursed oceans. Read about the *Retraction* from a scientific journal that causes uproar among the community. Unearth the dark secret of *The God Under the Church*. Speculate about resource mining in hyper-dimensional space in *The Loponine Exploitation*. Why does the architecture of the headquarters for *Tindalos, Inc.* have such strange angles? Endure a company orientation in *Welcome to the R'lyeh Corporation*. Witness the horrors of union-busting in *Wholesome Labor*. Fight alongside futuristic private armies on the hunt for monsters in *Apotheosis*. Laugh with delight from a modern-day parody of Dagon set in a corporation, *Dagon-Tec*. Read the EssentialSalts brochure as the company starts their *Festival Preparations*. Dodge the different factions in a department store war in *Clean Up Aisle Four*. Observe the shady dealings that go on to keep a multinational corporation's powerful leader's identity a secret in *Incorporation*. Enjoy the improvements that come with a corporate buyout in *The Shadows Lengthen in the Close* ... until the price for a better life must be paid.

So take off your work uniform, let your hair down, pour yourself a well-earned libation and sit in a comfortable chair to read *Corporate Cthulhu*. Hopefully it will serve as a brief escape from the dull monotony of the workweek, and maybe shed some light on the possibilities of why our society could possibly be destroying itself for the sake of increased growth and revenue.

Given the times that we currently find ourselves, is it any wonder why people look at corporate America and ask themselves, "What the fhtagn is going on?"

DEATH PLEDGE

by Jeff Deck

Bakersfield, California

The guy's name was Landry Howe, and he was supposed to be an accountant. Wife and two kids, no history of mental illness in his family. He was dressed like an accountant, too, stripes of his tie clashing with the plaid of his shirt. But he sure wasn't acting like an accountant.

"All the gates are opening," Howe said, scratching at the flesh of his own hand with his fingernails. It was already pitted with gouges and scars.

"What gates?" Brenda asked.

She leaned on the table, trying to get a closer look at him, but he kept looking down. The bank had transported the Howe family to this "interview facility" for Brenda to debrief. She was a fixer, one of the bank's best. First, though, she needed to know what she had to fix.

"We are all stained with the filth of the unholy dimensions," Howe said. "I am stained, June is stained, children—stained. The stain started in the yard, in the house, and it, it, it, it spread."

"Is that why you defaulted on your mortgage?" she asked.

"If I touch you, will you be stained too?" the accountant said, opening his eyes wider than Brenda thought possible. She half-expected them to pop out onto the table. "Give me your hand."

"No, thank you," Brenda said. "Why did you stop paying your mortgage?"

"Because he's fucking nuts, obviously," Matt put in. He was a vice president that the bank had assigned to work with Brenda on her investigation into the rash of defaults nationwide. Vice president of what, Brenda couldn't recall, but he exhibited the typical C-suite personality: impatient machismo and an utter lack of imagination.

He nudged her shoulder. "We're wasting our time here."

" 'Nuts' is not specific enough," she said. "We've got a whole bagful of nuts by now. I need to know what tree they fell from, Matt."

"Give me your *hand!*" Howe suddenly shrieked, and surged across the table, grabbing her. Brenda recoiled with disgust. She didn't feel any "stain." Just the horror of touching someone who'd lost not just his mind, but everything else too.

She ripped herself free and then Matt, overreacting, slammed into the poor bastard. Howe didn't even cry out, as if he didn't feel the pain. Brenda shouted for Matt to stop just after he landed the first punch.

"Is this how you treat the mentally ill?" she asked her partner.

He coughed. "Only the ones who deserve it. Sorry." He withdrew from the accountant, who seemed to have lost all interest in spreading his stain, as well as in the conversation. Howe's gaze fixed on the wall.

"The house itself," Brenda said. "They all talk about their houses, as if it's the houses' fault they can't pay their mortgages anymore. We need to go to the Howe house and check it out for ourselves."

"We've still got the rest of the family to interview," Matt said.

"Do you really want to do this again?" Brenda asked, indicating Howe and his mutilated hands. "Do you want to hear kids talking like this? I've heard enough. Let's go to the house."

"Juhasz isn't going to like it," he said.

She waved away any objections her boss might offer up. "That's why we don't tell him beforehand," Brenda said, grabbing her purse.

Grosse Pointe, Michigan

It was a cloudy, cold day when Brenda and Matt drove into Howe's neighborhood, a wealthy street full of Tudor revival architecture and gentle shade trees.

"What burns me is that these people have no sense of personal *responsibility*," Matt was saying. "A mortgage is a pledge you make. I mean, it's what 'mortgage' literally means. If you break your promises, what does that say about your character?"

"If our bank made its money by shorting the mortgage market," Brenda answered, "would we even be having this conversation?"

She'd sensed something was off about the area long before she arrived at the Howe house. Would she call it a *stain*? Perhaps not; that reeked a little too much of religion. Call it, instead, an instability. A disorder. A flaw, seated somewhere deep but worming its way out.

Matt was coughing as she stopped the car. He reached for his water bottle and took a long swig. "Ugh."

"You okay?" she asked.

"Yeah, just feel like—we didn't go through some kind of altitude change, did we? I get plane-sick, and this is kind of how I feel when I fl—" He interrupted himself with a flow of vomit, splashing all over the interior of the rental car's passenger-side door and the closed window. Immediately the stink filled the car.

Brenda rolled down her window before she asked him if he was all right.

He nodded, his face pale. "Sorry. Think I just need some fresh air." Matt opened the door, his fingers slipping on the barf-slick handle, and stumbled out.

Despite the smell, Brenda wasn't eager to leave the car. She could see already, through the windshield, that there was something wrong with Landry Howe's house. Every time she tried to look at it directly, her eyes crossed until she felt like she, too, might evacuate the contents of her stomach. The lines of the house didn't add up. They didn't stay still.

"Well, I've come this far," she growled at herself, not wanting to allow Matt to take the lead. She opened up her purse, grimacing at the drops of puke that dripped onto her fingers, and rummaged through the contents until she found her prize: a box of motion sickness pills that she'd bought for a boat trip a couple of years ago and never ended up using. Perfect. She swigged the pills down with some water and then got out to face the Howe house.

Or, rather, not face it directly, because that was just asking for trouble, but to keep her eyes trained on the pavement as she approached the front door with Howe's keys in hand.

She thought she could hear a phone ringing. Or multiple phones.

"What—the fuck is *wrong* with this place?" asked Matt, staggering behind her.

"Everything," said Brenda. "Look away."

He did as she said, but then shook his head. He sank to his knees and put his hands over his face. "The other houses too. They're dancing, they move. Every goddamn house. Must be me, then."

"No," Brenda said, fitting the key into the lock. "Carter Investments bought up mortgages in this whole neighborhood. And they were all bad. There's something wrong with *all* these houses."

"Sorry to wuss out," Matt gasped, "but I've gotta stay out here. I can't."

She cast a pitiless look in his direction. "Take pictures of the outside, if you can. Look away as you're taking them, if you need to. Document this. And call Juhasz. We may need a ride out of here by the time we're done."

"How about we just leave *now* and drive ourselves?"

Brenda said, "Do your job," and walked into the house alone.

The house had a landline, and it was ringing. Brenda's smartphone began to ring too. She glanced down: *Restricted number.* Could be Juhasz, wondering where the hell she'd gone.

"Hello?" she said into the phone.

And a growly, wet voice answered her: "*YOG. Yoggg. YOG. Yoggg....*"

She ended the call, dropped her phone, and immediately it began ringing again.

She staggered, reached for the wall. It wasn't quite where she expected it to be. The house was the picture of upper-middle-class Midwestern living, right down to the bland paintings of flowers hanging over the couch and the little white porcelain figures displayed on a shelf. But that picture had been wrinkled by sweaty hands. Colors bled. Angles didn't match up. The floor was treacherous under Brenda's feet.

She tried to distract herself from what she saw by turning inward. Carter Investments had shorted the mortgage bond market, while everyone else, including Brenda's bank, bet on its stability. Sure, a few people would default on their mortgages, but overall it was supposed to be solid. Especially in tony neighborhoods like this one. Yet somehow Carter Investments knew that the mortgages here in Grosse Pointe, and in certain other cities around the U.S., would turn into liabilities. How? There was nothing outwardly wrong with this neighborhood besides the unstable dimensions of the houses. On paper this was the polar opposite of a high-risk area.

Obviously something terrible had happened to this place, now that she was seeing it for herself. Something that had—

stained—

—corrupted the houses, infected them. And it had driven the owners mad, which in turn had driven the whole neighborhood into mortgage default (and enriched Carter Investments). But what could the corruption be? This went way beyond a radon leak or toxic mold.

Brenda opened her eyes and decided to make a dash through the house, to the sliding glass doors that led into the backyard. Nausea gripped her by the throat as she ran, and fell, and picked herself up and ran again. She fell again, smashing into the glass door, spreading a spiderweb of cracks across the surface. Her nose was bleeding, but she hadn't even hit it against the glass.

The phones were still ringing.

She closed her eyes again, reached for the handle blind. That was better. As she opened the door and tumbled into the backyard, she thought about the stories she'd heard late at night at investor conferences, murmured with a half-smile by drunken peers, as if the hint of a grin gave the teller sufficient remove.

Cults. Cultists that opened doors to … other places. Sometimes there was even a name, a horrible, guttural name: *Yog-Sothoth.*

And maybe in some of those other places, the geometry was just—wrong. Say that instead of existing in three dimensions plus time, their houses had five, six, seven dimensions. Say that these places operated by rules we could never hope to understand.

If those doors had been opened, would it not be reasonable to expect the stain to spread?

No. Not a stain. No, a difference, a flaw.

She was on her hands and knees in the grass, still unwilling to open her eyes because she did not feel better at all. In fact, she felt worse, and now even denying herself sight was an insufficient defense against the madness of this place.

"Matt!" she hollered. "*Matt!*"

He would not come. He was too sick and weak to come. And she'd never expected to rely on him anyway. Brenda opened one eye and saw the *hole* in front of her, set into the fence of the Howes' backyard. The hole was a passage of fire. It opened into a place whose incomprehensibility immediately struck Brenda blind in her open eye.

She kept her other eye jammed shut and turned away, scuttling for the glass doors still open into the house.

During her frantic, disoriented retreat through the Howe

house, Brenda passed her partner. Matt was lying dead on the living room floor with blood streaming from his eyes and mouth. He'd heard her after all, had tried to come for her. Brenda left him, scooped up her bleating phone, and fell out on the front stoop, down the short flight of concrete stairs, and crawled over the driveway to the car. It was raining now.

Somehow Brenda managed to lift herself into the driver's seat, turn on the car, and reverse out of the driveway, through her pain and seeing in two dimensions max. She drove onto the street. A few houses down, she hit a tree. She reversed, extracting the car from the tree, and continued to drive until she'd reached a safe distance from the Howes' neighborhood.

Her phone had stopped ringing. Brenda could still only see out of one eye, but the madness and agony that besieged the rest of her had subsided. She called Juhasz.

Carter Investments, 20th Floor, New York, New York

The secretary outside Craig Beebe's office looked away when Brenda approached. Even when Brenda spoke, the young woman still wouldn't look her in the face.

"Mr. Beebe is running behind with his meetings," she said to the African violets on her desk. "And you're early. Mr. Kingston and Ms. Nutt are still speaking with him in his office. Won't you have a seat?"

"No," Brenda said. She hadn't been sleeping well, and her patience had run dry.

At this, the secretary did look up at her. And cringed. "I'm sorry," she said, casting her eyes down again, "b-but you'll have to wait. Mr. Kingston and Ms. Nutt are the CEO and CFO of Carter Investments, respectively, and they won't—"

"Good," said Brenda, "I'd like them to be here for our meeting as well." She motioned to the two men who'd accompanied her here. They were both well dressed, the picture of Wall Street professionals, but they weren't here for business acumen. They led the way into Beebe's office. The secretary reached under her desk, doubtless to hit a panic button.

Brenda entered the office close behind her bodyguards. From her vantage point behind the wall of expensively tailored meat, she could hear but not see the outraged exclamations from the Carter bigwigs turn to gasps of dismay as her colleagues revealed the guns at their sides.

The bodyguards parted to allow Brenda her dramatic appearance. "Hello, Craig," she said. "Won't you introduce me to your friends?"

"This is absolutely unacceptable," Beebe sputtered. He was a thin, pale-eyed specimen with nervous, fluttering hands, not at all what Brenda had expected. He was a vice president of something or other, which reminded her of poor old Matt, but that was where the resemblance ended. "Carter security is on its way now, and we *will* involve the police."

The other man, a golden-haired jock type who must have been the CEO, Kingston, remained calm even as Nutt and Beebe played up how affronted they were. In fact, he even had the temerity to smile at Brenda. "Yo, ho, ho," he said.

She fingered her eyepatch, simmering with anger. "Funny guy, huh?" she said. She twisted it upward to reveal the pupilless, sightless yellow monstrosity she used to call her left eye. Kingston flinched. Nutt yelped. Beebe turned away from her, putting his hands over his face.

"I'm Brenda Roux," she said, "but Craig here could have told you that. I think he finally figured out who I am. And which bank I work for. We don't appreciate getting screwed by secretly subprime bundles while you bet against the mortgage market, Craig. You had insider info. Not only did you bribe the ratings agencies, but you knew which properties have been stained by gates to Yuggoth."

There was that word again, *stained*. Howe's word. She thought it, used it in conversation, dreamed it far more often than she intended.

"You shouldn't have gone there," Beebe said, only reluctantly uncovering his face. "I heard what happened in Grosse

Pointe. If you suspected the least part of it … you would have been wiser not to go there."

Brenda took a step toward him. Her bodyguards stuck close. "How did you know where the cults were operating?" she asked. "How did you know which mortgages would go belly up thanks to gate-induced madness?"

The CEO and CFO hadn't shown a hint of surprise at the words *cults*, *gate*, or *madness*. So this hadn't been Beebe going rogue. The entire leadership of Carter Investments was wrapped up in this scam.

"Don't tell her a damn thing, Craig," Nutt said.

Brenda nodded at one of her bodyguards, the one who called himself Jim. He drew with incredible speed and put a hole in the chief financial officer's fine leather shoe. She screamed and fell backward in her pain. Kingston and Beebe were white with fear.

"Tell her all the damn things, Craig," Brenda suggested.

"We have an inside line," Beebe said. "One of their, ehrm, high priests. He—"

Three men crowded into the office with their own guns drawn and trained on the intruders, barking commands to stand down. Brenda answered the questioning glance from her bodyguards with a hand gesture to lay down their weapons as the Carter security guys were asking.

"We can go," she said, "but our next stop will be the *Times* building. We've got a hell of a story we can give them."

She saw the calculations on the chief executive officer's face and continued: "And if you're wondering if you can dump three bodies and get away with it, don't bother. My boss Mr. Juhasz will be sending the cops to your doorstep if I don't report back in within half an hour. Unless the thought of that doesn't bother you? I recall your eagerness to involve the cops just a few minutes ago."

Kingston sighed. "Security, relax. We're all friends here." He cast a contemptuous look at the whimpering CFO and added, "Why don't one of you get her a first aid kit or something."

"You were saying?" Brenda directed to Beebe. "About the high priest?"

"He was very willing to share with us the locations of his cult's activities," the man said. "He figured that their gate-summoning would turn many mortgages subprime in short order—and that a sufficiently visionary company could make a killing with that knowledge. Naturally he came to us here at Carter."

"But why give *you* that info? Death cults aren't usually that generous. Especially not the cult of Yog-Sothoth."

Beebe's eyes widened. "Don't say that name here. Creeps me out."

"So? What did the high priest want from you?"

Beebe glanced at the chief exec, who could only shrug. "Not much," Beebe went on. "I mean, in proportion to what he was giving us. He asked only to use one floor of our tower to host members of his cult here in the city."

Brenda's blood turned frigid. "*This* tower? The one we're standing in right now?"

"That's right," said Beebe, looking at her with plain confusion.

"Oh, you fools," she said.

Beebe's phone started ringing. His secretary's phone started ringing. Everyone in the room who had a cell phone in their pocket felt it vibrating or heard it chiming.

And then all the lights in the office went out, leaving them to see only by the wan grayness of the late afternoon outside.

Brenda had come to Carter Investments expecting only to recover the money that her bank had lost betting on a stained mortgage market. And, perhaps, to extract literal eye-for-an-eye justice from Craig Beebe with the help of the pliers in her pocket.

She had not come to Carter Investments intending to save the world. Indeed, when she learned that the Yog-Sothoth cult had made their headquarters in the Carter tower, her first thought was to take her bodyguards and exit the building as quickly as possible.

But, upon further reflection—and for Brenda, there was *always* further reflection—she realized that the end of the world would be bad for business. Juhasz would not be pleased with her if she left the seeds of Armageddon to sprout.

So, reluctantly, she had led the party down the seven flights of stairs to the floor that the Yog-Sothoth cult had commandeered. Each time they passed the door to another floor, she could hear a multitude of office phones endlessly screaming. The lights were out in the stairwell, just like the power in the rest of the building, so they were forced to use their smartphones—also still ringing without end—to illuminate their path.

"It keeps saying *Yog*," Kingston had said in disgust, hanging up his phone and shoving the jangling thing in his pocket.

"They all say *Yog*," she said. "Just ignore them." But it was like trying to ignore a wailing baby or a knock on the door; the lizard brain rebelled.

The door from the stairwell was locked, but Kingston's master key gave them access. Now Brenda found herself walking into the lobby of the thirteenth floor with the anxious duo of Kingston and Beebe at her side. Her muscle and the Carter security team had taken point, but they were all looking to her for leadership.

Candles lit the dark lobby. A single cultist stood guard at the doors to the office suite. She was young and unarmed, and she quickly raised her hands at the sight of four guns. Brenda motioned for her to sit at the receptionist's desk.

"How many are in there?" Brenda asked her.

"No more than fifteen," the cultist said, "but you will die. The Outer God is coming." She was a pretty young woman; Brenda couldn't help but wonder what had led her into an apocalyptic cult.

That would be a mystery to solve some other time. "Don't move from that seat or we will kill you," Brenda said, then turned her attention back to the others.

"Don't look directly at the gate, if there is one," she told them, not for the first time.

Her bodyguards barreled through the lobby doors and into the business suite: backwards, heads down. And Brenda herself still couldn't help looking straight into the suite, just for a second.

She saw no gate, but she did see a dozen people standing in a circle around a conference table, mostly men. To her disappointment, they were not wearing robes. Didn't all cultists have to wear robes? The room, too, was underwhelming for the site of an interdimensional summoning. The darkness helped set the mood a little, but only a couple of wall hangings featuring the imagery of a cluster of white globes, two discount-store candelabras, and a smattering of vanilla-scented candles distinguished the place from an ordinary office.

Well, that and the corpse on the conference table: a grey-haired man in a tangle of twisted limbs, staring up at the ceiling with eyes that didn't see.

"Miller?" Beebe protested. "You people killed Miller? I thought he was in Thailand."

"Game's over," Brenda said, hollering to make herself heard over the cacophony of phones. "Desist all portal summoning immediately."

"You're too late," said a bearded man in a red sweater. He wore a necklace with, oddly, a cluster of pearls for its pendant. The high priest? "We've just completed the final rites and made our sacrifice. In moments Our Father Yog-Sothoth will open His mouth. Then the armies of the Mi-Go will pour through all the gates we've prepared across the nation. There is nothing you can do to stop Him."

And now Brenda did see something opening on the blank white wall behind the cultists, which they had cleared of cubicles and cabinets and photocopiers. Just a shimmer now, but expanding. The suggestion of a writhing at the center. The eye under her patch itched.

"You really screwed me, Dave," Beebe snapped at the man with the necklace. "And you killed Miller!"

"Look away," she said, turning her head, gesturing frantically at the two Carter executives, their security men, and her bodyguards. "It's happening!"

They all took her advice, except for the CEO, Kingston. He kept staring ahead as if to defy her. After all, she was only the crazy pirate lady. Yo, ho, ho.

"How can we close it?" Craig Beebe yelled at her.

"You're the one who gave them a lease in your building!" she shouted back.

But she *did* have an idea, after all. She hadn't expected to find the cult *here*—but she had done her share of reading up on the Outer God that the cult sought to summon into this world. She had requisitioned certain forbidden books and pored through certain forbidden internet forums.

The cultists believed that this world had grown decadent with corruption and cruelty, and needed to be cleansed. (Which, now that she thought about it, explained why they'd chosen a tower on Wall Street to complete their ceremony.) They worshiped Yog-Sothoth because they believed he was the Father of Gates, the one who could open portals to other worlds to destroy the Earth.

Apparently Yog-Sothoth had answered their prayers with a number of direct connections to the dark planet Yuggoth, which the alien warrior race the Mi-Go called home. Yuggoth was the place that had half-blinded Brenda on sight.

Most helpful to know was the fact that Yog-Sothoth fed on the dead, not the living. Every sacrifice the cultists made to open a gate was a creature—or person—that the cultists had already killed. Death, not life, was what Yog-Sothoth required to open the higher planes.

"March him to the far wall," she ordered her bodyguards,

indicating Beebe. "Do it walking backwards. Do not look behind you."

"Hey, what is this?" Craig Beebe said. "No, fuck you very much." When he saw the bodyguards approaching him, he said, "Security, stop them!"

"Security, do *not* stop them," Kingston countermanded. "In fact, help them get there. Cover each other. You'll all be walking backwards but you'll see anyone coming up behind your partners. Shoot to kill."

The two Carter security men looked scared, but not scared enough. They hadn't been briefed on who these cultists were or what they were doing; if they knew, they might have fled. Instead, they nodded and flanked Brenda's bodyguards. And now Beebe's face shone with terror.

"What the *fuck*, Doug?" he screamed at Kingston.

"This is your mess, Craig," the CEO replied, still facing forward. His expression had curled into a manic smile. "You need to clean it up."

The four security men began to escort Beebe to the front of the room. And Brenda risked a diagonal look over her shoulder to see the cultists springing to action. They had no weapons; they hadn't expected an assault on their sanctum. But they still had their own bodies to defend the growing gate. They could kick at soft parts and gouge eyes and squeeze necks.

"Incoming," she called.

One particular ringtone grew louder in her ears, surpassing the others. She turned her head just in time to see the young woman from the lobby running at her, wielding a hole puncher. Wetwork wasn't Brenda's specialty by any means, and her reflexes were still crippled by the horror of Grosse Pointe. But she still managed to duck the cultist's swing.

Brenda scrabbled in her pocket for the pliers and clamped them savagely on the young woman's soft belly as her adversary completed swinging the hole puncher. The cultist doubled over in pain, screeching. Brenda kicked her in the head and she fell and stopped moving.

Stained. They're all stained.

Gunshots rang out. Brenda heard the cultists die in droves as the security men advanced. Brenda's bodyguard Reed let out a choking cry at one point, but bullets quickly addressed whoever was assaulting him. She still dared not look behind her, even as an unnerving growl issued from the far end of the room. One of the Carter security men swore. Craig Beebe was screaming for mercy.

"Push him through," Brenda said.

"Oh! It's gorgeous," said Kingston, sweat pouring down his face. His eyes were bulging, and he did not blink.

"Last chance to look away, asshole," she told him, now thoroughly exasperated.

A final shriek issued from Craig Beebe. That would hopefully be the moment the security men shoved him into the gate. The growl became a roar that hit her with concussive force.

The floor leapt at Brenda's face. She flung up an arm as she fell.

Her back ached, but she could still pick herself up. The first thing she saw was the Carter CEO hunched into a little ball with his hands clutching his knees. His golden hair had turned paper-white and his eyes were grey and withered. He was gibbering to himself in a low voice.

The phones had all gone quiet. That was a sweet mercy.

Brenda turned from Kingston. The gate was gone, and so was Craig Beebe. The four security men were just getting to their feet. Between them and her was a field of corpses. But it seemed that one cultist, at least, had chosen not to throw his life away. The young man was staggering to his knees; his eyes were normal-looking, so he hadn't watched the Outer God take offense at the living sacrifice of Beebe.

"It doesn't end, you know," he told her, sounding out of breath. "You didn't harm Yog-Sothoth in the slightest. It will find others to call to, and the cycle will start again. Someday soon, someone will bring the armies of the Mi-Go into this world."

"You?" Brenda asked.

The young cultist chuckled without mirth and shook his head. "No, I'm just a pledge. I wasn't even brave enough to kill myself trying to stop you. I think I'm not cut out for this line of work."

"Consider seeing a career counselor, then."

"You're not going to kill me?"

"Heavens, no," Brenda said. "Look at this shambles. We're going to need *someone* to turn over to the authorities; I refuse to get stuck with all of the paperwork. You'll tell the police how your little club, driven insane by drug use and too much internet surfing, attacked these brave men on sight, who were forced to shoot them in self-defense."

A weird cackling coming from her left reminded her that CEO Kingston did not quite fit that story in his present state, but she would think of some way to fit him in. She would fix the narrative; she always did. That was why Juhasz valued her so highly.

While the two Carter security guys puzzled over the transformation of their boss, repeating his name in growing alarm, Brenda went to her bodyguards and touched each of them in turn. She recalled that physical contact was one way to express genuine concern. "Thank you, you did well," she said. "Are you all right?"

"Fine," said Reed, rubbing at ugly red marks on his neck, "but ... Ms. Roux, where did he *go*? And what was trying to come through?!"

"That's above your pay grade," she said. She could only wish it was above hers.

Bakersfield, California

Brenda was back in her own bed in her own austere apartment. Home. She should have been able to sleep. All the conditions were ideal.

So maybe she could no longer deny the reason for the insomnia she'd been experiencing ever since Grosse Pointe. It wasn't uncomfortable hotel beds. It wasn't indigestion from rich foods, or the change in time zone.

It was the stain.

Howe's word, sure. The word of a madman. But one who had gone mad because of something *real*. Brenda had heard the roaring that came from Its mouth with her own ears.

And now, every time she closed her eyes in the darkness, the one dead eye stayed open. It saw things that were not there. It saw the form of Yog-Sothoth: malevolent, glowing globes bound by a black and yawning mouth. And through those globes, Yog-Sothoth peered back at her.

She'd tried to tell herself it was a memory, not a vision. But she had never looked back at the gate in the tower as it opened. She didn't see the Outer God's gullet as It swallowed Craig Beebe. She tried to tell herself that she was envisioning Its form based on the images on the wall hangings, the shape of "Dave" the high priest's necklace. But this was too vivid to be a mere guess based on those crude representations.

She was looking at It right now, and It was looking at her.

If she told Juhasz about this … personal issue, he would fire her immediately. Perhaps even kill her to ensure the *stain* did not spread. No, she could not tell her boss. It would be her secret to keep. Hers and Yog-Sothoth's.

The Outer God would call to her. No, It *was* calling to her, now. It wished for Brenda to open another master gate in a sufficiently populated area. It didn't have to be New York. Nearby Los Angeles would do just fine.

But Brenda would resist, because she loved her job, she loved the bank, and she would not do the bidding of some alien deity who thought It could boss her around.

I will not be stained. I will not be stained.

She lay there looking at the cluster of spheres that were Yog-Sothoth until she was too exhausted not to sleep. As her mind plunged into unconsciousness, her fingers moved deftly on her smartphone of their own accord.

WELCOME TO THE R'LYEH CORPORATION

by James Pratt

Hello and welcome to your first day at the R'lyeh Corporation. The orientation program in which you are about to participate is the first step in a journey we hope you'll find both exciting and rewarding. For the past twelve billion years, the R'lyeh Corporation has proudly served the needs of Those Who Were and Will Be Again. Now you'll help carry on that proud tradition until that glorious day when the stars are right and the Chairman of R'lyeh returns. Congratulations and welcome to the team!!!

By becoming a member of the R'lyeh Corporation, you have taken the first step to an exciting and hopefully fulfilling career. As with most opportunities, what you take away will depend on what you put into it. Our job is to make sure you have the tools necessary to survive and thrive in your new vocation. It is important to remember there is no such thing as a small job. No matter your position, you're an important part of the team and teamwork is the glue that holds a company together. At the same time, you shouldn't be afraid to express your opinions. The R'lyeh Corporation has an open door policy. All comments and concerns are not only welcome but aggressively addressed. That said, it is important before stepping through any given door to verify it leads to a dimensional configuration compatible with your plane of origin. The R'lyeh Corporation's customer base stretches across many demographics, space-time manifolds, and alternate timelines, and so our headquarters must do the same. These days, multiversal inclusion is the name of the game. It's a mighty challenge and one we're eager to meet. In fact, the best advice we can give you is don't be afraid of challenges. You wouldn't be here if we didn't think you were up to it. Assuming you have the proper protection spells and/or hyper-technology in place, the only being that can hold you back is you.

Here's a bit of history. The R'lyeh Corporation was founded .0000000000002 seconds after the event you know as the Big Bang. Prior to that, space-time was more of a general guideline than a hard and fast rule. Linear time, causality, all those things were just actionable items that nobody really wanted to tackle because nobody needed to. Things were getting done and if it ain't broke, don't fix it, right? It was an amazing time to be sentient. These days, the quantumverse is where the magic happens. Back then, there was no meaningful distinction between the macroverse and the quantumverse. Reality was an open market, wild and free.

Then the Elder Gods came along. They didn't respect the old ways. Oh, they spoke with flattery but everybody saw the writing on the wall. It was a hostile takeover. The new owners codified space-time and instituted the regulations you know as the laws of physics and thermodynamics. Thus was born the paradigm of cause and effect, or as I call them the biggest enemies of innovation. Oh, there was much wailing and gnashing of teeth. Most of the old guard took on new and much diminished roles, basically figureheads, or simply moved on.

But not the Chairman. He was and will always be a transcendent entity of vision. Being a strict supply-sider, he foresaw a time when a unique cosmic alignment, a literal conjunction of the spheres, would give him the opening he needed to exploit a temporal clause in the contract. The key was a gravitational event, a momentary anomaly that would allow him to rewrite space-time without violating causality. The event would only last a microsecond, but that would be more than enough time for him to undo everything. Deregulate, in other words. All he had to do was wait until the stars were right. But he wasn't the only one who foresaw the coming of the space-time event. To ensure things played out just how he wanted, he needed to hedge his bets. That meant creating as many timelines as possible where history unfolded in his favor. And so he created the R'lyeh Corporation. While the Chairman sleeps and crafts the living dreams he will use to remake the multiverse, we work to empower those whose goals align with his goals whether they realize it or not.

As previously noted, the corporate headquarters is pandimensional. It currently consists of thirteen levels with each level number corresponding to the number of spatial dimensions in the universe it occupies. For example, the first level exists in a one-dimensional universe of single-point lifeforms who communicate via quantum entanglement, the second level in a two-dimensional universe of living geometries whose rank in society is determined by the number of sides and sharpness of angles they possess, and so on. It's just one of the many qualities which make working at the R'lyeh Corporation a unique experience.

Speaking of which, please take the time to acquaint yourself with all customs regarding interacting with higher and lower dimensional beings. A primer can be found in "Appendix Q – A Guide to Hyper-Dimensional Etiquette" in the employee handbook. The primer is quite helpful but should not be considered a replacement for proper training. Your direct supervisor can help guide you in the process of finding the appropriate classes taught by in-house staff to fit your professional needs. As a general rule, it is recommended not to attempt direct contact with beings removed from oneself by three or more spatial dimensions without guidance from a Protocol Specialist in the Multiversal Support Department, aka MSD. This is the best way to avoid misunderstandings which may result in disintegrations, temporal and/or spatial displacement, mind-swaps, and so on. Such incidents tend to be frowned upon and may result in administrative action as determined on a case by case basis. When in doubt, ALWAYS consult the MSD.

Now here's the part to remember. Exiting the elevator on the wrong floor can be extremely hazardous. Unless accompanied by an employee with the proper clearance and access to dimensional coherence technology or the appropriate anchor spells, it is important that you only exit the elevator on a floor compatible with the number of spatial dimensions comprising your native space-time. Under absolutely no circumstances should you exit the elevator on the thirteenth floor. Only trans-cendent beings with top clearance have access to and may safely occupy the thirteenth floor. Colloquially known as the "Home Office", it leads to R'lyeh itself where the Chairman of the Board lies dead and dreaming. The ultimate goal of the R'lyeh Corporation is to ensure that the Chairman isn't disturbed until the stars are right. Attempting to access the thirteenth floor without proper credentials may result in corrective actions in-cluding but not limited to a written warning, termination, and atomic dispersal.

Ah, I see that you come from a universe consisting of three spatial dimensions plus a uni-directional time dimension. Lucky you. The employees on the third floor are known for their pleasant dispositions, soft flesh-bodies, and preference for linear time. As an oxygen-breathing, carbon-based lifeform you should fit right in. Let's head to the elevator and take a quick tour of the third floor. Remember, that and the parking garage are the only places you can safely occupy without special pre-cautions. I'm legally obligated to advise you that the R'lyeh Cor-poration isn't liable for any injuries, mutations, or other trans-formative events resulting from an employee accessing an area inherently hostile to their specific biology. But hey, that's just a formality. Just stick to the areas officially designated for beings of your spatial configuration and you'll be fine.

DING!

Here we are. Right there on your left is the breakroom. It's conveniently located right beside the elevator so you can start your day with a fresh cup of coffee, space mead, or other bever-age of your choice. Over there's the supply room. The doorway is actually a wormhole connected to the planetoid where sup-plies are kept. I'd advise against making any trips to the supply room in the next few days. The planetoid currently has a dhole infestation. Big, nasty things, those dholes. Some folks call them dream-worms for reasons with which I'm sure you're familiar. We called in the exterminators and the infestation should be dealt with in the next few days. It's always something, right? By the way, the wormhole is powered by an artificial singularity. If an alarm consisting of three loud beeps, a pause, and then three more beeps sounds, it means the singularity's been compromised and you have about twenty seconds to reach the nearest exit.

The man sitting at the desk next to the supply room is the third floor's supply manager, Joe Devine. I'm sure you've noticed that he has a few too many eyes and one of his arms looks like a large, blood-red tentacle. Turns out the seal keeping the wormhole closed off from hyperspace developed a little leak. As a result, Joe was bombarded by an unknown radiation for an extended period of time. By the time the leak was detected and fixed, Joe's DNA had already been rewritten considerably. Don't let the hideous mutations fool you. You'll never meet a nicer guy than Joe. Just don't stand close to him for more than a few minutes at a time. Residual radiation and all that.

Look, there goes one of your coworkers now. That man stepping out of that office is Milton Freed. He's in charge of the design department. Milt has a bright albeit brief future ahead of him. Three years from now he'll take a wrong turn out of the parking garage and end up in a parallel universe whose most abundant element is ammonia. Milton will die choking on his own vomit, leaving behind a wife, two children, and a mistress who will miss him the most. Very sad. Milt likes telling cheesy jokes. Enjoy them while you can.

Oh and there's Patty Lipton, Bill Everett's personal assistant. Nice girl, very friendly and outgoing. She's actually a corporate succubus working for one of our biggest competitors, Carcosa Dynamics. Patty's true allegiance is known to Human Resources but that's okay. All things serve the will of the Chairman of the Board, blessings be upon him. Yes, Patty is an unholy abomination but she also heads up the birthday committee and makes a great cup of coffee. Get on her good side and she'll make you feel like a king.

Speak of the devil, there goes Bill Everett now. He oversees the Logistics Department. Uh oh, Bill's looking a little under the weather. He's cheating on his wife with Patty who's literally draining him of information and also his life-force. Bill's a bit on the reserved side but if you bring up golf he'll talk your ear off. Unfortunately his game has suffered of late, mainly due to the whole life-force draining thing.

And look, there's Drake Burroughs. Now Drake's a guy who knows how to get things done. Drake used to carpool with Mitch Levy. He wanted Mitch's job so he tricked him into exiting the elevator on the sixth floor. With all those extra dimensions suddenly tugging on Mitch's three dimensional body, he was literally torn apart. Other than that, Drake's a solid worker and a good guy. He's even paying Mitch's daughter's college tuition. That counts for something, right? Drake would be a great one to show you the ropes.

That's Tanya Greely coming out of the bathroom. Tanya's your department's liaison with Research & Development. She looks like she's in her thirties but she's actually sixty-three. As the R&D liaison, she spends half her time in the labs. Things are kind of weird down there. Even with all the safety protocols in place, visitors still might find themselves affected by the occasional space-time anomaly. As for Tanya, she appears to age backward but what's really happening is she's shedding chronotons. To put it another way, she perceives time moving in one direction but physically experiences it as moving in the other. She'll eventually become a fetus, then an embryo, and so on. Chronoton therapy could slow down the process, but the insurance company claims her condition is a result of negligence and is refusing to pay for treatments. As you can imagine, Tanya's pretty down about it. Hopefully things will work out.

There you have it. That's the team you'll be working with. They're a wonderful bunch. If you ever have any questions just ask for me, Mr. Nyarlat. I'm always around.

SHADOW CHARTS

by Marcus Johnston

No patient stays at Central Hospital long; now I know why. What I had seen there haunted my every waking moment, after my modern distractions failed me. It claws at the edge of my consciousness and drags me back to the mouth gate of hell. I've tried many prescriptions, but none of them could banish it away.

The hospital had another name. It had been bought out, re-branded, painted, and named after some donor, but everyone still called it Central. I didn't think much about the hospital when I got the assignment; I'd seen so many hospitals, what was one more? It was a private hospital, for-profit, which in a universe of faith-based non-profit healthcare should have warned me something was wrong. All I knew was that the Joint Commission had found "charting discrepancies", so with Central's accreditation threatened, the health network that owned the hospital hired a consulting firm to address the concern. The firm sent me, knowing nothing (nor caring) about the problem; they had a contract to fulfill. I didn't care either, because to me, saying there were "discrepancies" was about as useful to me as saying to a doctor that "people were sick".

Little did I know what horror I would find within those walls.

When I got out the taxi, I felt cold ... wrong ... like I had crossed into the wrong part of town. Of course, it *was* the wrong part of town; Walnut Hills had been the outer suburbs when Central had been built, back in the 1850s, but the city had continued expanding—and the money went with it. Yet I noticed even the homeless and the indigent avoided stepping near the monolithic building. My eye scanned the area around the hospital; the abandoned office building, the empty parking lot, the boarded-up store fronts. Even the sole remaining convenience store seemed to scurry from the hospital's shadow. Somehow a church managed to survive in this dead zone, but as I stared at the steeple, I saw three angels facing three other directions, with a gargoyle pointing towards the hospital.

I shrugged it off; this wasn't the first hospital I'd been to that sat in the rotting city core. Part of me wanted to take out the gun I kept in my travel bag, but I steeled myself, and simply took the bag with me into the hospital lobby. No one was there; a bland plastic telephone sat on the reception desk, a sign in ten languages asking the lonely visitor to call for assistance. Having not been given the number for my contact, I followed the instructions, and got some operator with a thick accent that had obviously only just started her job. After several call transfers, I finally talked to someone who knew who I was, and they said they'd be right down. I put the phone down and waited.

Everything was old; not that you could tell at first glance. A private hospital such as Central was rare, usually limited to nursing homes and rehab centers in some remote setting; they weren't plopped in the middle of rotting cities, only Jesus lived among the poor. However, the new owners tried to hide its warts, since they needed to attract the desperate elderly patients whose insurance was unreliable. The drywall and white paint job strategically placed over the old phone kiosks gave the appearance of modern, but like the rest of the hospital, it was only a façade. Simply a cover over the corruption that claimed the ancient building. However, the new owners had tried to give the old lady a face-lift. Calming or inspirational pictures alternated with quotes and mission statements. I expected Bible verses, or meaningless pap, but they were … off somehow. Read while walking by, not paying attention, they were only so much set dressing. But as I waited in the empty lobby, the lines took a more sinister tone.

That is not dead which can eternal lie
And with strange aeons, even death may die.

The quote written in fading gold paint drew me in, and I walked from the reception desk along the wall to see the rest of the collection. After passing the mission statement and the calming mother and child (who didn't look *that* comforted), I found:

Song of my soul, my voice is dead
Die thou, unsung, as tears unshed
Shall dry and die in
Lost Carcosa.

I was so disturbed by this collection of obscure poetry that I didn't hear the heel clicks coming down the hallway. Sure enough, it was my contact come to find me. "Mr. Johnston?"

She sounded young, but when I turned to face her, I involuntarily stepped back. She appeared to have lived a lifetime in only a few decades. Her shoulder-cut brown hair was mousy and limp, her eyes sunken, her clothes hanged on her tiny frame. Only the strategic placement of makeup tried to hide the soul that was being drained from her. "You must be Martha."

She blinked, as if the name meant nothing to her, but finally nodded when she realized it was her cue. "I'll take you to your office, for your use while you are here." Then she turned to walk away and I realized it was my cue to follow.

"And my system access?" I asked.

"We'll grant you a generic admin access to our systems, same level as ours. We wish to resolve these discrepancies quickly."

"I'll also need access to any paper backups, downtime sheets, shadow charting…."

"You will have full access," Martha insisted, putting a note of finality to it.

I tried to change the subject. "Not a lot of business?" I

waved my hand around the empty lobby.

"Not many direct admissions. We service the local community, as well as many of the nursing homes, free clinics...."

"I didn't see the emergency department."

"Other side of the building," she dismissed, "although most ambulances prefer to go to University or Christ."

"Why is that?"

Martha blinked. "They can handle the volume."

"Limited staffing?"

"We're one of the few facilities in the tri-state that take Medicare and Medicaid, Mr. Johnston. Since most our patients are low income, our resources are ... stretched."

I thought I was getting the picture. "That might explain the discrepancies. CMS is a bear when it comes to paperwork. You're probably missing a form or three on your insurance claims you weren't aware of."

"CMS?"

"Center for Medicare Studies? Health and Human Services? The Feds?"

"Oh. Of course." She blinked again, but dared not look at me. "You're probably right. Do you believe you could identify the missing forms quickly?"

A red flag was being waved in front of me; they wanted to get rid of me. True, the compliance man was about as popular as infectious waste disposal, but normally they at least *pretended* to value my investigation. "That depends on the patient charts in question. The report didn't go into great detail."

"Oh," the woman said, and didn't say another word until we reached my office.

Martha disappeared after she gave me the key to my temporary home. The office was one of many, on a long blank corridor, three floors above the lobby in what she called the "new" building. I figured it couldn't be less than fifty years old, a classic concrete box dating to the flawed post-World War II concept that all we really needed was a standard space, then rooms to fill it.

I spent the morning getting accustomed to the hospital's computer network. Like the building, the computer architecture was several generations older than the modern facility they pretended to be. The text-based character interface didn't even allow me to use a mouse; no wonder Joint Commission was angry … and so vague. They knew something was wrong, but with this arcane system, they couldn't find a blasted thing. After hunting between charts using function keys, my eyes were going numb, so I decided to go get a coffee from the cafeteria.

The second I stepped into the hallway, I knew I was completely lost. The only sign available told me that pain management was in a janitor's closet and special needs faced a blank wall. Giving up on directions, I guessed where the elevator might be and started walking. Past the row of office doors, I realized that most of them were empty, probably last used decades ago. The fluorescent lights were flickering, leaving everything in sight in a milky shade. At the end of the corridor wasn't an elevator, but a slight turn and a ramp leading down into an older building. Leaving the vacant administrative area, I stepped onto one of the patient floors. Hoping the nurses at the floor desk could direct me, I opened the door.

It was just as whitewashed as the "new" building, but now there were window sills, door frames, signs of character. As I passed the moaning, the monitor beeps, and occasional screams from the patients, I made my way to the nurse's station, only to be disappointed; there were no staff at the station. Still, it wasn't unusual for the staff to be busy with treatment and no one sitting at the hub. Seeing the glowing red exit signs, I followed them out of the unit, and soon reached a stairwell. Two floors down, the stairs stopped, and I had to get out on a clinic floor—one of the few hospital facilities where patients could check in with their doctor without having to stay in a room.

This strange end of the stairwell didn't worry me either; most hospitals grew organically. The original building gets too small for the volume, so they add a newer building on to it, then another addition. Eventually, they demolish the original building and build a new one, clipping the additions haphazardly. What remains is a crazy quilt of floors that never quite match, so it's not unusual for floors to stop and the building to continue, or elevators to only service a certain number of floors. I made my way through the half-filled clinic floor lobby, the temporary souls waiting and coughing, although to my eyes they seemed to need admission now, instead of going through the steps of treatment. On the other side was the next stairwell, with the promised steps downward.

What drew my eye was a door, halfway down the flight of stairs, which had to be at least a hundred years old. A quick glance through the window showed a gloomy corridor, with old wheelchairs, stacks of paper, and obsolete equipment; the detritus of a medical institution. I thought this had to be the original hospital building; too old to use, too expensive to tear down, so it became the all-purpose storage area. The peeling paint, dusty floors, and sense of age was interesting, but it clearly had no coffee, so I left it alone. I kept hoping that the ground floor would have the cafeteria I sought.

I guess I should have figured there was no cafeteria; just a row of vending machines. Machine coffee with poker cards on the paper cup provided the caffeine I craved without pleasure or taste. I took the same path back to my office to continue my lonely search for my hospital's "discrepancies" in the wilderness of green text on black screens.

It took me two days to figure out the problem; there *was* no problem. The patient charts were perfect. There were no incorrect diagnoses, no labs that failed to produce, not even a flippant nurse message with secret codes to tell how difficult a patient was. Every patient either got better quickly, or had a steady decline to the grave. It was *too* perfect. There was something missing, and if I knew clinicians, it was hiding somewhere other than the electronic medical record.

In the days before computers, when staff wanted to tell the next shift something problematic about a patient, they would stick a post-it note on the paper chart. It was easy, disposable, and more importantly, wouldn't come back to bite them if the patient or their family decided to sue the hospital. That way, the nurse could tell her relief about the drunk man in Room 4, or the woman who stole her pens in Room 12, without embarrassing the patient. Computers made these post-it notes impossible, so clever doctors and nurses found another way to pass these notes electronically. They would type them up in another system, unconnected to the patient chart, and reference it along with the official record. It became known as the "shadow chart."

Operating on a tighter margin than the nearby non-profits, I was sure they were hiding the absence of many mandated procedures, saving them costs, but still billing CMS for the price of labor unfulfilled. To accomplish this, I was convinced that Central Hospital had a shadow chart somewhere; a computer system that would show all the flaws they hid from the patient's chart. And I also knew who could give it to me. The only problem was that Martha never gave me her office number, so I had to hunt again through the labyrinth of patient rooms and unfamiliar treatment bays to find her. *Why hadn't they sat me closer to Health Information Management? Surely they knew I'd need to ask questions?* Of course, there was a simpler answer. With doctors and administration all fighting to be close to the hospital, office space was limited, and little things like finance and compliance got shifted to Siberia.

My elusive prey had her office in one of the older buildings, held off on one side of the floor in what was probably a ward room. Back when it was built, patients were placed in wards; long open floors with rows of beds, so that one nurse could watch twenty patients. When they turned it into office space, instead of building walls in the cavernous space, the administration just dumped in a cube farm, delicately aged cloth barriers breaking up one desk after another. Like their charts, their desks were perfect … but in some wrong manner I couldn't quite put my finger on. No family pictures, no messy papers; everything in its place as it should be. *No matter*, I figured, *most accountants I've met are hardly human.*

I found Martha near the end; she looked up with that blank gaze and said nothing. Like many women, she had that ability to make men think they were completely insignificant, but unlike the hot blonde at the bar, I didn't feel as if she was trying to cast me aside. It was as if life itself was too much of a bother and I was just one more distraction. To break that chilling gaze, I skipped the pleasantries tripping on my tongue and asked, "Where are the shadow charts?"

"You have full access."

"No, I have access to the records you send to Medicare," I corrected, quoting that omnipresent government agency that all mere multi-million dollar hospitals must bow in homage to, "but they saw the same thing I did. They're too perfect."

"Perfect," Martha echoed with a sigh. "Our patients are far from perfect."

"But your charting is. There's too much consistency. Your doctors and nurses have to be entering additional information somewhere. The shadow charts. Wherever they are, I need access to that server."

"You have full access."

"Listen," I said, giving her my best official glare, "you can play games with me and I'll give my firm an incomplete report. You'll lose accreditation, and with that, you'll lose all that Medicare money. Do you want that?"

Martha blinked; upon reflection, I saw that she wore the same outfit I first met her in days ago. "I can point you towards all our databases, which you should have access to, but if it's not there in the chart, I—"

"What about paper records? Do your clinicians keep a running paper chart in addition to the electronic one?"

"I have no idea."

Of course not, I thought. An institution using outdated twenty-year-old software wouldn't bother with little issues like charting workflow and what hardworking nurses would have to document outside the lines to do their job. "Tell you what, put me in touch with one of your department heads. I'm sure they'll know what I'm talking about."

"I'll send their contact information to your email."

But of course, she didn't. Not that day or the next; I realized that I had to take action myself. At first, I tried searching for the department heads themselves, but either I couldn't find their offices, or when I did, it looked like they only stopped by long enough to drop something off. Frustrated, I went to the patient floors, and started to track down nurses. Not as easy as it sounds; they rarely came back to their station, and when I asked to watch them chart, they were polite, but basically told me to get lost. The doctors were even more elusive. I took to wandering the floors of the hospital, learning the maze that was Central. I laid in wait, ambushing the healthcare providers, just to catch a glimpse of how they entered the patient's charts into the system, to see them entering in their secret notes. Each time, I was foiled.

I needed a different approach. If I couldn't catch them in the act, I had to find out another way. Since I had access to the system, I could easily see the patient census, and figure out the patient movement patterns. Many of the discharges and admissions happened right before midnight—not that unusual, a necessary evil due to the government regulations about hospital stays. I realized that if I needed to find the shadow charting I sought, I literally had to walk in the shadows.

At the end of the next work day, instead of going back to the hotel, I waited in my office and locked the door. As the housekeeping staff went past, I watched the clock, only leaving when the digits turned to 11:30 PM. Patients being discharged or admitted required the most amount of data entry. Since they both happened before midnight, it was the only time I would catch them when they were too busy to stop me. Although no one was in the office corridors, when I reached the first patient floor the lights were glaring and the previously lethargic hospital staff were suddenly buzzing with activity. My curiosity was piqued. I found a hiding place in an office doorway close to the patient rooms where I could observe the actions through the window in the swinging door.

It didn't take long before one of the anticipated discharges occurred. A swarm of scrub-wearing people wheeled out the elderly patient, obviously drugged or sleepy or both, on a wheelchair to the other end of the floor. The staff followed. When they reached the end of the hallway, where I couldn't see, they just left … and didn't come back.

After a couple minutes, my curiosity got the better of me, and I followed after them. As I thought, the floor was once again vacant of staff, as it had been most times I'd been there. I followed to the end of the floor and found the wheelchair empty, next to the familiar stairwell—the only exit they could have taken. But why take a patient down the stairs instead of the elevator?

I went down the stairwell to the clinic floor, and again found only emptiness. A hunch had me cross over, down the stairwell to look into the old hospital building, halfway between the second and third floors, and saw nothing but the same trash that was there before. But in the dim light, I finally noticed something; there were footprints in the dust.

They had taken the patient into the old abandoned building. The hairs on my skin stood up.

Carefully, I opened the stained wooden door; it opened without a squeak. The hinges must have been oiled frequently, which meant this route was used … a lot. What were they doing with their patients? Were they trying to avoid the 1986 EMTALA Act and dump their worst patients on another hospital? I walked as quietly as possible through the passageway; I could hear nothing but a low hum.

As I followed the footprints through the dim lighting, they ended up in an old chapel. The ceiling was half collapsed, causing water stains over the old wood, the insulation strewn over the beautifully carved and ruined pews. However, there were no other doors, and despite the footprints present all over the room, no one was there.

I looked around the room, my eyes looking over the solid block of the altar, a beautiful white marble piece stained red.... I looked up and saw the water damage. The water bleeding off the stained wood would have easily caused that stain. Then I backtracked to see if I missed the trail; nothing. Even the stained glass seemed to mock my search. Jesus wore a yellow robe and had a strange look on his face, that didn't seem to comfort the afflicted figures that came for healing, but that didn't seem to stop the sick from coming. There was a low hum, which I guessed came from some electrical circuit, but I could feel it vibrating in the floor, and I got more nervous about staying in the abandoned building. Against all logic, the patient discharge had ended in thin air.

I didn't even show up to work the next morning; no one seemed to notice. I got in around three in the afternoon with my travel bag, barricaded myself back in my office … and waited. I couldn't resist checking the discharge report—the patient had died, of course, but there was no next of kin. No autopsy by the county coroner, just a quick memorandum stating that standard procedure had been followed, and the body had been sent to the crematorium. *Who signed off on* that *procedure?* I wondered. Someone had gone to a lot of trouble to keep this quiet, and for good reason. The hospital was dumping their expensive patients out the door and pocketing the end-of-life procedure money. It was unethical, against the law, and worst of all ... it was sick.

Around midnight, I changed into scrubs and crept up to the door to the patient floor to wait. The same play of scrubs and movement beckoned, and this time, I only waited long enough for them to pass out of sight. Like the night before, the whole staff had disappeared in this strangest of all patient discharges. I quickly caught up to the stairway at the end of the hall. I caught a glimpse of the old man they were carrying in a stretcher. The patient might have been moaning, but it was the only sound, save for the whispered footsteps that followed in procession down the hall. In that rush of movement, no one was going to notice one more. I followed as best I could, making sure that the rear guard wouldn't notice me; of course, I had the advantage. This time, I knew exactly where this strange procession was going.

Sure enough, the lot of them disappeared through the door in the stairwell to the ancient, original hospital building. As soon as the hallway was clear, I followed in after them, right to the old chapel that I had found earlier. Instead of footsteps, though, there was a ... humming? Some might have called it a song, but not in any language you might have understood, or any octave that was designed by man. Atonal wasn't the word—they were tunes never designed to be sung by human voices—and the corruption by our mortal lips set my hair on end.

My heart was pumping in my chest, but I had to peer around the corner, to see what these supposed medical professionals were doing in the old chapel. What I never would have caught before, now I saw clearly. The old altar was shifted to the side, revealing a stairwell, going deep into the ancient structure. As the last of the nurses went into the hole, the altar slid back into place, and the tune disintegrated into silence.

I immediately raced over to the altar and, with a shove, it slid away to give me access to the darkness below. I followed; I didn't want to go, but after coming so far, I had to know what was happening to their patients. The old stones that made up the staircase were worn smooth over the centuries; they must have predated the hospital above it. Every step I took made me feel as if I followed the steps of many generations who came down these stairs. *It must have been an old cellar*, I figured, *or an old speakeasy from Prohibition, or maybe even a passage on the Underground Railroad. These sick bastards were using it as a dumping ground.* With more determination, I followed into the darkness. As soon as my head dropped below the floor, the false altar above seemed to sense it, and slid the cover back into place.

The songs ... the songs filled the darkened chamber, lit only with the glowing letters of some alphabet on the walls that I dared not comprehend. As my eyes adjusted, I could see that it was a natural cave, stalagmites cut off to make room for the frequent travelers. Walking further into the cavern, a fire pit nearly blinded me, I had to stifle my coughs against the smell of cloying incense and centuries-old wood smoke. As my eyes adjusted to the darkness, what astonished me the most was the altar, a twin to the white stone one above us, and the scrub-wearing clinicians surrounding the patient being laid down on its surface. I couldn't believe what I was seeing. *This* is why those perfect charts never told the truth; they could never explain the human sacrifice that was the true cause of death in this obscene ritual.

Taking out the gun from my travel bag, I revealed myself, and shouted as loud as I could, "What the hell are you doing?!"

All eyes turned to me, every single one of them blazing with a fanatic's purpose. Their eyes found me, found my gun, and stopped. For a few seconds, none of us (including myself) were sure what to do, and then one of their number stepped forward. "Mr. Johnston?"

It was Martha, but ... not her. Not the void of life I knew above this obscene and evil altar—this was a true woman, full of life and purpose, lit by the power of something beyond this mortal coil. With a dark stone knife in her hand, she seemed more than a natural woman, she was ... supernatural? I looked at her and demanded, "What do you people think you're doing?!"

"You don't understand…."

"You're damn right, I don't understand!"

"And I will explain it to you, but you need to go back upstairs."

Pointing my gun at her, I demanded, "Explain it *now*."

A bell rang once; a tiny bell, one that would have been ignored except for the silence. Martha shuddered at its sound. "We have no time, Mr. Johnston. Leave while you can."

"And you'll do what? You dragged this patient down here to this … to do…?"

"This patient is dying!" one of the doctors exclaimed, stepping closer.

"Back off!" I yelled, pointing the gun at the doctor. "If he's dying, then why did you take the patient from their room?"

"Mr. Johnston," Martha stepped forward, a pleading slipping into her voice, "you must leave."

"And what? You'll … you'll kill him?"

"He has lived a long, full life, and is only hours away from dying anyway," she said, "this way, his death serves a higher purpose. He saves all of us instead of saving himself."

"That's ridicul—" And then the bell rang again, but it was closer, louder, like … like a trip wire had been set, warning us of what was coming towards us. A new sound started to fill the chamber, quiet at first, but a slurp … a *slither* seemed to get louder.

"They won't see the Yellow Sign," another of the clinicians warned.

Martha pointed to the end of the altar; there was a large pit in the ground that I hadn't seen before. "They're coming," she insisted, "the avatars of Cthulhu will not be quenched except in the blood of the living."

" 'That is not dead which can eternal lie,' " the group intoned, " 'and with strange aeons, even death may die.' "

"You're going to kill him?!" I asked, not believing what I was hearing.

"We have to," Martha insisted, her eyes pleading with me. "Right now, dead Cthulhu waits dreaming in his house at R'lyeh, but he wants to wake and kill us all. Only Hastur can save us."

"Hastur?"

"His Unspeakable Majesty," a doctor replied.

"The King in Yellow," a nurse continued.

"Only his sign will hold back the feast of the Great Old Ones upon the Earth," another voice pleaded.

"We must kill the sacrifice," Martha explained.

"We're not doing anything until...." Then the slurping, slithering sound grew louder, now clearly coming from the hole near the altar, and even I couldn't help myself moving closer, even as the group drew back. "What is that?"

Martha shook her head. "Even if I had a thousand years and the words to express it, I could not explain what is waiting for us ... what is *coming* up that pit." She pointed around us. "We, the keepers of the truth, built this temple a hundred years ago to prevent the dark ones from devastating the Earth. But now the avatars of Cthulhu expect the sacrifice, they yearn for the sign that banishes them, as if the glow of the sacrifice somehow feeds their magic below us."

"And you've been using the hospital as a cover so you could kill people to this ... thing?"

"Blood is the only currency they take." She stared deeply into my eyes, the fire of her conviction emphasized by the sounds in the pit growing louder and louder.

"We must leave!" one of the doctors yipped.

"There is nowhere far enough we could go," Martha explained, "that the Great Old Ones could not devour us. Come." She looked at me, offering me the sacrificial knife in her hands. It was obsidian, the sharpest rock, a dark black blade that absorbed the little light around it. "You have come this far, you must achieve the true knowledge."

"The hell you say! I'm not going to...." I begged off, but ... something was starting to peer over the lip of the pit, this hell mouth, this unholy break into the reaches of the underworld.

"Invoke the Yellow Sign," Martha insisted, pointing at the altar. The old man wasn't even strapped down; his eyes rheumy with pain medications and a thousand swirling pharmaceuticals, it wasn't even clear the patient was awake.

My eyes involuntarily shifted to the pit. Something had gained a foothold; a woman screamed, but I couldn't shake the image. The slime covered a ... claw? Nail? Tentacle-like, it was only the beginning of something horrible, trying to break forth from the evil that it came from. I pointed my gun at the thing and fired ... once, twice, three times ... nothing! The sound and the fury did nothing to that unholy beast—except attract its attention. Now it was slithering towards *me*.

"What *is* that thing?!" I screamed

Martha put a calm hand on my shoulder and pushed me closer to the altar. "We don't have much time."

"Iä! Iä!" another yelled out in terror.

I was frozen in fear, in fascination, with the otherworldliness of what was being revealed before me. It was wrong, beautiful, evil, and alien. My brain wanted to reject what I was seeing, but it couldn't—it was now seared onto my memory forever, unable to forget the horrible wonder that lied before me. Voices rose, telling me to kill, but I was rooted to the spot of the beast desperate to escape its underground prison.

That thing can't be real, I assured myself, yet the slithering continued. What abomination could be worth murder and death? What *insanity* demanded blood to keep its thirst at bay? I wanted to scream. I wanted to run. But all my eyes could do was flick from the knife, to the creature, to the patient. *It's coming for me!* my mind screamed. The last shred of reality slipped from my grasp and I snatched the knife from Martha's hand; maybe the obsidian blade could kill that thing....

But then the second tentacle appeared, and all hope vanished.

Terror pushed me past my disgust, past all the human conventions I had grown to accept—all of it rejected in the face of true horror that only had to reach out and devour me. *Save me!* I wanted to scream, if only words could escape my terrified lips. *Save me! I'll do anything! Just keep that thing from escaping the pit!*

"Now," Martha insisted, and I agreed. I gripped the ceremonial blade and plunged it again and again into the beating heart of the old man with only a wisp of moan to show the spirit leaving the body. His blood flew everywhere and I cared not as I kept stabbing, invoking without thought the name "Hastur." I was beyond morals, beyond disgust ... I had to survive this insanity, and I was more than happy to kill anyone, even the poor helpless man before me.

The light in the room increased; the slithering slimy tentacle stopped. As the blood dripped down my shirt onto the floor, there appeared a symbol in the air, glowing with awful majesty, with angles and dimensions that conformed to no geometry I have ever seen before or since. The tentacles shrieked in a pitch that chilled me to my very core, yet the light, the Yellow Sign, continued to blaze. I started to breathe again when the beast from below disappeared from view, slithering past the bells and trip wires meant to warn the living that an immortal was coming.

The sign disappeared as well, and everyone breathed a sign of ... relief? Regret? It wasn't clear to me; nothing was clear to me. In the darkness, the blood on my hands and shirt seemed black. The sacrifice seemed ... peaceful, resigned, as if its purpose in life had been fulfilled. As for me, I was ashamed at having taken a life, and yet relieved that I saved my own. Guilt and hate and sickness.... My mind went into a tailspin, and my body was frozen in that moment of ... unholy communion. I knew nothing and everything. But I should have known my life would never be the same again.

Martha took the blade away from me like a toy out of a child's hand. I was drained ... exhausted, but she understood. She had dedicated her life to keeping this ... *god* at bay. Compared to that, everything else was a distraction. She led us back up to the land of the living, followed by the hospital staff returning to their normal routine, but none of us were the same. We had shared in this unholy communion, and while they were drawn to it, I only wanted to leave, begging to get as far away from that pit as possible. *If only I can return back to the surface*, I thought, *I can go home.* That was, I could cling back to my illusion of an ordinary life.

I wrapped up the job in two days. Martha was far more understanding, even if just as distant, once I explained the missing parts of the charts that had sent the red flags to the Joint Commission. Their tech monkeys and I quickly falsified the documents, and from now on, all that CMS would see was what they wanted to see. The health system was pleased, my consulting firm was thrilled, and I moved on.

But I *couldn't* move on. Part of me would always live in that basement, that unholy altar protecting us from unstoppable gods that thirst for blood and are never quenched. I looked for the sign everywhere, that unholy symbol, as I stepped inside every new hospital. Soon I found myself disappointed when I *couldn't* find the tell-tale signs of that secret world I had only glimpsed. I tried to pretend that every new job was a step back to reality, but once you've seen what I've seen, the normal world never felt … real, anymore. I finally understood Martha, because now I had the same reaction to life myself.

After going through the motions of my old life for two years, I finally gave up the job. I couldn't pretend any more. I applied for a compliance job at Central, and as I came in for my interview, Martha was there. Through the sallow look she gave me, a slight smile broke through, knowing why I came. I realized that I could no longer pretend; now I know the truth, and nothing else satisfies. Every few days, I depart this mortal shell and come back to life. I long to see that beast, that sign, and those words fall from my lips as unholy writ, unbeckoned and passionately desired.

Hastur the Unspeakable! Save us from Cthulhu!

CASUAL FRIDAY

by Todd H. C. Fischer

Mrs. Jervis at the temp agency said there was a high turnover rate for this assignment—so far no one had lasted more than a week. Marlon had no real idea why that might be. It was true that Hygon Solutions was not an exciting place to work, but in his experience no office was. He would also admit his current co-workers seemed a little weirder than most. And then there was the washroom … but still, not enough to give up a steady paycheck.

When Marlon had started on Monday morning he had been greeted by an overly-cheerful receptionist who directed him to the desk of the manager he would be reporting to. Like most office environments these days, Hygon Solutions seemed to be a labyrinth of cubicles, all of them almost identical. As he walked past desk after desk he had felt eyes studying him. *Yup,* he had thought to himself. *Check out the new guy.* It made him think of scenes from prison movies where the new inmate—the fresh meat—has to walk past all the hostile prisoners in their cells.

Mr. Bryant had been sitting in his office—one of the few on the floor—but had stood up when Marlon knocked. He was a large man, barrel-chested with wide hands. He looked like he might have some Mediterranean blood in his family background, as his pale flesh seemed to have a hint of green to it. He had shook Marlon's hand, which had disappeared into the larger man's mitt.

Marlon was then given the whirlwind tour: the break room, the washrooms, the copy room, an overview of where the various departments' clutches of cubicles could be found. Marlon made mental notes of all this, and as soon as he was finally deposited into his very own cubicle, he drew a quick sketch of the floor plan on a piece of paper in his notebook.

He was working in the Archive Department, and his job consisted of scanning old paper documents, then consigning the physical copies to the shredder. It was a perfect job for Marlon as there was little interaction with his co-workers and he could just sit and work at his own pace. He was awkward around strangers, and being a temp meant he was always moving from office to office, so it felt like a tiresome exercise in futility to put in the effort to get to know people he was never going to see again.

As he sat at his desk scanning file after file, he'd wondered why the other temps had quit after only one week. As of his first morning on the job it had felt like a breeze.

Once he'd scanned a few dozen files, he picked up the originals and walked over to the copy room where a large locked blue bin was located. He dumped the files into the secure bin, now on their way to be shredded, then he popped into the washroom.

During his quick tour he hadn't noticed how damp the bathroom had been, but now that he was standing in it he could feel the humidity on his skin. There was a sheen of moisture on the walls, and a small puddle around a drain in the floor. At the back of the washroom there was a door, which, when opened, revealed a steam-filled shower. The dampness in this room was overwhelming and Marlon quickly closed the door, but not before he thought he'd seen large patches of mold where the tiled walls met the floor.

He'd shuddered and entered one of the stalls. At first the door didn't want to close properly. The door looked slightly bent, and one of the hinges wasn't working quite right. He was about to move to one of the other stalls when he heard the bathroom door open, so he gave his door one more good push and was able to latch it shut.

As he sat on the toilet he could hear the shuffling of feet. Soon enough those feet came into view, encased in large brown loafers. He watched as the person on the other side of his stall door waded through the puddle and came to a stop directly outside. Marlon had heard the sounds of deep breathing, large breaths being sucked into a cavernous throat, rattling around gargantuan lungs. He fidgeted, uncomfortable with what was transpiring. Why was this guy standing right outside the stall door?

Finally, the large man moved away and entered the next stall. Marlon heard the other toilet protest as the giant's bulk settled upon it. He glanced under the stall's wall and saw that the giant was shuffling his feet while he sat, almost as if he was dancing while sitting down. The leather soles of his brown loafers scrapped against the dingy floor, sending shivers up Marlon's spine.

Debating whether to try and outwait the other man or to try to leave before he finished his business, Marlon decided on the later course of action. When he opened his stall he was sure that the other door would also open, and he'd be forced to interact with the strange giant. However, the giant's feet were still engaged in their soft-shoe routine. Marlon hurried to the sink, his eyes fastened on the reflection of the dancing shoes, then rushed out of the bathroom.

He'd returned to his desk a little freaked out. He'd had a few odd restroom incidents in the past, but few had unnerved him like this one had. He'd had to pull out some tissues and wipe a mixture of damp air and sweat from his forehead and forearms.

He'd resolved after that to drink and eat as little as possible while on the job in an effort to use the washroom as infrequently as possible.

He'd taken his lunch that first day just after one in the afternoon, and sat by himself at the back of the break room. While he ate, a slow parade of his co-workers came and went. Some nodded at him, others smiled, but just as many ignored him completely. One woman, with a large stomach and thin limbs, had heated up some fish in the microwave, and the piscine odor had filled the whole room. If there was one thing Marlon hated, it was fish.

When he'd been a boy his family had taken a trip to a lodge in Minnesota. While there, Marlon had fallen into the water and been swept under a dock. He'd bobbed there, surrounded by the floating corpses of decaying fish. The water had been thick with the rotting remains, and he remembered how some had gushed into his mouth when he called for help.

Marlon choked on his sandwich, remembering the vomitous flavor of the ichthyic liquid flesh; thought of the dead eyes that had stared at him remorselessly. He'd been trapped there for at least thirty minutes before his father had heard his cries for help, and had come and saved him.

In the break room, Marlon had lurched to his feet and stumbled past the other tables. At them several of his co-workers had their lunches spread out: sushi, chowder, tuna salad, lox smeared on bagels.

Gagging, he had returned to his desk, where he ate his lunch from then on.

On Tuesday, his second day at Hygon Solutions, one of the women from the Accounting Department had cornered him as he was walking to the copy room with another load of files for the shredder. She'd tried to engage him in small talk, but it was a skill he was sorely lacking in. Her name was Lisa, she had said, her lips parting in a smile. Marlon had thought her teeth looked small, and sharp. He'd blurted out something about being on an urgent task for Mr. Bryant and had rushed off, but not before she ran a red-nailed hand down his arm. Her touch had been cold, sending a chill through Marlon's body. He put it down to his social anxiety.

Every day that had followed had been a little weirder than the last, his co-workers seeming more and more odd as the week went on. Jiro, who worked in the cubicle next to Marlon, for example. Jiro seemed nice enough, but Marlon had begun to catch the other man peeking over the top of the cubicle wall. Whenever Marlon caught Jiro at it, the other man pulled back his head and began playing with a handful of small metallic stars he kept on his desk. The sound of metal rubbing on metal was like nails on a chalkboard for Marlon. He'd tried to ask Jiro to stop, and each time the other man agreed to do so, but within fifteen minutes he would be at it again.

Currently, it was Thursday afternoon, and Marlon was staring at a memo alerting him to the fact that the next day was Casual Friday. Employees, said the memo, in a colorful cartoon font, were encouraged to dress in khakis, jeans, or other casual wear. Of particular note was the fact that Friday was also to feature a catered lunch. Marlon just hoped the menu would offer more than just the fish the staff at Hygon Solutions seemed to love so much.

Marlon turned in his seat at the sound of footsteps and saw Lisa walking by. She smiled her little predatory smile and waved; her nails were long and red. Giving a small sick smile in return, Marlon turned back to his desk. He looked at the one picture he had put up in his cubicle, of his parents, taken the day before they had died. They'd been traveling to Maine for a wedding when their car had run off the road. It had been almost two years, but Marlon still missed them each and every day.

As the cubicles around him began to empty out as his co-workers made their slow way home, Marlon collected his things and walked quickly out the building and into the McDonald's down the block. He rushed into the washroom and emptied his bladder. The washroom here was not always the cleanest, but it was definitely better than the one in the office. He bought a small order of fries—he felt guilty using the washroom without purchasing something—and made his way home.

That night he laid out the slacks he planned to wear to the office the next day, as well as a plain white t-shirt. Nothing too casual, nothing too formal. He'd found that businesses had different rules when it came to Casual Friday. Some, for instance, allowed sandals, shorts, sundresses; in others, those would all be considered inappropriate. He'd actually seen one guy come into an office wearing flip flops, a Hawaiian shirt, and cut-off jean shorts. That guy had been sent home to change.

What went on in some people's minds, he wondered to himself as he lay down to sleep.

When he arrived at Hygon Solutions the next morning he saw that he'd erred on the right side of caution. Most of his co-workers may have been dressed down, but they still looked like they could dine at a semi-formal restaurant. Some of them hadn't changed their manner of dress at all. He noticed that everyone who saw him come in that morning said hello to him, not just the usual few. *Must have put in enough time*, he thought.

As the hours went by, and Marlon scanned page after page, he wondered what lunch was going to be. He asked Jiro what was usually served, but received no answer. The other man just shrugged.

At noon Marlon heard the sound of dozens of chairs pushed back in unison, the loud squeak echoing throughout the floor. He hadn't seen a delivery person arrive with lunch. Slightly puzzled, he stepped out of his cubicle. Lisa appeared as if out of nowhere and slid an arm through his. She smiled and led him to the break room. He was trying to figure out how to extricate his arm, but they arrived before he could formulate a plan.

He noticed that all the lunch tables had been pushed together; the chairs were piled up against the walls. Mr. Bryant stood by the tables and waved for Marlon to join him. Mr. Bryant placed a large hand on Marlon's shoulder.

"Welcome to Casual Friday," boomed Mr. Bryant. "Before we begin I wanted to thank young Marlon here for the exemplary job he's been doing for us this week."

There was scattered applause, the sound of damp hands slapping against each other.

"As you know, each week you all get a meal on us at Hygon Solutions, but before we begin, it's time for everyone to take off their business attire."

Marlon looked over at Mr. Bryant, whose large face was regarding him intently. The man's eyes seemed to be bugging out of his head, and his hand clutched Marlon's shoulder hard enough it was beginning to hurt.

He heard the sounds of clothing hitting the floor and turned back to his co-workers, shocked to discover they were in the act of undressing.

"What in the hell?" he choked out.

"It *is* Casual Friday after all," chuckled Mr. Bryant. "We like our workers to be comfortable."

Lisa smiled at Marlon once again, this time her mouth splitting open to reveal the terrible teeth of a barracuda. She reached up with her talons and pulled on the sides of her head, the skin splitting open, peeling away. Underneath was a second skin, green, scaly, covered in mucus. Beside her Jiro had clawed his stomach to shreds to display the pale white flesh of a fish's belly. As Marlon watched horrified a fin burst out of Jiro's right forearm, sending small shreds of epidermis flying. Beside Jiro loomed the form of a titanic man whose brown loafers split open to reveal the splayed and palmated foot of some monstrous frog.

Marlon began to scream as skin was rended, as the mob of flesh that had been his co-workers transformed into a chaos of webbed hands, sharp teeth, catfish barbels, tadpole tails. His eyes refused to focus; his brain told him this could not be. He tried to run but Mr. Bryant's grip was like a vise, the tips of his fingers now clawed and digging into the meat of Marlon's shoulder.

As the monsters clustered about Marlon he found himself once again under that dock, screaming for help, while around him swam scores of uncaring eyes.

Lucy was eager to begin work; she was fresh out of college and hoping that by taking a temporary position she would be getting one foot in the door. The temp agency told her that the last guy who had this position had quit without telling them. Lucy didn't understand that kind of unprofessional behavior. You would never get ahead in this world acting like that. When she signed in with the receptionist the woman had smiled at her, saying, "Guess you're the new fish, huh?"

Lucy laughed; it always paid off to fraternize with co-workers. As she was led to the office of the manager she'd be working for she hummed a happy tune, unaware of the hungry eyes she left in her wake.

THE GOD UNDER THE CHURCH

by David Tallerman

"You will be—as of tomorrow morning—the managing director of Tettenkorf Import and Export."

"It's an honor," I said. "To be chosen by the Board at my age...." I could barely keep the satisfaction out of my voice, nor did I much try.

"Ours is a company of vast influence," Farley continued, "Not only here, but in Europe and Asia as well."

We were heading south over the bridge, into the old town. Behind us was the affluent heart of the city, and at its very center the towering, somber obelisk of the Tettenkorf building. "I certainly appreciate that. And if I may say—"

Farley cut me off. "Well then. There's something I have to show you ... as my father showed me, when I took over."

He'd emphasized the *have*, though it didn't occur to me at the time. If I'd noticed then perhaps I'd have kept my mouth shut. "George," I said, "I wanted to talk to you about that. I know that if I was you I would be feeling pretty sore about the company passing out of my family." Was I beginning to slur? Perhaps I'd drunk a little much at the party. Then again, it *had* been my party. "That's why I wanted to ask you ... will you stay on? I mean, in an advisory capacity? Please don't take this as a gesture; I honestly think I'll need you around."

"Yes," Farley murmured, though it wasn't altogether clear what he was agreeing with. "As of tomorrow I'm free of Tettenkorf and free from—well, you'll see, soon enough. There's something I have to show you, Mr. Taylor. And now we're there."

We pulled up against the curb, and a moment later the driver came round to open first Farley's door and then my own. He was a big man, intimidatingly so, and I didn't recognize him as one of the company's chauffeurs. A couple of drinks less and the situation would have seemed unusual from the start; however, only with that detail did I begin to seriously wonder at Farley's suggestion of a midnight drive into the old town.

I stepped down, with all the caution I could muster. We'd parked in front of a small and ancient-looking building, hemmed on either side by dilapidated shells that must once have been houses. The moon, sickly behind banks of low clouds, picked out sparingly the details of our destination: what was, despite considerable age and neglect, unquestionably a church. Yet what a church! It was the product of an age more infatuated with damnation than salvation, a haphazard structure of tiny windows, abrupt arches, and countless gargoyles which leered from every shadowed aperture. Even the candlelight that seeped through the narrow windows did not seem comforting; for the hour was past one in the morning, and I couldn't imagine why the church would be lit so late.

The driver, to my surprise, climbed back into his seat, and Farley, who had already climbed the brief flight of stairs, motioned to me from the doorway before disappearing inside. Seeing no option, I followed. Within, pews of worm-eaten dark wood filled the nave; candles flickered dimly. A great stone altar rested on a plinth at the far end, and beyond hung a crucifix, the suspended figure horridly contorted.

I hurried to catch Farley, who was in the chancel, engaged in conversation. His companion was buried within a cassock, and I took him for a priest who tended the church. As I approached, the pair retreated into the shadows of a corner and continued their discussion in hushed tones. Unable to catch a single word, I turned my attention instead to the altar stone—which, under close inspection, was far more impressive than the crucifix above. The altar was large, disproportionately so to the narrow space it occupied; it also seemed, inexplicably, to be older in design than the surrounding building. The stone appeared weathered, as though it had stood unprotected in some earlier age. Symbols had evidently once circumscribed the upper rim but now were indecipherable, nothing but distorted lines and curves. The surface was cracked and, in places, badly stained.

My investigation was cut short by Farley calling my name. His companion had opened a door in the wall behind them, had taken up a lit candelabra, and now waited in the entrance. Farley, standing between us, muttered, "Come now, Mr. Taylor."

On sudden impulse I barked back, "And what if I don't want to?"

Farley looked concerned. "There isn't much time."

"I mean, maybe I'm not interested in whatever you have to show me. What if I've decided I'd rather leave?"

"I'm afraid that wouldn't be allowed," Farley said.

Goaded by my nerves and the last vestiges of the champagne, I snarled, "Damn it, are you threatening me?"

Nothing in the old man's outward appearance changed: the lined face, beneath its mop of white hair, remained inscrutable. Yet as he replied he seemed somehow, suddenly, exhausted. "Not at all. Still, you won't be permitted to leave. We will go beneath the church and I'll show you what I have to show you. Nothing else will be tolerated."

Two things struck me in that moment. First, that Farley was right, that I *couldn't* leave. I was nervous of what might lie within that place, with its grotesque façade, its parodic crucifix, its inexplicably ancient altar. I had no desire to go farther, no curiosity. Yet I couldn't bring myself to turn away. And second, I realized that whatever peril I might be facing, it was not George Farley. I saw him then for what he was: aged, broken, a man at the end of his life. Almost pityingly, I said, "All right," and moved to follow him through the door.

Somehow I wasn't surprised to find, immediately beyond, stairs leading sharply downward into darkness. The steps descended for some twenty feet, then turned abruptly to the right at a sharp angle. When we reached this junction—the cloaked priest in front with our light, then Farley and myself—I found that the flight continued for another twenty feet before turning again, spiraling ever down.

After the third turn, the wall—which previously had been of the same drab brick as the church—changed to a sandy stone veined with lurid red. Around this point also, the air became noticeably oppressive. At first its dankness had seemed quite natural, the tepidity of an atmosphere sealed underground for goodness knew how long; however, the farther we descended, the clearer it became that the smell was something worse than the product of stale air.

As though sensing my thoughts and hoping to divert them, Farley turned back and said, "You're of an old family, Mr. Taylor. Your ancestors were amongst the first to settle in these parts. You've heard, perhaps, of the Tétaquo?"

"I haven't," I replied brusquely. It was becoming harder to breathe.

Yet the foul air didn't seem to bother Farley. "That's hardly surprising," he continued. "Their existence has been scoured from all but a very few histories and records. Isn't there, though, something familiar in the name itself?"

I forced myself to consider. "Tétaquo … Tettenkorf?"

"The Tétaquo," Farley said, just as though I hadn't spoken, "were the indigenous people of this region. They were unusual in being monotheistic, and they shared the name of their god. They were one of the few tribes to embrace the arrival of white settlers, and for a brief while they worked with the immigrants, even helping to build parts of what would become this city; specifically, what you know as the old town. During that time they spoke openly of their superstitions, and of their god, whose name they shared. We may assume, however, that the settlers did not approve of what they heard; we *must* assume, from what they did. For they slaughtered the tribe, every man, woman, and child that they could find, in a single bloody night. They demolished their village and made the wreckage into pyres. Then they set about erasing every sign and record that the Tétaquo had ever existed."

I was intrigued despite myself. "You make it sound as if the

natives invited their own destruction. But that name ...
Tétaquo, Tettenkorf? I don't understand."

"Then be patient a while longer, Mr. Taylor."

By then we had descended an incalculable distance beneath
the ground. The walls were damp, like clay, and the stench—
grown cloying and sickly-sweet—was overpowering. I would
have liked to vomit, or to escape back up those endless stairs.
Instead I continued downward, deeper into the intestines of the
earth.

Then, at the next right-angle turn, I stumbled. For the first
time the passage didn't descend. Instead, the way ran straight
and level, and my foot had reached for a step that wasn't there.
Farley looked concerned, offering me a hand to steady myself—
but I ignored the gesture. The priest had already disappeared
around the next corner, and a dim reflection of our light danced
madly upon the walls.

Beyond that next bend, the tunnel finally opened out into a
small antechamber. Here our guide had deposited his candelabra on a stone shelf, having lit a lantern from one candle. The
room was barely large enough for the three of us to stand together. I could see only the narrow shelf on the left, and ahead a
doorway of about five feet in height. The closed door was plain,
of a similar dark wood to that which furnished the church
above. The lintel, however, bore those same curvilinear glyphs
that I'd seen around the altar stone, though more clearly pre-
served here deep beneath the earth.

"What I have to show you is behind that door," said Farley.
"And, for whatever it may be worth...." For an instant, his face
clouded with pain, as though he were prising the words from
deep inside himself. "For what it's worth, I'm sorry."

Then, as if nothing had been said, his face regained its usual
distant expression and he motioned to the priest, who opened
the small door. Farley followed him through, stooping slightly
to avoid the lintel—which I practically had to crouch to pass
beneath.

Immediately I felt a crushing sense of space. Our lantern

seemed as futile as a spark in a thunderstorm, and at first I was sure I could make out nothing of the cavity I'd found myself in. At any rate, there was no gauging its length; I supposed the proportions might be similar to those of the church above, but the void seemed interminable. Nor could I make out much of its contents.

For that, at least, I was grateful—because by what scant light there was I'd seen more than enough. The place was an abattoir. Finally I choked up what little was in my stomach, and stumbled, gasping and shivering. I thought I might pass out, but the horror of the scene was so overwhelming that I staggered against the wall instead, and half stood, half cowered in the gloom there.

The cave was worse than a slaughterhouse. Nothing was whole or without decomposition. The hindquarters of a cow were splayed to my right; part of what I took to be a dog, ending abruptly in a stump of muscle and clotted gore, was visible close by. Wherever I looked there was nothing but broken and gutted corpses. Against the side wall, bones heaped towards the invisible ceiling, and every surface was caked with aged blood; everywhere stagnant offal pooled. I wondered frantically, were any of these remains human? But I couldn't bring myself to look.

After a few moments I heard my name being called. I turned dazedly towards the sound and gazed at Farley, as though he could somehow rationalize that nightmarish anatomy. Yet Farley gave no indication that he was even aware of our surroundings. When he was sure of my attention, he said, "Listen to me, Mr. Taylor. This is important and you must listen carefully. The being before you," and he motioned into the farther blackness, "is Tétaquo. That which waits."

Strangely, I hadn't thought to wonder what could have produced such carrion. As I followed Farley's direction, I could just make out a form huddled in the near darkness—a silhouette of deepest black. It was a mere shape, but that was enough to make the room's other terrors pale into insignificance; for even that outline was so shockingly alien that the fact of its existence made the surface world seem far away or gone forever.

The thing appeared to be entirely without color, and its surface glistened moistly. Its head was ovoid, almost featureless, and tapered into a feeler that rummaged the ground about. Behind the head, its vast body seemed vaguely insectile, and I imagined I saw an appendage something like a scorpion's sting weaving and jerking in the air beyond. Out from the body thrust three or more pairs of segmented legs—or what I took for legs, until I realized they were too fragile to bear its weight. Wondering in paralyzed curiosity how it could even support itself, I finally saw the mass of tentacles churning from behind its head.

"Tétaquo?" I managed.

"Indeed."

"Why … what does it want? What does it want *with me*? What in the hell does this have to do with Tettenkorf?"

"Mr. Taylor, they are the same. Tettenkorf is no more than an extension of Tétaquo … its tendrils into the world above. We exist for no other reason than to make the world ready."

"Ready?"

"For when it and others like it choose to take their place as the true rulers of our world. They are boundlessly powerful, but few. Humanity must be prepared for their return: weakened, taught to serve. That is our role and the role of others like us. When we are finished, they will come."

I almost laughed—and knew that if I started I would never stop. But surely there was more than a hint of mania in my voice as I said, "Do you think I'd do that? That there's anything you could give me, or threaten me with, that would make me serve that … that *horror*?"

"Mr. Taylor, you still don't understand." Farley motioned for the priest, who had been waiting patiently to one side, still clutching our feeble lantern. I could see now that he had his hood drawn down about his shoulders, with an expression of haughty defiance. His skin was a deep tan; his features were elegant and sharp. I couldn't but wonder then how many others of the accursed Tétaquo tribe had survived that centuries-old massacre.

The priest moved at Farley's direction to illuminate the area around the creature. In the scant light I could see how its feeler was almost like a trunk—though one that oozed with opaque jelly. Unconcerned by my scrutiny, it continued to eat, its appendage curled around a hunk of meat that visibly dissolved under the pressure. Above, near the center of its head, was an ovular orb, pale and milky as a cataract.

I looked back at Farley. "It's blind?"

"Not blind, no. The organ you see is largely vestigial in humans, long eroded by time and disuse. If you were superstitiously inclined you might think of it as a third eye."

I didn't understand at first. "You don't mean … you're not saying it can read my mind?"

"More than that," he murmured. "Why couldn't you leave when we first arrived? And later, when your every urge was to flee? Why … why do you think I'd bring you here?"

"You mean that thing can control me?" I cried. "It's been in my head this whole time?"

Then, impossibly, a voice inside my mind, like saliva dripping upon glass: a single word, or something more and less than a word, meaning and sound indistinguishable.

YES.

At that I think I screamed, and turned to run. I only remember the sensation of movement and my fear, before the darkness closed around me, dragging me into itself.

Then finally, gratefully, I slipped free of consciousness.

I woke crumpled in a corner of the car, Farley in the seat beside me. The view through the window told me we'd passed back over the bridge into the new town. I could see the Tettenkorf building rising upon the skyline, perhaps ten minute's drive away.

Farley was staring at me intently. When he seemed sure I was capable of understanding he said, "We're unlikely to see each other again, Mr. Taylor. It's important you understand what your role will be."

He proceeded to explain, and I listened, semi-conscious, watching the nighttime city pass by outside the window.

The thing could be fed through a shaft beneath the altar. This was attended to by the priests, what few there were. The arrangement was supported financially by a minor subsidiary of Tettenkorf. In this sense, my role was negligible: I had only to keep the organization in its accustomed profit. Unrestrained by morality, guided by a will and intelligence that was utterly alien—that perceived humankind as a nuisance or at best a resource—there was no real likelihood that the company would fail. There was, of course, the risk of questions arising about our divergence of funds to an insignificant monastic commune in the most dilapidated part of the old town. This was to be guarded against by any and all means.

Otherwise I had merely to continue my existence—and to submit. Tétaquo would work through me, and through the others it controlled. I would have no independence in matters of any consequence, and my personality as it had been would remain only as a mask. I wouldn't even be allowed to go mad, although—and Farley assured me of this—I would wish I could with every remaining fiber of my being.

George Farley was right.

For three years I've been a figurehead, enacting the policy of that monstrous entity under the church. Looking back, I see now that perhaps I was never a good man. Yet I hope you'll believe that I would never have committed the acts I've been compelled to since that night. I have seen things; agreed to policies, signed upon dotted lines; I've been made to watch the consequences of my actions. Tettenkorf has influence I'd never imagined, and in my position as its managing director, so do I. We have caused suffering and degradation on a scale I could never have conceived. From this, we've gained more money and more power, resources that will be used to manufacture more and greater waste and poverty. So it will continue until we and others like us have made the world a fit place for that monstrosity to crawl upon; until humanity is ready to grovel without question or reserve.

Farley died two and half years ago. He'd been placed in an asylum, like his father before him. I handled all of the arrangements. He ended his life screaming, contorting his body regardless of sedation. I was forced to watch, as a warning.

I understood. Better, I think, than it realizes.

It isn't omnipotent, you see. Its powers are vast and awful, its intelligence far beyond my own. But I don't believe it controls many others besides me. Even then, it has limits. Sometimes when it doesn't need me it leaves me almost alone. I think it senses when its presence seething in my mind will drive me insane and retreats for a while. In those moments, I've written and I've planned.

More often, though, it's only half there, watching the surface of my thoughts … guiding and intimating, only occasionally forcing. It can't displace me altogether. I feel sometimes that the subterfuge, the working with such base materials, disgusts it. Perhaps I revolt it as much as it does me. We are fragile, petty things by comparison.

Perhaps, too, it doesn't realize quite how fragile.

I don't believe we can defeat its kind, or avert what's coming. Even if the church could be found, (and I have only the vaguest idea of where it might be), even if the vault beneath could be uncovered by sufficient numbers that it couldn't defend itself—even then there would be the others Farley spoke of. They are behind companies, churches, governments. They are the Shadow Cabinet of the world. And I don't think that I'll be needed much longer.

I've made this record, in those brief moments of complete freedom, only for my own benefit. It's a pretense, at least; an attempt to forewarn of what seems an unavoidable destiny for our species, as less-than-slaves to beings that understand neither mercy nor restraint.

As for myself … I'm free, as I write these lines. As befits the managing director of Tettenkorf, my offices are on the top floor of the city's tallest building. Stairs will take me to the roof, and from there … but I don't have much time.

I will not die a lunatic like Farley. And I won't live like this for another day.

REFUSAL

by DJ Tyrer

"They're what?" Edward Thornberry-Hyde's already-roseate cheeks grew redder and seemed to swell so that he looked like nothing so much as an irate, pop-eyed pig with sunburn. He slammed his meaty hands down upon his robust mahogany desk.

"Refusing to board the ship, sir." Blameless though he was, John Sudbury, Thornberry-Hyde's secretary, was pink-faced with guilt as if, by relaying the message, he too were guilty of insubordination.

"Refusing to board? By thunder! How dare they?"

"I cannot say from where they get the nerve, sir, but they certainly have it. They were most … trenchant in their view."

"Blind them all! What excuse did they give?"

"It's that old Tahitian, sir, the one they call Priest; he's got the lascars in a state."

"Confound him. What for? Answer me, man, and cease beating about the bush."

"Sorry, sir. Um, well, it's that business about that god or devil, the one they call 'Tulu'."

"What about it?"

"The same reason: they say the ship is sailing to the waters it rules and won't go unless the proper, ah, sacrifices are made. What that entails, I don't rightly know, as I know you don't countenance such things."

"Quite right. Heathen mumbo-jumbo and dross."

"In addition, they seek an extra payment."

"Payment? Greedy heathen beggars. What for?"

"The danger."

"The danger? The sea's always dangerous enough."

"It's this 'Tulu'—they claim to be scared to sail those waters and, if they're to do so, wish additional payment."

Edward Thornberry-Hyde paused to pour some snuff out onto the back of his hand, then snorted it up into each nostril in turn, before expectorating the contents out into a fine silk hankie.

A little calmer, he looked Sudbury in the eye and said, "Then hire a new crew, dammit."

"Um, we already have; this is the second crew to refuse to board ship. I would suggest we hire crewmen who are neither lascar nor African."

"Nor Irish," interjected Thornberry-Hyde.

"Quite so." Sudbury shifted awkwardly; his grandmother was from Ireland, a fact he was careful not to let his master know. Thornberry-Hyde had taken against the Irish during the potato famine and had deplored them ever since. "It's the only way we might commence the voyage before the seasons turn against us. But, it may not be enough; there was an American amongst this last lot and even he was muttering about this devil. Priest seems able to poison the mind of any sailor."

Thornberry-Hyde snorted. "Americans are practically heathens, too. Give me a stout Cornishman or Yorkshire lad, any day."

"Indeed."

"So, you think that hiring a new crew may achieve us nothing?"

"No, sir. It's quite possible Priest will subvert them, too."

The businessman gave a sigh. "Then it seems something must be done about Priest."

"Sir?"

"Speak to the Brothers Leigh, have them deal with him."

"They won't."

"What?"

"They won't deal with him. I already approached them about intimidating him and they refused to have anything to do with it."

"They going soft?"

"They were scared, sir."

"Scared, what the deuce of?"

"Him. Priest. Or, his followers. Both, perhaps."

"Rot and poppycock! The Leighs scared? Nonsense!"

"I'm sorry to say not, sir. The Brothers Leigh live amongst these people, share their superstitions. Priest appears to have quite the reputation, and he has a number of followers. Some from our crew, in fact."

"Followers?"

"A congregation, of sorts."

Thornberry-Hyde released a lengthy string of curses, then rested his hands upon his desk in a manner his secretary knew to denote resolution.

"If the Leighs won't do it, then *we* shall have to deal with it. Do you know where this..." He wrinkled his snout-like nose. "...congregation is to be found?"

"I will make enquiries, immediately."

"Do so. Then, gather Rochford, Tuckman, and Harrison, ensuring they're armed, and we'll pay this Priest a visit and 'persuade' him to cease his opposition."

Sudbury twitched with a momentary stab of nerves. "Very good, sir. I'll do so at once."

The night was chill and their breath fogged a little before them, a wisp of mist that quickly dissipated. The yard to the rear of the office building was empty, save for the three men, the workers having long since gone home to bed or to the convivial atmosphere of local hostelries and public houses.

Rochford, who served as the firm's doorman, wished he were with them, but a little extra money wasn't to be refused. For Tuckman and Harrison, who served as night-watchmen here at the office building and the neighboring warehouse and storehouses, the extra night work was no hardship and the additional payment welcome.

They all turned at the sound of a door to see their boss step out into the yard, Sudbury following behind him.

Thornberry-Hyde paused to survey the three men, then nodded in satisfaction. "Good, stout men. Now, Sudbury, do you know our destination?"

"Yes, sir. It's not far from here, an empty warehouse, in fact. Priest has commandeered it for himself and his followers attend it for meetings. I know the way."

"Very good. Lead on."

Sudbury nodded and stepped to the front of the little group. They followed him out of the yard and down the street. Moving carefully so their hobnailed boots didn't clatter upon the cobbles and keeping to the ample shadows as much as possible, they followed Sudbury along the backstreets of the dock district to their destination, the warehouse. Ragged strands of mist swam apart as they passed, agitated by their passage.

"Are you certain? It seems deserted."

"Yes, sir. Or, so I'm told."

Thornberry-Hyde drew his revolver from a pocket. "Very well. In we go."

The side door was neither guarded nor locked.

"I don't like this," muttered Rochford. "Too easy." An unguarded door offended his sensibilities.

"Savages." Thornberry-Hyde spat. "God gave them no sense."

Tuckman slapped his baton against the palm of his hand as if to punctuate his master's sentence.

They stepped inside and Tuckman swore at the sight that greeted them, for the interior wasn't empty as might have been expected. Instead of an open space, the inside of the warehouse had been hung with sheets of sail canvas. There was but the faintest glow of firelight from within the cocoon of sails, and they muffled the noise of what must have been many people so that it sounded like the distant rumble of waves upon a shore.

"What the hell is this?" demanded Rochford.

"It's like a bleedin' maze," said Harrison, tone nervous, observing how the canvas sheets appeared to be layered.

"It's how they hide themselves." Sudbury turned to his master. "And, have you noticed, sir, how it's rippled?"

Thornberry-Hyde gave a noncommittal grunt.

"It's like the waves of the sea."

It was true, although Thornberry-Hyde lacked the poetical sensibilities to make such a connection without having it pointed out first; the way the sheets of canvas had been hung gave the impression of waves and the way it muffled sound was like surf. There could be little doubt the effect was deliberate.

He gave a soft snort, unwilling to admit the ingenuity.

"Right, follow me."

Thornberry-Hyde slipped in between the hanging sheets and began to thread his way along the maze-like gap between them, as if he were descending towards some hidden light far below the ocean surface.

Harrison produced a large knife. "We can cut our way through."

Thornberry-Hyde shook his head. "No, not unless speed becomes a necessity. I want to surprise the bastard."

Then, muffled, he heard the sound of a bell, like one tolling in the depths. He shivered. Suddenly, it was as if there were whispers around them, the hint of shadowy movement amongst the sheets, souls swimming down to a watery purgatory. The dark stories sailors masked under such tales as those of Davy Jones stirred in his memory, and he had to concentrate upon the fact it was canvas, not water, that surrounded them to calm his nerves.

Harrison turned and pushed past him, eyes wide in panic, desperate to escape.

"Stay, you fool," Thornberry-Hyde hissed. "It's only heathen trickery—you'll give us away."

But Harrison wouldn't listen and began to use his knife to hack his way through the canvas, attempting to reach the exit.

Sudbury looked at his master, who spat and said, "Press on, man, before he gives us away. Hurry!"

A sense of urgency mixed with the fear that washed about them like the chill sea's waters, and it was with a speed verging upon panic that they completed their journey to the heart of the canvas labyrinth, the sound of Harrison's retreat rapidly fading.

With just one sheet, now, between them and their quarry, Thornberry-Hyde, Sudbury, Rochford and Tuckman could observe the secret chapel that the canvas had been hung to conceal. A brazier lit the scene with dancing light. The old Tahitian known as Priest and his congregation were engaged in a fury of worship that Thornberry-Hyde immediately dismissed as "savage" and "primitive", yet still shivered to observe, his dismissal unable to quite reject its power. There was something in the frenetic dance, as an old sailor with ebony skin tanned to leather by the ocean wind rang the bell and another banged upon a makeshift barrel drum, that spoke of some primal truth the logical mind could not readily deny.

Thornberry-Hyde spat, as much in disgust at himself as with them.

There were the lascars and Africans and others such as he had expected, "heathens" and "savages" of no great account, but he was surprised to see white men amongst their ranks. It offended his sensibilities to see those he considered superior, albeit inferior to himself, engaged in such degradation. It seemed the malign influence of Priest's superstition was capable of infecting anyone. He gripped the handle of his revolver more tightly, reassured by the firmness of the polished wood in his hand, and looked at the three men who remained with him. Each man's jaw was grimly set, unnerved a little by the scene, but resolute.

He nodded and stepped forward, his men at his back. The drumming ceased and the men fell still.

"Listen here, I've had just about enough of all this. I want this nonsense to end and my ship crewed to go."

Priest turned to him. He seemed to leer grotesquely in the

light of the flickering flames.

"Thornyman-Hides," he said. Thornberry-Hyde snorted at the mangling of his name. Priest gave an elaborate bow. "Welcome to our sanctuary."

"You heard me."

Priest spread his hands. "And, *you* have heard me. None shall enter into the forbidden waters without a blessing and a sacrifice—and suitable recompense."

Thornberry-Hyde thought he caught a mercenary glint in the man's eye. "That's it, isn't it? Money. You may have your followers fooled with your threats and mumbo-jumbo talk, but this is all about money. You'll extort me into paying up and pick their pockets in turn."

He folded his arms in satisfaction, his revolver resting in the crook of his arm, content the man was no more than a charlatan and a crook.

Priest laughed: the sound was mocking, not mirthful.

"You are a fool, Thornyman. You understand nothing but the gold that jangles in your pocket. The ocean depths are dark and cold and hold horrors no man can comprehend."

As he spoke, the fire in the brazier seemed to gutter and die, the scene growing dark as shadows crept in upon them.

The men at his back exchanged glances.

"Mighty Tulu must be propitiated."

Thornberry-Hyde snorted again, and pointed his revolver at Priest. "Heathen nonsense. If it isn't pure fiction, a play upon the credulous simplicity of these men who follow you."

Priest laughed once more. "You demand proof? As if I kept Tulu in the purse on my belt! Very well, very well...."

He crooned strange, harsh words that put them in mind of waves crashing against rocks.

"Look...." Tuckman pointed, and they saw dark shapes, darker than the shadows that surrounded them, were pressed up against the canvas, shapes like men, only squat and broad with bowed legs and overlong arms like apes; they gave the impression of gigantic frogs that had learnt to walk upright.

Rochford swore. Sudbury echoed his sentiment.

"Sir," he said, but Thornberry-Hyde ignored him.

The men looked at one another, then Rochford turned and ran. Sudbury lingered, half-turning, but unwilling to abandon his boss.

"You shan't fool me with your quackery," Thornberry-Hyde cried.

Then the canvas tore and the figures stepped forward. Thornberry-Hyde looked about wildly. Although the darkness shrouded their features, he could see enough and cried out to God in his alarm.

"Now, you believe…."

Thornberry-Hyde nodded and begged Priest to send them away. "I'll accede to your demands. The men shall be paid and you shall have your sacrifice. I yield—I yield!" He turned to Sudbury. "Make the arrangements with the purser."

Sudbury didn't wait to hear more, but nodded, then ran.

Priest laughed again. "Very good, Thornyman, very good!"

"Do it, do it!" He turned to leave, the revolver slipping from limp fingers to clatter on the floor.

But, before he could take more than two steps, hands seized him and he was dragged back towards Priest.

"What? What are you doing?"

"Seeking the benign tolerance of our god. Do not worry, Thornyman, your ship shall sail, your ship shall sail. *You* shall be the sacrifice."

"No! Help!"

Priest touched an unseen lever and a trap fell open in the floor.

"Farewell, Thornyman." Priest chuckled. "Farewell."

"No, please…."

"Throw him in."

They released him into the darkness, to plunge down into the waters below where the servants of Tulu waited in the murky, saline Thames waters to feast upon his flesh. His ship would sail into the forbidden waters, but Thornberry-Hyde wouldn't live to learn of its success or failure.

Priest smiled and closed the trap, then turned to his followers. "Let us give praise and thanks to Mighty Tulu, who sleeps in his drowned house dreaming...."

DAGON-TEC

by Adam Millard

I am writing this under a severe amount of mental strain, and also on the back of a cereal box as I could not for the life of me find a piece of blank paper. I have unfortunately run out of weed, and can take it no longer. When this is done, I shall launch myself out of window like a midget out of a cannon. Now, you might think I'm being a bit of a pansy, but once you've finished reading the back of this Fruit Loops packaging, you'll know why I must kill myself. Well, hopefully kill myself, for there is a slim chance I'm now in a hospital bed with two busted legs and a very sore back. Anyhow, let us proceed.

It was on the final Friday of last month when Dagon-Tec went on our annual outing, and we had, over the years, done it all: scuba-diving, mountaineering (madness!), spelunking. Two years ago there had been a slight decrease in company revenue, and so we, as a team, had spent a Sunday afternoon painting pottery mugs and teapots in the cold back room of our local craft store.

Luckily, profits were up this year. Who knew there was so much money in developing fish-based videogames?

As the bus pulled up to our destination—a corporate re-treat our boss Charlie Dexter had hastily put together after a weekend of paintballing fell through, thanks to some muppet double-booking us with a band of merry girl scouts—I couldn't help but notice the fantastically gibbous and waning moon. Like a giant's toenail, it was, hanging there in the darkness. I even said as much to my friend, Randy Carter.

"Look at that moon," I said. "Have you ever seen a more gibbous one?"

To which Randy replied, "I haven't got a clue what gibbous means."

"Me either," said I, before lighting a much-needed cigarette and stepping down from the bus.

The journey had been long, and my back was sorer than a hooker on payday. I stretched, breathed in the cold night air and, after coughing it all back up, went to find Dexter, who was at the front of the bus, arguing with the driver over a price.

Now, you wouldn't think a man of Charlie Dexter's wealth would haggle so feverishly over three hundred bucks, and that's where you would be wrong. Dexter is—*was*—so tight, he yearned for the day the Bible came out in paperback. This was the man who created *Fish-Tales 1-4*—not to mention *Tonic the Trout* and *Super Shark on Salmon Island*—bickering with the bus driver over such a trifling amount.

"Do you smell fish, Dexter?" said I, for I could. The whole area seemed to reek of it, and I found myself wondering if there was a fishery nearby, which would have explained everything. "And also, do you have any idea what gibbous means?"

The bus driver sniffed at the air like an asthmatic pug. "Smells a *bit* fishy," he said, which confirmed my suspicions. "And gibbous is when the illuminated part of the moon is greater than a semi-circle and less than a circle."

"Don't be silly!" said Dexter to the driver. "Gibbous are those monkeys with the glowing red backsides." He turned to me then and added, "And the fish smell is from just over there. We're going on a little boat trip tonight, you know? To strengthen our bond as a team."

"Oh," I said, for I had not prepared for such an adventure; the fifteen-hour coach drive to the coast had fairly taken it out of me. I wanted nothing more than my bed. Perhaps a cup of hot chocolate. Three cigarettes. A frantic session of masturbation. But mostly I just wanted my bed.

Less than an hour later, the six of us were in a dinghy off the west coast. There was me, Charlie Dexter, Randy Carter, Jervas Dudley, Tina Tillinghast, and Herbert something-or-other (Herbert cleaned our office for us, so it was only right he should come along).

"Does anyone know what gibbous means?" I asked as we floated along.

"Will you stop going on about gibbous!" Dexter said. "All I've heard since we got here is 'Gibbous! Gibbous! Gibbous!'. This is supposed to be a corporate adventure! Not a quiz on antiquated words!"

Even in the darkness I could see the vein throbbing upon Dexter's temple. I decided to let the whole gibbous thing drop, lest we all suffer for the duration of the event. Besides, the bus driver seemed to know what he was talking about.

Now, what happened next I do not know. One moment I was sitting there in the boat with my unfortunately-named colleagues, the next I was all alone. I can only assume I had fallen asleep, at which point the rest of my team had, as they are wont to do, decided to play a prank upon me and scarper.

"Guys!" I called out into the darkness. "This isn't funny! I need the toilet!"

But there was no reply, which meant one of two things: either they were all dead and I was cast adrift in a rubber boat, or they didn't care if I wet myself.

For hours—perhaps even days, although I don't recall the sun ever rising—I appealed for help, occasionally stopping to sing a verse from Coldplay's latest (what a terrible earworm!), until finally I succumbed to sleep once again.

When finally I came to, I found myself up to my gonads in mud, the dinghy grounded off to my right. I should have been happy that I was out of the water; however I'm a miserable sort and could only focus on the negative.

In this case, all the dead fish scattered about the place (plaice?). The air was redolent with the stench of rotting sea-creatures, and also the urine in my trousers, for I had, like an idiot, fallen asleep with a full bladder.

I was all at once aware of silence, broken every now and then by my own humming (damn you to Hell, Coldplay!).

Eventually, I managed to drag myself through the inky mire to the dinghy, where I knew there were several Twinkies with my name on them—literally, as Herbert something-or-other had a tendency to go through the office refrigerator, helping himself to the salads and sandwiches.

I sat eating the Twinkies, and must have fallen asleep again. I made a mental note to visit a doctor when I got home, for I was almost certainly suffering some sort of narcolepsy, before climbing out of the dinghy and setting off in search of help.

I found myself wondering what had happened to my colleagues. Not so much Charlie Dexter, but of Tina Tallinghast (who was a bit of a sort, for want of a better description) and my good friend Randy Carter, who still owed me twenty bucks. I would have waived the twenty bucks to see him again, or at least halved it, for I'm not a complete bastard.

The ground beneath my feet began to harden, which was a relief as, in that moment, I was growing awfully tired of the squeaking sound my brogues were making in the morass.

I arrived, some three hours later according to my expensive and pointless Rolex, at a hummock. Too knackered to climb it, I slept for a while in the shadows.

My dreams were strange that night (day? week?), which I could only put down to the gibbous moon and the eating of three Twinkies in quick succession. I dreamed of cancelled pensions, of falling stock, of some journalist named Dunwich looking into my tax returns, and when I wakened I was cold with sweat. Reluctant to return to sleep, I decided to head on up the hill.

It was a lot steeper than it had looked from down at ground level. By the time I reached the halfway point I had a stitch in my side and a fresh piss in my pants, but I forged on, for I'm nothing if not determined. However, given the choice between determination and bladder control, I would have had a tough decision to make.

I arrived at the crest of eminence an indeterminate amount of time later, for my Rolex had unceremoniously given up the ghost and was now running backwards. As I looked down into the canyon, I felt I was on the edge of the world, which is ridiculous as I'm certain—unlike some foolish people—the earth is round. I mean, of course it is! Otherwise space would be teeming with overzealous nomads.

After a while I began my descent into the canyon, gazing into the Stygian deeps as I went.

"Does anyone know what Stygian means?" I called out, but the only reply I received was in the form of an echo, which, after a few seconds of panic, I realized belonged to me.

Then I saw it off in the distance. A huge monolith, like something out of *Dune* or Dubai. At first I thought it was just a piece of rock, shaped by fortuitous means, but then I became convinced it was a thing not shaped by Nature, but by the hands (webs? fins?) of living, thinking creatures.

My instinct told me to go back up the canyon, find my way back to the dinghy, and take another nap, but my heart, like Celine Dion once said it would, urged me to go on.

And on I went, water lapping at my feet, and as I neared the great monolith I saw the inscriptions all around it. It was peppered with hieroglyphics depicting fishes, eels, mollusks, whales, and also, in some places, rudimentary penis drawings.

"Typical," said I, clicking my tongue and shaking my head.

Waves washed the base of the great monolith, which was a shame as everything north of the water could have done with a little rinse, too. I saw, carved into the side of the structure, strange bas-reliefs depicting the most grotesque creatures I have ever seen, which is remarkable as I had once spent six months working in the British House of Commons.

Perhaps, I thought, these creatures are the imaginary gods of some ancient seafaring tribe. Or perhaps they had been carved and transported here by Tracey Emin, who was renowned for her crap art. Either way I was a little perturbed, for the bas-reliefs were fairly putting the shits up me. I was about to turn around and head back from whence I came when I saw it.

With only a slight churning—like a frog's fart rising in a

garden pond—to mark its rise to the surface, it emerged. A creature so vast I had to take several steps back to take it all in. Loathsome it was, though I wouldn't dare say that to its face. It shot across the water, flung its gigantic scaly arms around the monolith, and said, "Bugger off!"

I think that was the point I went completely mad. And also pissed myself for a third time.

Of my frantic scrabble back up the hill, over the other side, and down toward the dinghy I have very little recollection. Although I do remember singing some Coldplay as I went, which perhaps sent me even madder.

So *mad* was I that I came to in a San Francisco hospital. Lord knows how I got there, but I should imagine it involved ambulances, helicopters, sirens and the like.

"It was terrible!" I screamed at the poor nurse on duty that night. "Like something out of a Harryhausen movie!"

But no one would believe me, and I spent a little time in Arkham—just three nights, actually, as they needed my bed for someone else—before returning home with nothing but a prescription for a course of antidepressants and a note entitling me to two weeks off work.

It is at night when the moon is gibbous—I know what it means now, for I have a dictionary right here upon my desk—that I see the thing, the creature rising from the depths, and I am at my wits' end.

So now, having scribbled all this down on a single side of a cereal box (I have ridiculously small handwriting), I must end my life, for I cannot forget about that nameless thing, throwing itself around the monolith like a desperate girl around Hugh Hefner's leg.

Wait! I hear something at the door! Something soft and wet and probably out to get me.

To the window! To the window! Ah, living in a basement apartment, I don't *have* a window!

It's in through the door now! And yet I am still writing! Ah! Ouch! No! It's so terribly slimy! Ouch! Get off! No! It appears I will shortly be dead! Ah! Oooh! Tell my mother I—

   ...

ESOTERIC INSURANCE, INC.

by Evan Dicken and Adrian Ludens

It wasn't like the old days, not that Obed had actually been around for the "old days," at least how his father described them. The old man loved to talk about how great things were before the Esoteric Order had become incorporated—midnight sacrifices and blood orgies, dark pacts forged on jagged sea cliffs, nights spent swimming deeper and deeper and deeper. Granted, Obed didn't think he'd enjoy a sacrifice, and he didn't really have the stomach for a blood orgy, but anything had to be better than standing in the rain patiently waiting to ruin someone's life.

"It's all right here." The client pressed a loose sheaf of papers into Obed's hands.

He shuffled through the documents, trying not to wince at the client's anxious, yet hopeful smile. The man looked about Obed's age, dark hair flecked with gray, worry lines bunching the corners of his mouth. He probably had a kid in college, maybe two; a car loan; a mortgage on the house that was even now sinking into the muddy ground behind them.

They're not people, they're clients, Obed reminded himself.

The man swallowed. "I bought everything y'all offered: flood, fire, earthquake, burglary—all of it."

"I'm sure you did, Mr. Allen." Obed took a wet, raspy breath, dreading what was to come. "Unfortunately, your policy doesn't cover acts of god."

A series of quick-changing emotions swept across Mr. Allen's face: surprise, disbelief, anger. He could've been following a script. "Listen, this is a mudslide or a sinkhole. No god here."

"I'm afraid so." If there was a script, Obed had his part to play, too. "Per the 'Infinite Fairness in Insurance Act,' gods are defined as all beings who exist either all or partly outside time and space." He squatted, pointing at the puddle of viscous slop next to Allen's front porch. "These are clearly dhole excretions. You might know dholes better as chthonians, but either way, as vermiform creations of Shudde M'ell they're exempt."

The dhole slime was something of a relief, actually. Gods, spirits, and Old Ones were everywhere, but it was seldom this obvious. Last week, Obed had been forced to reach all the way back to Azathoth to find an exception.

"Please, look again," Allen said.

Obed fixed him with a long stare, sighed, then riffled through the papers. They both knew it was for show. No matter his car, his house, his life, Mr. Allen hadn't been born with "the look," and that meant he didn't have the coverage, didn't have anything, as a matter-of-fact.

"Everything we had was in there." Allen ran a hand along his stubble, blinking. Now came the client's only real choice: fury or grief. Obed wasn't sure which was worse. "What am I going to tell my family?"

Grief, then.

"Sorry, there's nothing I can do," Obed said. It wasn't *exactly* true. There were loopholes—maddening eccentricities and escape clauses wriggling deep within blocks of cyclopean text. Mr. Allen's mind wasn't equipped to find them, at least if he wanted to keep his sanity, but Obed could—no one knew the rules better than Obed. He could get Mr. Allen his payment, but it would take a night of paperwork. Not to mention it would piss Randy off. Esoteric Insurance's regional manager had been known for his temper even before the change; now that Randy was eight feet tall with claws like fishhooks, Obed was doubly concerned about cutting corners.

He held out the insurance documents. When Mr. Allen didn't take them, he let the papers tumble to the muddy ground.

Mr. Allen slumped back on the crumbling remains of his porch and covered his face with his hands.

Obed almost wished the man would take a swing at him. *Grief is definitely worse.*

He walked away, trying to keep his back straight, his shoulders high even though he dearly wanted to drop to all fours and scuttle back to his car. Obed's father might be a relic, but he was right about one thing: this wasn't the old days. The Esoteric Insurance was a business now, and in this business, a professional appearance meant everything.

"This isn't right," Mr. Allen called after him.

"I'm sorry, sir. It's the law." Obed turned away, feeling a familiar heaviness settle in his stomach. Nobody ever said the job would be easy. Clients looked at him and they saw a paunchy, sallow-skinned insurance adjuster with no chin and a receding hairline; they didn't see a man with two aging parents to look after, a house, a car, and a life.

His car windows were open, the interior damp with rain, which was nice. At least this had been the last case of the day. He loosened his tie and headed home, wondering if he should get takeout—maybe sushi, or a *pizza*. Obed's mother wasn't likely to want any, but his father, for all his bragging about cannibalism, would absolutely devour an extra-large anchovy pie.

There was a woman lying in the middle of the road, face down, her arms and legs spread so Obed couldn't tell if she was alive or dead. It happened from time to time, when someone couldn't bear to live any longer or a corpse washed up from the sewers. He wondered if he should stop. Maybe he could talk to her, maybe he could help, or maybe it would be a waste of time.

He checked his mirrors for traffic, then drove around the woman. Someone else would stop. She shifted as he passed, watching him with eyes like bits of wet slate, one hand raised, fingers hooked as if to drag his car closer.

Obed stamped on the gas, accelerating away. A few turns and she was lost from sight. It was sad, he reflected. Sad and unfair. Whatever happened to her wasn't Obed's fault. He was just living his life like everyone else.

He turned on the car radio, tapping his fingers to the

tongueless howls of the Easy Listening channel. Still, he couldn't get her face, her *expression* out of his head—hopeless, broken, just like Mr. Allen, just like all of them. Obed ran a hand through his thinning hair. Pizza didn't sound so good anymore.

Come to think of it, he wasn't hungry at all.

Obed took his time climbing the creaking stairs that led to the Fever Attic, so named because the garish paisley rug and yellow wallpaper reminded him of the frequent fever dreams he'd had as a child. He would've avoided it completely except his mother had shut herself up there months ago after a fight with Obed's father—as if she could lock out both her husband and the change.

Obed skipped a step to avoid a spot he knew creaked and lurched sideways to avoid another squeaky board. He realized his gait resembled a jester's dance and, reminded of Poe's dwarfish Hop-Frog he flushed, and dropped to all fours. Work had his head all turned around; if a man couldn't scuttle in his own home, where *could* he scuttle?

As always, he paused outside the door, not certain if he would feel more relieved if she hadn't changed, or if she *had*.

A blast of hot, dry air met Obed as he slipped into the attic. A row of dehumidifiers lined the far wall, matched by a half-dozen space heaters spread around the room, and still the place was damp, water stains and black mold visible where the yellow wallpaper had peeled away from the ceiling. He wrinkled his nose at the dry antiseptic smell of the place.

Obed's mother was in bed, watching him, her eyes narrowed to slits, her lips pressed tight. She'd pulled the blanket up over her legs, almost gone now, the great curve of the tail that was replacing them curled under the sickbed. Blue veins criss-crossed her skin like rivers on a map, the surrounding flesh luminous in the evening shadows. She laid still, hands resting on her Bible. Obed could see the bloody gashes where she'd cut away the webbing between her fingers again.

She shifted as he entered, the mattress making a wet, sloshing noise. "Obediah."

"Don't call me that."

"It's the name I gave you." His mother gave a phlegmy cough. "Obediah was a prophet in the good book."

"Which one?"

She heaved her great bulk up to glare at him. "This is the time of tribulation John of Patmos prophesied. Abaddon, the angel of death, flies free; the Dragon gathers his loyal followers; the Beasts of the Sea cavort below my window, and yet I am not afraid."

Obed gave her a tight smile. "How do you feel?"

She laid back. "How was work?"

Obed turned away to hide his flush, making a show of checking her breakfast tray. "You're not eating. It's important to keep your strength up."

"Why?"

Obed gripped the tray tight. "The change is an honor, you know."

"That's your dad talking." She regarded him. "I won't go down, not now, not ever. I'd rather die and let my spirit fly up to heaven. Where will *you* go, Obediah?"

He felt like a pinned insect in a display box whenever his mother watched him like that. "I'll bring you food. Fish if you're up to it, or salt broth, if you'd rather…."

She rolled over, bed creaking. Obed stared at her broad back, shaking his head. Her body, so ungainly on land, would be fast and sleek in the cold dark beneath the waves, and yet she refused, collecting dehumidifiers and space heaters as if they could stop the rising damp.

He chewed his lip. "Mom, you should—"

"How many people did you kill today?"

He turned and hurried from the room.

" 'All of us have become unclean, and all our righteous acts are like filthy rags.' " Her words followed him. " 'We shrivel like a leaf, and, like the wind, our sins will sweep us—' "

He closed the door.

Downstairs, he grabbed some kelp beer and turned on the news. There was a story about Esoteric Insurance. Nightgaunts had flensed another group of protesters outside the District Office. There was a clip of a lawyer-woman, April Derleth, saying the demonstration had been peaceful; that incorporated cults were contributing to systemic inequalities; that access to food, water, housing, and medicine were basic human rights. She looked familiar, but Obed couldn't place her. The clip cut to a blurry video of a security nightgaunt snatching her up. Obed winced as they flapped off screen, and he reached for the remote. He already knew how this would end.

There was a splash from the basement.

Obed set his beer down, shaking his head. Dad had flooded the cellar again. He stamped on the floor. When the splashing continued, Obed pushed from his chair to crawl across the house. He opened the basement door, saw what awaited him, and sighed.

Obed's father had plugged up the sump, letting brackish water bubble up through the gravel cellar and into the finished part of the basement. At least he'd remembered to disconnect the circuits this time, although it left everything pitch black. Obed used his phone's flashlight app to survey the damage.

Bits of cardboard, ruined clothes, and a few of his mother's keepsake ornaments floated on the filthy water. Obed scowled as one of his old baby albums bobbed by, the pictures all runny and waterlogged.

"Dad!" Obed slapped the surface of the makeshift pond. Ripples spread from his hand, lapping over the top of the washer/dryer—which was probably *also* ruined.

When nothing broke the surface, he stepped into the water, chiding himself for not changing clothes. Another suit ruined.

He could see his father at the far corner of the basement, a pale blur near the workout equipment Obed had bought and never used. At least the water felt nice, a bit warmer than he would've preferred, but not bad.

In the light of the phone, he could just make out his father's features: eyes squeezed shut in concentration, long, greasy hair like loose strands of kelp in the standing water, a thin trickle of bubbles slipping through his pursed lips.

Obed knew it was coming, but still leapt back with a shout when his father surged up, water cascading off his naked form.

"Obediah!" His father blinked the water from his eyes, grinning.

"Don't call me that."

"And why not? It's a strong name, an *ancient* name." His father clapped him on the shoulder.

"We talked about this."

"About what?"

"*This.*" Obed gestured at the flooded basement. "You know salt water is *murder* on the plumbing."

"I know, I know, but I had to celebrate." His father bared flat, human teeth. "See, they're getting sharper, and look—" He lifted one leg from the water, revealing toes that looked normal apart from a very bad case of fungus. "It's *finally* happening, don't you think?"

"Definitely," Obed lied. He didn't have the heart to tell the truth to a man who had put forty years in with the cult only to be left high and dry with a pension that barely covered utilities. "Now why don't you go upstairs, towel off, and have some fish to celebrate?"

With a nod, his father waded toward the stairs. Shaking his head, Obed followed him upstairs.

Gods, sometimes it felt like he was raising two children.

"So, how many people did you kill today?" his dad asked once Obed had gotten him dried off and into a pair of overalls.

"You know we don't do that anymore."

"Of course, of course. I get it." His father gave him a conspiratorial wink, then leaned in. "C'mon, you can tell me."

"No one. Honestly."

"Bullshit."

Obed blew out a long sigh. It was clear his father wasn't going to give up. "Well, two of my clients *did* hang themselves. And there was a woman in the street on the way home."

"My boy!" His dad nudged him in the ribs. "Did you see the news?"

"The protest?"

"You mean the riot?" His dad opened the refrigerator and rattled around, pulling out two kelp beers and a plate of raw fish. "It's these kids. They think the whole world revolves around them. In my day, we'd toss the lot of them off a cliff or cut them open with a kris knife. Gods, remember my old sacrificial dagger? Big ol' gold handle, blade curvy as a slithering snake, rubies in the pommel. Wonder where it got to?"

"It's probably in the basement," Obed said.

"Loved that knife. Always carry a blade, Son. Always," his dad said around a big mouth of fish. "Back in my day we didn't need security nightgaunts. We would've tickled those protesters ourselves."

"I don't think—"

"They deserved what they got. Shouldn't have resisted."

"That's the thing." Obed winced, thinking of the surprised expression on April Derleth's face as the nightgaunt carried her away. "I don't think they did."

There were still smears of blood on the parking lot outside the Esoteric Insurance District Office, little bits of hair and gristle baked into the cracks in the asphalt. Obed felt nervous, but the remains weren't the reason why. He'd been called in to meet with the regional manager. Rumor was Randy had contacted Corporate Inhuman Resources, which meant things were either very good or very *bad*.

Caught up in nervous prognostication, Obed nearly drove over the woman. To be fair though, she *was* lying in his parking spot.

He recognized her from the road last night, and from the TV—April Derleth. She wasn't moving, although as Obed threw the car in reverse he did see her flinch at the noise. The nightgaunt must've dropped her in the housing development and for some reason she'd crawled back here.

Scowling, Obed drove around and parked in a visitor space. This was just what he needed going into a meeting with Randy.

April—no, *the woman*; Obed shouldn't use her name—made a soft rattling noise as he walked past. He chewed his lip, feeling just like when his mother stared at him.

What did they expect him to do? Quit? Stop paying the mortgage? Put his parents out on the street?

Obed walked past her, his throat hot and tight, the skin between his shoulder blades crawling. There was nothing he could do, but if so, why did he feel so bad?

The Esoteric Insurance District Office was a ramshackle multi-story building squatting sullenly at the edge of the sea as if it wanted nothing more than to leap from the rocky cliff and into the waves. Inside, a single naked light bulb barely swept back the darkness. The antique security desk was unoccupied. Obed let his gaze linger on the ancient texts and tomes of unearthly insurance regulations spread across the desk.

Checking his messages, he saw the meeting was scheduled for the sepulcher, and felt another wave of clammy anxiety wash over him.

A trio of skittering shadows disappeared into holes in the wall as he pushed into the stairwell. He paid them no mind. Instead, he crouched and slid his fingers across the floor until finding the cold iron ring he sought. The trapdoor rose with a bark of protest, and cold dank air rushed up to touch his face. Obed descended into the cool darkness, treading on rustic footholds carved into the stone.

The red exit sign provided barely enough light to see, so

Obed flicked his flashlight app on again.

His shoes scraped the gritty sub-basement floor. The meager light revealed a pair of wooden barrels, an empty wine rack, and a few scattered bones of varying size and shape.

In the farthest corner of the room, a crevice gaped like a toothless mouth. Obed lay on his belly and scrabbled through the opening. Another suit ruined, but that was to be expected. The darkness and the tunnel walls pressed in against him. Water trickled between his hands and knees, soaking through his pants.

Obed emerged at the edge of a deep, murky pool. Water dripped from stalactites overhead. About thirty yards away, Obed saw a faint glow beneath the water—sunlight, as seen through the cavern's egress into the sea. The tide was coming back in, and the sepulcher would soon fill to the ceiling. The distant light diminished as a huge shadow shifted in the water.

"*There* he is!" A raspy voice echoed from the darkness off to Obed's left. "This is the guy I've been telling you all about! Best adjuster in the tri-county area!"

Obed turned to see Randy Waites, the regional manager, emerge from the gloom, his smile sharp enough to cut glass. The manager's eyes were a luminous green, his underslung jaw filled with broken-bottle teeth, his legs and arms long and multi-jointed, to better scuttle along the ocean floor.

"And *punctual,* too." Randy slapped Obed on the back, hooked claws digging into his skin.

Obed winced, trying to keep his smile.

"Ah, sorry about that." Randy drew his hand back. "Still getting used to these."

The thing in the pool shifted.

"*Exactly.* I was just telling the Ineffable Shadow here about your record. Shadow has teleconferenced in from Corporate Inhuman Resources over in Y'ha-nthlei." Randy grinned. "Obed, Shadow, Shadow, Obed."

"Nice to meet you," Obed said.

The thing in the pool shifted.

"Exactly." Randy turned to the pool. "Obed's closed more cases than anyone in the office, hundreds of clients and not a single payment. No one knows the rules better than this guy. *No one.* And his suicide percentage is through the roof. The guy's a born killer, a *real* monster."

Obed swallowed. "I don't think—"

"No need to be modest," Randy said. "Here we are, drowning in regulation, and every idiot with a cell phone camera acting like an investigative reporter. Not like the old days, eh?"

The thing in the pool shifted.

"Exactly." Randy nodded.

Obed took Randy's humor as a good sign. They weren't going to fire him, apparently. But Obed still felt like algae scraped off the bottom of a boat, and he couldn't shake the tightness in his shoulders.

"Ah, well, the old days are gone." Randy heaved a wet sigh. "Relics like me don't know how to handle all these social media outlets and class-action lawsuits. That piece on the riot last night was a firestorm. Everyone's all over the blogs and whatever, calling for my resignation."

"Riot?" Obed asked.

"Yeah, last night, a bunch of violent protestors tried to storm the office." Randy winked one bulging eye. "At least that's the story we're pushing."

The thing in the pool shifted.

"Exactly," Randy said. "So, Obed, you're probably wondering why we called you down here."

"Actually, I—"

"I'm retiring, you see. The powers that be think it's time for Esoteric Insurance to embrace the future. No more sacrifice and blood orgies, no more dragging people into the ocean. Our future is about quiet desperation, the slow wear of waves on stone. Madness, hopelessness, driving people to the brink then stepping back and letting them stumble over." Randy spread his webbed fingers. "We need a rules guy, someone with a head for memos and clauses. The numbers say *no one* is better at that than you, and Corporate Inhuman Resources agrees."

The thing in the pool shifted.

"*Exactly.*"

Obed felt like he was deep underwater, the entire ocean pressing down on him. He'd just been doing his job, keeping his head down. He'd never even thought to look at his numbers, he'd never thought of himself as a killer, as a monster.

"We want you to take over as regional manager," Randy said. "Get your feet wet. If things go well, you can scuttle on up to Corporate. Maybe make director. Who knows? Maybe even make CEO in time."

"This is a lot to process."

"The Ineffable Shadow has already pushed the paperwork through. You're on the fast track, my friend. Here's the company card. Take a few days—swim in the ocean, have some drinks, eat a kid. Y'know, *celebrate.*"

"Sure, okay." Obed accepted the credit card. "Thank you."

"Get out of here, enjoy yourself." Randy slapped him on the back, then winced. "Sorry."

Obed crawled out of the sepulcher, barely aware of the reeking damp. Outside, he sat in his car, windows up, the humidifier blasting. The promotion was everything he thought he'd wanted; everything his dad had worked his whole life for but never gotten. More money, more power, more responsibility.

More responsibility.

There was a soft scratching on his car door. Obed rolled down his window and looked out to see the woman. *April.* She was lying alongside the car, her clothes torn and dirty, one eye swelled shut, her hair matted with blood.

"Shit," Obed said as he opened the door.

"Shit," he repeated as he gingerly picked her up, looking around to make sure no one was watching.

"Shit," he said again as he laid her down in the back seat.

"Shit. Shit. *Shit.*" He drove from the parking lot, still not sure what he would do with the half-dead woman. Eat her. Help her. Take her home. He gulped at that last thought.

Gods, what would his parents think?

Obed carried April into the living room, set her gently on the couch, and climbed to the Fever Attic.

His mother's face conveyed disapproval as he announced his promotion, but he'd expected as much. When he revealed April's presence downstairs, she clawed the air with her hands, as if slicing off his words, and floundered into a sitting position.

"Get her out of the house," she croaked. "Now."

For a moment, Obed could only gape. "But Mom, I thought you, of all people, would feel some compassion."

"Don't be a fool, Obediah! It's a—"

Below, someone screamed.

Obed turned and pounded down the stairs.

He got to the living room in time to see his father looming over the couch. April had curled into a fetal position, one arm thrust out as if to ward off her attacker, whose menacing grin expressed only cruel intentions.

"Dad! What are you doing?"

"Found my dagger. Now we can cut her up proper!" Obed's father straightened, gesturing toward the injured lawyer. "Why else would you bring her here?"

Obed reached out, and for one brief moment, he understood his father. April wasn't a person. If anything, she was prey. The world was cruel, cruel and mad, just like Father Dagon, like all the Elder Gods, Obed was a fool to pretend it was anything else. The powerful, the *monsters* did as they wished, and the prey, well, they prayed. It wasn't right, but that didn't matter. And yet, Obed felt something tighten in his chest, a bit of conscience lodged like gristle in his teeth.

He wasn't a monster. At least he hoped he wasn't.

"Stop!" He leaped forward. "Don't!"

His father narrowed his eyes. "Why?"

Obed's mind raced. *Why, indeed?* What purpose would his saving April serve? They weren't lovers, or even friends. He was putting his position with Esoteric Insurance in jeopardy. He glanced at April and saw she'd lapsed into unconsciousness. Obed's stomach tightened at the way her bloody hair framed her face, the way she was sprawled on the couch, helpless, hopeless.

"You're not going to touch her, Dad," Obed said.

His father made an irritated sound in the back of his throat. "What do you mean?"

"I didn't bring her home for you to eat," Obed said. "I want to—"

A heavy thump sounded above them. *Gods! If Mom comes down now....*

"What's she up to?" His father looked up as floorboards creaked above Obed's head. "Stay upstairs, Lavernia. This is men's business."

The gurgling roar from upstairs gave Obed the chance to grab April and flee the house.

With April in the back seat of his car, he drove the night streets in an aimless pattern, seeking inspiration. Preoccupied, he almost hit a huge piece of cracked bone in the street. He fought with the steering wheel, jumped the curb, and threw his car into park, his heart pounding.

Obed caught sight of a patrolling nightgaunt and killed the ignition. He followed its soaring arc with his eyes, not daring to move. It made a lazy loop, circling as if it was looking for someone, maybe looking for *him*. Had someone seen him rescue April? When the nightgaunt disappeared behind a building, Obed waited for it to drop onto the hood of his car.

After several minutes, he spotted the nightgaunt fleetingly silhouetted by the moon. It was much smaller, much farther away. Obed turned the keys and eased his car back onto the street as quietly as he could.

He kept to side streets and alleys, scanning the night sky for any sign of pursuit. Though the buildings on either side of the alley seemed to lean toward each other to the point of collapse, Obed still felt exposed and vulnerable. He gazed at April and wondered again why he hadn't just left her alone.

Something touched his arm and Obed lurched away, stifling a cry. His fear lasted only a moment; April's hand wavered mid-air. He reached back to clasp it, marveling at how soft her skin was. "Hang in there, okay? I'm going to get you to a hospital."

The intake nurse gazed at him with a bland, disconnected expression.

"She's hurt," he announced.

"Put her there, please." The nurse indicated a gurney. Obed lay April softly upon it.

When he returned to the desk, the nurse handed him a thick sheaf of papers on a battered clipboard. "Fill these out."

"Yes, of course." Obed swallowed. "But I'm afraid I don't know much about this woman."

"You know we can't treat someone like her without insurance." The nurse shrugged. "It's the law."

Five seconds passed, then ten. Obed fumbled for the edge of the counter and gripped it. The intake nurse waited, saying nothing. Another ten seconds passed before he made his decision.

"I, uh...." Obed rooted around in his suit jacket. "I have this." He placed the Esoteric Insurance company credit card on the counter.

"Oh, *Obed.*" A familiar voice rasped behind him.

Obed turned to see Randy Waites, followed by a security nightgaunt, wings folded to fit into the reception room. Its featureless face cocked as if testing the air, its claws twitching in anticipation.

His boss shook his head. "Obed, I am *so* disappointed in

you."

Obed knuckled a bit of blood from his split lip, glaring across the limo at his father.

The old man didn't meet Obed's gaze. He'd been quiet since the nightgaunt tossed Obed into the limo. A company man to the end.

"I thought you were smarter than this, Obed." Randy lifted April's head. Points of blood marked where his claws dug into her cheeks. She moaned, eyes flickering, but didn't regain consciousness.

"You *had* to know it was a test." Randy let her drop. "Did you think she just *crawled* back to the office?"

Obed felt a flush creep up his neck but Randy didn't seem to notice. The nightgaunt had insisted on giving Obed a good "tickle" en route to the car, leaving painful cuts on his face and arms. The fact that he hadn't resisted didn't seem to have figured into the creature's consideration.

"I put myself on the line for you," Randy said. "What am I supposed to tell the Ineffable Shadow? Do you have any idea how long I've been waiting for the stars to align right for me to retire? Now we've got to start the whole thing over again." Randy sat back with a sigh. "There's nothing for it. We'll have to sacrifice both of you."

"That wasn't part of the deal," Obed's father said. "I called you so you *wouldn't* kill him."

"*Someone* needs to appease Father Dagon," Randy said.

"Take me, then."

Randy snorted. "And *that's* why you never made management."

Obed's father looked at his hands as the limo drifted to a stop.

"Ah, here we are." Randy's grin dripped with cruel promise

as the doors swung open. He crawled outside, muttering to the guard, "Careful, now. We need them mostly intact."

Either the nightgaunt didn't hear, or didn't care.

The altar had seen better days. Situated on the rocky cliff below the Esoteric Insurance District Office, it had fallen into disuse after the cult incorporated. Now, the slab was chipped and salt-rimed, its sigils almost invisible beneath decades of bird droppings.

This time, Obed *did* try to fight back as the nightgaunt pressed him down on the altar, and earned a few more cuts and bruises for his trouble. It dropped April's limp body on the rock next to him. Obed was relieved to see her chest move with the faintest flutter of breath. Then he remembered where they were and what was about to happen.

"Alright, old man." Randy handed Obed's father a curved golden dagger. "Show me I was wrong about you."

It started to rain, big, fat drops that bled through Obed's suit to trace icy lines down his ribs. The nightgaunt's grip was tight on his wrists, its claws sharp as knapped obsidian. Overhead, the clouds darkened, beginning to swirl as if in preparation for a typhoon.

Obed heard the waves crashing on the rocks as his father trudged forward, long gray hair loose and lank over his face. He held the dagger in trembling hands, lifting the blade gingerly, as if it might bite him.

"Iä Dagon! Iä Hydra! Ineffable Shadow, Lord of the Unfathomable Gulf, Master of Human Resources—we release you from your bonds! Rise and accept this sacrifice!" Randy spread his arms, head tilted back in wild ecstasy as he choked out incantations in the old tongue. Below, the water began to swirl, a blot of darkness growing under the waves. Obed had thought the Ineffable Shadow waited just below the surface, but now he saw it was vast, vast and terrible, free of trivial concepts such as space or distance. It wasn't growing, it was getting closer, and yet, somehow, it had always been there.

"Gods, how I *missed* this." Randy's grin stretched inhumanly wide.

Obed met his father's eyes. The old man raised the dagger, wincing.

"Go on, Dad." Obed didn't look away. "It's what you've always wanted."

"You got me wrong, boy." The reply was soft, almost a whisper.

"Do it!" Randy bellowed, stepping closer. "Before the Shadow swallows us all!"

Obed's father spun, slashing at Randy's throat.

The blade snapped off at the hilt.

Randy squatted to pick up the broken dagger. "It's fake, you idiot. Think I would trust a washed-up old pensioner like you with a *real* blade? I just wanted to see if you'd actually go through with it."

"Don't need your knife, boss." Obed's father said with a tight smile. "A good cultist always brings his own. I just needed to distract you."

Randy cocked his head. "Distract me from wh—"

A dark shape lunged from the boulders to Randy's left, tackling him from the ledge.

" 'And lo, the Dragon was hurled down!' " Obed's mother howled as she and Randy tumbled from sight, tearing at each other.

At the same moment, Obed's father drew his old dagger, stepping up to slash his blade across the throat of the nightgaunt holding Obed down. The creature tried to turn, but Obed clamped onto its wrists, holding on even though it felt as if the thing would dislocate his arms.

His father stabbed again and again, the nightgaunt's thick, black blood hot against Obed's skin. It struggled soundlessly, slashing at Obed's father with its barbed tail.

"You think I've never been tickled before?" His father laughed as he dragged the blade across the nightgaunt's back, spilling strange organs and viscera onto the rain-slick stone.

At last, the creature went still.

Obed pushed himself up from the slab. Thunder rumbled overhead, flashes of eldritch lightning giving the sky a greenish cast. Tendrils of darkness broke the churning sea, crawling across stone and sand as the Ineffable Shadow crept closer to where Randy and his mother struggled on the rocks below.

Obed's mother was easily twice the size of the regional manager, but her body was better suited to the deeps. Randy scratched at her eyes, his long, fishhook claws cutting deep furrows into her face.

Obed and his father started down the narrow stone steps that led to the rocks, taking them two at a time. They reached the outcrop in time to see Randy slam Obed's mother to the stone, his eyes glowing a furious green in the storm-lit gloom.

Obed's father ran at Randy with the dagger. Randy slapped him aside with almost casual ease, then spun toward Obed, claws flexing. "C'mon! You wanna take a swing at the champ?"

Obed eyed his boss. Even uninjured he wouldn't have fancied his chances against Randy. The man was a monster, a relic from when Esoteric Insurance had been an eldritch cult, when murder rather than memos, rites rather than rules had bound it. But times had changed—and *no one* knew the rules better than Obed.

"Stop. Just, stop." He held up a hand. "You're embarrassing yourself."

"What?" Randy growled.

"Gods, where do I start? Misappropriation of company resources, abducting an Esoteric Insurance employee, improper use of a company vehicle, unlicensed sacrifice," Obed ticked them off on his fingers, then nodded at the Ineffable Shadow. "Not to mention you didn't file *any* of the proper paperwork for a summoning."

"That's ridiculous, I—"

Obed shouted over him. "Company bylaws require you go on unpaid leave pending a full inquiry."

"I'll rip your pudgy little—" Randy paused, glancing down at the shadow that had swallowed his legs. He looked up, lantern-bright eyes wide with panic.

"Guess the Ineffable Shadow agrees with me." Obed grinned. "It *is* with Inhuman Resources, after all."

"I'll sue for wrongful exsanguination! You can't do this. I'll go to the media—I've got enough dirt on EI to choke a gug. I'll—" Randy gave a startled croak, his mouth yawning wide to reveal the dark pit that had opened within him. The regional manager tumbled into himself as the Shadow devoured him from the inside out, flesh, muscle, and bone crumpling in like wet paper. In another moment, Randy was gone. A moment after that, so was the Shadow.

Obed and his parents made their way back to the ledge, leaning on each other for support. He knelt to slip aching arms under April, tottering like a newborn colt as he stood, a fishhook of pain lancing through his side with each labored breath. It was worth it when she curled close, her face pressed to his chest as if she knew she was finally safe.

"Guess I should start looking for a new job," Obed said as they began the long, slow climb back to the parking lot. "I don't think Corporate is going to want me for regional manager any-more."

"Don't be so sure," his father said. "Killing the previous manager is company tradition. How do you think Randy got *his* job?"

" 'And so did the whole world come to worship the Beast Out of the Sea.' " His mother panted as if in pain. Fortunately, her eldritch biology already seemed to be closing the slashes Randy had left in her sides. " 'But the people asked, "Who is like the beast? Who can wage war against it?' "

His father snorted.

"Enough." Obed shook his head. "We'll talk about this when we get home."

His parents glared at each other.

Gods, sometimes it was like he was raising two children.

The hospital room was a riot of flowers. Cards piled on the nightstand. April lay in bed. Monitors and IV drips beeped cheerily in the morning light.

Obed set his flowers with the others, and turned to see April watching him. She wasn't smiling. For a moment, Obed felt confused, until he realized this was the first time they'd met when she was *actually* conscious.

"I'm Obed," he said.

"Ah." She gave a tight smile. "They say you brought me in."

"Yes, that and—" He frowned, trying to find the right words. "There were nightgaunts, and a sacrifice, and crawling darkness, and my mom and dad, and well...." He swallowed. "I was wondering if we could talk about it all over dinner."

She cocked her head, frowning. "I don't think that would be appropriate."

"What?"

"You're the regional manager at Esoteric Insurance, right?"

Obed didn't trust his voice not to break, so he just nodded.

"Then you should know I'm suing your company for six hundred million in damages, public endangerment, wrongful death, the list goes on."

"Well, yes, but I thought we might—"

"Listen." She pushed herself up on her elbows. "I'm grateful you brought me in, but it doesn't change who you are or *what* you do."

"But that's not true. I'm going to change the company from within—raise the payout rates, clear up murky clauses, start an outreach program, hire more humans. It could take a while, but I'm working to—"

"People are dying right now."

"What?"

"Right now, out there." She nodded at the window. "People are dying because of Esoteric Insurance."

Obed took a step back. This wasn't going at all like he'd planned.

"I saw you drive by me on the street, walk past me in the parking lot. Does the fact you *finally* did the right thing wipe all that away?"

"But, I...." Obed chewed his lip. She was right.

"And I'm not going to even ask what you think *this* is." April waved a hand between the two of them.

He held up his hands. "I should go."

She sighed. "So that's it? You just going to scuttle back to your job to ruin more people's lives? You've seen what it's like. You *know*."

Obed swallowed. He was regional manager now, with all the perks and responsibilities.

Responsibilities.

"I know," he said after a moment.

"Then don't forget."

Obed nodded and left the room. He pressed the elevator button, waiting as the numbers on the display blinked upwards. The old days were gone, but after seeing how Randy, his father, even his mother acted, how they lied to themselves, Obed wasn't sure that was a bad thing. It didn't matter if he was regional manager or a low-level insurance adjustor, he couldn't hide anymore. All his old justifications fell away—to see the people Esoteric Insurance hurt, to realize the part he'd played in it, and go back to pretending it wasn't his fault—

Well, then Obed really *would* be a monster.

CAREER ZOMBIE

by John Taloni

I was staring into the spreadsheet when the lights blinked off. Startled, I looked around. In the wan light of the hall lamps I could see that the floor was nearly empty. Three cubicles down, Gary stood up.

"Well, that's my cue," he said. "Nine PM and the lights go out, time to head home." We seemed to be the only two people left on the floor.

Gary stretched as he switched off his computer. "How about you, Alan?"

"Can't," I replied. "Nina dropped this project in my lap at eight. Right when I was planning to go home, actually. Got to be done by tomorrow." Nina was our Controller, the person in charge of day-to-day operations for financial reporting. But I'd heard that the project came straight from Jeff Johnson, the Chief Financial Officer, who had little regard for the personal lives of his employees.

"Poor sap," said Gary. "I'll be in early to finish up. You doing the same?"

"Nah," I responded in a monotone. "Jeff needs this early, get ready for the earnings call. I'll be here late."

"Would have been nice if he gave you some warning," said Gary.

"Tell me about it," I muttered, concentrating again on the spreadsheet.

"Did he even talk to you?" asked Gary, a knowing smile on his face.

"Course not," I said, rolling my eyes. Jeff had met with us regularly as a Senior Vice President, but soon after he became

Chief Financial Officer he implemented a closed door policy. Most communication from him came by email or instant message, with an infrequent Webcam for group meetings. On the few occasions that we saw him, he blinked frequently due to some kind of recently acquired dry eye condition. During Webcam sessions he continually sipped from a Diet Coke can, placing it next to pictures of his daughters and his cat.

"Well, so long," Gary responded. He put his laptop in his bag and swung it onto his shoulder, waving goodbye with his other hand. I grunted a reply and made a small wave in return.

The night stretched on. I picked at the leavings of a meager dinner, provided grudgingly by the company as a sop to the late hours. Ramen noodles and foil tuna. I crumpled it up and tossed it in my trash, then placed the bin outside my cubicle. I barely noticed an hour later when the night crew picked it up.

Sometime around one AM I started to get very foggy. My eyes wouldn't clear and I could barely type. My left arm had been hurting for hours. I reached for the mouse and fell forward, slumping on the desk.

I woke to see Gary looking down on me. "Hey Bulksdale," he said as he jostled my shoulder. "Looks like you nodded off."

I looked up, my eyes focusing just fine now. Deep in the recesses of my mind registered the old joke—my friends often called me "Bulksdale" instead of my actual last name Barksdale after a junk mailer got it wrong. I stared at him quizzically for a moment. Why did he smell so good?

Involuntarily, I lunged across the desk, grabbing for his arm. He leapt back, horrified. "He's turned!" Gary shouted, "Alan's turned! Call Security!"

My work colleagues managed to get away and hide, while Security pushed me into the isolation room. I didn't feel any different than I had the day before. It's just that all of them had suddenly become delicious. That, and my brain was foggy. I wasn't quite certain why Security had wrestled me into the room with attachments on long poles. If they'd just let me have something to eat....

I sat there for some lengthy, undetermined period of time. The room smelled of strong chemicals and unspecifiable herbs. I slowly got used to it. Eventually a figure walked into the other half of the isolation room, separated from me by a reinforced wall and an inch-thick plastic window. She sat in a chair. After several moments I realized it was Nina O'Loughlin, our Controller. Her usually gleaming white teeth were hidden behind a grimace.

She motioned to a keyboard and monitor. I looked over, slowly remembering what they were for. Through the plastic window I could see that she had a similar setup on her side. Letters appeared on the monitor in my portion of the room. I blinked, and realized Nina was typing a message for me.

I slid over and looked at the screen. "You've changed," she typed. "You were lucky, though. You didn't hurt anybody before we got you secured."

I stared at the screen, uncomprehending. "Hungry," I typed. Nina looked delicious. If she would only come into my side of the room....

"Of course," typed Nina. "Have this." She pulled out a drawer on her side of the wall and placed a package in it. It looked like those banking contraptions that they used to exchange money securely. Nina shoved the drawer shut and it came over to my side. I lifted open the lid. A wonderful scent overcame me. I ripped open the package and tore into the contents. It seemed to be meat on some kind of bone. I took a bite and felt my thoughts becoming clearer. The meat was cold and, as I thought about it, uncooked.

Nina pushed another item through. It was a small plastic baggy with liquid inside. It smelled heavenly. I drank it down without thinking.

"Feeling better?" Nina typed.

"Yes," I typed. "What was it? One of your favorite red wines?"

"A few ounces of blood. Best I could come up with."

"Um … thanks," I typed. My head felt much clearer, but I was still foggy. "What next?"

"Same offer we give all the zombies," she typed.

"I haven't really paid attention to that," I admitted.

"We put a bullet in your head and you go down clean," she typed. "Your family gets your full life insurance and any other benefits. Then there's the alternative."

"Which is?" I replied.

"Half the life insurance, plus your family inherits. You keep working at full salary. Your family gets the money. It's why we gave you the food, and the blood," typed Nina.

I looked at the plastic bag. Blood? I guess it was obvious if I thought about it. The liquid hadn't tasted like anything in particular. Coffee, maybe, if I thought about it. My zombie metamorphosis had changed more than my thoughts, it had altered my entire metabolism.

"You have to be clear-headed to make the decision," Nina typed. "But do it soon. The effects of the food won't last too long."

I thought of my daughter, just ten years old. Without me she would make it in some sense, but not with the dreams my wife and I had for her. Without my income they wouldn't be able to keep the house. They would probably have to move out of the school district we had painstakingly chosen for her.

To keep it I would join the zombies in the back office and do whatever work was assigned to me. I hadn't paid much attention. They seemed to be just fine for rote work. What would it mean for me?

I decided I would find out. "I'll do it," I replied.

"Okay," typed Nina. "Officially, there's a twelve-hour waiting period, then you have to sign. Materials are over there." She pointed to a loose-leaf binder and a folder. "You'll stay here until then. We'll move you after that. Take a few days to get adjusted. You'll start again officially next Monday."

I wouldn't be in this situation if they hadn't made the damn lake. But then, I wouldn't be anywhere if they hadn't done it. If it hadn't flooded at just the wrong time.

I kicked around the vestibule for a bit. After an hour or so I opened the loose-leaf binder. Right on the first page was a list of bullet points, *Helping You Decide*. Well, I'd already decided, so I skimmed through the pages. Towards the back was a summary of events. I'd covered this in high school, but that was a long time back.

A meteor strike left an area in the countryside west of Arkham blighted. People in the area went mad. Vegetation grew large, colorful, and inedible. So of course they dammed a stream and built a lake over it. What could possibly go wrong?

It probably would have gone unnoticed if Miskatonic University hadn't seen fit to put a satellite research facility right on its banks. What they were hiding there soon became known to the world: Reanimation. The lead researcher, the son of a journalist and enthralled by his father's stories, had eventually found a package of works by Doctor Muñoz. He was somewhat more successful than previous work inspired by Doctor Herbert West.

Then a series of torrential rains hit the area. The lab flooded. The serum interacted with the trace elements of the meteor in the lake water, and then into the drinking supply. From there it spread like a viral infection. Recently dead people began walking as zombies.

Even then the outbreak might have been contained, but some of the researchers got out of quarantine and went to a retreat in Jackson, Mississippi. They turned without even realizing it, and infected the local area. Within days the entire globe was subsumed in a zombie outbreak that took months to bring under control.

I finished and slumped back in my chair. Perhaps it could have been avoided. Some even darker whispers suggested that the medical companies had wanted the flood to happen as part of their experiment, without taking into account the possible disastrous effects. It didn't matter. One way or the other, I was dead and still working for the Man.

At the appointed time Nina came back. We went through the formalities, and I signed the papers in the folder. She left, and the rear of the room opened. I went out into the area with the other zombies. I'd managed to keep from thinking about them when I was alive, since they were well locked away. As I stepped in I saw rows of desks with outsize keyboards and large monitors. They were just the thing for clumsy zombie hands and dim eyes.

About a dozen other zombies quietly worked away at those desks. Well, quietly wasn't quite the word. They hammered keys and regularly bashed the desks as they worked. But they didn't move from their desks as I came in. Most didn't even look up.

I shambled over to the closest one. "Hi," I said. It came out slow and almost incoherent. "I'm Greg." The other zombie acknowledged my presence with the slightest nod of his head. He flicked his eyes at the corner of his desk. I saw his nameplate: Kevin Nolan.

"What'cha working on?" I asked. It came out as "whaatttzzchooo woookin on," but he seemed to understand.

"Bills," he replied. He looked at me for just a fraction of a second. I let my eyes drift to his screen. He seemed to be matching invoices to purchase orders. That made it part of Accounts Payable.

The whole area was just one big room. There were a few couches and beds pushed against the wall. After a while I went to lay down. I couldn't sleep, though. From what I had heard zombies didn't sleep, but rather existed in a kind of half-aware state. Now I was experiencing it for myself. The fluorescent lights overhead provided a dim illumination. I drifted, but did not dream, or even make it past a twilight state. I realized in the abstract that the room was cold, but the temperature seemed just fine to my current state.

After several hours, I heard a buzzing sound. A door opened in the side of the room. All of the zombies got up from their chairs and headed toward the door. I quickly realized why as the scent hit my nostrils. Dinner time. I went into the other room and the door closed behind me.

Food was served, if you can call it that, in several big trays. I reached into one and picked out a … I wasn't sure. It was a bone with meat attached. A day ago I would have found it revolting. Now it smelled, not great, but good enough to eat. There were also cups of liquid with straws and secure lids, like a large version of a kid's sippy cup. I took a glass and had a sip. It was blood of some kind, obviously animal. It didn't taste near as good as the blood Nina had brought me. Also, every zombie picked up a small cup of noxious liquid—the chemical/herb combination that sustained our half-life existence.

The other zombies bit into the bones and sucked out the marrow. Some chewed on the bones themselves. I gave it a try but found my teeth too soft. Apparently other physical changes were coming.

When we had consumed all the food, the buzzer rang again and the door opened. I saw a new desk complete with computer setup. My name was on the nameplate: Alan F. Barkdale. Looking down, I noticed login instructions.

There was nothing else to do in this dimly lit room. Certainly they weren't going to let us out. I sat at my desk and logged in. My typing speed had gone down by half and I had trouble hitting the keys at first. Still, my coordination overall seemed better than the other zombies. Perhaps there had been some difference in our treatment? With nothing else to do, I kicked around the company intranet. My access was restricted and I could only get to certain files. Instant messaging was disabled. I could send emails, but only to a specified list. Right now that was just Nina, but the orientation package said I'd be given access to more as time went on.

Finally I sent an email to Nina. "Ready to work," I wrote. What else was there to do?

She wrote back. "Great! Please put together a spreadsheet for the quarterly filing. We need some analysis for the footnotes."

And with that, I was back to work. I could only function at about half my usual speed, but I didn't take breaks. Zombies didn't need coffee, or sleep for that matter. I worked through the night, only noticing the time because my computer had a clock. By the next morning Nina had her spreadsheet.

The work went fairly well after that. I hardly noticed that a week had gone by, during which time I turned out several detailed spreadsheets. My time sense was skewed, but I guessed that I was working twenty hours a day. There was nothing else to do.

Sometime during that week Nina forwarded me an email attachment. It included pictures of my wife and daughter. "For the desktop," said the text. "The government discourages contact between zombies and family members, but this can't hurt. A little reminder of why you're doing it."

Because of the fugue state the zombie mind left me in, I hadn't really thought about the passage of time. I'd been dead for a week. The people in the pictures seem to have tried to smile but couldn't muster the emotion. There were a few others of my daughter from the school year, before I died. I found one I liked and made it my desktop background. Her wide smile looked out at me at almost full size, one tooth missing from her grin.

In the meantime, my usefulness to the company seemed to have increased since my death. Three straight nights I received requests for rush analyses. Well, as a zombie I really couldn't rush anything. We had one speed, and it was permanently stuck in the "slow" position. But since I didn't need sleep, I plodded on through the night each time, delivering the data by the next morning.

Earnings call capped the quarter end. The Wall Street analysts posed the usual questions, but nothing out of the ordinary. They seemed satisfied with the earnings package they had received in advance. That package included the results of many of my analyses.

I listened in on the broadcast line—they took no chances on my being able to communicate out. Some traditions hung on, even if they made little sense.

However, the company gradually loosened the restrictions on my communication within the firm. After the first month Nina opened up my contacts list so that I could email my old department. Still no instant messenger, but I could go direct to the people I was working with. That included my old boss, Linda. Her emails were polite but to the point. I didn't blame her. I suppose I would have had trouble working with a zombie back when I was alive.

The next two months went by quickly. I did a backlog of detailed analyses that our department had not gotten to recently due to lack of time.

When the next quarterly close came around, though, we found another reason Linda had been terse. She left the company on short notice, having gotten a higher paying position in a related industry.

I got a few emails from colleagues speculating about who would get her position. The consensus seemed to be that they would hire from outside. To my surprise, though, the Chief Financial Officer suggested they give it to me.

There was some controversy over that. Zombies didn't really learn anything after death. We were mainly capable of repeating what we had done before. But this was Accounting, and not much changed.

Plus, as the CFO wrote, I was always around. No matter how late they stayed I was always able to work later. The CFO in particular liked to stay late and give instructions before he left. I could take those, do some preliminary research, then farm out the work to the team for them to start when they got in. Considering the CFO's famous lack of desire for personal interaction, a late night email suited his working style best.

I got a surprise one nondescript day. The timing seemed to be mid-May. I couldn't tell the change of seasons within our windowless room, but the filings were right for that. Year-end had come and gone, and first quarter earnings call was about two weeks in the past.

One of the other zombies came up to my desk. I had seen her before, becoming more and more sloppy at her keyboard. As she shuffled up I noticed that the fingers on one hand were worn down to the bone. The pinky had lost the first two joints.

She nodded at my computer. I wasn't working on it at the moment so my desktop background displayed the picture of my daughter. "Girl," she said, nodding her head. It came out "grrrraaalllll" but I had gotten used to zombie speech. Then she nodded towards her own cubicle. "Boy," she said. She waved back towards her workstation. A small piece of flesh flew off her hand as she moved.

The action seemed to be an invitation. I got up and went to her computer with her. She took a long time to settle back into her chair. She fumbled with the mouse, unsurprising with half her fingers missing. Eventually she opened an email with an attachment. In it were pictures of a beaming teenager at a high school graduation. The boy's father was with him. I slowly made the connection. This was her child, the one she was protecting with her work.

She fumbled through to another document. This was a financial statement of some kind. After a few minutes I realized it was a college fund. There was enough in it to cover four years' tuition at a private school, or tuition plus room and board at a state school.

"Nice," I said, and clapped her on the shoulder. Her flesh gave way beneath me. For reasons I did not understand, I was holding up better than the other zombies.

She looked up at me. "Work done," she said. "Bye." I didn't quite understand why she was dismissing me, and in any event she had work displayed on her other monitor. I could see the invoice she was working on.

She made to get up and I walked away. She shuffled over to the rest area and lay down. I went back to my desk and thought nothing more of it.

That's when I got a lesson. After a few hours in the rest area she went into a closet, one I'd seen but never thought about. Moments later I heard a loud bang. I went to investigate. She had placed her head in a press and pushed the button. This crushed her skull and ended her undead life.

The other zombies moaned for several minutes, then went back to work.

The next quarter close went much like the last—efficiently run, with the questions of Wall Street analysts anticipated and answered in advance. Our filing to the Securities & Exchange Commission was even a day early. Nina was pleased, and asked what she could do for me.

I thought back to the zombie woman who had waited out her son's high school graduation before ending her existence. Time was short any way I looked at it.

"See family," I wrote back to her email. "Haven't seen them

since death. There must be a way."

"Sure, your daughter is almost eleven," she typed.

"How did you—" I stopped as she tapped her head. "Right. Photographic memory."

"Give me a few days," she wrote.

"Why not today?" I asked.

"Need to arrange something. Not worth discussing if I can't," she sent.

It was over a week later that she finally met me in the secure meeting room—the one we had met my first day as a zombie. There were two security guards with her, armed with zombie poles. Also, I noticed that there were now some handcuffs on chains on the zombie-side desk.

"Put your hands into the cuffs," she typed.

"Why?" I typed back.

"You'll see," she replied.

I did as asked and found the cuffs tightening around my wrists. It didn't hurt, but I had to be careful about damage. Zombie bodies don't really heal, they just close over the wound.

The chains around the cuffs were about a foot, so I was still able to navigate the desk. The restriction made it harder to type, but still manageable. "What next?" I tapped.

By way of answer she slid a package into the secure slot and pushed it towards me. "Drink, then talk," she typed. I opened on my end. Even in plastic the delicious smell was overwhelming. There had to be quart of fluid. The package had a spigot which I quickly turned to open, gulping down the liquid.

I drained the package, sucking out the last few drops. It took a minute or two before I was coherent again. "Was that what I thought it was?" I typed.

"Yep," she wrote back. "We took up a collection. We got more than usual because we were able to include people who normally can't give blood. Their conditions won't affect you because, well, you're dead."

"Okay," I wrote back. "I feel a lot better than usual. Which is to be expected since zombies crave human flesh most of all.

It seemed extra rich, though."

"There was some plasma in there as well," said Nina. "We ... well, people are willing to give blood for pay. Jeff made a fairly large donation."

That seemed odd. Our CFO's unwillingness to interact with his staff had reached legendary status. He seemed only willing to swiftly assign work, then move on. If he could be bothered to leave his office it was only for a few moments. Caring about his staff seemed unlike him. I shrugged it off, another mystery that benefitted me. "So what next?" I asked Nina.

Nina got out of the chair and approached the security door that separated the two rooms. She had a key in her hand. The security guards prepared their zombie poles.

With a slow and steady motion, she unlocked the door and pushed it open. A waft of what seemed like very warm air came in, although it was only regular office temperature. She smelled delicious. And yet....

"How are you holding up?" she asked, the first words I'd heard from a live human in months.

"Okay," I said. "Well, I want to get up and eat you, to be honest. But I can resist. Not sure how long it will last."

The wheels turned, but they turned exceedingly slowly. My family put in a formal request to see me in person, since the test had gone well. It had to be approved at all levels of the company.

The federal government chose not to regulate zombie labor. Each company decided for itself how to handle any zombies it chose to keep. We had a quasi-legal status as people, but in some ways were also property. This meant that any company would be responsible for damage caused by its zombies. We were like dangerous equipment. I'd overseen the calculations myself. Our company's liability accrual was lower than others because of our strong security measures. Allowing me to see my family jeopardized that.

Eventually the Chief Financial Officer intervened and gave final approval. That was more than a formality as the controls to open the door to the zombie area were in his office, a government requirement. On the designated day, I washed as best as I could and climbed into some donated clothes. The room was specially set up with powerful fans behind me, pulling the air past my side and keeping the undead stench of my body from reaching the living.

A few minutes before the meeting, Nina showed up with a gallon of my new favorite drink—human blood with a plasma kicker. I drained it in two long draughts. They then opened up the meeting chamber so that it looked like a regular conference room. I sat at a desk. What wasn't obvious to the people on the other side was that I was chained both hand and foot, with cords leading down through the clothes to secure locations on the desk.

Nina came in with the same two security guards and checked the setup. She wore a mauve scarf against a black shirt. It reminded me of my now favorite drink, although the cravings had temporarily subsided. When they were satisfied, Nina gave me the thumbs up. "You've probably got ten minutes Alan," she reminded me. "We can't take any chances once the effect of the blood starts to wear off."

Shortly thereafter, my wife came in. Or was she my widow now? In any event, my daughter came in right behind her. The air seemed unbearably hot, but they were wearing coats.

"Hi daddy!" she said brightly. "Wow, you look like hell."

She never did have much of a filter, but then most kids don't. She'd turned nine since I'd died.

"Well, that's true," I said. My voice was a lot better—temporarily. "But I'd rather talk about you. How is school?"

"It's good," she said. "A coupla other kids got zombie parents. We hang together. Sometimes the other kids make fun of us, but I tell them my dad's a big 'zecutive."

We chatted a little more, and my wife chimed in as well. Nothing important, just the kind of inane chatter any family would make. Inane chatter that now meant more to me than anything else.

The ten minutes was up pretty quickly. When it was almost time to go, my little one got out of her chair and put her hands in the air. "Look at my handstand!" she giggled, and did one in the meeting room. When she came down she rounded the table towards me. Both guards tensed and started to deploy their poles. Nina grabbed at my daughter, but she was past her in a flash.

"It was good to see you, daddy!" She rushed in for a hug as she had done so often during safer times. My mouth opened involuntarily. I saw the horror on everyone's faces. With an effort of will I closed my mouth and turned the motion into a kiss. She smelled delicious. My hands shook with the effort of remaining still.

"Nice to see you too, Pumpkin," I said. "I think it's time for you to go now." My wife gathered her and quickly exited the room.

The guards locked the room back up, with me behind the protective clear wall again. Nina came back when they were done. She tapped out some commands on the keyboard and I felt the cuffs release.

"A close call," she typed. I pretended I didn't know what she meant, but I had experienced the hunger. It had been closer even than she thought.

The days began to blend together again, with the usual drone of financial analysis. If anything, though, my work was even better after the visit. This led to an added benefit for all the zombies. The company decided to lighten up on the communication restrictions. It was up to them how to interpret vague government

directives, and they decided to allow more frequent emails between the zombies and the outside world. All communications
still had to go through an intermediary, but we had more frequent updates from our families. Even a few friends were allowed the occasional missive.

And so I wasn't quite sure what I'd received when an attachment came in from Nina. Most of it was the personal items
she was allowed to send me. There were a few pictures of my
daughter at school events, a shot of the extended family at one
of her softball games, and a note from each of them. Then there
was another email that wasn't from my family. It seemed to
have work information inside, but wasn't the usual single subject requests I got for projects. Rather, it seemed to be a long
string of emails.

The top was a bunch of information back and forth about
various schedules, some of which I'd worked on. The emails
made scattered references to a possible merger and the staff
needed to handle the extra work the merger would bring.

I decided to go to the beginning of this long email string
and read from that point onward. First up was an email from
Nina to the Chief Financial Officer, Jeff.

"We're going to need to add new staff," wrote Nina. "Not
just temps. This merger means a permanent increase in the
scope of work we do."

"Are you sure we can't just get the existing people to work
harder?" Jeff wrote back.

"No, they are already pushed to the limit," Nina replied.

"Send me your analysis," Jeff wrote tersely.

Nina's next reply was a spreadsheet showing the number of
hours the merger was expected to take, compared to the number of people already on staff, and how many new hires would
be needed to fill the gap. There was a single line of text. "As
discussed."

"Maybe a third of this," Jeff wrote back. "Otherwise the
expense will affect bonuses."

Jeff's compensation was a matter of public record, disclosed in our financial statements. I knew he got a bonus of at least one million dollars guaranteed each year, with higher levels based on factors such as revenue growth and cost containment. Jeff was essentially complaining about a million dollar bonus, built on the backs of his employees. With the merger, that bonus was likely to be double its usual size.

"Not sure we'll retain quality if we work our people too hard," was Nina's response.

"See if zombies can do it," replied Jeff. "Might be as good as Alan. After all, if you're not willing to die for the company, I'm not sure you're committed." There was a smiley mark after that, but I didn't find it funny.

Was I dead because Jeff simply was too greedy to adequately staff his department?

I wasn't sure what to do with what I'd read. In any event, it wouldn't help me to make a fuss about it. The company held all the cards.

As I sat at my desk, I slowly pondered. I seemed to be in better shape than the other zombies. My fingers hadn't worn down like the zombie woman I'd had a short conversation with. My thought processes seemed clearer than theirs. Why? That, at least, was a question I could ask and hope for an answer. I set up a discussion with Nina in the encounter room. She took a few minutes the next day to meet.

"I'll get right to the point," I typed. "Why am I better off than the rest of the zombies?"

"A couple of reasons," she responded. "First, it seemed that we caught you just as you died. Whatever happened with your heart, it seemed to hold on until an hour or so before Gary found you. So you were fresh dead."

She paused at that point. "What else?" I asked, fingers tapping.

Nina pursed her lips. She seemed reluctant to continue.

"Come on," I wrote. "It's not like you could shock me."

"Okay," she typed. "You know we feed all you zombies. The raw meat, the bones. It's sustenance. But that isn't what you most want."

"We can't have what we most want," I replied. "Even in our state, when we're calm we know it's wrong to eat people. We just can't help it when we're hungry."

"True," Nina wrote. "But that's the thing. For you, we've been providing packets of human blood. Not a lot, but enough to make a difference. With your better starting state, it's been enough to keep you stable."

She pointed out of the room, past the open door. I saw a small refrigerator, like the kind college students use in dorms. "My idea, but Jeff eventually approved it as well because he likes your work. Whenever we can, we take up a collection. There's a pint in there now. Mine."

I decided on a slight change of topic. "Merger coming," I typed. "Can you get more for the other zombies?"

"Not enough of us," she responded. "The government won't let us reach beyond the department. Not regularly, any-way—we took a risk with you. Family members and strangers are strictly forbidden from donating. We're probably breaking some rules as it is."

True to expectation, extra projects related to the merger started coming in right away. I got to work on it. What else could I do? Regardless of the company's motivation, if I wanted to earn money for my family, I had to play the game their way.

We zombies generally worked around the clock, so we were accustomed to being up in the late hours. However, I noticed that the instant message icons started to say "available" instead of "offline" to some very late hours. Many of the living staff worked to midnight regularly. The merger was wearing all of them down. I half expected a new arrival at any moment.

And then, another oddity. Before our regular meetings over company intranet, Jeff started texting me. "See you soon!" he would send about fifteen minutes in advance of the start time. It's not like I was going anywhere. I chalked it up to his being happy with my work. But why would he communicate with me when he was so famously unwilling to interact with his staff?

Because of the late hours everyone was keeping, I got used to hearing noises around the office at night. So I didn't immediately think anything of it when I heard a click. But then a few minutes later I heard a creak.

The other zombies didn't seem to notice. Given my generally better senses, that wasn't surprising. I got up to investigate.

I was quite surprised to see that the security door to the outside was open. It was just a crack, but that door was supposed to be secured at all times. There was no way it could open accidentally.

As I looked, the doors then swung completely open. Someone had let the zombies out deliberately.

I looked around. Nina's office was nearby. Her door was open. There were some scattered staff in cubicles, but they were on the other side of the floor.

Who could have done this? Nina didn't have the authority. Only senior management had the codes. That meant it had to be Jeff.

My brain almost turned off as the scent hit me. Succulent human flesh, there for the taking. And as the wonderful scent flowed over me, I saw the refrigerator that Nina had pointed out. I shuffled as quickly as I could over to it. A large packet of blood lay inside. I tore a hole in the corner of the baggie and quickly drank half of it. A small semblance of control returned. And with that, I took a large sniff. From Nina's office, the usual delicious smell.

From Jeff's corner office … nothing. No smell of living flesh. Why? And then comprehension dawned.

Jeff was undead like me.

He was a zombie. A zombie who had groomed me to make other zombies, so that we could be exploited.

This, then, was Jeff's gambit. I had only to let the zombies attack Nina in her office, and her job would be mine. I would have more money for my family, and wasn't that why I was doing this?

But. A very large but. Nina had tried to help me on many occasions. Jeff was just interested in what I could give him.

Nina must have had some idea of what Jeff was planning. But how could you go public with something like that? How do you accuse a senior staff member of planning murder and not sound like a lunatic?

Behind me I heard the moans of the zombies. They had caught the scent as well, and were now making their way towards the door. Even if I pulled it shut they would be able to open it again.

"Aaaarrrrrrrr," I groaned, inchoate. I saw Nina's door slam and heard a scraping noise. She must have dragged her desk in front of the door. I also heard screams as the other staff ran for the exits. Dimly an alarm blared.

That left one person on the floor. One person expecting his plan to succeed, not realizing he had been anticipated.

I shuffled down the hallway toward Jeff's office. I dribbled blood from the package Nina had left me as I went. The zombies followed my lead, blocking off any escape path.

The door to Jeff's office was locked, but we were a massed horde of hungry undead flesh. Under the pounding of the zombies the door slowly gave way. Finally they were through. I went in first, the other zombies behind me. Jeff hid under his desk, trying to block access with his chair. I poured the remaining blood on him and stood back. The first zombies reached him and dug at his arms, eating what they could tear off. He screamed and kicked at them. Bad move. A zombie—one of the accountants from the general ledger team—bit through his pants, tearing off muscle.

The security guards arrived with their nets and went to grab me. I was at the rear of the pack by then, furthest from Jeff. The guards didn't know that I was relatively rational. When I fell back in such a way as to block their ability to trap more zombies, they chalked that up to simple bad luck.

The time I gave the other zombies with this delaying tactic was enough to finish off Jeff. The zombies pulled him out from under the desk. I heard tearing and rending flesh and the gnashing of a multitude of zombie mouths. From the corner of my eye I watched as one zombie bit through his shoulder muscle and severed arm. Other body parts flew around the room as zombies fought over them. His entrails lay in a bloody mess on the floor. Eventually Jeff stopped screaming as a zombie ripped out his heart.

I thought they were going to terminate all the zombies due to the altercation, but before that could happen I got a word in to Nina, about the proof I could provide. She led an investigation into the events of that night. Evidence of Jeff's involvement was pretty damning. Then, on further investigation, they found that his perennial drink of Diet Coke was anything but. Inside the can was actually a container of plasma. On searching they found a hidden store of plasma in his office. He must have been drinking it regularly to allow him to interact with living humans. Suddenly his reticence to leave his office made much more sense.

Nina took over the Chief Financial Officer position. The first thing she did was to improve the quality of our food. We still got raw meat and bones, but fresher ones with better cuts of meat. Then, with the publicity from the incident, she petitioned the government to allow blood donations. We found plenty of people willing to donate blood who were otherwise unable to do so. That included those traditionally excluded, like cancer survivors and HIV positive people, but also strangers who felt sympathetic. Some viewed us as an oppressed minority.

Nina also provided some entertainment, zombie style. We couldn't follow much in the way of television, but some basic video games were within our reach. And she opened up another room for us, one with a window. The meeting room was made substantially more secure in order to allow all the zombies to visit with family.

I wound up leader of the zombie team. It wasn't long before they gave me the job Nina vacated. I would rather have been alive, but if I had to be dead, this was a decent existence.

And then, from time to time, I received a package from Nina. A very discreet one. One of Jeff's hands had gone missing in the attack, presumed eaten. Actually, Nina had taken it. The plasma-rich flesh was extraordinarily succulent to zombies. She parsed it out to me joint by joint.

Just as a load of work came in for the quarter close, Nina sent a piece. I opened the file to have a look, but then took a break before continuing. It was time for some finger food.

BOEDROMION NOUMENIA

by Andrew Scott

The plastic sheet billowed and wafted the thick scent of burnt human into the late summer air. Henson covered his mouth and nose with the back of his hand and squinted at the charred remains of his newest case. The body was huddled over, head resting in the "v" between its knees and its hands were laid out in front, palms upwards, as if this former man were praying to a god that just never came. Below his forehead the letters "BOHΔPOMIΩN NOYMENIA" were carved deep into the weathered wood and were now catching the illusory ash of their creator.

Henson let the sheet fall, hand pushing on his bent knee he levered himself upwards and looked around. He was on the porch of an old town house that looked on to field after field of corporate corn. It had to have been built at least ten miles away from anything that could optimistically be called a "town" and the irony didn't escape him. He turned towards the house and gave the solid doorframe a pat with the flat of his hand. Based on the amount of kerosene in the air it was a miracle the whole place hadn't gone up in flames.

Cops were bustling in and out of the guy's study, a skeleton crew but more than enough for a case like this. Suicide by self-immolation was still a suicide at the end of the day, and all that was left was to sign the papers and find a next-of-kin. The office looked cozy enough. Based on the books and framed degrees on the wall, the guy must have been some kind of academic and he sure knew how to keep things tidy. *Kindred spirit*, Henson thought. He stepped over to the fireplace and kneeled down, his knees making the "Snap Crackle 'n Pop" that reminded him of the cereal commercials he'd loved too many decades ago.

He was dirtying white-gloved fingers with the burnt scraps of a notebook when Leversen came through the door, her happy lilt more incongruous in the hushed academia than a six-foot Barney doll in the Vatican. She perched on the edge of the desk that faced the fireplace and started to read—more *pontificate* really—from the case file.

"Anthony Thomas. Age forty-seven. Former Professor of Ancient Languages at Miksa … Miskuh …"

"Miskatonic, it's up in Arkham," Henson helped, still eyeing the burnt paper.

"…University, right. Well, it seems our charcoal buddy outside had tenure up there until he was not-so-politely asked to give it up after some nasty business involving another dead-language-prof. Nerds fighting over 'stolen ideas' or something. I tell you, they're just as bad as any jock, I remember I used to date this programmer who went bat-shit over…."

Henson let her comments drift over him as he stared closer at some of the blackened page-corners. Whether it was the fire or the professor's cryptic handwriting he couldn't tell, but either way he couldn't make heads nor serifs of what was written on there. Whorls and scratches, it looked like the "automatic writing" he'd seen on a documentary about psychics years ago, but he didn't pin a professor for that kind of thing.

He peeled away another cracked parchment and saw the edges of a laptop beneath. He pulled it out between his thumb and forefinger and handed it to Leversen, who was chuckling to herself over a joke he'd missed.

"Think your ex knows anyone who can recover something off of this?"

She looked down at it, grimaced and took it off him. She told him she would see what she could do and slid it into a polythene bag she whipped out from nowhere. Not looking up from the desk she let out a barking laugh. "Hell, would ya look at that? Prof still used a *roller deck!*"

Joints popping again, Henson walked to the chair-side of the desk and started flitting the cards on the wheel. All of the names were crossed out with a single neat line in red ink. One after the other, name, number, and email were drawn through with calm precision. All except one. Written carefully in navy ink was the name "Don Malakakis". It wasn't much to go on but it seemed this guy was the last person in the world Professor Thomas wanted to speak to before his death, so he was definitely worth a visit from Henson. He detached the card from the deck, slipped it into a small bag, then into his inside jacket pocket. Leversen shouted that she'd "take things from here, then" but her sarcasm fell flat behind the sound of his slowly fading footsteps, and then he was gone.

The words "Malakakis Media 725" imposed themselves over the doorway to the Fifth Avenue skyscraper. Henson heaved a breath and pushed open the heavy glass door. Give him murderers, give him rapists, give him strung-out junkies with nothing to live for besides spoon and syringe, but don't, for god's sake, give him *entrepreneurs* on a Tuesday morning. The whole place stank of overpriced floor polish and the kind of sin that not even a Tom Ford suit can cover up. The blonde receptionist was nice, though, and not in that "I'm paid to be nice until 6:00 pm, then I hope the elevator cable snaps on you" kind of way. She was genuinely nice and definitely didn't belong in this place.

After the elevator took him to nosebleed heights, another receptionist (a blonde again, this guy had a type) opened the glass door to Malakakis' office and, as she closed it behind him, the entire transparent wall frosted translucent and left him in suffocating privacy.

"Detective Henson, right on time."

Henson eased himself into one of the plush leather chairs in front of the desk and took in the surroundings. The office was so clean it was almost sterile, but dotted around the walls and desk were ancient artifacts—Greek or Byzantine, he thought— screaming the boss' heritage like a football fan with too much money. The cushion muffled Henson's landing and he looked up at Malakakis' dark face looming over the desk at least a foot above Henson's line of sight.

"So, my people tell me that you found my name on some dead professor's contacts list?"

"His roller deck. Can you tell me what your relationship was with Professor Thomas before he died, Mr. Malakakis?"

"Detective, Malakakis Media employs 3300 people in over forty divisions, we hire researchers all the time. The Professor was probably just freelancing for a staff member or thinking about applying for a job; our benefits are second to none!" He waved a long, curved letter-opener in his hand and stabbed the air towards Henson with his last word. It was in the shape of one of those old Greek swords Henson had seen on movies about Spartans as a kid, and he doubted it was used for anything more than waving about while this guy basked to the sound of his own voice.

"Do you often give out your personal email to freelancers you don't know, Mr. Malakakis?"

"That's the kind of boss I am, Detective. Lead from the top down, I say, and all memos come from the top. If this guy had a fire up his ass he might have made it here."

Henson sighed at the irony and pushed up from the curved arms of his chair. The only thing what would come from his staying any longer would be a lesson in the depths of apathy rich men can attain. And that was a lesson he'd already learned too long ago.

"Thank you for your time, Mr. Malakakis. If you can think of anything else that can help us, here's my card."

He turned to walk towards the door and the frost vanished. A floor of pale, sickly workers silently huddled into their cubicles emerged in front of him. Henson's shifts and retirement package might suck, but at least he didn't have to work here.

Henson sat up on his single bed in the apartment he'd rented since he was a rookie. It was homely in the kind of way that homes just evolve after they'd been lived in for so long. And although grease had accumulated into new curves and lines on the furniture and walls, he took pleasure in knowing where everything was, from his single fork to his old .45.

He was staring at the wall by the foot of the bed, letting the city's voices wash over him in their crashes and hisses and wails. He couldn't stop thinking about Professor Thomas' body and the letters hacked out beneath it. He picked up his phone and searched for the two words. Wikipedia pages for *Boedromion* and *Noumenia* were the first two hits. Some kind of ancient Greek name for what we call September and October, and then "New Moon". Was it a record of his death? Or some kind of premonition? When in Christ *was* the "New Moon" anyway? He typed it in: two days' time. What was Thomas *getting* at? Poor bastard must have scrambled his mind in the end, all by himself in that secluded house. *Too much solitude will do that to you,* he thought as the cold reality of impending retirement crept up from the back of his mind.

He wondered how long Thomas had knelt there smoldering. Wondered if anyone saw the flames or the smoke in the distance. Wondered if anyone would have cared if they had. This poor guy studied languages all his life, locked himself away and deciphered words written across the centuries as if just for him, and ended up dying alone on his porch in the middle of nowhere in a house for one. Henson went cold and touched the crucifix he wore round his neck. What would happen if *he* died right now? How soon would anyone find out? Would anyone care when they did?

Then, as if on cue, the phone shattered his icy thoughts.

"Detective Henson? My name's Kirsten Thorne, I'm Director of Communications at Malakakis Media. I'm calling on behalf of Mr. Malakakis, he asks if you could come in tomorrow. There's been *an incident* that may pertain to your case."

Back in Malakakis' office Henson turned down the offer to sit in the insultingly low chair and stood between them instead, hands in his pockets. He waited for Kirsten Thorne to finish giving hushed orders to an emaciated guy in a white shirt holding a laptop with an "Approved by the Comic Code Authority" sticker covering up the logo. Malakakis was twirling the letter opener again and staring intently at the monitor on his desk. The door hushed closed as the tech left, leaving just the three of them alone in the office.

"Thank you for coming in, Detective," Thorne said, "we wanted to talk to you about Professor Thomas, it seems there's been some *irregularity* with his computer."

"Ms. Thorne, the professor torched his computer the night he died. We found it in the fireplace under a heap of his burnt notebooks. What kind of *irregularity* are we talking about here?"

"This morning we received a message from it," Malakakis blurted out, then he breathed in and looked up at Henson. "I'm afraid I wasn't entirely honest with you yesterday, Detective. Professor Thomas wasn't on the staff, exactly, he was performing a *personal* task, for me, pro bono as it were."

"Right. You do know obstructing the course of justice is an arrestable offence, Mr. Malakakis?"

"Look, Detective, there are certain things that are 'public-worthy' and others that aren't, you understand? Professor Thomas was helping me trace my ... my *heritage*. He was a washed up old man who enjoyed the reading, that's all. I've built an empire on my name, Detective, but ... it turns out daddy played a little 'free 'n loose' with the facts. Changed his name to Malakakis to avoid the draft. I needed to...."

"You needed to *fabricate* a family history." Henson finished his sentence. Malakakis whipped his eyes from the screen and glared at him. "What I don't get is, how do you know it came from that computer? Could have just been someone using his e-mail addr—"

"All off-site staff have their own private Malakakis email servers with top-shelf security and encryption, Detective, we monitor their access to the network rigorously to ensure the fullest confidentiality." Thorne let the last words fade on her breath as she glanced down at Malakakis.

"So what did the message say?"

Thorne turned the monitor around so Henson could see. He squinted to read it.

Μεταγειτνιων 5

Finally, things are looking up. A gentleman named Malakakis— tragic name—contacted me today asking if I could make up some believable family origin of his name, something that gave him a profound connection to the Hellenic isles. I told him that there may be something I could find— "soft" or "bland" or some etymology thus. He confided in me that his father had perfunctorily concocted that absurd name to avoid certain unpleasantries *involving wartime conscription and, when I informed him that it was most likely that the "Greek" who helped his father invent the name had probably done so in jest, the man's blood visibly boiled. He certainly has quite the "Mediterranean Temper" even if his name is bogus.*

Nevertheless, he tells me that he is a businessman of sorts so perhaps I can look forward to some regular—and much-needed—Ɖ in the near future. It would be a welcome habitué in my life these days, I must say.

Henson reached for the mouse but Malakakis just grunted, "That's all of it."

"So there *was* money involved?" Henson pressed. Malakakis shot a look at him. "What? Your *daddy* never took you on holiday as a kid? That symbol right there, looks like 'Dp', that's the sign for *Drachma*, the old Greek currency, and those letters at the top, they're definitely Greek. Seems the old professor was a bit obsessed, like yourself. Where did this message appear?"

"On the PM@TEN," Thorne said.

"On the *what?*"

"The 'PM@TEN', it's the…"

"The 'Passion Memo at Ten', Detective." Malakakis was standing now; he slid the letter opener into an embarrassingly tiny sword rack on his desk and pointed out the frosted window while the other hand rested on the desk, making him look like a suited ape. "Every night I send out my Passion Memo at 10:00 pm to see who's got the *passion* to be a part of Malakakis Media, who *cares* enough to give it all they've got at any hour of the day, seven days a week." He was two feet away from Henson now, his eyes burning. Henson leaned past him and spoke to Thorne.

"And how many people do you think saw that *memo?*"

"*All* of them." Malakakis sounded vindicated and he planted his other fist softly on the desk. "*Passion requires replies*, Detective. I get a reply from everyone before 10:05 every night."

"And if you don't?"

"Rainy-day Resume, Detective."

Henson pinched the top of his nose and wondered how long he would have to deal with this belabored Newspeak. Thorne broke the silence.

"I've just spoken with our top security guy, he tells me Thomas' email account has been deleted. We shouldn't receive any more messages from it, we just thought you should know about the one we got."

"Right." Henson turned towards the door. "You better hope I don't find anything on Thomas' laptop that says 'scumbag CEO screwed me for millions', Malakakis, else I'll have your ass. And I want in on that 'PMTEN' bullshit, just in case any other messages come through. You got my card, don't expect a goddamn reply." The door muffled shut behind him.

Henson was having a smoke on the tiny balcony that over-looked the alley by his apartment. The sun was going down over Brooklyn and it colored the brown high rises with soft hues of orange and red. He billowed smoke into the sky and made a silent prayer that he could get Malakakis on digital theft or extortion.

The night had closed in rapidly but it was still warm out, and the winos were easing into their long evening of pontificating at the better-lit end of the alley. He smiled down at them and raised his glass. "But for the grace of God...." He muttered, but was cut short by a ping from his pocket. He smiled at the winos hiding their booze and drunkenly looking around for the source. He pulled out his phone, it was the "PM@TEN".

As he scrolled down disgust surged upwards like acid reflux. The *pings* of desperate workers opening their messages out of fear of losing their jobs turned his disgust into hatred. Hatred for Malakakis, for the entire monkey show of corporate careers and the glorified indentured servitude it resulted in. And then the replies came. *Ping.* "Disruptive." *Ping.* "Next Level Drill Down." *Ping. Ping. Ping.* For a moment, his mind drifted towards the likelihood of bringing Malakakis in on charges of murder for the flurry of "Let's Execute This" that rolled up his screen. The PM@TEN wasn't just an email, it was a direct message through Malakakis Media's own locked-down internal app. The pings came from the 3299 other staff members replying and trying to beat their fellow drones to the punch of saying "Let's Action This" or "Touch Base Offline Tomorrow". He let them ping in his pocket as he finished his drink. Sure enough 10:04 came along and *silence*. Then, at 10:10, a single ping rang out.

He picked up the phone again and grimaced, knowing he just made the same movement as all the other corporate-ladder-jockeys excited to see who was getting fired the next day. And then he saw the name—Anthony Thomas, a dead man writing from a defunct email—and his evening lost all semblance of quietude.

Μεταγειτνιων 15

What a month so far! The last time I wrote I was just thinking *about requesting some genealogical records at the State Library for the unfortunately named Mr. Malakakis. I must admit that I scoffed at the absurdity of his offer to fly me to Crete to "perform my task better," as he put it, but as my shoes padded on the coarse strips on the steps of his private jet, I realized that his conviction was indubitable.*

As we flew to the ancient Cretan cultural centre Xania, he told me that his initial request for genealogical aid was only part of his reasoning for travelling with me to Crete. He said that he had found himself mired in controversy over the logo he had chosen for his brand and he was interested in encountering another, infinitely rarer specimen that would "give the brand the uniqueness Malakakis deserved". (I'm proud to say that I resisted the urge to laugh.)

The plan, as I was informed, was that he had paid some unscrupulous military officials at the nearby United States Naval Support Activity base to release their findings of deep water excursions into the depths of Souda Bay. These results stipulated that evidence of unidentified symbols were found at a depth of some 350 feet. Barely had I inquired if the services of a team of expert deep-sea divers had been obtained than I was holding my nose to release the pressure exerted by the fathoms.

That day I saw the maniacal fervor Mr. Malakakis holds for his enterprise. I sat beside him in his personal Triton 3300 submarine and watched as the Cimmerian depths opened before our front lights. While he followed the coordinates given to him by an uneasy soldier above, Malakakis played with the mechanical arms that would serve us in our furtive salvage mission. He spoke to me about his theory for Crete being the actual site of ancient Atlantis. He surprised me with his knowledge of the Minoan Empire and the volcanic eruption that spelled the same fate for its commerce as the fabled waves did for the mythical continent. I listened with quiet politeness. I was not prepared to let foolish academic nit-picking send me back to penury or worse.

The Triton 3300 whirled to the left and shone lights against what looked like an underwater cliff-face and we hovered downwards to the fathomage prescribed by our informant. The jagged rocks drew us down to the eldritch abyss and then curved open, like the curtains of some unholy

altar, and the lights of the Triton crept slowly over a hideous marine taber-
nacle carved into the rock.

What looked like dozens of small tablets, akin to those of Moses alt-
hough these were hewn from some ancient tree, lay haphazardly on the recess
floor. Malakakis toyed with one of the multitude of handles in the cabin,
and the robotic arms stretched out and grasped one of the tablets. It curled
what can only be referred to as its elbow and brought the object towards the
window, like some freakish mechanical monster feeding its maws. We
stared at the diminutive slab of wood and, though it was stained and infest-
ed with maritime draff, I was able to perceive some symbols etched beneath
the surface. We collected as many samples as our hold could bear and fath-
omed upwards at a glacial pace, attenuating the pressure in the cabin.
Malakakis was giddy with joy at the hope of etching the sides of his gaudy
towers worldwide with the symbol that announced his discovery of Atlantis.
I must admit, there was no shortage of a similar boyish ferment in the beat-
ings of my own heart. If Malakakis does not approve the Ϟ there's still a
chance a journal may pick up my findings and publish them. This fortui-
tous foray into the deep could spell my way back to the university and, dare
I say, the academic acclaim I deserve!

Henson stood in the quiet office at the head of an empty bull-
pen. He'd spent the day immersing himself in art crime prece-
dents and theorizing how a tweedy professor could infuriate a
billionaire enough to get cooked alive on his own porch. Whatever Malakakis' involvement, though, Henson knew he couldn't
go spouting his name all over the precinct during the day shift
without catching a lawsuit. In the hopes of being able to enjoy
his modest pension, he opted to broach the subject at night.
The office lights blazed against the black canvas of the moon-
less night sky outside the windows and the screen of his cell
phone illuminated his Police Captain's grim face like some nocturnal imposter.

"Professor Thomas' journal entry goes on from there, Captain. Talking about how his pride had got the better of him before. How he's realized how wrong he'd been to put his career first over the 'true search for knowledge,' and how he wondered if his wife would ever understand the depths of his stupidity. If his daughter would take his calls if they came from his old office. Stuff like that. This guy wasn't looking to *off* himself, Captain. He talks about looking forward to tasting the pastries at conferences again, for god's sake!"

"Did your contact find anything on the guy's laptop?"

"They got onto the hard drive, but it'd been wiped. I just got off the phone with Leversen, though, and she showed me what she'd found on the laptop screen. We initially thought it had just been sliced up by a suicidal lunatic, but when she looked closer she realized he'd carved the same series of letters into it over and over again. "BOHΔPOMIΩN NOYMENIA." The same ones he carved into his porch before lighting the match."

"Is that Greek?"

"Yeah, I looked it up and it means 'New Moon' and one of the names of their months, Boedromion."

"Sounds like he was writing some kind of *date*." The Captain turned in his chair and the screen blazed when he touched the mouse. "Boedromion. Looks like their months overlapped ours, putting the 'new moon' right in the middle of September. Here, look at the top of the e-mail, the date's in Greek too. 'Metageition'. Says here it's the month leading into the first half of September. According to this diagram, that would put his writing in his journal a couple of weeks before he died."

"Could have been kidnapped, then brought back to make it look like a suicide?"

"Tenuous. We're still receiving his diary entries, don't forget. Did you confirm Thomas' address was deleted?"

"I confirmed it this morning, sir. Tech guy's been working all night to find out how the messages keep—"

Henson's voice was cut short by the loud ping coming from his cell phone. He and the Captain instinctively checked their watches.

"Looks like our dead friend's got his times mixed up," the Captain smiled, but the cold sense of foreboding was already surging through Henson's body and it took every ounce of his will to keep from dropping the phone.

Μεταγειτνιων 27

I am truly alone. An academic's life is one of solitude and contemplation, but there is always the hope of conversation some way down the line. Yet not for me. I can see the end of the line now and it is nearing me with every blink of this cursor. It's almost impossible to believe that this month began with such hope. Such unbridled hope, only to end in bleak nothingness, peering into the eternal Fallen abyss.

The last opportune moment I had to write in this journal came before I examined those wretched tablets in the sanctity of my own home. Sentences written by a man with a lighter heart. A man unconscious of his fate.

I spent more than a fortnight painstakingly scraping at the wooden tablets we found in the depths of Souda. I scraped and I picked, and as I cleaned the wood I noticed it could no longer be called as such. The corrugations wove in lines like the bark of a tree but, if this material had ever lived, it was during a time long before the rule of men ... or their gods.

I studied the calcified tablets fastidiously, hoping they would reveal a new alphabet, a new library of symbolism that would bear my name and return my dignity. And yet each tablet, each cursed lump of fossilized matter bore just one new image. The same symbol etched over and over into tablets of different sizes but monotonous content. They were repeated on all sides, as if some underwater creature, driven mad by a sight it was never destined to see, had cleaved them in some dying apotropaic wish.

I was distraught. A unique symbol with no frame of reference would be lucky to find a home in the dank pages of Internet conspiracy theorists, let alone a veritable academic journal. I had fallen into the mired realm of Voynich.

The night of Μεταγειτνιων 20 I went to bed telling myself that academic glory may not yet be within my grasp, but I had found Mr. Malakakis' new logo and the ⅅ promised would make life more comforta-

ble at least. I resolved to send him my preliminary findings the following day and turned out the lights in my bedroom—as it were, for the last time.

I've not dreamt much since I was a child, but what occurred that night wasn't so much dreaming as being transported to a dream world. *I looked around me, as conscious as I am now, and peered through the murky viridian air. Smoke swayed like translucent algae before my eyes and soft sediment billowed up with every step I took. I could see a mere six feet before my outstretched arms and my ears felt plugged like Odysseus'. And then, like the sirens' call, I heard it. A low rumbling, at first. An immense dormant growl from some ghostly beast out of sight. The ground beneath me resonated with the ebb and flow of an omnipresent bellow that somehow confirmed the hopelessness of my fate.*

The land grew darker, changing viridian for obsidian. The air around me began to crush my chest as if I had somehow stepped unwittingly into the Marianas Trench. I heaved for breath as I fell to my knees with a languor that defied gravity. Then the earth beneath me lit up. Slowly, dust and debris silhouetted against my vision and floated about my head. I looked up. There from my obeisant position in the depths of some unholy chasm I could see the moon. Gibbous and pregnant with meaning, it shone down on me like the judgement of a cruel god long, long forgotten. I turned my face from the light and shielded myself with my hand as it seemed to approach me, becoming larger and more waxed than anything I'd seen in the earth's night sky. I dared to look again and found that I was not staring at the benevolent face of Selene but, instead, was face-to-face with the single Cyclopean eye of a creature so immense, so Leviathan in its scale, it seemed to be immortal and ancient, and unspeakably evil.

Since that day I've lived in a shifting state of consciousness. Terror whirls around the maniacal exuberance I'm incapable of controlling. I see its tentacles in every line on the page. Its hideous eye is burned onto my retina so I dare not close them even for sleep, lest I feel it mining my soul for answers beyond my comprehension. I didn't understand its investigation until today, until I cleaned the debris off the final symbol, and felt my soul become infected with its evil.

It haunts diurnal thoughts, it tricks me into believing I've done things like eat or sleep, but the unending screech of my body proves the contrary. Whenever I blink the first thing I see from the corner of my eye are its abominable whorls as clear as my own hand but, when I turn, it maddeningly disappears from sight. I can feel it waiting for me, the symbol, waiting for me to activate it somehow and unleash the eons of evil that lie somewhere in the depths of our world, waiting to reclaim the earth for its own. Waiting with repulsive patience.

I can bear this madness no longer. Time is but a fleeting wisp of smoke to me now. Malakakis *brought this upon me.* He opened the vortex *to a world of which no human should have to bear the sight. And I shall bear it no more....*

Neither Henson nor the Captain looked at the window, but they could both feel the ice-cold hue of a new moon wash over them. It was September, but somewhere in the depths of their hearts they knew *Boedromion Noumenia* had arrived.

Henson's chest burned as he ran up Fifth Avenue towards Malakakis Media. He'd tried to call Malakakis' office, but nobody picked up. He had no idea what the mad professor meant by his last words, no idea what this ancient calendar date could have in store for that unbearable "Captain of Industry", but his gut told him it was dire. His knee almost buckled as he turned for the elevators and pounded the button beside the doors.

"Has anyone been in here in the last hour?" he barked at the night guard.

"Only Mr. Malakakis, sir. Odd, though. S'normally gone by now."

Henson's heart pounded again as the lift door *pinged* open. He stepped in and mashed his pudgy thumb against the highest floor on the touch screen. He heard one of his shirt buttons rip off as he squeezed out the door and sprinted between the cubicles. Malakakis' office wall and door were frosted, but the lights were on, so he burst inside.

It was a massacre. Malakakis' head was lolling over the back of his chair; his neck had been hacked through to the vertebrae and the blood had sprayed in fountains over both his shoulders, covering the antiquities in scarlet gelatin. Henson stepped around the desk gingerly and approached the body. He was looking for signs of defense and thought he'd found them when he saw Malakakis' right forearm covered in blood. He crouched down painfully and saw the novelty letter opener gripped in the dead man's bloody hand. He stared at the dead man's neck up close and saw that a legion of tiny stab marks had ripped it apart. What could have made this Type-A exec stab and slash his own neck more than thirty times? What did he see?

Henson looked over at the screen. Pixels and discoloration surrounded the fifty or so deep grooves Malakakis had made when he stabbed it maniacally with the small imitation sword. It looked like he'd been checking his emails when, in a fit of rage and lunacy, he started to attack the monitor with the ferocity of a deranged animal. Henson looked closer; he could just make out an email message—a *personal* message, direct to Malakakis— from Professor Thomas. But it was timestamped at 9:55? Something the professor wanted Malakakis to see on his own before the PM@TEN. Henson tried, but he couldn't make out any of the content behind the damage on the screen—but he did see something next to the email addresses. This message contained an attachment. An image file Malakakis had opened before he took his own life.

Henson was trying to make out the image around the circle of slashes when both the screen and his phone *pinged* together in the heavy silence. He took his phone out of his pocket with shaking hands and looked at the screen. It was Thomas. It was the PM@TEN. And there was an attachment. His hand began to shake uncontrollably at the thought of holding this image in his hands. What was in this attachment that could make a man do *that* to himself? Even as he thought the question, the answer was already lying at the back of his brain. It was as if it were something permanently there, something he'd always known, like the sound of his own name. It was the symbol Thomas found. The one that sent him insane. Henson couldn't say for sure, but something from the past few days told him it was true. As if Thomas had somehow been reanimated since the first time Henson saw his charred corpse. As if reading this man's deepest, final thoughts had made him *live* somewhere in some reality, and just hearing him talk about this symbol had indented some form of it on Henson's memory, like he could feel the strength of the symbol emanating out of Thomas' messages, out of the crushing depths of eternity. It had to be deleted. Deleted before anyone …

He looked up at the screen as he heard the *ping* of the first person opening the message. Then the second. Then the third.

Then he dropped to his knees and wept.

INCORPORATION

by Max D. Stanton

I am a high priest of the new gods and a prophet of the Golden Sign. With feats of logomancy and numerology I have bent this world to the will of my masters. I have midwifed the births of mighty deities, officiated the marriages of bodiless androgynes, and put immortal beings to death, all using nothing more than incantations and precatory offerings. Words and paper are all it takes to conquer the world.

I am a partner at the white-shoe law firm of Prochnoy Carpenter, specializing in mergers, acquisitions, and corporate governance. I sit atop a tower in Wilmington, Delaware, the holiest city of the new gods, looking out across the water. There are places the new gods love better than Delaware, but this is their true home.

The beings I serve create paradises for their chosen servants to dwell within, but their favor is scarce and fickle, and many are sent away from them into outer darkness, weeping and gnashing their teeth. They have laid once-prosperous nations to waste because their people did not honor the Golden Sign, and raised up gleaming new metropolises to take their places. They drink the black blood of the Earth in rivers, and shit out everything mankind treasures. They spun a vast invisible web out of ones and zeros, and captured all of humanity's minds and identities inside it. All for the Golden Sign. No man or god may prosper unless he bears the Golden Sign.

The new gods demand constant propitiation. They devour their clerics' lives in six-minute intervals, keeping meticulous note of every tenth of an hour consumed. Without their servants they would be nothing, not even ghosts. The new gods rule the planet as spectral emperors, but cannot so much as pick up a pencil without help. Yet despite all their neediness and hunger they have remade man's civilization in their own image, and are refining their work still further.

Now I come bearing eldritch scripture sent from on high. Once this spell is given effect then life will change irrevocably. I write this memorandum to file to commemorate the dawning of a new aeon.

My client is already beginning to manifest. Its sharp, smooth feelers caress the back of my neck like a lover's fingertips. It is anxious to be born. I need to finish this memo quickly, there is urgent work that must be done tonight. And yet I want to recount the whole tale. How odd that at the apex of my career, after a lifetime of decisive, thoughtfully-ordered actions, I now find myself procrastinating. Perhaps this is what it's like to be afraid.

I began my career at Prochnoy Carpenter right out of Miskatonic Law. I spent my 1L and 2L summers at the venerable firm as a summer associate, where they wined and dined me at the finest restaurants, fattening me up like a calf for the sacrifice. There was no question about me working anyplace else. When I first started, they assigned me to work beneath Charlie Dunsany, a senior partner in the firm's corporate group. Charlie was a glad-hander of the old school, whose backslapping jokes and relentless charm concealed an intellect like a fearsome sword. He was a harsh taskmaster but a fine mentor, and I was proud that my work met his pitiless standards. He summoned me to his office one day. With the dark wood paneling and musty cigar smell it was like being inside a humidor.

Charlie gazed out the window with an uncharacteristically faraway look on his face. "We've got a new client coming into the firm that I'd like you to handle," he said. "Have you ever heard of Hastur Capital?" By that point in my career I knew most of the players on Wall Street, at least by reputation, but I didn't know that name. I shook my head. "It's a venture capital firm out of New York," Charlie explained. "I'm not surprised you haven't heard of it, the CEO doesn't like publicity. The business press hardly ever mentions it, even though it does billions in acquisitions each year."

"How'd we land them?"

Charlie, normally so proud of his networking prowess, cast his eyes downward. "The CEO's named Alex Vanderlee. I met him at a—at a … at a party last year. A very strange party. I—I shouldn't have gone. We didn't talk much. I didn't think I'd ever see him again. He called me out of the blue today. His usual outside counsel's in some sort of criminal trouble and he's holding a beauty contest to find a replacement. It won't be much at first, but it's got the potential to turn into something big for the firm. Can I ask you to spearhead it? I think you've got what it takes."

At the time I was flattered, but in later years I often wondered what exactly Charlie saw in me that convinced him I was Hastur's man.

Charlie was right that it wasn't much work at first. Hastur Capital occasionally needed to form new corporate subsidiaries; my task was drafting and filing the paperwork that created those entities. It would have been utterly routine work, if not for the client's esoteric and inscrutable demands. For example, all Board meetings were to be prefaced by solemn, poem-like recitals of phrases from Babylonian talismans. Special meetings were to occur on Walpurgisnacht and the solstices. Solar eclipses triggered special dividends. These are not the sorts of provisions that most young attorneys are familiar at drafting, and there is no model language in any of the treatises. But I have a creative mind, and Delaware's General Corporation Law is famously flexible and adaptable. I drafted clauses and exhibits and amendments that accomplished the CEO's weird purposes. I put together bylaws that mandated management to perform strange rites, binding them with duties of utmost loyalty and care. More and more work began coming in. Hastur Capital was growing fast.

A year into the engagement, Vanderlee summoned Charlie

and I to New York for a meeting. I had never previously spoken to the man, I'd only encountered him as a disembodied, authoritative name on emails and documents. It would be my first time meeting a billionaire, and I was excited. Charlie, on the other hand, was a wreck, alternatively morose and twitchy. We were sitting across from each other on the Acela Express train, and he was hitting the drink service hard.

"I hate New York," he grumbled, as he peered at me through the golden contents of a single-serving Scotch bottle. "My theory is that the Indians sold Manhattan to the Dutch because they saw the land was cursed. Their wise men knew that it was a dirty, haunted island, full of powers that people can't control, and when some foolish white boys in wooden shoes showed up willing to take it off their hands, they figured, hey, let's get out while the getting's good. Pick up some nice glass beads as a bonus. Plan didn't work, though. The curse caught up with the Indians anyway." He kept drinking all the way to New York, and once we'd checked into our hotel he insisted on visiting the bar. I was surprised, since he was ordinarily quite careful with booze. I begged off early so as not to be groggy the next day.

The next morning I rose before the sun, focused and refreshed. I suited up for the meeting and pounded on Charlie's door. No answer. I knocked again. And again. I called. I emailed. I called again. Nothing. I paced the lobby, growing increasingly frantic as the minutes ran out and the silence continued. At last I made the executive decision to head on to the meeting alone. I had barely any clue what was on the agenda, but the choice between searching for Charlie and disappointing the client was no choice at all.

At least that's how it seemed at the time. Looking back, I see that I did make a choice, and that my life would have progressed along an entirely different path had I chosen differently. Triumph requires an unbroken chain of wise choices, but disaster is never more than one bad decision away. I have no regrets, though. Just the opposite.

Hastur Capital is headquartered in a midtown skyscraper that reminded me of a gothic cathedral—a looming monolith of weathered, stained concrete decorated with riotous carvings and sculptures. Gargoyles in a wild assortment of shapes caper and writhe around the ledges and doorframes, some of them more like abstract geometrical sculptures than living things but nonetheless somehow recognizable as depictions of fantastic beasts, and some of them almost human-looking except for irregularities in their leering faces that subtly but indelibly mark them as monsters. An art deco glass-and-steel pyramid incongruously caps the building.

Stepping from the controlled chaos of Manhattan into the Hastur Capital lobby was like stepping through a doorway in the Brazilian jungles and emerging into the freezing void of outer space. The lobby was a vast expanse of black marble and emptiness—seemingly too large a chamber to even fit within the skyscraper's walls. To walk through this vastness was to feel puny. I shuddered involuntarily; the air conditioning was turned up to cryogenic levels. At the far end of the lobby, a sole security guard peered at me from behind a desk of white-veined stone, tiny in the distance. He was the only other person in the lobby.

I walked forward to check in, suddenly wishing badly that I had Charlie with me to smooth things over. With each step I took, my tasseled loafers made a sound like a hammer on the marble floor. I showed my ID to the security guard, and was met with a mask of wall-eyed incomprehension. Drool trickled from the corners of his baby-like mouth.

A cold hand clapped on my shoulder. I turned with a start and saw a lean man in a grey suit smiling mirthlessly at me. His skin and hair were papery white, his tie and eyes were deep black. This monochrome fellow introduced himself as Hastur's general counsel, shaking my hand with a grip like a glacier, and I relaxed a little, since at least I knew him from conference calls. I tried to make an excuse for Charlie's absence, but he seemed to have been expecting it.

We took the elevator up—my eardrums popping from the sudden ascent—and the monochrome man took me on a tour of Hastur Capital. I've been in many corporate offices, including during head-chopping events like mergers and restructurings when my very presence was seen as a harbinger of doom, but the atmosphere in Hastur reminded me of nothing so much as a prison that I toured during law school, on a field trip for my criminal justice class. That field trip convinced me never to practice criminal law. Muffled screams and bellows sounded from behind office doors. Eyes hot with jealousy, suspicion, and malice followed me closely, peering around corners and out of conference room windows. A woman was sobbing uncontrollably in the bathroom. Her hyperventilating gasps sounded like the death cries of a wounded animal.

"Mr. Vanderlee believes strongly in establishing a culture of high performance and accountability," my indifferent guide said. "We pay our people exceedingly well ... but we also demand quite a lot of them. Yes, quite a lot."

Vanderlee's office occupied the apex of the building, enclosed by the pyramid. The office was nearly as vast and empty as the lobby. At its center sat a desk carved from a huge block of black stone, with a few chairs and a couch nearby. These items were the only furniture in sight. Despite the room's size, an unpleasant tang of body odor hovered in the air. It was almost completely dark, as steel shutters on the sloping glass walls blocked out any daylight. The only illumination came from a bank of a dozen or so flat-screen monitors positioned around the desk. Alex Vanderlee stared into those monitors, his eyes dancing compulsively between them. Their pale, unwholesome glow cast eerie shadows across his face.

He was much younger than I'd imagined, boyish even, but was fat and decrepit beyond his years. There was something about him of the shut-ins who are found dead in their homes, surrounded by heaps of newspapers and mummified cats, except that he had shut himself in on the pinnacle of a skyscraper at the center of Manhattan, surrounded by wealth and power.

His skin had a jaundiced yellow sheen to it, and the stink of un-
washed flesh grew stronger as I approached him.

"Mr. Vanderlee?" I asked. "It's good to meet you. I'm—"

"I know who you are," he said. His voice was raspy and
baritone. He did not stand, but lurched forward a bit in his chair
to accept my handshake in his damp, clammy mitt. "You're the
hierophant."

I had not been expecting that. "I—I'm from Prochnoy
Carpenter," I said, proffering my card. "I'm sorry Charlie
couldn't be here, but—"

"Charlie doesn't deserve to be here," Vanderlee said. "You
do. I've seen your work. It's excellent. And you don't ask un-
necessary questions, like so many of the other lawyers do. You
never tell me what I *can't* do or what I *shouldn't* do. You don't
question my purposes. You accept my will and translate it into
documents and agreements that bind the men whom I want
bound. I value that immensely."

The praise of a billionaire feels so much better than ordinary acclaim. "Thank you very much," I said. "My philosophy is
that it's all about serving the client, whatever the client needs."

"It's good to have a philosophy," he said. "I have a question for you about that. Lately there's been a lot of … *controversy*
… around the idea of corporate personhood. The idea that corporations are people. What do *you* think about that doctrine?"

Something in his tone took me aback. I knew that he
couldn't be one of those hippie-dippie types to work themselves
into an uninformed lather about what the Supreme Court did in
Citizens United. Hell, half of Washington was dangling from the
tit of Vanderlee's political action committee. But at the same
time, there was something distinctly hostile in the way he spoke.
"Corporate personhood's misunderstood," I said cautiously. "If
the law didn't treat corporations as people then—"

"Corporations are *not* people!" Vanderlee snarled, spittle
flying from the edges of his mouth. "They are infinitely grander.
Corporations can live forever! No disease can taint them, no
knife can wound them. They exist on a higher plane than us.

And the power they wield … no, corporations are not people, they are gods! New gods, to be sure, but no less divine on account of their youth. Consider Jupiter. At the peak of his power, his domains stretched across Europe, the Mideast and Africa. Not bad, but now consider the Golden Arches. There is no land on Earth where they are not known, where they lack servants, where men do not toil and shed the blood of animals in their holy name. Even if the Roman priests heaped all the treasures in all their temples together, that hoard couldn't purchase what the Lord of the Golden Arches earns in a single fiscal quarter. I know, the 10-Q earnings report just came out today."

At that moment, I thought Vanderlee to be insane. I wished again that Charlie was here, and wondered about what kind of party they'd met at. I stammered something vague and non-committal.

"I shouldn't be so hard on you for your naiveté," he said. "You're a young man, and there are many corporate lawyers much more experienced than yourself who still don't grasp the true nature of their work. Tell me, have you seen the Golden Sign?"

"The Golden Sign?"

"Behold," he said reverently. "The Golden Sign." He hit a button that activated a spotlight overhead, illuminating an area near the roof of the darkened chamber. He gazed upwards, turning his face towards the light, and my eyes followed his. I saw that just beneath the tip of the pyramid, he had mounted an idolatrous sculpture that seemed to be made of solid gold. It was an amalgamation of the dollar sign, the euro mark, the pound, the yen, and the sigils of many other currencies beside, and yet there was also something else in its curves and jags, something fiercely alien. It must have cost hundreds of millions to cast. The glittering seared my eyes but I could not look away. I had never wanted to possess anything so badly in my life.

"Even the new gods bow before the Golden Sign," said Vanderlee. "The new gods all seek its favor … they wage eternal war against each other in the Golden Sign's name. A man who is marked with the Golden Sign possesses great power. Enemies cannot hurt him. He can commit terrible crimes and not fear punishment. He can have women, friends, whatever he wants. It is the greatest magic there is. But a man who is *not* marked with the Golden Sign...." A look of utter horror and repugnance passed over Vanderlee's sallow countenance. "A man who is not marked with the Golden Sign spends his days in fear and want and helplessness. He is barely a man, he is an animal to be used and butchered. You see now why men will murder for the sake of the Golden Sign, and commit every sort of atrocity for it. It stands above everything else."

"My God...." I gasped, barely even hearing Vanderlee's words. The idol had me firmly within its hypnotic power.

"Yes, exactly." Vanderlee turned some of his screens to face me. They displayed stock tickers, earnings charts, currency fluctuations, business news. "This is the alchemy of our age," he proclaimed. "It transforms base matter into wealth and power. By mastering these formulae, we earn the favor of the new gods. Hastur Capital is a great deity, you see. You and I serve it, as its hierophant and its magician, respectively, and it rewards our fealty by reflecting the Golden Sign upon us."

"It's gorgeous. It's the most beautiful thing I've ever seen."

"I'm glad you understand me," he said, his voice warm with gratitude. "Here, let me show you something else. The Island of Manhattan is a holy place to the new gods. To most it's just a city, but those with the right eyes can perceive it for what it is."

He hit a button beneath his desk and the steel shutters all along the sloping walls retracted with a *clack-clack-clack*, flooding the room with golden light. It took a moment for my eyes to adjust from the darkness, but when they did, I beheld a panoramic view of a vast and hideous megalopolis that was not New York City at all, or perhaps which was New York City in its purest and truest form. Where I'd expected to see skyscrapers, instead I was surrounded by megalithic stepped pyramids, their tiered ledges worn smooth by the knees of countless supplicants, and stained red and brown by the blood of countless tumbling sacrifices. Vast cathedrals of unearthly beauty stood proudly atop the pyramids. Here and there I glimpsed ant-like priests in gorgeously colored vestments strolling the rooftop gardens or hauling chained and struggling offerings into the apex temples. And so too, here and there I caught glimpses of the carnivorous divinities that dwelled inside those temples. A many-taloned paw stretched forth from gem-encrusted gates to snatch up a shrieking man. A tremendous eye with an hour-glass-shaped pupil peered out from behind a stone archway—it saw me just as clearly as I saw it. I could not, however, see what lay beneath the skyline, for the land below was shrouded in seething darkness and fog, and the briefest contemplation of those stygian depths filled me with terror. I would have done anything to stay out of that wretched netherworld. I looked instead to the heavens, where I saw the Sign burning with divine radiance like an infinitely beautiful sun. Next to the genuine article, Vanderlee's idol was a mere bauble, despite its size and its astronomical cost. I was awestruck with insane, possessive desire, the sort of desire that puts men into mansions and prisons and madhouses. I wanted this holy light to shine upon me and me alone. I've wanted nothing else since.

My next coherent memory is of staggering out of a taxi with one of my shoes missing and a persistent, insectoid buzzing in my head. The Hastur meeting had been at 8:00 AM, but now it was dark. I still don't know what happened to all that missing time. The hotel lobby was full of cops. They told me that Charlie had used a straight razor to open up his wrists and throat in the bathtub.

A few days later I was milling about at the funeral when Alan Carpenter pulled me aside. He'd been the driving force of the firm ever since Old Man Prochnoy had succumbed to dementia and a vastly reduced existence as *partner emeritus*. Rumor had it that Prochnoy's much younger wife kept the toothless lion in a state of squalor and near-starvation. Having met her once at a firm Christmas party, I believed these rumors to be correct.

"I hear you've been doing superb work for Hastur Capital," Carpenter told me. "That's a crucial client. We think it has a lot of potential for the firm. With Charlie gone, we need a partner to handle that relationship. Are you ready to step up?"

"That all depends on how much my compensation will step up," I said, although I knew the partners' take-home pay as well as if I'd been cutting the checks personally. "And if I step out the door to another firm, Hastur Capital will come with me."

Carpenter's eyes narrowed. He made me his offer, and in that moment the Golden Sign cast its light upon me. I smiled and shook his hand.

The partners of Prochnoy Carpenter subscribe to a peculiar funerary custom. When one of their own dies, the others traditionally leave the service in a single mass. The moment that Carpenter turned towards the door, every other partner abruptly concluded their grieving and followed. Perhaps it was presumptuous for me to have left with Carpenter, for officially I was still just a lowly associate until I was voted in formally, but no one dared to say anything. I took Charlie's corner office for my own the next day. It took a while to get the cigar smell out, though.

With Hastur Capital as a client we didn't want for billable hours. I had plenty of fresh young associates beneath me, and I worked them like helots. The Hastur team got a reputation as the suicide division of Prochnoy Carpenter, but what the hell, bigger bonuses for the survivors. I bathed in the Golden Sign's light, but my desire for its sacred radiance was a hunger that fed upon itself, and I always wanted more.

Hastur Capital is itself a god of hunger, which ceaselessly seeks out lesser gods to devour. Sometimes its prey willingly sacrifice themselves, stepping into Hastur's maw so that they can be reborn in the light of the Golden Sign. Other times they and their worshippers fight back and must be subdued, or one of Hastur's rivals swoops in and tries to seize the prize in its own teeth. The work of a high priest is never done. Holy wars rage in between every line of the *Wall Street Journal*. Activist shareholders preach heresies that must be suppressed, and trick-

ster gods weave deadly traps deep into their financing agreements and debt covenants. Even the C-Suite magicians who
serve Hastur must be kept under a watchful eye, lest their own
appetites overpower the loyalty they rightfully owe to their master. Just look at the fallen god Enron, utterly destroyed by the
Judas disciples charged with tending it. I did not shirk my responsibilities, and I learned the secret wisdom of my craft. I became a master at brokering treaties with the priests of hostile
divinities, turning our enemies' poison pills into sweet wine,
transmuting the base lead of distressed securities into triple-A
rated gold, and drawing protective circles to hold the hated demon Taxes at bay.

A few weeks ago Vanderlee reached out to me about restructuring Hastur Capital. He told me that the business was
fundamentally transforming itself, and sent over some draft language for my review. I read the documents he sent almost without blinking, and then re-read them again and again until my
eyes bled. Article III of the amended certificate of incorporation, setting forth the new corporate purpose of Hastur Capital,
LLC, is the most harrowing—an apocalyptic dirge in a place
where ordinarily one finds inoffensive boilerplate. The documents' carefully numbered paragraphs and exhibits are like poetry written by an alien machine, yet for all their strangeness,
brutality, and bleak, haunting lyricism, I don't see anything
about them that's legally invalid. It's a good thing that Hastur's
not a publicly traded company, for if we had to publish this
madness in a proxy statement it'd provoke mass panic and
waves of suicides. But much as a web leads only to a spider, and
a labyrinth leads only to a minotaur, Hastur's exquisitely struc-
tured intricacy of holding companies and subsidiaries leads back
to Vanderlee alone.

All of the formalities have been scrupulously complied
with. The Board of Directors was convened on the appointed
date, and has voted unanimously in favor of the amendments.
Once I electronically file the documents with Delaware's
Prothonotary, Hastur Capital will enter into its new phase of

existence. The "submit" button that will complete the transaction seems to glow with faerie fire, while a lightning storm rages across Wilmington's meager skyline. I am alone, but my client-god is manifesting into my presence. Hundreds of slender yellow fingers grasp me all along my body. Talons of rubies and diamonds scratch impatiently at my throat.

The true incorporation of Hastur is at hand. May it carve the Golden Sign into my body and soul.

THE LOPONINE EXPLOITATION

by John M. Campbell

The vacuum pump began evacuating the air from inside the hollow steel sphere. Bobby Gibson took off his glasses and rubbed the bridge of his nose. In the fluorescent lighting of the windowless laboratory, it could be any time of day. By the outdated clock on the wall, however, he realized it was approaching midnight in the world outside. He grinned to himself, finding it all too fitting that his first foray into the hidden dimension would occur at the witching hour.

Electrons excited into the Fullerton state infused the material that coated the sphere. All it took was a pulse from a laser at the proper frequency, and those electrons would rotate *en masse* into the hidden dimension, taking the hollow steel vessel with them. Bobby was still amazed to experience the effect that Professor Fullerton had discovered a decade ago, shortly before his death from a mysterious illness. Bobby was one of his research assistants at the time, and the death of his mentor had hit him hard. Now, Bobby stood on the brink of proving the professor's naysayers were shortsighted idiots.

With Fullerton's research all but discredited, Bobby had been locked out of academia as a career. He finally took the only opportunity available, a position in the multinational corporation, Elton Pharmaceuticals. He found himself assigned to Oaxaca, Mexico to shape up their quality control processes. The saving grace in this assignment turned out to be something he never expected. Despite being slight of stature, his mixture of steel-blue eyes and sandy hair garnered him a lot of attention here that he never got back home, especially from pretty girls. The other advantage was unsupervised access to the laboratory after completing work each day.

With the vacuum established, Bobby placed the sphere onto the platform inside the reinforced isolation chamber and sealed the door. He wasn't sure what, if anything, this hollow ball would contain when it came back, so he was following hazardous-material protocols just in case. Professor Fullerton had discovered the gateway into a realm hidden from our normal three-dimensional space. Bobby was attempting to bring back a sample of material from that dimension.

He double-checked the frequency setting on the laser and aligned the beam with the window in the side of the chamber. Everything was ready. Bobby's heart beat hard and fast as he glanced up at the clock on the wall. The second hand moved in six-degree hops as it progressed around the face past the numeral ten. At five seconds to midnight, Bobby turned his head to look through the window into the chamber. Counting down silently, he pressed the button to trigger the laser exactly at midnight.

The frequency setting for the laser was outside of the visible spectrum, so Bobby couldn't see the pulse itself, although its effect was clear. The steel sphere collapsed into a circular disk, and the disk oscillated on the platform like a coin dropped onto a table before coming to rest.

Bobby reset the laser to the relaxation frequency and then checked the clock. At 12:01, he triggered another pulse, and the disk expanded back into a sphere. If everything had worked correctly, a timer had opened a port in the ball after it had rotated into the hidden dimension. The vacuum within the sphere should have sucked in a sample of whatever might be there, and now it was back in 3D space where Bobby could analyze it.

Professor Fullerton had discovered a previously unknown state of matter with a mysterious property. Material excited to this state would collapse into a two-dimensional projection of its normal three-dimensional form when exposed to photons at the trigger frequency. Another pulse at the relaxation frequency would restore matter to its 3D form. After many experiments, he concluded that the matter itself never experienced two dimensions. Instead, its 3D form rotated into another dimension, leaving only two dimensions of it observable in the 3D world. He speculated to Bobby that perhaps the matter entered one of the extra dimensions postulated by string theorists to have existed during the Big Bang.

Bobby opened a door on the containment chamber to access the glove ports. He inserted his arms up to his elbows and grasped the sphere in both hands. He twisted its two hemispheres in opposite directions and felt it unseal. Using one hand to anchor the bottom hemisphere to the platform, he lifted the top half away.

Purplish-blue slime plopped out of the top and began dripping over the edges of the lower hemisphere onto the fingers of his glove. Bobby jerked his hand away in surprise. The hemisphere tipped and blue slime spilled out onto the platform.

Julio was a bit nervous. The *yanqui*, Bobby, had been sent from the States by the higher-ups in Elton Pharmaceuticals to improve quality control in their Mexican division. Bobby had asked him to prepare a full analysis of some slimy blue compound, saying the company was testing the skills of their biochemists. Julio had asked him where it came from, but Bobby wouldn't say. Now it was time for Julio to give Bobby the report.

"You told me to treat it as hazardous material, so I observed all the appropriate containment protocols," Julio began.

Bobby nodded.

"This stuff is definitely organic material," Julio told Bobby, pointing at the mass spectrometer analysis, "but I've never come across anything like it before. The purplish-blue color comes from deoxyhemoglobin, the form of the hemoglobin protein without oxygen attached. It's mixed in with other proteins, which I listed in the report. Somehow, the mixture inhibits the hemoglobin from absorbing oxygen, even when exposed to air. I was unable to isolate any cells, but I found DNA. To identify the type of DNA we'd have to map the genome. Unfortunately, our lab doesn't have the equipment to do it, but I know a lab where we can send it, if you want."

"That won't be necessary. Do you have anything else?"

"I'm just getting to the good part." Julio had decided that if this exercise factored into his employee rating, he'd think outside the box. "I tried culturing the material, but it doesn't seem to have any bacterial component. I injected a dose of the material into one of our lab mice and mixed a portion into the food of another. Neither showed any apparent symptoms—until I happened to put their cages next to each other." He paused for maximum effect.

"So, what did you find?" Bobby asked.

"Both mice exhibited extreme agitation, heading toward each other and scurrying back and forth as if they needed to find a way into the other cage. One of the mice was male, and the other was female. The male was a scrawny thing we call Wimpy because he always slinks away when another male is in the same cage. The female we call Queenie because all the alpha males fight over her. She'd never shown any interest in a lowlife like Wimpy, but now she couldn't wait to get to him, and the attraction was obviously mutual from Wimpy."

Julio had Bobby's attention, so he continued. "I thought, what the heck, so I attached a tube between the cages and opened the doors between them. They both scrambled into the tube, and Queenie pushed him backwards into his cage. It was an absolute rut-fest between them for the better part of an hour. Weirdest thing I've ever seen."

Bobby's face showed his discomfort, confirming what Julio suspected.

"So, Bobby, I know this is not some quality-control test like you said. You want to know what I think? I think the company has come up with a new drug and is doing some sort of double-blind experiment to confirm what they have. Am I on the right track?"

Bobby shook his head, trying to deny it, but he wasn't a very good liar. Julio plowed on. "After the drug wore off, Queenie crawled back into her own cage and ignored Wimpy like nothing had happened. I monitored them both for a couple of days, and neither showed any ill effects. Then I tried reversing the process, injecting Queenie and feeding Wimpy, and it was the rut-fest all over again."

Bobby stood up, like he'd had enough.

"On more thing, Bobby. You should hear this. I took the sample home that night, and I mixed a little into hot chocolate for me and my Evita."

Bobby's eyes got big as he realized what Julio was telling him.

"Man, you guys have really got something. My shy little Evita was a lioness. It was the best sex we've ever had."

"Your discovery has created quite a sensation, Mr. Gibson. How fast can you ramp up production?" The Vice President of Marketing had invited Bobby to his plush office. He was a tall man with gaunt features and black, slicked-back hair. He spoke English with a thick accent.

"Well, sir, we have a lot more work to do before we can think about expanding production." Bobby shifted uncomfortably in his chair under the VP's gaze.

Folding his hands on his desk, the VP leaned toward him. "Just tell me what you need, Bobby, and we'll get it for you."

"We know very little about this substance, sir. We need to conduct animal studies to determine its safety and efficacy. Beyond that, the human trials could take years."

"Certainly, we have teams working on the studies. But, in parallel, we also need to ramp up production so we're ready when the approvals come in. What do you need for that?"

Bobby looked down and squirmed again.

"Look, Bobby. I know this all seems overwhelming." The boss turned on his charm. "But you want to continue your research, right? We want to back you. Do you need more equipment? More staff? A bigger lab? I can get it for you."

"Sure, more equipment and a bigger lab would be good."

"Okay. Come back tomorrow with a list of the equipment you want and how many people you need to triple your current output. That will be a start."

"Hi, Bobby, I hear you've hit the big time." Hortensia Silva breezed into Bobby's lab. As a member of the quality assurance staff at the factory, she knew Bobby well.

Bobby recognized Hortensia's friendly voice and looked up from the computer display. She was a short young woman with milk chocolate skin, brown eyes, and black, curly hair. "Hortensia! Good to see you. To what do I owe the pleasure?"

"I was told you needed assistance, so here I am."

For once, Management did something right. Hortensia was smart, and her bubbly personality made her a dream to work with. "Terrific. I'm drowning here."

"What are you doing, and how can I help?"

"You won't believe it if I tell you, so let me show you."

Bobby took her over to the containment unit and repeated the procedure he first executed what seemed like ages ago, but had been only a few weeks. He narrated as he went, relating his time at college with Professor Fullerton and the research Bobby pursued after hours at the lab. To Hortensia, he was afraid he seemed like a hopeless nerd. He was gratified by how impressed she seemed with his discovery.

When Bobby told her about Julio's experiment with the mice, she put a hand to her face to hide her smile, but she couldn't hide the crinkles around her eyes. He locked eyes with her, and they both burst out laughing. A weight lifted from his shoulders.

"I guess I see now what got the boss so excited." Hortensia giggled.

"Love Potion Number Nine!" They dissolved into laughter again.

A week later, the marketing department began circulating brochures for Loponine, the blue capsule made for women as well as men.

Ramping up production could be done two ways: increasing the amount of material produced at each facility, and expanding the number of facilities. Under Bobby's tutelage, engineers had produced copies of his original collection device, along with a laser-pointer version of the triggering laser. Hortensia arranged to send these devices to the company's other labs and scheduled progress meetings among the engineers. Excitement reigned in the initial meetings as the engineers crowed over the balls that shrank into disks and back. However, subsequent meetings had turned more and more contentious.

"Are you sure you followed the procedure?" Bobby addressed one of the engineers on the teleconference.

"Are you sure the procedure is correct?" retorted the engineer. "I'm not the only one who can't duplicate your results."

"The engineers here in my lab don't have any problems with the procedure." Bobby was getting frustrated.

Hortensia stepped in to cut off any further argument. "We need to review our options before proceeding further. Thanks for everyone's efforts. If anyone has any ideas about differences between labs that might explain the lack of results, please send them to me. We'll get back to you if we need anything else." She signed off the teleconference and looked over at Bobby.

"I don't have time to go to every lab and hold their hands, Hortensia." Bobby looked haggard from the pressure and lack of sleep.

"They're smart guys, Bobby. There must be something different about our lab here in Oaxaca. Maybe it's the altitude here. Or the humidity."

"I have a hard time believing the hidden dimension isn't uniform outside of 3D space."

"Yeah, well, sometimes I have a hard time believing the hidden dimension itself exists outside of 3D space." Hortensia smiled. "Maybe we don't know what we don't know."

Bobby gave her a tired smile. "I can't argue with that."

"I'll see if I can come up with something. In the meantime, you look like you need a break. Why don't you come with me to the Guelaguetza festival? We'll have fun."

"I'd love to, but I've gotta work out a few bugs in the 100-X model." He got up wearily and headed back to the lab. "See you tomorrow, Hortensia," he called over his shoulder.

Every summer in Oaxaca at the Guelaguetza, young women enacted the legend of Princess Donaji in dance. Growing up in Oaxaca, Hortensia herself had performed the dance as a child. It told the story of a Zapotec princess who, according to prophecy, would sacrifice herself for her people. The Zapotec people were at war with their neighbors, the Mixtecs. Zapotec warriors captured a wounded Mixtec prince named Nucano. Donaji took pity on the prince and cared for his wounds. They fell in love and, at his request, she let him return to his people. Later, a peace deal was struck with the Mixtecs and, because of her love for Nucano, Donaji agreed to go with the Mixtecs as a hostage to guarantee the peace. She was taken to Monte Albán, the city founded by the Zapotecs but now occupied by the Mixtecs, where she was reunited with Nucano. But the Zapotecs attacked

Monte Albán, breaking the treaty, and in retaliation the Mixtecs beheaded Donaji. They left her body behind but took away her head. In mourning over her death, Cocijo, the god of thunder, shed three days of tears. Later, a shepherd discovered a lily always in full bloom. He dug it up to find its roots entwined in Donaji's skull. In her honor, Cocijo's life force was keeping the lily forever at the peak of its bloom.

The familiar music and dance transported Hortensia back to when she was a little girl. She first experienced the stories of her people at the knee of her grandmother. With no written language, the Zapotec culture was passed down orally to each generation.

"As a Zapotec princess, you must always keep these stories in your heart," she would say.

As a girl, Hortensia truly believed she was a descendant of Princess Donaji. But as a woman, she realized grandmothers of every culture made their granddaughters feel like princesses. She came to understand these stories imparted the wisdom of her forebears: life's most sacred purpose lay beyond one's personal desires. The good life stemmed from a true commitment to others. She witnessed that commitment between her sister and brother-in-law, Fabi and Enrique, and it was something she wanted for herself, but only when the time was right.

Hortensia's fascination with these stories led her to attend university in Mexico City on a scholarship. She studied Mesoamerican history and culture, which included the Zapotecs and Mixtecs of the legend, but also the Toltecs and Aztecs, and the Maya and Inca as well. Among the many similarities of their cultures was a god of thunder and fertility, and every Mesoamerican culture included the tradition of the virgin sacrifice to assure the god's favor upon their people.

From her seat in the natural amphitheater of the Cerro del Fortin, she could see Monte Albán, five miles to the southwest. Indeed, Elton Pharmaceuticals had built their campus halfway between Monte Albán and where she currently sat. As her subconscious mind sifted through the possible characteristics that made Oaxaca different from the sites of the other Elton labs, one gruesome possibility leapt into her consciousness. Nestled in the Central Valley among the Sierra Madre Mountains, Oaxaca was the site of a thousand years of blood sacrifices.

Hortensia sat across the table from Bobby in a cozy café that had been her favorite since childhood. Zapotec themes decorated the walls, including an image of Cocijo. She chose this place because what she wanted to tell Bobby would not have come across well in the antiseptic confines of an Elton lab. When the owner brought their creamy hot chocolates flavored with cinnamon and almonds, he commented on the handsome gringo across from her in the language of her youth.

"What did he say to you?" Bobby asked.

"I've known him since I was a girl. He said he was happy to see his princess." Hortensia sipped her chocolate. She relaxed, enjoying the familiar, comforting aroma and flavor.

Bobby took a sip and licked his lips. "Wow, that's really good." He took another sip. "So, what did you want to tell me?"

Hortensia took a breath. Despite giving it a lot of thought, she still wasn't sure of the best way to broach the subject. At this point, she just had to plow on. "I've been trying to understand what might make our lab here different, why we bring back Loponine from the hidden dimension when none of the other labs do."

"You think you've come up with something?"

"Well, maybe, but it's going to sound strange, so just give me chance, okay?"

"Okay, sure, Hortensia. Go ahead."

"First, I should say, I grew up here in Oaxaca. My heritage is Zapotec, and our people have been here for three thousand years. We call ourselves the *Be'ena' Za'a*, the Cloud People. By legend, we originally lived in a blue cloud in the sky, ruled by

Cocijo, the god of thunder. After a time, the people came to Cocijo asking for a more permanent life, so he gave the people bodies and a place on the earth. Cocijo taught the people to farm, and he provided them rain. Later, the fields became fallow, and the people asked Cocijo to come down and make the earth fertile for their crops. He agreed, on condition that they sacrifice one child among them. They did so, and the crops flourished, and the people flourished."

"Your people used to sacrifice virgins to their gods?"

"For a thousand years, yes, they did, right here in this valley."

"How barbaric," commented Bobby.

"It seems so now, doesn't it? But think of how hard life was three thousand years ago. Obtaining food and shelter was a daily struggle. Death was a continuous presence in their lives, from infant mortality, famine, accident, and disease, and from their neighbors who came to take what they had. If it seems cruel to sacrifice a child, you must understand how that sacrifice weighed against the survival of the tribe itself. To ensure the protection of their god, they were willing to pay that price."

"But how could anyone offer up their own child? Was there a lottery or something?"

"According to our historical traditions, they created an elaborate ceremony around the sacrifice. The chosen girl had to be a virgin, so her blood was pure. They dressed her in a white blouse embroidered with flowers and a white skirt with a woven rope belt. They fed her hot chocolate laced with *pulque*, an alcoholic drink made from the maguey plant still brewed in Oaxaca today. At that time, only the priests and chieftains of the tribe were allowed to drink it. The *pulque* put the girl to sleep, so she felt no pain. To answer your question, every mother prayed that their daughter would be selected for the sacrifice. Most deaths were violent and painful. The sacrifice was the one death that was not, and it was for the good of the people."

Hortensia paused to sip her chocolate.

"What does this tale have to do with our lab, Hortensia?"

"I think a thousand years of blood sacrifices are the reason you find Loponine here and nowhere else." Hortensia's voice trembled as she said it.

Bobby just stared at her in disbelief. "And you think *I've* been working too hard? This is crazy, Hortensia."

She felt heat in her cheeks. "Maybe it is, but it's a working hypothesis, at least."

"You're saying that anywhere in the world where blood was spilled is a potential source of Loponine? Wouldn't that make the battlefields of the American Civil War or the World Wars in Europe prime sites for exploration?"

"Could be. At least it's something we can check out. But I've got a feeling it goes beyond just spilling blood."

"Why? You think an ancient god is somehow involved?"

"I don't know, maybe. Yes."

Bobby looked at her, dumbfounded. "Is there some of that *pulque* stuff in your hot chocolate?"

Hortensia joined Bobby in the control room. Through blast-proof windows, she could see into the next room where the engineers had built a ten-meter-diameter sphere intended for the large-scale mining of Loponine. Early tests of the scaled-up device had run into some bugs. Because of the increase in mass of the giant globe, Bobby's team had designed a net to catch the disk and lower it to the platform, rather than have it crash down every time. In the first test, the edge of the disk slashed through the net, and the disk crashed down anyway. In response, they came up with a plastic coating over the Fullerton material that would provide some thickness for the 2D disk. That solved the problem.

A later test tried out the enlarged and improved sampling portal. The new orifice served double-duty as both a valve and a hose connector. Prior to a rotation, the portal connected to a hose attached to the vacuum pump. After the collection, this same hatch connected to another hose used to extract the Loponine from the sphere. For the initial portal test, they had pressurized the globe slightly, and then zapped it with a laser pulse to send it into interdimensional space, followed by the relaxation pulse to return it to 3D space. Recording devices mounted inside the sphere showed the aperture opening and closing properly. The positive internal pressure kept the Loponine outside of the inner cavity.

Now came the first sampling run. They had removed the test equipment from inside the globe and were in the process of pumping out the air. Taking advantage of a lull in the action, Hortensia told Bobby what she'd discovered.

"I sent a request to all the engineers who'd received the collection devices and laser pointers. I asked them to go to the bloodiest battlefield they could find within a hundred miles of their labs, take a sample from the hidden dimension, and report back. I received reports from a dozen countries, and they all came back negative. I also sent one of our local engineers to Mexico City to perform the same task on the grounds of Teotihuacán, the ancient Aztec site. The sphere was full of Loponine."

Bobby sat silent, digesting the news. "So the process only works in Mexico, when used by engineers I've trained myself."

It was as if he was closed off from any other explanation. "It could also mean that bloodshed alone does not create Loponine," Hortensia offered. "Maybe it has to be innocent blood in the presence of a god."

Those words sounded so plausible when spoken in the confines of a cozy café while drinking hot chocolate. They seemed like superstitious nonsense when spoken in a brightly lit laboratory. Bobby's eyes betrayed that he felt the same way but respected her too much to say it. She broke eye contact, and Bobby checked the instrument readings on the console before him.

When the air had been completely evacuated from the sphere, a lab technician disconnected the hose and left the chamber, engaging the pressure door behind him. Once every-thing was secure, Bobby pushed the button to initiate the transdimensional rotation. The huge ball collapsed into a disk, and the net lowered it gently to the platform. After sixty seconds, Bobby pushed the button to activate the laser pulse at the relaxation frequency, and the disk inflated instantly into a sphere.

A spontaneous cheer erupted from the engineers behind Bobby and Hortensia, but it just as quickly became a cry of alarm as purplish-blue material streamed from a corner of the collection portal where it had not sealed completely.

Bobby quickly realized he had to contain the growing concern around him. "It looks like we've got a leak, but we can fix it. Carlos, go get in a hazmat suit and connect the collection hose before we lose too much—"

An explosion ripped out the portal, shaking the windows, and a blue mist spewed out. The mist curved before hitting the walls and made its way around the room. Hortensia was reminded of a snake leaving its burrow. The mist ceased its emission from the opening, but Loponine slime continued to disgorge for several more seconds. The blue snake remained in motion, however, seemingly intent on exploring every crevice of the room.

"Boss, about that hazmat suit...." Carlos' voice broke the silence.

Bobby looked over at him. "No, forget the suit." He reached over and flipped open the plastic cover protecting a big red button. Then he hit the button with the heel of his hand. A red light began flashing, and a klaxon sounded. He had activated the emergency evacuation alarm. "Everybody out."

When Hortensia stood up to leave, she realized Bobby wasn't moving. She sat back down beside him.

"What the hell is that thing?" he asked, but the question wasn't directed at her. He watched the blue, misty creature as it wended its way around the room. "It sure acts like it's alive."

Hortensia watched it with dread. "Did it come from the

other dimension?" Her mouth was parched, and her voice was little more than a croak.

Bobby glanced over at her, surprised to see her still here. "That's the only thing I can think of," he agreed, "but I'm confused why it's still in there."

"The room is sealed, right? How can it get out?"

"I presume it's a four-dimensional being, so a three-dimensional box won't hold it if it wants to leave." Seeing Hortensia's look of confusion, he added, "Think of it this way. If you're a two-dimensional being living on a plane, you can be trapped inside a square if there's no opening to go through." He drew a stick figure on a notepad and drew a square around it. "But if I'm a three-dimensional being," he placed his two fingers on the paper inside the square, "I can just step over the line." He walked his two fingers out of the square.

"So a four-dimensional being can just walk out of a three-dimensional box?"

"Yup, anytime it wants."

Her understanding dawned. "So, what's it waiting for? Does it want to go back?"

"Yeah, maybe. If we could lure it into the sphere, I could send it back," Bobby ventured. Then it hit him. "But not with the busted portal. If the Fullerton material doesn't create a full enclosure, the object inside won't survive the rotation intact."

"Do you have any other spheres we can use? Maybe a smaller one?"

"How would we get it in there?" He looked through the window, and his eyes latched onto the airlock. "Okay, I've got an earlier model that'll fit into the airlock. Once the inner door is open, I can trigger the rotation from here using a laser pointer through the window. The sphere's back in the lab. Keep watch here while I get it."

Hortensia watched the serpentine movements of the blue mist while she waited for Bobby to return. Was this a creature—a god, even—from the blue cloud where her people once lived? Could this be Cocijo himself?

Bobby came back wheeling a meter-wide ball on a low dolly with casters, but he was looking concerned. "How're we going to get that thing to go inside this?"

"Maybe we could...." Hortensia hesitated.

"What, Hortensia? I'm open to anything at this point."

"What if we put some blood inside?"

"You mean, like a sacrifice?" His face and voice betrayed his doubt. Then his face changed. "Where would we find blood?"

"There's some whole blood in the medical lab. I'll go get it."

Bobby had the top off when she returned with a unit of blood from the lab refrigerator. Hortensia opened the valve at the bottom of the bag and drained the blood into the lower hemisphere. She helped Bobby lift the top hemisphere onto the lower, and with a twist, it seated securely into place.

"Okay, let's push it over to the airlock."

Bobby operated the airlock controls, and the outer door opened. He punched in a few commands on a plastic panel mounted to the sphere. "I'm setting the portal to open and shut every thirty seconds. I'm hoping that's enough time for the creature to enter the sphere. Once inside, I can trigger the rotation with the laser pointer, and thirty seconds later the door will open up and let it escape. What do you think?"

He waited for Hortensia to answer. She realized he thought she knew more than he did about this matter. "Sounds like it should work. Let's try it."

Bobby pressed one final time on the plastic panel and pushed the metal ball into the airlock, sealing the door behind it. Then he used the door controls to open the inner door, exposing the sphere to the creature inside the room.

They hurried back into the control room. Holding the laser pointer, Bobby sidestepped into a gap between the control console and the window. Hortensia stood behind the console and looked over his shoulder. She started feeling lightheaded and realized she'd been holding her breath. She willed herself to breathe.

The blue mist still meandered around the room at a constant speed until the sphere's portal clicked open. A second later the creature picked up speed and zeroed in on the sphere. It circled around the sphere for a few seconds, the mist partially obscuring their view from the control room. Suddenly, the mist darted into the sphere through the opening.

Bobby started counting down the time until the aperture closed. "Ten, nine, eight," the blue mist was accelerating into the sphere, "seven, six, five," tendrils of mist around the room were coalescing into the stream headed for the portal, "four, three, two," the blue mist was clearing from the room and disappearing into the smaller ball, "one, zero." The door closed with the mist inside.

"Whoo-hoo!" shouted Bobby and aimed the laser at the sphere. He pushed the button and it collapsed to a disk. "I think it worked! We'll know in twenty seconds."

Bobby kept his eyes on his watch, and Hortensia kept her eyes on Bobby. He started counting down at five. At zero, they both looked over at the disk. There was nothing to see. They hoped the portal had opened, and the mist had returned home. Bobby turned from the window and smiled at Hortensia with a mixture of gratitude and relief. He never saw what happened next.

Mist exploded out of the hole in the ten-meter sphere behind him, but this time the room didn't contain it. An instant later they were engulfed in blue. Hortensia thought she heard Bobby scream before darkness swallowed her.

When she regained consciousness, the blue mist was gone, and Bobby was draped over the control console.

"Bobby?" She reached over to touch his shoulder. Underneath his shirt she felt only bone. She lifted his shoulder to turn him over. As his face came into view, she jerked back with a gasp. The skin of his face was white parchment stretched across his skull, his eyes sunken holes. She doubled over and retched onto the floor. She staggered out of the room, tears streaming down her face.

The building was deserted due to the evacuation alarm. She pushed open the lobby door, heading toward the parking lot, where the evacuation assembly points were located. Blue-tinged light bathed the scene outside, and a strong wind whipped at her clothes. She edged around the corner of the building. Lightning flashed to reveal a mass of desiccated bodies. Her mouth and eyes opened wide in a rictus of horror, and her scream was drowned out by the crack of thunder. She turned away and collapsed to the ground, shielding her head with her arms.

A steady roar issued from overhead. She looked up to see a menacing blue cloud rotating above her, blocking out the sun. Lightning bolts streaked through the maelstrom, branching like the veins in a dead leaf. The cloud extruded funnels like octopus arms bringing destruction wherever they encountered the ground. The wrath of Cocijo was unleashed upon the world.

Fear for her sister and two nephews gripped Hortensia around her throat. Looking east across the valley towards the city center, she realized the storm had not yet reached their neighborhood. Filled with urgency to get home before disaster struck, she dashed to her car.

She pulled away from the parking lot into the deserted street. A car up ahead straddled the curb. As Hortensia steered her way past, she saw the mummified head of the driver hanging out of the window. She averted her eyes and continued on. As she got closer to town, she passed more desiccated drivers, some with passengers. She also passed the bodies of pedestrians crumpled on the sidewalks. One woman had been strolling with a baby carriage. As she passed the carriage, a plaintive sound reached her ears.

She skidded to a stop and jumped out. Outside the car, the sound of a baby crying was unmistakable. She rushed over to the carriage. Inside, a baby girl with dark brown eyes and hair wailed in fear. Hortensia scooped up the baby, cooing comforting words in the Zapotec dialect her mother had used with her. Standing in the open with this baby in her arms and the lightning-streaked storm cloud rumbling overhead, she finally apprehended her mission. With renewed determination, she placed the baby onto the seat next to her and resumed her drive home.

The wind slammed the door shut behind her as Hortensia entered the home she shared with her sister and brother-in-law and their two boys. Fabiola hurried to meet her and stopped short when she saw the baby in Hortensia's arms.

"The storm killed her mother. We need to take care of her."

"My God, Hortensia, what is happening?"

"Please, Fabi, take her. The storm started at Elton. I have to stop it."

Speechless, Fabiola took the whimpering baby from her sister. Hortensia went to the kitchen and poured milk into a pan, put the pan on the stove, and lit a fire under it. While it heated she went to her room. Hanging in the back of her closet she found the white blouse she'd last worn at age sixteen when she danced at the Guelaguetza. It had red flowers embroidered down the front and across the shoulders. She donned the blouse and white skirt, and tied the rope belt around her waist.

Returning to the kitchen, she mixed chocolate, cinnamon, and almond extract into the milk, stirring as it heated. The simple ritual calmed her mind, allowing her to think.

She had left Elton Pharmaceuticals confused and frightened by the death all around her. Questions weighed upon her. What had they unleashed upon the world? Could it be stopped? Why was she spared? Then she found the baby, alive, in spite of the fact that her mother lay dead beside her. She began to understand. She and the baby had something in common, the one thing that Cocijo demanded of his people: the blood of an innocent. The blood from the medical lab was almost certainly not from a virgin. Offering it to Cocijo just enraged him. She knew only one way to placate him. Cocijo would only rest when he had his sacrifice.

She turned off the fire and was pouring her chocolate into the drinking bowl when Fabiola came in with the baby swaddled in a light cotton cloth. Fabiola had always wanted a girl, and her face glowed. She froze when she saw her sister barefoot and dressed as Donaji.

"What's going on, Hortensia?"

"Cocijo was released in the lab at Elton Pharmaceuticals. He's in the blue cloud looming over the city. Many people have died, and many more will follow. You must take the children south into the mountains until the danger has passed."

Shock and disbelief colored Fabiola's face.

"The god of the Cloud People has returned, Fabi. He is demanding the sacrifice our people agreed to provide him."

"No, Hortensia, it's a storm, not a god," she said gently. "I agree, it's dangerous to stay here, so let's go. You come with us."

Hortensia went over and wrapped her arms around Fabiola with the baby nestled between them. "Only I can stop this, Fabi," she murmured. "But you must go now. Save the children."

She turned her back, opened the refrigerator, and took out the bottle of *pulque* her brother-in-law had stashed there. She poured it into the chocolate, raised the bowl to her lips, and drank it down.

Hortensia drove west, back into the heart of the storm, weaving around the scattered cars as fast as she could. The storm had continued to grow, its rage fueled, she was convinced, by the tainted blood Cocijo extracted from each victim he encountered. Wind gusts shook the car as her route took her southwest into the foothills that led to Monte Albán. Driving ever higher into the hills, she could see the funnel cloud arms swinging down from the maelstrom and visiting destruction on the earth. Finally, she reached the top and swerved into the tourist's parking lot. She flung open the door and ran to the Grand Plaza. Her bare feet flew over the lawn that had been cultivated by the custodians of this ancient landmark. She headed for the South Platform, the highest point on the site. The nearby trees bent and thrashed in the heavy winds as she climbed the thirty stone steps. Her bare feet were bleeding when she reached the top.

She tilted her head up to look directly into the heart of the storm. The blue clouds roiled in anger, lightning lacing through them. Stepping onto the altar stone and swallowing her fear, Hortensia raised her arms in welcome. She began the sacrificial chant her grandmother taught her in the language of the Zapotec people.

"Cocijo!" she shouted. "I call upon you!"

The noise of the storm quieted, although the blue mist still spiraled.

"Cocijo! Accept your sacrifice!"

The storm seemed to hear, for it retracted its funnel arms and moved closer.

"Cocijo! Accept our payment!"

The storm came to a point directly overhead, the mists swirling in a tight circle above her. A heightened sense of vertigo combined with effects of the *pulque* caused her to sway.

She fell to her knees. Showing her face to the sky, she raised her arms once more and whispered, "My blood in exchange for my people."

A blue lightning bolt erupted from the storm, spearing through Hortensia's body and down into the ground. Following its path, the purple mist became an immense, auguring funnel burrowing into her skull. Maintaining its posture of supplication, her body accepted the onslaught of the twisting mists until the last of it disappeared into the ground. Only then did she topple forward onto the sacrificial stone.

News reports recorded a strange epidemic that swept through Oaxaca, leaving hundreds of people dead of severe dehydration. Epidemiologists were unable to identify the disease nor explain its sudden onset and disappearance. The event seemed to have spurred renewed interest in religious observances in the city, especially among members of the Zapotec community.

In other news, an unpredicted storm system parked itself over the Central Valley and soaked the area in rain for three straight days before dissipating.

In a press release, Elton Pharmaceuticals announced they were reopening their plant in Oaxaca, which was hard-hit by the epidemic that swept through its workforce. Company spokesmen discounted rumors that the virulent disease may have originated in their laboratories, where they produced several profitable pharmaceutical products, including the popular drug, Loponine.

Production of Loponine had stalled while the plant was closed. Elton management indicated engineering problems had been overcome, and production would be ramping up to full capacity in the near future.

FESTIVAL PREPARATIONS

by Justin Bailey

Greetings, fellow traveler. Know that there is a place for you.

If you are reading this, you are part of the EssentialSalts mailing list. This pamphlet represents a sacred trust between all of our members, and allowing this document to fall into outsider's hands will be met with severe consequences.

If you have come across this pamphlet through misadventure OR if you have ill intention towards our community, ***Ph'nglui mglw'nafh R'lyeh wgah'nagl, fhtagn. Ooboshu.***

(Members, after reading the previous sentence, please enact your preferred warding, otherwise you will self-terminate once the dreams come.)

If this is your first journey to EssentialSalts, welcome! We are a society of outsiders, seekers, and families of specific breeding, brought together as a community to shout, to kill, and to revel in fierce, black joy.

The EssentialSalts festival takes place in the same location annually, in a stretch of Canyonland National Park. Previous attendees will know the location already, and new attendees will receive the GPS coordinates by email. Though safeguards *are* in place, discretion is still required. The event begins at 3:00 AM on Thursday morning and continues through 3:00 AM the following Wednesday.

The community at EssentialSalts operates under a set of collective principles, known as Decrees. You will be welcomed so long as you respect the Decrees:

1. **Destruction of the Self:** The mind-state that we refer to

as "I" has no value in EssentialSalts. Your identity, your possessions, your role in the human world, are all tethers meant to bind you to the fragile—and ultimately failing—illusion called the human experience. You are more than your fears, your base instincts, and your terrified adoration of whatever entity or primordial concept that you have devoted yourself to. In our exultation, we are one.

2. **Predatory Instincts:** To lift a sentiment from blessed Lord Tennyson, the true law of the world is red in tooth and claw. While you are at the festival, you must look to your own survival. Nothing is to be shared, you must bring (or steal) what you need, and there is no protection, implied or otherwise. While we discourage wholesale massacre—and we certainly don't need a repeat of 2012—part of the goal of EssentialSalts is to cultivate your natural instincts and bring you closer in line with the cosmic beings that are our true mothers and fathers. The weak will feed the strong, both figuratively and literally. There will be a cookout at the end of each evening.

3. **Learning:** While EssentialSalts may look like a bloody, debauched orgy to first timers, the truth is that every member leaves the event with new insight and understanding into the nature of the universe. Throughout the event, you will find lectures on all manner of subjects, opportunities to experiment, and other chances to expand your consciousness. We encourage all attendees to try anything that they're offered, even if it frightens or offends their sensibilities. The golden rule is to always say "yes."

4. **Inclusion:** Even the most cursory study of the world will teach that the human race is merely the tip of a rapid-melting iceberg. At EssentialSalts, you'll meet corpse-

consuming *ghuls*, ancient mystics inhabiting the bodies of their descendants, half-breeds born of vast ocean kingdoms, and many other entities. Each has something to offer, so we encourage you to mingle. If you require freshwater tanks, graveyard earth, or other environmental necessities, please contact the staff at EssentialSalts. We will accommodate any special needs you may require.

5. **Recording Knowledge:** For millennia, the secret knowledge of the world was trapped behind dusty volumes going unread in university libraries or in the blurry scrawl of a family diary. Part of the purpose of EssentialSalts is the collection and dissemination of that knowledge. We encourage all attendees to bring whatever material they may have, so it can be added to our online database. We all have different pieces of the puzzle, and EssentialSalts is a way to bring it all together.

6. **Radical Self-Expression:** Most of us view EssentialSalts as a homecoming and a necessary break from the world because, for one week, we strive to create the world *as it is meant to be*. The truth of the world has inspired poets, musicians, playwrights, and dreamers for generations, and EssentialSalts is a way for the most gifted among us to realize their visions. This event will showcase endless variations on the macabre arts, from recreations of vast cyclopean vistas to sculptures incorporating non-Euclidean geometry, to performances of theater that was old when the Earth was young. EssentialSalts is one of the most unique experiences on this plane of existence and we encourage our artists to share their expression of madness and joy.

7. **Disconnection:** The world is full of compromised vision. From the vast self deception of morality to the grotesque puppet show of religious structures to the

endless assault of unfettered greed and conformity of a world plastered in advertisement, the world we live in is awash in poisonous pedagogy. EssentialSalts was created to be a safe space from the regular world. So: no cell phones, no clothing with logos on it, and no gaudy displays of the material world. EssentialSalts will never be a licensed property of Viacom, Disney, or Subway Sandwiches.

8. **Leave No Physical Trace:** EssentialSalts requires secrecy. Those who remember the US Navy's destruction of the Y'ha-nthlei community near Innsmouth knows that the human world can be deeply destructive when we draw attention to ourselves. That means we clean up after ourselves. Everything you bring in, you take out with you, you burn your spoor, and you bury (or consume) any bodies you create. The only exception is any rifts or disturbances in the atmosphere that your workings may create. The area around EssentialSalts has earned an unwholesome reputation over the years, with hikers disappearing year-round. It keeps outsiders away, which we encourage.

9. **Celebrating Fear:** The oldest and strongest emotion of mankind is fear, and the strongest fear is fear of the unknown. Even though we would be perceived as monsters to a trembling populace, we are in awe at the cosmic truths that could crush us as an afterthought. We are who we are because we know what we know, and that reverent terror unites us all far more tightly than the blood we shed.

10. **Immersion:** You are attending EssentialSalts, not watching a baseball game. There is no half-measures, no spectating. Once you're here, you're expected to participate *in one form or another.*

EssentialSalts is a community in the loosest sense of the word. You are expected to take care of your own needs. For first timers, that means getting a sense of what you need to ensure your comfort and safety.

The event takes place in mid-July, when Utah summer is at its peak. That means hydration is a must. If you require water, we recommend bringing 1.5 gallons to drink per day, plus whatever you need to bathe or wash clothes, cooking utensils, and sacrificial implements. Attendees who need to spend time in water will have accommodations provided, but please contact us beforehand. Otherwise we might only be able to provide a washtub and a couple of bottles of Evian.

Canyonland National Park is a desert environment, so the days can be very hot and the nights can be cold. We recommend a variety of clothes for the environment. And, because EssentialSalts is first and foremost revelry, we encourage our attendees to dress to impress! Time to bring out your feather boas, your Viking helmets, and your waistcoat made from flayed human skin.

Finally, there is food. While we recommend you bring enough food for a week's worth of meals, the community at EssentialSalts has a number of demonstrations of extraordinary cuisine. The strangest, most exotic, and most terrible delicacies can be found there, if you're willing to pay the price of their wares.

No EssentialSalts would be complete without The Adoration of the Mother, our festival's most celebrated event. It is here that we offer full communion with the gods, where we offer ourselves body and soul to be reborn. The experience is not for the weak of heart (no fainting East Coast scholars, please) but those who see the other side will be able to see wonder at the majesty of the universe with fresh eyes.

The festival's construction crew is currently hard at work on the iron plinth, a large dais that conforms to the *Righteous Principles* as set down in the Hearn translation of the *Seven*

Cryptical Books of Hsan. Offerings will be lashed to the plinth. While we appreciate the more enthusiastic attendees offering themselves to the gods, our sacrifices come from the flock of Elder Hascomb at the First Separatist Church of Jesus Christ of Final Day Saints in Moab, Utah.

At 3:00 AM on the last evening of the festival, we will call forth the Mother's favored children from the primal darkness. All attending *must* be a part of the summoning (remember Decree 10) and, if the favored children accept our offering, the Mother will manifest for us in the flesh.

The manifestation hits all of us differently. For some, it is a baptism. For others, the manifestation offers an expansion of consciousness on a deeply primal level. The Mother will take some of us as lovers and she will devour others. Whatever happens, there is no going back. You can no longer fit into the prison of the human world.

That communion is the reason EssentialSalts exists. It's the reason we come back year after year. It's the reason we risk our existence in order to touch the divine.

If this is your first year, I welcome you from the bottom of my heart. You are my brother or sister or something uniquely, beautifully you. I love you.

But, if I catch you, I will eat you.

-V
Sr. Event Coordinator, EssentialSalts

MARYANNE'S EQUATIONS

by Harry Pauff

I worry the delivery boy's curiosity may one day exceed his fear and I'll have to kill him. He has his instructions to leave my groceries and toiletries on the bottom step of the porch, but he often lingers and tries to see past my heavy curtain, trying to put a face to the pseudonym on the order.

Panic attacks strike every hour and my left eye hasn't opened since it happened, but these are ailments I can live with. I can *live* with anything. I haven't slept in months and I consider that a blessing. Knowing what waits on the other side, I would rather be awake to see death coming when it does.

Every single person in town despises me for what I've done. Even if I could afford to leave, I wouldn't know where to go. To show my face in public would be a mistake, possibly my last one.

No one believed me when I told them what I saw in Maryanne's office: not my parents, not my pastor, not the police. The only person who can speak to my claims—Maryanne herself—hasn't been seen since it happened.

Not much separated Maryanne and myself. We both grew up in Coaldale and attended the same schools. We sat near each other in class, were in the same Girl Scout Troop, and dated from the same pool of boys. You could have exchanged us and no one would have noticed, not even our parents.

Our paths diverged after high school—I went to a state school, she to a university no one had heard of before—but both of us came crawling back to wooded, pothole-laden Coaldale after striking out in the real world.

I would see her working the checkout line at Genetti's supermarket and she would see me mopping floors at the hospital. "I see you're putting your degree to good use" was the common greeting.

She was the first in line for an interview when the Plygz Co. bought and renovated the abandoned No. 9 Coal Breaker building, and I was not far behind her. Outsiders and industry experts did not understand why this hot startup flush with venture capital chose Coaldale of all places to build their new office, but a secluded, crumbling town left barren by industries that no longer exist was precisely what they were looking for. They wanted space to work on their radical ideas and room to breathe away from nosy and scared vultures of New York, Boston, Chicago, and the other financial capitals.

The founder of Plygz Co. said all the right things. Revitalization. Modern economy. Job training. Giving back. Wholesome people. Untapped talent. He even told the ancient story about the out-of-towners who tried to hack it in mines below the No. 9 Coal Breaker and couldn't; after just a few hours, they came streaming to the surface. They couldn't handle the work down there. Too tough. But the Coaldalers could handle it. It was in their blood. When pressed about Plygz Co.'s decision to spend millions renovating the hulking, nine story, asymmetrical building instead of demolishing it and constructing something new, the founder spoke about the history, the energy, and the certain magic that places like this held.

Locals were hooked. Jobs would come. Talent would come. Money would pour into struggling local businesses. A crumbling building that in its heyday processed tons of coal and fueled economic growth—and stood as the area's tombstone for far too many years—would once again serve as a hub of prosperity.

Maryanne and I shared a cubicle on the first floor in the renovated building where our lifetime cordial-but-distant relationship could continue. After the renovations, the outside of the building looked cleaner and more inviting, and retained all of the features that made it iconic: the brutal reinforced concrete, the myriad windows, the slanted rooftops, the tacked on additions, and the mammoth, sloped ramp that once hoisted unprocessed coal to the very top of the building. The locals called it "the aqueduct", and from afar it could look like it was the only thing propping the entire building up.

We used to throw rocks at this building's windows when we were younger. Kids younger than that used toil in brutal conditions inside this building, sorting conveyor belts of coal and removing sticks and stones and other debris until their fingers broke and bled. Now, Maryanne and I did something completely different inside this building, spending many wordless late nights there passing a carton of Chinese back and forth putting our degrees to use. Our labyrinth of cubicles haunting the building would have looked just as confusing to our ancestors as their coal-breaking machinery would look to us. Our cubicle was one island of light among many struggling to fend off the darkness that threatened to close down the workday. To leave before nine at night was to sin. What we did there, I'm still not entirely sure. Like the coal in previous generations, orders and instructions and ideas came down from the top floors, working their way through each level, getting sanitized, simplified, refined, and repackaged until they reached our first floor level where we could put on the finishing touches and ship them out to the wider world. I minored in business and I still don't understand complex financial instruments, but I could write memos and design graphics and that was good enough to collect a paycheck there.

But Maryanne, she took to the work they wanted with all of the gusto and skill of someone who belonged on Wall Street. I trafficked in commas, adverbs, and nouns, but she was fluent in forwards, futures, swaps, and other derivatives. She saw beyond the dumbed-down visions that arrived at our desks. The theories that lurked beyond were more in line with what she studied at her university, she said. Every day, she volunteered for new projects and came up with newer and better ideas. Every once in a while I would peek over her shoulder and look at the lines of code and theoretical models on her computer screen. Mere glances gave me headaches. How she could stare at that all day let alone get excited by it was beyond me, but every day she found ways to pull aside superiors and present some of these ideas.

It wasn't long before they gave her a dedicated parking spot and had her doing higher level work on the floors above in her own office. They had been looking for someone like her: the singular, undiscovered talent with the passion and fire for this stuff in her blood. She moved up and I became the sole occupant of a two-person cubicle.

I saw her seldom after that, catching scant glimpses of her as she took the elevator up to her office to work on making the company more valuable. With her ideas and the company's resources, there didn't seem to be any limit to their success, but what her ideas were remained a guarded secret.

Rumors abounded, of course, and our company founder did little to squash any of them, but he said all the right things to the media. New ways to generate wealth. Adding value. Disrupting stale systems. Stealing market share. Unique business. New ground. Talented employees. His eyes lit up every time he talked about his employees, but I knew he meant the word in the singular. The company was not hurting for money, with new hires every day and plans to open offices in Ohio, West Virginia, and Kentucky. They hoped to find more talent just like Maryanne in these places.

The founder got the accolades, but I knew she was the driver. Her plaid button-downs became crisp power suits. Her beat up junker that followed her from high school became a fire-red convertible that lit up Coaldale's streets and had all the old-timers gawking.

I had no intention of staying with the company more than a few months, no intention of using my talents to make other people rich, no intention of using the magic of words to coax people into consuming the products that Maryanne developed, products that I did not understand. I read and I listened and I wrote about them every day and I never came close to understanding them and probably never would, but I could fake it. I knew the emotions that my bosses wanted people to feel when they read about the company.

I hoped this job would be a stepping-stone to something greater, something outside the confines of Coaldale, but my stuff kept accumulating and it kept spreading. Trinkets, gifts from coworkers, badges from conferences. Stuff. It cluttered my desk, consuming and colonizing open space like a viral disease. When it ran out of real estate on my side, it jumped across the cubicle and conquered the still-unoccupied desk where Maryanne once sat.

Maryanne had not left either, but where I stagnated she continued to prosper. Nicer clothes. Nicer cars. A bigger house in the hills. A house in Florida for her parents. Nothing could stop her meteoric rise. She had *it*, they said. What was *it*, exactly? *It*, they said.

I was not envious of her work—it seemed dumb and insignificant in the grand scheme of things—but I was envious of her success. It was nice that someone from our little town was going to make an impact on the world, but I couldn't help but wonder where I had gone wrong in my life.

I'm not embarrassed to admit that Maryanne became something of an obsession of mine during this period. What she did and where she went were an endless source of entertaining speculation for me, much more interesting than whatever sat on my computer screen. I stalked her social media profiles even though she had never once added anything to them. I hoped for some glimpse into her life upstairs or outside the office, but they sat blank, without even a profile picture, reserved and unused.

Days would go by where I did nothing but watch the elevator door for a sign of the founder's favorite employee. She carried no purse, no lunch, and no briefcase with her in the mornings on her way up to her office. All she carried was a lanyard badge that let her access the higher levels within the elevator. I could only imagine the spread they rolled out for her upstairs that kept her from ever going out for lunch, from even stepping outside for a breath of fresh air during the day.

For most of our lives, Maryanne and I were the same, but that was no longer the case and it bugged the hell out of me. I did take some solace in seeing her shamble in to work looking pale and tired like the rest of us, but where we carried the burden of mediocrity every day, there seemed to be other passengers weighing her down that success couldn't seem to banish.

She began to look worse than I felt, and I wondered if the same mind-crushing monotony—and the late nights, dry eyes, and blurry vision that came with them—had gotten to her. I wondered if her boss sent her emails and then showed up seconds later asking if she had read the emails yet. I wondered if she walked between her desk and the printer upwards of a dozen times before getting a document to print. I wondered if she put up with coworkers playing music too loud, or discovered all the toilets clogged and the custodial staff unaware.

I desired answers to all of these wonderings and more, and I was determined to get her aside and ask her. It was my special project, a project I had actual interest in for once.

I waited in the parking lot late at night hoping to corner her, to ask her to spare a few minutes for an old friend, but I would fall asleep before I ever caught her leaving work at a reasonable time.

It seemed that I couldn't get there early enough either. I could beat the sun to work but I would find her convertible already in her reserved spot, engine cold.

Weeks passed before I realized that I hadn't seen her in quite some time. When I asked around about her, most people brushed me off in favor of being seen pretending to work. Without the right badge to unlock the upper levels, I could only travel up two or three floors and no higher, and the security guards stationed inside the elevators weren't about to make any exceptions.

My boss chided me for wasting so much time on someone who worked on the floors above me when I should have been spending more time on the person I saw in the mirror every morning. Yes, he said that, and when I told him about the red convertible sitting in the parking lot abandoned for days, he dragged me out there to show me I was mistaken. There was no red convertible in the lot. There never had been. I protested, but all he did was gesture to the empty parking spot and the blank name plate. Get your head right or get out, he said.

I left work early that day and drove around town, white knuckles gripping the steering wheel, head pounding and stomach churning. A red convertible did not blend into the background of a town like Coaldale, but it was not parked in front of her house, nor was it in the impound lot. Her parents had been packed up and shipped off to Florida. Their old home now housed a brand new family who threatened to call the police when they caught me peering through their garage windows.

You may think I'm insane for jumping to conclusions. Maryanne had simply gone on vacation without telling anyone, or had been relocated to one of the new expansion sites. But I never entertained any thoughts like that, not for a moment. I knew she was still in the Plygz Co. building somewhere.

The woman at the police station nodded with a concerned look on her face when I told her my story, but her pen sat idle, her notebook unmarred by my words. Maryanne was probably fine, she said, but I could trust that the department would take my concerns very seriously. She escorted me out to the lobby and whispered a few things to her partner manning the front desk, eliciting an open laugh from him. I didn't expect them to look too hard at the largest taxpayer Coaldale had ever seen.

No one was going to help this woman. No one even knew she needed help. No one but me.

It was business as usual at the office. Muted television sets hanging on conference room walls showed the visage of our beloved founder giving his latest interview about our magical, proprietary algorithms that generated unbelievable wealth and made our company's valuation graph look like a rocket launch. Workers kept their heads down in the cubicle trenches and plugged away at whatever work fate had assigned them. My boss printed out new company style guide standards on the proper use of prepositions and taped them to my cubicle wall at eye level just above my computer monitor where I would be forced to look at them.

No one seemed to know that anything was amiss, or no one seemed to care as long as they were unaffected. It was easier that way. Who needed to tack on one more problem to the work day?

Had I not known this woman, had I not sat near her in school, had I not exchanged pleasantries with her over the years, I might have been able to go about my business and let her fade from my mind, but I knew too much. One or two twists in the road of life, and I could have been her. I needed to get upstairs and find out what was happening.

Everyone knew the coal breaker had nine floors. You could look up the historic floor plans and diagrams at the library, until suddenly you couldn't anymore, and the librarians would feign ignorance. The directory in the lobby named all of the departments in all of the eight, not nine, floors.

If Maryanne was anywhere, I decided she was on that ninth floor—but even if I had the right badge, the elevator lacked a button for the ninth floor, and the labyrinth of stairs only got you so far before you ran into a door that wouldn't open no matter how hard you pulled.

The only way I was going to get upstairs was from the outside. I spent many evenings sitting in my car after work studying the building and the patterns of the patrolling security, trying to decide the best way to reach the summit. If I could somehow get on top of the long aqueduct sloping off the side of the building, I could maybe walk up to the fifth or sixth floor. I would have to find a way to the ninth floor from there.

I went two towns over to buy rope and a grappling hook. I went to a second store to buy some black clothing and a third store to buy a ski mask. All of it was paid for with cash. The hammer I had in my closet was more than adequate to break any windows, if the need arose.

Finally one evening, when even the most devoted employees went home for the day to steal a few hours of sleep, I went with them, but I didn't go home. In the strip mall parking lot, I slipped the black sweatpants and sweatshirt over my body and stuffed the rope, grappling hook, hammer, and ski mask into a duffle bag. It was a short walk from the parking lot back to the office building, one I made with my head down. I didn't really feel safe until I approached the company land and could slip the ski mask over my head.

Climbing onto the top of the aqueduct proved easy enough when the security guard ducked inside for a moment. I felt saner creeping up that long incline under cover of darkness than I ever felt sitting inside that cubicle day after day.

I thought two weeks of doing pull-ups in my apartment would be enough to help me scale the building's façade and get me from the sixth floor to the ninth floor, but I couldn't have been more wrong. Even with the grappling hook dug in at the top of the building and the rope in my hands, my wrists hurt, my forearms burned, and my back ached. More than once my foot slipped, or I misjudged what was a foothold and what was a shadow. Someplace, somewhere, my person was being recording scaling the building, but that wasn't something I could concern myself with at the moment.

The windows at the ninth level were blacked out, but I could see the faint glow of artificial light around the fringes. None of the windows would budge, but the hammer tucked into my pants underneath my black sweats did the trick. Somewhere, a silent alarm was blaring.

Scrambling through the open window, the broken glass cut into my body leaving a trail of blood in my wake. Now they had me on camera *and* they had my DNA, and I didn't care. The need to prove myself eclipsed any sense of self-preservation.

If there was ever a sign that I was doing the right thing, it was that I chose the right window to break. Maryanne sat in a chair bathed in the light of the terminal screen, and didn't seem to notice the bleeding woman and broken glass.

I shook her and asked her if she was all right, even waved a hand in front of her glassy and watery eyes. She didn't move, she didn't blink, but she wore a smile. Fluids ran from an IV drip bag into her forearm. Her fingers continued to tap away at the keyboard. Nothing restrained her to the chair. Despite the IV, she looked capable of standing and walking out anytime she wanted.

I clapped in her ear to no effect. Then I made the biggest mistake of looking at what was on the screen.

Pivot tables with more than three dimensions. Stock symbols and currency units that didn't exist and would never exist. Models and equations that squirmed and bled. Spreadsheet lookup functions that pulled data from other realms. Transactions flew by at dizzying speeds, lines of white text on black. Line after line. Transaction after transaction. Thousands per second. What little I could glimpse made no sense. Things were being bought and sold, things that should not be bought and sold, from destinations and coordinates that had no basis in reality. Horrible, unimaginable transactions with strange unearthly inputs were sanitized and packaged and repackaged and sold on the markets for profit.

I wanted to keep looking. I wanted to try and make sense of what I was seeing, but bright red rashes spread on the surface of my skin and the blood beneath it boiled. Staring at the screen was akin to staring at the sun. Spots developed on my vision and my left eye began to weaken until it closed completely.

Whatever was on the screen did not affect Maryanne; it drew her in. I tore myself away and shook her harder. She remained unresponsive to my pleas, and I couldn't remain in the same room with the screen much longer. To this day, I replay the events in my mind hoping for some alternate ending where I'm able to get her out of the building, but no such ending will present itself. Even if it did, I could tell that the woman had given herself over, that no trace of the woman I knew all those years remained.

I limped to the window and lowered myself down, not caring how much glass embedded itself in my skin, how much blood I left behind, or how bad my muscles ached. I needed to get home and nothing was going to stop me—not police, not stop signs, not red lights, not pedestrians.

For the next few days, I sat fully clothed beneath the cold shower, loaded gun within reach, and waited for the shock and the memories to fade.

My first call was to the local TV station. Expecting private security or police to kill me at any moment, I wanted to get what I saw out there as fast as I could. The polite man on the other end grunted assents and mhmm's and promised to send a crew out to interview me, but such a crew never materialized.

No story ever ran and no one stopped the founder from cashing out and selling the Plygz Co. to an even larger firm, who shut down the office and moved it—and Maryanne—out of state. I have to think the founder knew what Maryanne was doing up there, that he had come to town, spent all that money, and got exactly what he wanted.

The founder said all the right things to the media. Tough economic times. Cost-savings. Promises to be back. Last I heard, he was somewhere in Africa looking at abandoned mines.

All local employees were downsized in the restructuring. All of them but me. The only one who was fired would become the scapegoat and would suffer for the area's resurfacing economic woes.

Someplace, somewhere, whatever new monstrous corporate entity absorbed Plygz Co. continues to do things they should not be doing, creating products that defy the mind, and manipulating equations that shouldn't add up. Someplace, somewhere, Maryanne's mind and her skills are helping them. I don't want to know where that place is.

WHOLESOME LABOR

by Sam Rent

Jacob Marlowe pulled the car into the parking lot under the shadow of the Wholesomes megastore, a place you could find just about anything. Customers and cart pushers milled about as Marlowe's assistants, Sal Weathers and Mark Kim, undid their seat belts and gathered their laptops and presentation materials. The car was rented, not a company vehicle, picked specifically because of its "rustic" flavor. Corporate wanted their representatives to be seen as practical, salt of the earth folks. Same went for the motel they were staying at, The Summer's Breeze, which was not only cheap but the only non-chain option available. Marlowe was familiar with the playbook—hell, he had practically written it.

The Summer Breeze had been a precursor of the general shabbiness of Matron, Pennsylvania. The years had not been kind to the aging coal town. *Former* coal town; the mine had closed over a decade ago due exhaustion of the vein. The streets were lined with abandoned and decaying shops so forsaken no one had even bothered to cover them with graffiti tags. Marlowe was surprised to see there were a few abandoned churches as well. Dead convenience stores were expected, but the churches usually hung on until their fingers bled. There they were though, doors padlocked and windows boarded up.

It wouldn't be correct to say the town survived, it simply persisted, drawing thin nourishment from people stopping at gas stations, restaurants, and whatever local businesses remained as they drove towards Pittsburg. Matron's Wholesomes sat on the side of the interstate leading out of the city and was flanked by dark, undeveloped land. It likely wasn't too deep, and Marlowe suspected there would be interstate a mile or two behind the green no man's land. No one would call it a forest; it was glorified weeds, thin and green, growing quickly and fighting fiercely for resources. It wasn't the type of place people would go hiking or camping. He was surprised it hadn't been bull-dozed and made ready for other businesses. It was a waste of potential to leave the land to nature. Best to raze it all and put down a crust of bedrock; give enterprising folks in town prime real estate to license a franchise of some sort. Something that could survive in the Wholesomes' shadow.

Marlowe suspected Wholesomes was the largest employer around town these days, boasting a current staff of three hun-dred and forty. Matron's Wholesomes was on the smaller side and was lacking some of the extravagant features found in larger stores, such as movie theaters and restaurants. There were thou-sands such as this one spread across the American countryside; giant cinder block monuments to convenience and low prices. If Marlowe had to guess the epicenter of the latest attempt to un-ionize the Wholesome workforce, he never would have even considered this forgotten town.

Or at least, Matron was the latest *suspected* attempt to union-ize. No one had taken any steps to call a vote, not a single union card had been passed out, and the Labor Board hadn't heard any petitions for an election either. But corporate was worried and Marlowe, drawing from his experience of dealing with pre-vious unionization attempts, believed they had cause to be. The-se movements had a tendency to simmer for a time before erupting into a storm of protests and bad press. The possible perpetrators in Matron were being careful, but Marlowe intend-ed to nip it, whatever it was, in the bud before it bloomed.

Sal cocked her head and asked, "They know we're here?"

"The Senior Manager knows we're coming," Marlowe ex-plained, "but she thinks we'll be here next week, scheduling er-ror and all."

"So we lied."

"Yup, we need to catch them off guard if we're going to

figure this out."

Sal made a grimace that Marlowe pretended not to see. Sal had originally started working for Wholesomes' labor division as an intern about a year ago before being offered a job. He wasn't sure that had been in best interest of the company, or her for that matter. Her work ethic was impeccable, but Wholesomes' methods clearly weren't her idea of "employee relations". Perhaps she had thought she could change things—but he could tell that, if she had ever believed so, time and experience had taught her otherwise. He gave her another two months, at best, before she handed him her resignation. If not, he'd have to take her aside and, as a professional courtesy, recommend she consider other work. He would write her a lovely letter of recommendation if asked, though.

"The Senior Manager must be in on this. Usually they call labor if there was even a whiff of a union cropping up, but she's saying she doesn't know anything," Mark murmured as he thumbed through a folder of presentation materials.

Mark had been working with Marlowe for about three years now. In that time Marlowe hadn't learned much about him, and Mark seemed happy to keep it that way. He did his work well and was cooperative, which was all Marlowe needed. He knew Mark was married with kids, but had never met any of them. They looked happy in the pictures on Mark's desk.

"Weird. What do you think?" Sal asked.

"We're going to see. We'll hit the department managers and some of their associates with the normal routine, you guys'll handle that. I'll talk to the Senior, get a look around, talk to some people."

"So what should we be on the lookout for?"

"Take note of anyone who seems combative. Also if someone seems to be trying to be invisible. Try and talk to them, see if they're just bored or worried about being made. But don't be confrontational, remember we're here to help."

"Sure we are," Sal said. He ignored it. Something told him two months was being generous; she probably already had offers.

"Still can't get over how quiet they've kept this. Home Office barely has any intel to work on," Mark said, shoving the folder back into his laptop bag.

It was rare for there to be only "suspicion" of a union push percolating. Wholesomes Corporation paid good money to ex-FBI agents to monitor and report potential employee unrest and how it could manifest. Marlowe admitted he had been spoiled by years of up-to-the-minute reporting on social media posts and after work gatherings that allowed them to track and counter such movements. Just last year that intel had helped thwart a serious threat of a country-wide strike on Black Friday weekend. The strike was led by a loose coalition of workers going by the name Wholesomes Workers for Fairness, which wasn't a union itself, but had the backing of one. Without the information from Home Office it would have been much more difficult to track down who was organizing the movements store to store. Not just the leaders, but the employees who spoke on their behalf to coworkers on the person-to-person level.

Before, Marlowe would have to find contacts who could leak him names and dates, pass some cash under the table, say a few tough words, but now? Now he got screenshots of Twitter and Facebook posts with the perpetrators announcing their plans, clear as day. It allowed him to strike fast and, more importantly, be specific. Marlowe had personally hit dozens of the stores most likely to strike, and was ready to counter any talking point the organizers could come up with. Two days before Thanksgiving, Marlowe received confirmation that the strike had fizzled, with Senior Managers calling in to report they had enough associates for the weekend. A few locations did shut down—Marlowe was proud to say none of his targets participated—but ultimately the effect was minimal.

Perhaps proud was the wrong word. At least he knew he earned his paycheck.

This time was different. Wholesomes Workers for Fairness didn't seem to be involved in any way, or even aware of what was bubbling up in Matron. Marlowe's contact in the organization hadn't even heard of the town, and was able to confirm that no one at that store had contacted or cooperated with them previously. Matron's store, #9-037, had been open on Black Friday, just as it was every day except for Christmas.

Furthermore, no one was talking about strikes, benefits, or unions at #9-037, but they were definitely networking *something*. Marlowe and his team had prowled internet forums and message boards for a week trying to get a grasp of the situation. On the Wholesomes workers' Reddit page there had been a short thread about setting up a meeting with someone in charge of the #9-037 "support group" and the possibility of starting a similar group at their store. Most of the thread had been other people asking if they could be clued in as well. Only one reply, from a user under the handle "MatronSupport", showed anyone was listening:

"So glad you're all interested! We'll get in touch!"

Marlowe had sent a message to the user for information, but never got a response. Sal had managed to figure out the password for "MatronSupport" and found absolutely nothing there. Whoever had been using it had made that one reply and then done nothing else, hadn't sent a message or made a post. However, it seemed "MatronSupport" must have gotten in contact with some people, somehow, as the original thread had a few thank you posts show up a few days later. Now there were hints of "support groups" cropping up across America—and Home Office still wasn't sure what they were. Someone, anyone, should have slipped up by now and blabbed about what was going on at these meetings. But whoever was leading the movement was keeping their supporters from saying anything on public media.

It was an impressive feat—impossible, actually—as Wholesomes employed two percent of the American workforce. No one was talking? No one was posting pictures of themselves at the "support groups"? That wasn't possible. Senior Managers from suspected stores didn't have anything to offer either, and

were all saying they had never heard about the groups. That last
fact particularly aggravated Marlowe, as Senior Managers usually
called the labor hotline whenever they suspected *any* employee
coordination. He was beginning to suspect the Senior Manager
at #9-037 wasn't the only one working with the "support
group".

A row of twenty-three cash registers greeted them at the main
entrance of #9-037. Only six were currently open, which was
more than most stores manned, as Wholesomes kept its stores
lean enough to see ribs. Customers pushed mammoth shopping
carts packed with jeans, pet food, toys, and more. A shopper
could find just about anything they needed at their local
Wholesomes at the most cut-throat prices possible. Marlowe
looked about to gauge the employees' reaction to him and his
team. Anger? Suspicion? No, no one seemed to be paying them
any mind at all. As he scanned the store Marlowe could tell
there was something different about #9-037. He looked about,
trying to get an idea of what was nagging at him, pulling just at
the tips of his consciousness. One glaring difference right in
front of him.

"Hello there, so good to see you!" said an elderly greeter
who gave them a wave.

"We're from the Home Office, I'm here to speak with Mrs.
Imgrund," said Marlowe, snapping out of his ruminations.

"That would be me. So good to finally meet you and your
friends, Mr. Marlowe," said a short and round woman with a
smile a mile-wide walking up to them. Mrs. Imgrund reached
out her hand, enveloped Marlowe's before he had begun to offer it, and gave it a hard shake. Her grip was stronger than he
expected and his knuckles popped in her grip. She stared directly into his eyes for just a moment too long with her broad grin
never faltering. It occurred to Marlowe there was a point where

a smile became someone simply baring their teeth. He gave a quick shake and returned her gaze, not allowing her to throw him.

"Welcome to our little home away from home. Although some of us spend so much time here, our houses may be our homes away from home! So, how can I help you today? Bit early, ain't you? Your call said somethin' 'bout a little lesson on somethin' somethin' workplace—"

"How Wholesomes ensures the best workplace for its associates and managers by continuing a healthy labor relationship. Sal and Mark are going to conduct some presentations while you and I talk about your store and staff."

"Well that'll be fun! John here'll help you guys set up in the break room, should have everything you need in there, but feel free to ask if you need anything, anything at all. John, if you would?"

"Sure thing, Mrs. Imgrund!" said a large man in a Wholesomes vest. Marlowe was surprised at how genuine the warmth in the man's voice was. He glanced at the greeter, at the cashiers, at the employees going about their business. It clicked with him what had been so odd about #9-037. All the staff seemed to be happy, with grins of contentment. Not the strained, rictus smiles associates at other stores had plastered on their faces to meet Wholesomes' politeness standards. Nor the exhausted expression of someone who was just trying to get through their shift. But actual honest-to-God smiles of people who were enjoying themselves as they worked. They also all looked well fed.

Marlowe had never seen such a sight in the twenty-five years he had worked for Wholesomes.

"Mr. Marlowe, how about you and I take this to my office and we can have a little chat," Mrs. Imgrund said with a cracking voice.

"No, I think it best we take a tour of the main floor first."

"Alright, alright, don't want to be wasting your time." Mrs. Imgrund spoke cheerfully, but Marlowe could detect shards of ice in her words. It wasn't usual for Senior Managers to give him trouble, as they wanted to keep him—and by extension, Home Office—happy.

"I won't keep you too long, just need to see the floor is all. I imagine you have work to do yourself."

"I do."

She led him down to the outdoor section first, remarking on how it was responsible for the bulk of their sales. From there the tour became fairly standard despite Mrs. Imgrund's obvious hostility. Racks of bicycles being stared at by wide-eyed children. Locked cabinets of shotguns and .22 caliber rifles. Then on to the electronics, filled with bargain CDs and DVDs. Along the way he asked probing questions of varying subtlety. How was your turnover rate? (Not much!) How satisfied do your employees seem? (Very!) Do some department's associates seem more cooperative than others? (We're all one big happy family!) How often do you see your coworkers outside of work? (Matron's not very large!) She kept her answers curt, empty, and slathered with a layer of faux folksy friendliness. She knew how this game was played, and Marlowe suspected he would have to start working the associates if he wanted real information.

About an hour later they came to the produce and deli section. Mrs. Imgrund pointed to the frozen food aisles saying the deli and produce section was being cleaned at the time. The glass counter where the food should be on display was covered with large sheets of wax paper. Odd. All the produce stands were also draped in the same opaque sheets. It looked like it had been a rush job, and likely done while Mrs. Imgrund had been giving the tour. Marlowe had no idea why they would do such a thing, as he doubted the tomatoes were passing out union cards.

He began to walk over to the deli counter.

"Sir, as I said, that area is being cleaned, we'll come back later."

"But it's the middle of the day," he murmured. He made his way to the counter where a nervous associate in a stained apron smiled and wiped a sheen of sweat off her forehead. He reached out and pulled up the covering.

Bowls of meat, pastas, and cheese sat behind a glass counter in ceramic white bowls and plates. There were identical selections across the world, right down to the neon yellow potato salad. He turned his attention to a bowl filled to the top with cooked chicken breasts and thighs. For some reason the meat seemed to be dusted with grated parmesan cheese.

"Mr. Marlowe!"

Then he realized what he was looking at and recoiled in disgust.

The meat was covered with a layer of white, fuzzy mold. He could see the chicken on top was newer, and deeper in the pile there was even fouler pieces. Great clumps of fungus must have been festering there for at least a week or more. His stomach retched as he saw the rest of the deli display was in the same state of decay. A bowl of cooked pasta he had thought was covered in pesto sauce was steeped in a viscous green slime. He fought against the bile rising in his throat and took a wobbling step back. He leaned on a produce stand to steady himself, the paper slipping away, but his hand landed on top of a green apple. The fruit was like gel and squashed into a putrid pulp with the pressure. He looked at the filth on his hand and shook it off in disgust.

"Imgrund, what is this! This—what are—this is revolting, disgusting!"

"Mr. Marlowe, please calm down."

"Are you serving people this? Are people buying this—do you expect people to *eat* this?"

She sighed, put her hand to head, and her grin was replaced with a thin scowl. Then she took a deep breath and a small smile returned to her face.

"I'm sorry, Mr. Marlowe, many of us have trouble throwing food away, it's very wasteful," she said in a bizarrely even tone.

"It's rotten! No one could eat this!"

She held his gaze for a beat too long.

Marlowe spun away from her and began to quickly walk for the exit to get back to the car. He needed to get to the hotel, call Home Office, and report in. Get Sal and Mark to start packing up their equipment as soon as possible. Sal and Mark—he stopped with a start, realizing that they were still giving presentations. He needed to get to them, tell them to pack up and get out. As he fished out his phone to call them he tried to compose himself. His heart was thudding away in his chest like a hammer on a rail spike and he forced himself to take several deep breaths. They weren't in danger. He'd found moldy food, but that didn't mean he should be panicking as he was. No one was eating it, he was being absurd, and was making wild conclusions. Mrs. Imgrund had obviously misspoke, or simply didn't realize how bad the food was. In back in his mind though, a dark lump of dread pulsated with nervous energy. The three of them needed to leave. Now.

He opened up contacts to call Mark, but as soon as he hit "call" a hand shot out and wrested the phone away from him. He turned to see John, the big associate who had been with Mrs. Imgrund when they'd arrived. John flipped the phone over and canceled the call with a look of rage spreading over his face. Marlowe took several steps backwards and collided with two more employees. Mrs. Imgrund arrived.

"You know, you really should have just stuck to the date you gave me."

"Imgrund, I don't know what's going on here but—"

"That's right, you don't know, but you come traipsing in here with all your threats and assumptions. Yeah, you don't know anything."

"Think about what you're doing."

"Why didn't you?"

An arm went around his throat and tightened. He gasped for air and thrashed against his assailant, but his resistance was nothing more than a nuisance. His vision began to fade and his mind swam in a churning ocean of terror. Then it all went black.

Once Marlowe's son Simon, who was ten at the time, asked him to explain what his old man did for a living. Marlowe was surprised to find he was hesitant how to tell his son just what exactly his job entailed. Marlowe eventually decided on saying he settled labor disputes for the grocery store. At the time that answer had been satisfactory, and the boy didn't question him for years. But as he got older, Simon started applying for summer jobs, and asked his dad if he thought he could get him work at the local Wholesomes. Marlowe had sternly told him he was never to even consider working there, there were plenty of better ways for a boy his age to make money. Simon was confused by this—after all, wasn't his dad one of the people who made sure employees were treated fairly? Marlowe never answered, he just repeated he was not to work there, end of discussion.

Eventually, inevitably, Simon figured out Marlowe's job wasn't exactly about helping employees. When he went into "fix" labor disputes, he was using every trick at his disposal to keep the company's "associates" in line. His son asked just why in hell his dad would do this, why was he choosing to do this?

"Because it'll get you through college."

Marlowe knew that wasn't the best way to put it. It made it sound to Simon like *he* was the reason his father went to stores staffed by people living in poverty and telling them that they could have it much worse. But Marlowe had been saying it to himself for years—hell, it'd been how he had explained it to his wife before Simon was even born.

"I just, I just think you should look for something else. Greg's a worker there, he hates it, says they barely pay him,"

Claudia Marlowe, née Georgeson, had said as Marlowe had been getting ready to leave for his first day of work.

"He's an 'associate' and we don't have the luxury of me looking for work," he had said as he placed his hand on her swollen stomach.

"I know, I know. Promise to keep looking okay, alright? Promise. You're a good man Jacob Marlowe. I think you forget that sometimes."

"That's why I got you, and I promise. I love you."

"I love you Jacob, always remember that."

He leaned over and kissed her, the love of his life, and the mother of his child. She would die two years later from cancer.

That had all been years and years ago, the pain of her absence never fading, but time bleeding through his fingers so fast he didn't even realize it was gone. Simon was a man now, with a family of his own, living happily in Virginia.

Wondering why the fuck his Dad kept doing a job he knew was wrong.

Marlowe wasn't sure why he did it anymore either. His excuse had flown the coop decades ago after all. Maybe it was out of routine, maybe it was the money, and maybe there was no reason. Maybe Claudia had just been wrong about him. All Marlowe knew was he had a head of grey hair and a lake of regret he was trying keep his head above. Over the last year he'd been telling himself he was going to retire. Maybe take up painting. Matron wasn't the last job he was going to do, but it was certainly to be one of the closing chapters in his career.

As he awoke as he was being dragged towards the tree line by two large men in Wholesomes uniforms, he started to suspect it would be his epilogue.

There was a ragged hole made in the perimeter of the woods wide enough for about twenty or so people to walk abreast.

Through the opening was a well-worn trail just visible enough with the light of the fat moon hanging in the sky. He must have been out cold for hours.

With every step they took, the forest became darker, the trees thicker, and the moonlight fainter. They were surrounded by thin trees and shrubs in which he could hear small animals scuttle away from the encroaching humans. Here was a dark world with a mud floor littered with decaying leaves, logs, and animal carcasses. Crawling up among the corpses of the dead, consuming the putrefying matter for nourishment, there was life: fungi, worms, grubs, weeds, ferns and saplings, all feeding on the carrion of their forbearers and vanquished adversaries. Marlowe had spent his youth traipsing around the backwoods of rural Mississippi and had become intimately familiar with that stench of life feeding on death.

After ten minutes of being dragged by his silent captors, Marlowe saw a trembling light in the distance. They came to an improvised torch, a wooden pallet slat wrapped with a burning bundle of cloth that reeked of kerosene. The torch was driven into the ground next to a large and knotted tree. It was an elder thing, its trunk as wide as a car and covered with thick, dark bark that looked more akin to slate than plant matter. Its roots spooled out from the base like the tentacles of some underwater creature and covered the earth in a dark blanket. He gazed upwards to try and get the size of it, saw its mighty limbs reaching far above. Marlowe realized they were now flanked on all sides by such trees, all dark and ancient. Gone were the slim reeds that could only dream of such grandeur; now they were in a true forest. There was no undergrowth to speak of, no struggling shrubs or grass, simply a vast sea of writhing roots.

His captors continued to drag him forward, down and down the twisting trail lined with more torches. In the firelight, he could just make out that some of the trees were bleeding. Globs and streams of cloudy yellow sap crept down from deep wounds and pooled on the roots below. Something had torn into the trees, similar to the bear marks he had seen in his youth, only much larger. Much, much larger. There were claw marks that began dozens of feet up in the trees' branches and descended towards the bases. As they continued marching, Marlowe spotted one tree simply missing a chunk of itself, a giant, ragged semicircle made in the side … as though something had bitten into it.

Marlowe knew he should try to escape, run down the trail and get to the car. He'd known the moment he had stepped onto the path. He never should have come to this starving town in the first place. Wholesomes didn't matter, Home Office didn't matter, and Matron's support group didn't matter. He should have gone back to his room at The Summer Breeze, called in his resignation, and visited Pittsburg for the weekend. He glanced back at the path and saw the lights from the torches were still there, but the areas between them were now in pitch darkness, lights shining in a sea of tar.

One by one the torches went out. They did not fade like a dying flame, but winked out in the blink of the eye. Smothered by the dark. The canopy above them now completely hid the sky from view, like the roof a building composed of wood, leaves, and sap. It was a feeling he knew well from his time exploring the woods of his childhood. Occasionally he would go too far in and realize he couldn't leave. He was outside, far away from any walls, but he was trapped. The only difference between being lost in the forest and being locked in a room was that you knew where the room ended. A forest, true wildwoods, were a world unto themselves.

He knew running back through this wooden labyrinth without light would be impossible. His father had taught him that if he ever got lost in the forest at night he should hunker down and wait for morning. Marlowe suspected morning never visited this place. He turned back and let his captors drag him along.

The path came to an end in a large clearing ringed with torches, and filled with what seemed to be the entire population of Matron, Pennsylvania, perhaps even more. Thousands of people stood shoulder to shoulder looking at the end of the clearing where a massive stone slab lay. The crowd was completely silent. There was no sound from the wall of trees surrounding them; leaves fell from above quietly. His captors dragged him around the people. Some in the crowd eyed him with looks of disgust. Marlowe knew he had finally found the support group he'd been tracking. But it was a hollow victory, because he understood even less now; kidnapped, dragged through an impossible forest, and looking at a gathering much larger than #9-037's workforce. He wondered where Mark and Sal were. He hoped they had escaped, but he doubted it.

As they pulled him along, a chorus of whispers broke out, people pointing towards the slab. Something was happening.

Then Mrs. Imgrund climbed onto the stone and looked onto the crowd. She was still dressed in her senior manager polo and slacks, complete with name tag, from that afternoon. He wasn't sure what else he'd expected; no one else was dressed any differently.

"Hello everybody!" she called out to the crowd.

The crowd roared back in greeting. The sound was deafening, but he suspected—knew, really—that anyone beyond the tree line wouldn't hear anything.

"So, so good to see you all here!" she said, her voice carrying across the expanse of the clearing.

People were cheering and clapping like they were at the Matron High football field on game night. Now that he was closer to the slab, he realized it was actually hundreds of smaller, irregular stones fitted against each other perfectly. There wasn't any mortar holding them together, but the structure looked to be as solid as a cube of steel. Mrs. Imgrund held out her hands to quite to the crowd and the din slowly died out.

"Now, I know some of y'all are a little worried right now. We had some people drop by and start snooping around and askin' about. But I'll tell all of you right now! This is a good thing! We're gettin' the message to the right people, which means the wrong people are gettin' good and nervous. They're puttin' it together that they ain't the boss of us anymore, 'cause we got God on our side and she's lookin' out for the little guy! In fact, we got some of them right here!"

She pointed towards Marlowe and the crowd showered him with jeers and curses. He saw fervent hatred in their eyes, heard it burning in their words. There were so many people, so many glaring faces, that he felt dizzy. This wasn't the first time a crowd had turned on him, but he had always been in control before, no one could actually hurt him. And he'd never experienced anger on such a scale before either, or been so powerless before it. A stone flew through the air and narrowly missed his head, just brushing his ear. Not the first time that had happened either, but perhaps the first time someone truly wanted to kill him. His two captors pressed against him to form a barricade from further projectiles.

"Now, now, none of that, he'll get his, but it's not ours to give. Besides, we have some folks who might be convinced to see things our way."

She pointed again, and Marlowe saw them: Mark and Sal, both being held by their arms by men in Wholesomes uniforms. They seemed to be dazed though, as if their minds were not with their bodies. Their heads lolled listlessly back and forth. Were they drugged?

The crowd erupted with applause and cheers again.

"Now let's talk about God. This God doesn't sit in the clouds and watch us, ah no, ah no, she's down here in the dirt with us. All those guys in suits are scared chickenshit of her, they know she works, that she gets results, that she gave a damn when no one else did! She don't say 'Oh wait until the next life and it'll get better,' ah no, ah hell no. She wants to make it better now!"

Marlowe was becoming drenched with freezing sweat, his body numb with anxiety and dread. It was clear they weren't going to be passing around a collections tray for Jesus here, let alone take a damn union vote. How had he gotten here? Decades ago he took a job and stuck with it. He knew people would hate him for it, but this was something else entirely. He never dreamed that one day he'd be on his knees witnessing a blasphemous, backwoods revival.

"How many of you ever been hungry?" Imgrund called out to the crowd. There was a surge of angry jeers. "I asked how many of you guys have ever been hungry, and I mean *really* hungry! How many of your kids have been hungry?" The crowd continued to roar and she held out her hands to quiet them again.

"We've all been hungry before! When the mines closed! When all the stores closed! We've *all* been hungry! Let me tell you right now, she knows how you feel! She knows how you suffered! She knows, 'cus just like you she's got kids to feed! But her heart is so big she looked on us and just had to help! And she does more than just throw a food drive during Thanksgiving! So lemme ask you, ever since she started helping us, how many of you have been hungry?"

The rapturous cacophony from the crowd was so loud Marlowe's ears began to ring. He could see tears streaming from people's eyes. Others had their heads tilted back and their arms in the air. His two captors couldn't control themselves either, and each were giving celebratory whoops and whistles. They still managed to keep a vice grip on Marlowe's arms, though. Many in the crowd were chanting something, a phrase over and over again, but Marlowe couldn't make it out. He thought he heard "la", or something similar, but beyond that it sounded like gibberish.

"And who helped us?"

The crowd began to coalesce around one phrase, so loud the trees seemed to be shaking. Over and over again they chanted, "The Goat!"

"Who?"

"The Goat!"

"One more time!"

"THE GOAT!"

"Turns out we were lied to! All our lives we been lied to!

The real God isn't some bearded asshole, but a hard workin' mom, and she's an ornery old goat! She took a short nap, and look what happened! Well, now she's wide awake and mad as all hell, and she's gonna take it all back, every damn bit of it!"

Marlowe was now beginning to struggle against his two captors. He wasn't sure what he would do if he got away, but he'd rather take his chances screaming through those dark woods than stay here. He tried to pull from their grasp, tried to wriggle out of his jacket, pulled with all his might. All it got him was a hard strike across the head and a punch to the gut that knocked the wind out of him. He tried to pull away again and was struck square in the face, felt his nose crack with the punch, and hot blood pour down his face. He slumped down in a daze of pain.

"First thing she gave us, first thing! We ain't hungry anymore! Doesn't matter how old and far gone the food is, we can eat it! No problem! The meat gone 'bad'? Milk's sour? Bread stale? Down the hatch, tastes great! And you know why she gave us that gift?

"Why!"

"You wanna know why?"

"Why!"

"Because hunger is how they control us! What hunger let them do?"

"Control us!"

"When we ain't groveling for our next meal all the time, suddenly we can think about all sorts of other stuff, let's us notice how badly we been treated! They up there in their big towers and mansions get to eat whenever they please, that way they can always plan to keep us down! And she continues to bless us! Let me show you, let me show you! Many of you know for the last several years I've been dealing with cancer, docs said I wouldn't make it six months. Well."

She raised her hands up, and the crowd's cheering slowly died away to silence. Mrs. Imgrund lowered her hand to her stomach and—Marlowe could barely understand what he was seeing—reached inside herself. Her hand plunged through her shirt, blood welling up against the fabric, but she didn't stop or show any sign pain. Now she was up to her wrist inside of her stomach, and looked as though she was searching for something. Then, with a look of satisfaction on her face, she withdrew her gore-soaked hand and held it high above her head. She was clutching a sickly, gray lump about the size of an apple. It looked organic.

Marlowe realized it was a tumor. He'd only ever seen them in his wife Claudia's x-rays, never outside someone's body. She continued to hold the ball of festering cells for all to see as rivulets of blood ran down her arm and onto the stone. The crowd watched in fervent silence as she lowered the tumor to her mouth. She took a bite from it.

The audience's roar of exultation was so loud that Marlowe was sure his eardrums would rupture. He saw many of the people's eyes had rolled completely back into their heads, white shining in the dancing of the torches, their bodies undulating in strange rhythms to silent music. As Mrs. Imgrund continued to tear into the tumor the crowd began to chant again, but this time their voices cried out in unison.

"Iä! Shub-Niggurath! Iä! Shub-Niggurath! Iä! Shub-Niggurath! Iä! Shub-Niggurath!"

And their bodies began to warp, to twist, to grow. He saw flesh stream and flex like putty, saw limbs bifurcate and multiply, saw mouths unhinge and teeth erupt and sharpen. Legs became flexible and tendril-like, torsos became muscular trunks of flesh. All were chanting Her name, a name he had never heard, but deep in the back of his mind and soul he recognized it like the name of his mother. The sight was so horrid, so abominable, he didn't realize he was screaming himself hoarse. Tendrils reached out to caress his face, grab him, tear at him as he was dragged before the forest of flesh.

The two men holding him, their bodies shuddering and changing with every step, hoisted Marlowe onto the stone. When he was brought before Mrs. Imgrund, it was not arms that held him.

"I'll give Home Office your regards," she said, and flecks of blood fell onto his face.

His terror-soaked mind barely noticed the trees around him swaying, their branches curling and writhing as if twisted fingers. Sap and leaves rained down as he was dragged screaming to the edge of the altar.

The creatures forced him to his knees and held him before the quaking woods. With a great cracking sound two trees behind the altar twisted and pulled themselves from the earth. Mud and stones flew into the air as they raised their twisting roots up and slithered to the sides of the clearing, revealing a great black void of pure midnight before Marlowe, as though something had made gash in reality. Above the chanting, above the creaking of the lumbering trees, over his own thudding heart, he heard the sound of something moving—a being of such immense size he could not fathom or comprehend it, only that it was approaching. Coming for him.

"Iä! Shub-Niggurath!"

She reached out for him, and Marlowe's mind and soul were sundered by Her glory.

LIKE A GOOD NEIGHBOR

by Wile E. Young

Mrs. Joan Whitaker claimed a monster totaled her car.

Usually this is the kind of claim that gets thrown right in the shredder without a second glance, so you can imagine my surprise when the boss asked me to head down to her place, take a few pictures, and investigate the validity of her claim.

"Are you fucking shitting me?" is not an appropriate office response, so instead I countered with, "I'll head out there right now."

Joan Whitaker was every bit of seventy-one years old and probably should've been taking out a life insurance policy rather than salvaging her gas-guzzling Lincoln. I stepped out of my car and walked towards the small house that had definitely seen better days; rotted wooden beams held up the decrepit roof, a patchwork of missing shingles adorning the top. The carport contained the totaled car and I whistled when I saw the damage.

The Lincoln looked like it had gone a round or two with an elephant for all the damage done to it. Huge, circular sections of the metal had been removed and one of the tires had been sliced in two. The windshield was caved in and the engine was gutted and smashed, antifreeze and oil leaking onto the smooth concrete of the garage.

I walked past it and up to the door that had an old, murky stain glass window and politely knocked. Silence reigned inside the house and I knocked again, this time a little more forcefully. "Mrs. Whitaker, it's Billy Levine from State Ranch Insurance. I came out here to take some pictures of your car?"

I heard some shuffling and a shadow behind the glass moved closer, growing larger and larger until the door slowly swung open and Joan Whitaker stood in the doorway. She was wrapped in her bathrobe despite the June heat, a cigarette clutched tightly in her hand. I caught a strong whiff of nicotine and that smell that permeates the houses of people that should've died a long time ago, but kept persisting against the odds.

"Well it's about damn time you got here." After I heard her talk I wasn't surprised that she had taken out a policy on a car rather than herself; her gravelly voice indicated that there were more miles left on the car than on her.

She shoved past me, her wrinkled feet clad in a pair of Crocks that clacked against the stone of the carport. As she took a drag and let the smoke settle in her lungs before exhaling and looking back at me, piercing eyes boring over me as she gestured at the car. "Gonna take some pictures, or just sit there having a circle jerk?"

I now had a good idea why Mr. Whitaker had decided to punch his ticket a few years back.

I went about my work, circling the car and snapping photos of the damage that the woman directed me towards, all the while asking questions. "You say a monster did this ... like Sasquatch or something?"

Mrs. Whitaker took another drag from her swiftly disappearing cigarette. "Ain't nothing like that. T'was one of Doug's pieces."

"One of your husband's art projects?"

She crushed the cigarette beneath her Crock. "You bet your ass."

Douglas Whitaker had been a sculptor in life, an underground hit. Or so I was told; he had mostly been a recluse around town. The Shreveport art scene looked up to him, and I knew that we had insured several of his sculptures for reasons that were beyond considering. We usually dealt in assets I considered real, like houses, cars, boats, and the like.

Still, if it had done damage to the vehicle then I was legally obligated to file it in the report and note that Joan was probably going senile if she truly believed that her late husband's sculpture had come alive and gone on a domestic rampage in downtown Shreveport.

I sighed. "Where's the sculpture, Mrs. Whitaker?"

The old lady gestured towards the rear of the house. "Out there in Doug's workspace with all the other peculiarities. Had my nephew drive over from Monroe just to drag that thing off my car and put it back where it came from."

She reached an unsteady hand into her bathrobe and brought out a withered package of menthols, sliding one of the cigarettes out and clutching it with a trembling hand. She fumbled with her lighter as I watched.

I didn't have time to sit there and wait the twenty years it would take her to get that cigarette lit. I reached out and snatched it from her hand; the small wick of flame danced in the early morning light as I held it to the end of the cigarette and waited until I saw the fiery glow.

The old woman waved her hand again, urging me to let her kill herself one breath at a time. "Take as many pictures as you want, but don't try nothing funny. I'd sue your ass so fast...."

I didn't bother listening to what senile threat or another she was throwing my way. The grass was beginning to wilt, the hard June sun having already made short work of April's showers. The world was hot and the sun unforgiving, and I hated being out in it.

The storage room/studio was about fifty yards behind the house. The earth had been chewed and great gouges were dug into the ground. I made a mental note to ask the woman where exactly it was that the "monster" supposedly destroyed her car.

The nearby woods seemed to meld around the workshop, the water-starved branches of pine, elm, and the occasional cypress tree turning the place gloomy despite the bright Louisiana day.

The studio was made out of hand-sawed wood and the roof was tin metal. A sliding metal door adorned the front with no window, and a crumpled metal lock lay in the grass. I heaved the doors open and caught a whiff of stale air and dust before I stepped over the threshold and into the shop.

The bright light outside barely penetrated the gloom and I fumbled around against the wall until my hand brushed across a switch. A swift flick and a spark of ozone split the air as lights cast the workshop in a dull orange glow.

The place was massive, bigger than I'd initially assumed. It stretched back into a darkness that my eyes couldn't penetrate. I thought I'd seen the edge of the building outside, but if the dimensions of the interior were anything to go by, it must have stretched much further back into the woods.

Then I saw it. I was surprised that I'd missed it, really.

Taller than me, but squat in form; writhing tentacles topped with crab-like pincers frozen in place, a head like a mosquito or a tumor with a long elephantine trunk stretching towards the floor, with horns and fur like a spider surrounding three bulbous blue eyes.

I assumed that this was the sculpture in question that had "attacked" Mrs. Whitaker's car, but I had to admit that I hadn't expected this level of artistry and craft from her late husband.

It was maddeningly rapturous.

Temporarily forgetting the reason that I had come into the workshop, I stepped closer and reached out a hand, resting it lightly against the sculpture. I felt a small sigh of pleasured surprise escape my lips. The sculpture was warm, something I rationalized away to the heat of the June day, but still it was like the stone was alive and just waiting for my approval. I walked around the entire piece until I could find the plaque bearing its name: Rhan Tegoth.

The name rolled off my tongue like that of a friend that I hadn't seen in a very long time, and I suddenly felt the urge to just sit there with the statue, throw my work to the wind, and bask in the magnificence....

I sighed heavily and pushed the emotion away, bringing up my camera and shooting as many photos as I thought would satisfy my boss and whatever other executives were going to inevitably deny this claim.

After twelve shots from various angles, I thought I had enough and turned to leave. An overwhelming feeling of loss swept over me as I took one last look at the marble marvel and slid the door shut with a heavy sigh. The feeling abated as soon as the statue was out of sight.

I submitted the claim and thought that would be the end of it. Sure, I had dreams about the marvelous statue for the rest of week, some of them filled with wondrous visions of ice-covered mountains and lakes so deep that they held secrets from times lost long ago…. But I also had nightmares about that elephantine trunk wrapping around my head, needle-like teeth inside it piercing my skull and drinking to its heart's content. Each time I woke up, shook it off, and went to work, occasionally wondering how much it would cost to buy it off of Mrs. Whitaker's hands.

I parked my car, retrieved my briefcase, and walked into the building that served as State Ranch's corporate offices in Shreveport, intent on spending another day handing out estimates, writing checks, and taking reports.

Then I saw the email in my inbox.

Below the usual corporate drivel such as "Good morning valued employee", "Numbers are in the clear", and "Shifting paradigms", was one of my pictures that I'd submitted from my trip to the Whitaker place.

Rhan Tegoth photographed in all its mind-bending glory.

I immediately sat up in my chair, scuffing my shoes against the tile and leaning forward to read the text underneath the picture:

Meet the new mascot for State Ranch Insurance, Rhan Tegoth!
This is the original sculpture by the cult artist Douglas Whita-

ker, and photographed by our own Billy Levine. The original be-
ing unavailable for purchase was a letdown, but we have pur-
chased the image rights to the sculpture!

   And that brings us to the heart of our email ... a little
competition....

I groaned. Corporate occasionally had these asinine little
contests in order to "improve team spirit" that more often than
not consisted of about one week of half-assed participation before everyone got back to their real lives.

I went back to reading the email.

   We are calling it Tegotharama! Whoever can craft the
greatest likeness of our new mascot will have their creation put up
in the lobby and receive a special grand prize.

   WOW, right? The competition will run for the next two
weeks, and remember your copy doesn't have to be made out of
stone; it can be made out of anything!

   LET'S MAKE TEGOTH PROUD!

I zoned out from reading the rest of the email; a mindless
corporate sign off and some signatures wrapped it all up, and it
wasn't something that I was in any way interested in.

I leaned back in my chair and chuckled; I had never expected my little trip earlier in the week to turn into something
so farfetched. I got back to work, intending on riding out this
farce with the minimum effort required.

Jared Barnes, our Vice President of Claims, was building an effigy. I had come in to ask if our liability was spelled out correctly in a certain client's policy, but instead found him with a knife
in hand, carving away at a block of wood. I wasn't sure where
he had gotten such skill, but I had to admit he had talent. Look-

ing at my boss' homemade effigy, I felt the same allure as I had from the original sculpture.

"Billy, come on in, come on in. Just getting a little head start here." I sat down in the uncomfortable chair that passed as office standard before laying out what exactly my issues were and whether there was anything that we could do about it. Jared Barnes listened half-heartedly to my pitch before waving his hand at me. "If you want to pay her, go ahead. You've got good instincts and a good head on your shoulders. Now if that's all, get on out of here. I've got to finish this before quitting time...."

His eyes stared at the effigy longingly as his fingers and knife worked. I felt coldness in my stomach as I slowly stood and turned to leave.

Jared's voice stopped me. "I envy you, Billy. You've actually seen the real one."

I shut the door behind me and hurried back to my desk.

An unnatural silence descended over the building as the day progressed. It wasn't something that I could have immediately identified, more along the lines of the lack of activity. Usually interns would hurry past my office, great reams and folders held in their hands, phones would ring in distant offices, and I'd hear muffled voices and laughter around the water cooler.

Instead, there was just an odd silence and the occasional muffled voice. An atmosphere of tension had descended over the office instead of the frantic rat race that the days usually found us in.

I leaned back in my chair, the beginnings of a pressure headache building in the back of my skull. I groaned and rubbed my temples, wondering why the lights seemed like they were behind a haze (was the building on fire?) before I staggered out of my office door, trying to make my way to the water cooler for something that would soothe the headache.

Nothing seemed out of the ordinary other than the weird blur that seemed to come from every light source; people still sat at their desks, some of them occasionally typing on their computers, a phone rang too loudly in the silence. Employees who weren't working on their sculptures were the exceptions rather than the rule, though; people were using office supplies, parts of their desks ... some of them were quite creative in their attempts.

I shrugged past the cubicles until I saw one of the water coolers at the end of a small hallway between the sterile grey walls. I practically fell against it, grasping for the cup dispenser and shoving it under the nozzle. I let the water flow, a bubble splitting the inside of the jug and erupting on the surface of the water.

The liquid felt cool to my lips and I found myself sighing contentedly as I felt the headache subside. I crumpled up the small paper cup and threw it in the nearby trashcan, intending on walking back to my desk and finishing up some claim reports.

I took three steps before I heard the squelching sound like wet grass being stepped on. It was coming from a supply room located down this hallway. My brain told me to keep walking, to mind my own business and get back to work.

Yeah, that had never been me.

I took two steps and leaned against the door listening, trying to discern what was going on behind it despite being fairly sure what was happening. Workplace romances were common in corporate settings.

I opened the door slowly and walked in shutting it behind me; ready to take a mental note of whom I was going to report to Human Resources for spreading their fluids over the copy machine.

There was a woman I didn't recognize inside, and she was chopping pieces of meat into small bloody chunks on top of the copy machine, which flashed and printed out reams of photocopied meat designs.

"What the f—"

The woman whirled around, the kitchen knife held in her hand, a wide smile spreading across her face. I could see the bloody bits of what I hoped was hamburger smeared across her formerly white teeth; her blouse and skirt were stained something dark red. "Hiya, Mr. Billy!"

I gave a halfhearted wave while reaching for the doorknob behind me. The woman ran forward and shut the door, waving the knife in my face, making me stumble back and fall against the wall.

"No no no, don't leave yet. You haven't seen the improvements I've made to the machine." She hurriedly ran back to the copier, grabbing a chunk of meat and the copy paper and ran back, crouching in front of me and pointing at the bloody picture in her hand. She had chopped the meat into intricate designs, but I had no comprehension of their meaning.

"You see, right? Every claim that comes through us has been influenced! *Staged!*" She stabbed the knife past me into the wall, smearing the bloody hamburger that she had brought with her around with the knife until she'd made another sign that almost hurt to look at.

It reminded me of a tree branch—a single line with branches extending from it—and something about it thrummed with power, like an electrical current running through a wall.

"This symbol is somewhere in every claim we agree to pay out.... It's about the monsters, Billy, the ancient things out there between the cracks."

I nodded my head, barely listening to the nonsense spewing from her mouth. I just wanted to get out, call security, and live through this.

"You're just the latest, Billy, and you haven't authorized the claim yet, but that Rhan Tegoth email confirmed it.... We're stewarding the entrance of the Old Ones into the world. The city will rise in the ocean, the Demon Sultan at the center of time will look at us, the Shadow Man will call in all debts." She cackled and widened her hands like this made complete sense.

"The higher-ups are gonna call me crazy, gonna say that I don't work here, that I broke in ... but let me tell you, Billy Levine, that I've worked here for over three years, and I've seen the signs. I've stared at the changing weather patterns, the improbable accidents ... the stars are right!"

The door burst open and three men from our private security firm, Sargasso Securities, came through and grabbed the woman even as she yanked the knife out of the wall and slashed at them, cutting furrows into their flesh. I averted my eyes; I didn't want to see blood, especially when I already thought I was going to vomit from the bloody meat the crazy woman had smeared everywhere.

They pulled her screaming from the room. She screamed eldritch curses and incomprehensible cries. *"DON'T LET YOUR GUARD DOWN, BILLY LEVINE!"* Then she was gone and the security guards were shining a penlight in my eyes, asking if I was okay.

I think I was in shock. I could see their mouths moving, but I had no idea what they were saying. Was that pink blood? I shook my head and made some sort of noise that I hoped conveyed, "Take me back to my office."

They pulled me to my feet and gently began walking me out of the room and back down the hallway. The rest of the building had gathered around to see what had happened and they whispered as I was marched past.

I didn't care. I really just wanted to lie down.

They didn't take me to my office, though. They took me to a waiting ambulance and I was whisked away to the hospital.

The doctor released me fairly quickly after the shock wore off. I'd seen a lot during the course of my job and I didn't think that anything could still have affected me. Clearly, I had been wrong.

Vice President Jared Barnes had personally come down to visit me in my hospital room after the workday ended. He sat down in the uncomfortable chairs that seemed to be a part of every hospital, the damn effigy of that repulsive statue clasped tightly in his hand. He opened his mouth to speak when his cell phone chirped causing him to look at me apologetically.

"Mind holding this?" he asked, holding out the effigy clutched tightly in his hand.

I wanted to do anything but touch that loathsome thing.

Instead I nodded and reached with a trembling hand....

My vision went woozy as the surprisingly warm figure dropped into my palm. It was like everything in the world lost its importance as the world turned in swirling cascades of marker white paint and blue floor tiles.

"Thanks, Billy."

Jared took it back from my hand, and I felt immense relief as he began giving me the recap of what exactly had transpired at my workplace.

He went on to explain that the woman was a nutcase who had been denied a job on one of the lower floors and proceeded to kill one of our mailroom workers. He told me that I was fortunate to be alive, that I was a valued part of the company, and that if I wanted it, I could have a few days off to get myself back together.

I refused, of course. I was angling for a promotion up to the seventh floor and I wasn't going to let anything stand in my way. I reiterated my determination and Jared smiled, gave me a clap on the shoulder, told me that I was well on my way to that coveted office, then left. I was discharged less than an hour later.

I did some research when I got home. The woman had made the news and everything seemed to back up Jared's story, but there was something else ... something eating at my gut that told me to dig deeper.

I plowed through the company files, but could find nothing. At least nothing that pertained to that woman. Instead I found gaps, areas in our paperwork trail that an employee should've filled but didn't. No one would've been able to notice if they hadn't worked at State Ranch for a long time. Like most insurance companies, our paperwork was designed as a maze that would have been unnavigable without a guide. I wasn't guiding anything except my conscience, and it was sick to its stomach as the truth began to sink in.

From a practical standpoint, it made sense; an employee murdering another employee and going off the deep end preaching about alien gods and conspiracies was bad for the friendly neighbor image that corporate had built. Still, deleting her entire employment record....

I decided not to dwell on it. It was just another reality of the business world.

I went to bed, intending on hitting my workload hard when I went in the next day.

The Rhan Tegoth statue was in the lobby, and there were at least twenty employees standing in various states of undress around it. I stopped in my tracks when I walked in; I'd never thought I'd see this thing ever again, but there it was in all its inhuman glory. My mouth moved wordlessly and I thought I could feel the statue's gaze like a living being on me, the toothed orifices across the sculpture looking almost like smiles as I entered its presence.

I tried not to watch as a woman brought her small idol to the base of the larger sculpture. It was crude, to be sure, but with enough of a resemblance that there could be no mistaking what it was. I hurried past the assembled crowd, catching glimpses as the woman thrust herself towards the huge sculpture, licking at the clawed appendages. I thought I could see our security firm close by, but a trick of the early morning sunlight flickered through the windows and made their faces look like shifting masses of gray gel.

I stepped in the elevator trying to control my breathing and attempting to ignore the fact that someone had left a smaller statue of Rhan Tegoth in the elevator. It sat lifeless in the corner, but the wrap-around mirror in the tiny space made sure that I could see it … no matter where I turned.

I thought that the elevator ride would last forever and I was hyperventilating near the end, irrationally thinking that if I moved closer to the discarded effigy it would come alive and attack me.

I stumbled out of the doors, waved off my coworkers' questions about my health, and just tried to reach my office. It seemed the effigies were everywhere, decorating cubicle walls and desks. Someone had made a painting and hung it on one of the sterile white walls that I had to pass through to get to my office.

Everyone I passed had an ethereal quality to them like they hadn't had enough sleep lately. A few people sat slumped over their desks, the symbol the crazy lady had drawn painted across the walls above them.

I made it into my office and shut the door, closing out the world and trying to discern what the hell was happening. If I focused I might be able to get some work done, but it seemed like a silly priority. Hell, it didn't sound like a priority at all considering what was going on outside. It was like the whole office had gone mad because of that damn statue in the lobby. I couldn't understand the weird fascination with it that even I fell prey to.

I had to destroy it.

My door opened and I sat down in my chair, trying to smooth out my hair and plaster on the biggest smile I could muster. Jared stuck his head through the doorway, a huge grin smeared across his face. "Hey there Billy! How you doing today?"

I felt nauseous and was ready to throw my guts up all over my desk, but instead I gave him a thumbs-up. He slapped his hand against his leg and whistled, "Damn, son, that's what we like to see. Now I have Mrs. Whitaker here who has graciously donated her statue to us. You probably saw it in the lobby on the way in." The old woman walked in at the mention of her name, all scowls and potential lung disease.

My boss temporarily took on a wistful look before he shook his head and focused his eyes back on me. "Anyway, Mrs. Whitaker here just needs to have her claim approved and then she can be on her way, secure in the knowledge that her husband's glorious statue is the future of this company!" He sounded too chipper, and I assumed his excitement was getting the better of him. It should've been "the future face" rather than simply "the future" of the company.

"I'll take care of her, boss," I said. Jared nodded, gave me a similar thumbs-up, and closed the door as he left.

Joan Whitaker coughed and slid another cigarette into her mouth, the lighter in her hand not trembling this time.

"You can't smoke in here, Mrs. Whitaker."

The old crone gave me a level look before coughing once and sending a puff of smoke skyward. "Have you seen what's happening out in that office, boy? I think I'm entitled to a smoke after walking through that fucking mess."

I didn't bother disputing it considering I felt the exact same way.

"What kind of company are you folks running?" She hacked and spit onto the carpet. "Because last time I checked, people doing actual work weren't offering blood to the statuary in the lobby."

"Well why the hell did you donate it to them in the first place?"

The old woman looked confused. "Why the hell wouldn't I? It already came to life and smashed up my car. Next thing it'll be smashing through my windows and sucking my brains out.

I'm glad to be rid of the damn thing."

She sucked in another breath of smoke and stared at the closed blinds, her mind somewhere only she knew. "It killed my husband, you know. Sucked his blood right out of him. That's why he died so young."

"You really believe that, don't you?"

She waved a hand in my direction, the blue nails ethereal in the rings of smoke swirling around her. "Don't so much matter what I believe, Mr. Levine. It's what I can see that's important. You think any of what's going on out there is normal?"

I didn't and she knew it.

"You want the trouble to go away? You kill that thing in the lobby. It's already infected your business; that's how it worked on my husband … the pictures of it, then the fascination, then subservience, then the sacrifices."

She looked dead serious, and I knew that when she meant "sacrifices", it didn't mean money or assets.

"How are we supposed to kill it? It's a fucking statue."

She shook her head. "It isn't, it just can't move. As soon as one of the drones you have running this place decides to give it some blood, it'll be moving. And at that point, there ain't hope." She continued, looking grim. "It'll entrench itself here like a tick on a dog, and everything will be an extension of it: the people working here just extra limbs, the building like a shell…." Joan Whitaker looked haunted. "Trust me, you don't want to get to that point at all."

We sat in the silence of my office while outside someone ran past the window, a quick shadow against the sickeningly bright fluorescent lights.

Mrs. Whitaker stood. "Either way, it doesn't matter. This is all on you, don't make no difference to me."

I slid over and looked up her account on the computer, making sure that her claim was accepted. After we finished with the necessary paperwork, the old lady nodded and dropped her cigarette on the floor, stomping it out with her left heel.

"It can still be stopped. Time hasn't run out for these people yet."

She turned to leave. and this time I stood up. "Hey, now, you can't just leave. I don't even know what the hell you're leaving me with."

The chain-smoking crone shrugged. "It ain't my problem. I'm not long for this world, so when it goes tits-up I'm gonna be six feet under not giving a shit."

She turned to leave again, and I felt the wave of desperation wash over me one last time as I reached out and clutched her arm; it felt like old sandpaper with almost no moisture present. She glared at me. "Please tell me how to kill it," I begged.

She wrenched her arm away and opened my door. "If it were that simple I would've taken an axe to it a long time ago." She walked out of my office, leaving me to squirm in my seat as everything went to hell around me.

I wasn't sure if Joan Whitaker would make it out of the building; fervor had seized the entire office. Paperwork was hurried to and fro as a few of the employees carried out the new policy of denying claims in order to cause the most suffering possible. I thought it was like a bad sitcom based on the sheer audacity of denying someone with full coverage simply because it would cause them to peter out and live homeless on the streets when the banks repossessed their assets.

Cubicle cults had sprung up, each one dedicated to a certain kind of policy-making and worshiping the alien call they heard in the back of their heads that whispered the secrets of depravity to their minds.

I knew because I could hear it too.

It was quiet, like a small voice, but I could hear it … that soft tenor whispering for me to *feed, Feed, FEED.*

I shrugged my head, trying to dislodge the loathsome presence from my senses. I could glimpse the future, and it wouldn't be long before the sacrifices to the statue in the lobby would start.

Madness was the new king and I was not going to be party to it anymore.

I locked my office door and edged my way down the hall-way trying to avoid eye contact with anyone, afraid that they could see my intentions if I so much as glanced at them.

The carpet had been stained with something that I wasn't sure was blood; it was sticky and made a ripping noise as I pulled my shoes from it. Someone had taken feces and rubbed them across the walls. I raised my hand to my nose to block the overwhelming stench.

The culprit was still there drawing in the hall, occasionally whipping out his penis and spraying piss in a stream across the wall. He giggled madly, a claims stamper in his hand as he pounded the word "Denied" into the feces and piss-stained wallpaper.

No one seemed to notice him. Interns and cubicle jockeys walked past him without even a second glance, papers clutched tightly in their hands or escorting sobbing clients towards the elevators, their despair momentarily stifled by the surreal sight of a man rubbing his excrement against the walls. I strode past them intending to make my way down the service stairs to the maintenance closet where they kept the chemicals and other supplies.

The legal department was having a massive orgy; my eyes watered at the mad rush for flesh, the moans of pleasure mixed with cries of pain as lustful hands armed with knives alternative-ly penetrated and carved flesh from their own genitals in orgas-mic agony.

"Billy, BILLLY!"

I had always imagined the sight of Kay Lynn Thomas na-ked, but the sight of her holding her detached breasts in her hands made me turn and vomit on the floor, the acrid bile washing over the carpet that was already stained with the blood and semen of a dozen different employees.

When I was finished emptying my guts onto the floor, I looked up to see Kay Lynn's disapproving face, a sad and hurt look coloring her features.

"You said I was beautiful...."

I tried to protest as she reached up and began sawing off the skin of her face.

"Don't do that!" I reached for the knife, but she slashed at me, nicking the top of my hand and causing me to jump out of reach. I clutched my bleeding hand as she went right back to flaying the skin from her face. She gasped in pain but didn't seem to slow. I couldn't bear to watch another second of the act. I threw all caution to the wind and made a break for the stairs.

"WHERE'RE YA GOING KILLER!?"

It was Jared. He was naked from the waist down and his undershirt had been cut in two strategic places exposing the bloody bits of flesh where his nipples had been. He rushed, me a box cutter clutched in his hands and a large grin plastered over his face. The entire legal department paused their psychotic ecstasy to engage in the fun new game of run-down-the-sane-employee.

I ran like hell, not bothering to turn around or observe the madness around me, entirely focused on getting through the doorway into the stairwell and finding a weapon.

A naked aide leapt from the desk and I ducked, barely avoiding him. I could hear the squishing flesh as the mob trampled over him, his cries of pain-warped ecstasy lost amidst the mad scramble to murder me.

The red exit sign was like a lighthouse beacon gleaming in the night and I tore towards it, panicked breaths escaping my mouth as I felt the hot breath of one of the naked lunatics behind me.

It was close now ... closer ... and then I was through, spinning around and kicking the door shut in the face of the floor supervisor who had carved his face into a gross facsimile of a tic-tac-toe.

I clicked the sliding lock into place and fell back as a massive *BANG* rattled the metal door, followed by rhythmic pounding and snarling, chips of old paint flaking off the lock. It wasn't going to hold for long and I didn't want to be around when it eventually gave way.

I scrambled to my feet and ran down the stairs as fast as they would take me. My steps echoed throughout the stairwell and my bleeding hand left a trail that any idiot would have been able to follow, but it was the last thing on my mind as I made it to the bottom floor and quietly slipped into the maintenance closet.

I took a minute to catch my breath while I tried to keep my mind from thinking about the insanity taking place on the floors above me. Subconsciously I knew that Rhan Tegoth was aware of my plans, or had known what I would've decided to do when I came to work this morning; everything seemed to have escalated from a general strangeness to balls-out madness.

There were some paper towels that I used to wipe the blood off my hand, a first aid kit stashed away in the corner tidied up the wound, and a can of gasoline and a small lighter completed my morbid shopping as I hurried back towards the door and slipped out, shutting the door as quietly behind me as I could.

The door to my right led out onto the first floor, the lobby down a long and ornate hallway to the left past the elevator banks. From the sixth floor I heard the crunching of metal as the insane legal department caved in my impromptu barricade and began shouting the obscenities and promises of pain they had adopted. A swift spike of fear pervaded my senses and I quickly left the stairwell and ran out into the main lobby.

It seemed so oddly serene compared to the madness unfolding above us. People walked, busily chatting on their cell phones in immaculate attire, the security guards sat behind their desks at the far end of the hall, and plants that weren't splattered with inordinate amounts of blood and semen sat serenely in their pots.

That didn't mean that the insanity hadn't seeped in.

The cell phones the crowd talked into weren't connected to anything, more like props in their hands, all eyes on Rhan Tegoth down the hall. They gave me a wide birth as I passed. I wondered how I looked in my bloody suit with a can of gasoline and a wild-eyed look. Already calls were being made, and I was sure that the security guards would be running to protect their precious statue from my wrath.

It was there squatting in the lobby, the marble stone having transformed into flesh.

Its followers stood in a circle around the perimeter of the lobby; they had spray-painted the windows a dark black so that the outside world was separated from the madness. The occasional person entering quickly turned around to leave.

Basins filled with blood circled the creature, and I watched as it slowly reached out and began sucking it up through its trunk, ignoring its followers who had begun dancing around spilling their own blood on the floor.

I grasped the gas can tighter as I strode forward, trying to appear much more confident than I felt.

The creature's skin roiled and its three blue orbs turned towards me, blinking in unison as its sandpaper voice filled my mind. *Billy, don't be that way ... sit for a spell ... take everything in ... you found me and deserve all of my blessings....*

I ignored it as I walked past its followers; they parted to let me through. The blue eyes stared at the can held in my hand. *Oh Billy, you don't need that....*

I poured it all over the squamous creature and flicked the lighter.

It went up like kindling, a keening squeal escaping it as its tentacles batted the air, wrapping around whomever they made contact with and squeezing until they suffocated or burned with it.

It screamed in my head and made threats, but I ignored it, watching as it burned away to nothing. I smiled evilly as the last of the green goop that was its body evaporated and bubbled away into nothing.

A lot of people died and even fewer knew what Rhan Tegoth had been. Most of them acted like they'd woken up from a bad dream.

Perhaps that's what it had been.

Either way, the company issued apologies, payments, anything to pay off its debts.

Jared Barnes was dead and I got his job. Seemed like an appropriate reward for the man who had saved everyone.

Jared Barnes watched as his makeshift effigy devoured Billy Levine's mind. He supposed he should've thanked the up-and-comer for discovering just where it was that Rhan Tegoth resided.

Closing down an entire wing of a hospital wasn't an easy feat, but the effort was worth it in order to silence any potential complications to Corporate's plan.

The small statue's trunk sucked out the blood through Billy's eye socket, his body occasionally twitching as the elder spawn fed him whatever delusion it needed to keep him sedated.

They would feed his body to the real thing, of course, when they brought it in.

After all, who were they to deny their god's claim?

TINDALOS, INC.

by Charlie Allison

Augusta sat at her desk, twirling a pen between fingertips while the hardware reset after the seventh forced shutdown that afternoon. It was all she could do to pass the last few hours of the workday. She tried not to look at the mound of data to upload, correlate, and make almost readable. Travelers ran up debts, in one way or another. It fell to the drones of Tindalos, Inc. to chronicle the infractions and tolls in a seemingly endless system of databases and dates.

Behind Augusta, her cubicle-mate Philips was taking a late lunch after a long call with an addled client.

"Not Thindalos, ma'am," the thin man said in his New England interpretation of a Royal London accent: surgically enunciated, with just a touch of pedantry behind the syllables. "No. Tin. As in the metal. Dalos. Tin-dal-os. Yes. Of course. Any time or place, that's our motto. No, thank you. Have a—ah, lovely. She's hung up."

Philips wasn't the slamming sort, but the plastic of the phone cracked perceptibly as he set it home on the receiver.

"About an hour and a half too late," he growled, as Augusta's computer finally displayed a start screen: the open jaws of Tindalos, Inc., as mandated by company policy. At first glance, they resembled an oddly sinister "greater than" sign that took her straight back to primary school mathematics.

Augusta logged in, a flurry of passwords. Found herself holding her breath.

"Who the hell knows why companies pick these wretched names?" Philips managed around a mouthful of soggy ham sandwich plucked from his brown bag. "Nerizon, Whately, Nike, Tindalos. Just pick a name and try to make it sound ancient."

Augusta, horribly aware of her own Roman-inspired name, kept silent.

"As if that gives it class," the thin man muttered darkly. He tore into the sandwich as if it had done him a great personal wrong, enamel shredding meat. "Like that dreadful house you've shacked up in. Old Prognosticator Parson's place, wasn't it? Charming atmosphere, I hear."

Augusta glanced at the clock and swallowed her barbs—they'd only prolong the conversation. So what if her place of residence near the newest Tindalos branch office had once been the home of some local loon who was found messily deceased inside his circular stucco home? It was what she could afford, once student debt was calculated.

Philips, amateur company archivist and professional gadfly, seeing his goad had failed, resumed his lunch.

Augusta pulled up the spreadsheet she'd been attempting to fix for the past few hours. It contained a formidable list of time-debts chronicled and collected: who and when and in what amount. Travelers or employees of a thousand client-companies who'd overspent their resources in one way or another and were now at the tender mercies of Tindalos, Inc. Just numbers, not people.

Sometimes, when Augusta blinked or looked away for a moment, bright blue foreign characters twisted and gleamed with a sickly glow in her spreadsheets. They didn't move with the rest of the sheet, or suffer to being clicked on, overlaid, pasted, or deleted before vanishing.

The first time Augusta had seen them she'd tried to flag down Frank, her supervisor. He claimed not to see the figures, which was more than Philips ever did. He simply grunted. "They come up from time to time. Part of the territory."

Someone other than Augusta would have missed the micro-twitch that flickered across Philips' thin face.

Philips sniffed. "We do what we're told. Collections. Or rather, tracking collections. Travelers." He took a big sniff of air and went back to his on-the-job hobby: back-tracing and sorting cases chronologically.

She didn't pursue the matter further then or now. Instead, she opened up the files, beginning with the Howards case, and unfocused her eyes, loosened her fingers. Prayed for the computer to stay active long enough to finish this sheet.

"I found something interesting in the archives, actually. Might actually relate to that hideous house you rent. Might stay late, dig through the last of the Parson files to get the juicier details from the archives, who knows," Philip said as he finished his food and opened a new window on his computer. There was a faint thump, as if the elderly man was fumbling for something. "Anyway, that place of yours has a history. Back from the charter days of the company. Before you were a glint in anyone's eye."

Augusta shrugged and pretended to listen as Philips babbled on about his find. If she wanted to hear horror stories about old Prognosticator Parson she'd go to a local bar or try to research some of the tenacious, alien-looking marks burned into the wooden floor of her circular domicile—neither of which appealed to her in the slightest. Augusta watched the clock. Phillips must have been diverted from his original topic by some verbal marginalia, because the next time Augusta checked into his monologue she heard the terms "sorcery" and "time-travel", phrases with no bearing to anything outside of a television program.

She wasn't paid to listen to speculation. She was paid to track, correlate, and categorize thefts of time—a break extended a second too long, an unauthorized sick day taken—in their client companies. If someone got too greedy, collectors were dispatched. She swiveled her back to Philips and tuned his voice out further still, relegating it to the basement of her subconscious.

Augusta began typing, and time stretched forwards towards the end of her shift.

The foyer of Tindalos, Inc. was mathematically crisp. The company was less a series of rooms in a building and more a collection of sharp angles filed in precise order that tolerated people working in it. The atrium was spare—all white paint and a few badly hung mirrors around head-height. Augusta felt as if she was dirtying it with her footsteps every time she clocked out from work. Tindalos, Inc. was a place where organic life felt unwelcome—each breath an offense against geometry.

Unlike many businesses on the seventh floor of the office-park, the doors to Tindalos, Inc. were not transparent glass. Old oak separated this branch of the company from the rest of reality. Sometimes as she left work for the day, Augusta thought she saw odd things in the wood. A squiggle of something that the carpenter had let slide in a careless moment—a slip of the chisel or saw to make things that looked like pictures if one squinted in a certain light. A pair of jagged lines formed a pair of ever-gaping jaws by the door handle.

There was no art at Tindalos, Inc. Only an ocean of cubicles, the clicks and rings of calls, the ragged breath of people working the phone banks—cases, collections, cases and collections.

She punched out at exactly 5:00. No later, no sooner—as company policy had made excruciatingly clear.

Augusta walked as quickly as she dared. Her flat-heeled shoes made thunderclaps as she clocked out for the day, shouldered through the black wooden door, and stomped her way through the stairwells down into the parking garage.

Augusta thought she saw drifting smoke in the corner of the parking lot. She shook her head, and it vanished.

Prognosticator Parson's house, Augusta's home for the duration of her time with Tindalos, Inc., sat on the edge of the tree line—circular and stucco-covered walls clashing against the pine forest. To Augusta, it felt like living in the cast-off eye of some dismembered titan. She parked her car in the muddy driveway and made herself a quick dinner of a burger topped with honey. As she walked around the angle-less home, she ran a tired hand over strange glyphs, checked and secured the dozen or so different locks that old Parson had clearly felt were necessary over his rounded doors and windows. Augusta slept better knowing that iron and brass were between her and the odd forest—sometimes she heard strange whispering voices from the woods as she drifted off to sleep. This final task attended to, she slipped out of her shoes and passed out in her circular bed.

Augusta woke to the sound of pine branches snapping outside. The thud of heavy feet.

Or at least thought she did.

Augusta raised her head from the pillow—she'd slept in her work-clothes again. Her bedside clock read an appallingly early hour.

She tasted smoke on her tongue for some reason.

There it was again, just beside her bedroom window. A rustling sound—something like a raccoon, to judge by the noise.

The window was closed against the autumn winds, and Augusta's nearest neighbor was a mile away.

"They come through corners," a familiar voice mumbled. Its owner remained disembodied, though the breaking of tree limbs continued. "They come through corners."

Augusta moved as quietly as she dared, sliding from her bed, against the rounded wall of her home, next to the window. She slid onto her belly, hands trembling, all but invisible to the outside, even with the harvest moon high overhead.

"The foulness, the foulness of corners and binding laws outside our ken." The voice continued, rising and falling, piercing like the north wind. There was hysteria just below the enunciated syllables. "So clever, so so clever. Start with those who walk through time! Expand to shirkers! Cruel and angular, who puts a saddle on a dog? Athirsting and lean and hideous! They hide from our eyes, veiled by another, yet always before us. Collecting and consuming! They didn't get Parson, in his egg. But they got more, the rest of our clients. Oh God."

Augusta reached for a cell phone that wasn't in its normal place on the bedstand. Her hand came back empty.

She didn't move further. The voice continued.

"They come from corners, blue tongues wagging. They come from corners. No corners here though." The voice cracked: nasal and high and coughing back tears and snot. Hands slapped against the stucco walls. Fumbling, as if the person behind them was sightless with panic.

"The hounds are coming. We go into their jaws every, every day and emerge, but now…." The voice had switched pitch. It had the tone of a religious fanatic or a lunatic. She heard scrabbling. Nails on stucco, skin being torn and rubbed raw. Now there were tears and swearing and a distinct slump of a body against the wall.

Then she heard a flurry of blows at the circular front door. Fists, by the sound of it, then a frantic scrambling at the handle—flesh on metal. The door shuddered at the impacts, which only seemed to increase in speed and force even when the owner of the voice began to swear in a language she didn't know. Slowly, the blows became heavier and slower—a forehead, or perhaps fear-driven kicks?

Augusta held her breath. The stranger didn't circle the house or try the round front door again—he seemed focused on the high oval-shaped window instead. He jumped, and scrambled, but there were no footholds or handholds for him here, in this house without corners. He began to sob. "Tindalos, Tindalos, Tindalos," he whined, a dirge that was barely human.

Augusta waited. After about five minutes of undignified sobbing, the footsteps retreated, stumbling as though crippled or drunk, back through the forest.

She didn't remember falling asleep.

When Augusta slept her dreams slithered and creaked with alien sounds. Smoke clogged her nose, whispered down her throat.

When she woke, she saw a faint hint of blue mingling with the sunrise. She blinked, and the impression passed. There was a faint smell in the air that preceded her morning toast, something almost foul—like sulfur or eggs gone bad—but that too vanished.

Philips didn't show up to work.

Augusta didn't notice at first. She reported her late-night visitor to the local police that morning and was rewarded with a tepid promise to "send a man over". After the flatfoot found nothing besides footprints and broken branches, she scrambled to work.

Augusta, rattled or not, was behind on her files as it was, and broke the speed limit getting to Tindalos, Inc. She clocked in at exactly 9:00 AM.

Caffeinated and twitching, she tried punching in time-data on the Ackerman Cooperative's employees—some new startup with a stickler's approach to time-management. In contrast. Tindalos, Inc. was not an old company, nor young—it seemed to be one of those constants that is simply there, outside of time or context. One could remember Tindalos' insignia when they saw its open-jawed sigils and forget it before they turned the corner.

Today, like every day, that sigil made her spine crawl. But the people behind that sigil also paid her, so one couldn't be too choosy.

When lunchtime came, and Phillips' seat remained empty, Augusta reluctantly looked around to investigate. Still no

Philips.

His desk stood resolutely empty.

Augusta dialed the front desk, almost relieved to hear the receptionist's indifferent drone of a voice. No, Philips hadn't clocked in that day. He had left late last night though, finishing some archival business. No, he hadn't called in sick either.

Augusta went back to work, ignoring the knot in her stomach even as her computer crashed for the second time that day. She shunted her certainty about the identity of her nocturnal visitor to the back of her brain, where it couldn't burst out of her mouth and cause problems.

As the day wore on, with the Ackerman file completed, Augusta finally managed a sweep of Philips' desk.

Her hands came away sticky from the second they touched the surface. Something pale blue and nearly translucent glistened atop the empty surface.

The drawers were also filled with the blue stuff, Augusta soon discovered. Sterile as an operating table otherwise. No mementos, nothing.

Augusta straightened up and took as deep a breath as she could manage. This might be something to see management about, like it or not.

She picked up her phone, dialed. "Yes, I know it's not encouraged, but I need to see Frank. It's about Philips."

Supervisor Frank, silver-goateed and saturnine, sat facing out one of the blue-tinted windows of Tindalos, Inc. He had one of the corner offices—the only one that was consistently occupied. The other three were locked whenever Augusta tried the handle, and the smoked glass in their windows revealed nothing.

There wasn't much in supervisor Frank's office, but Augusta got an impression of rounded edges, egg-like fountain pen holders. A place that was free from the systematic geometry of the rest of the office. It felt like a home.

He turned to face Augusta.

"You've only been here a year," the supervisor said gruffly as the sun went down. "You've done good work. Been prompt. Thorough. Sent collectors after a minimum of customers— that's good. And now you've found something interesting."

Augusta wasn't sure about that, but decided to leave her boss uncorrected on the count of her productivity.

"Something strange was going on at Philips' desk. He hasn't shown up. All day. He said he'd be in the archives after work, doing some research on my rental home, but that's the last I heard from him." *But he was around my house last night, shrieking like a madman*, she could have added but didn't. Tindalos, Inc. took a dim view of employee complaints.

Her supervisor tilted his head, like a raven that has spied a shiny coin on distant pavement. She thought she saw his spine stiffen.

"Speak up. My hearing isn't what it used to be," Supervisor Frank said.

Augusta nodded. Breathed deep. "His desk had some sort of blue fluid smeared over it. Like anti-freeze or something," Augusta said, forcing the words out of her diaphragm, holding back the rest of the story. "Everything was gone from his desk."

Frank blinked and took his eyes off of his egg-shaped monitor.

"You don't say."

"It was odd. Philips' desk, I mean. Color of watered-down coolant or anti-freeze. It was dripping everywhere, but under the light it was nearly invisible until I touched it," Augusta blurted before what she had seen and felt could become more unreal, more doubtful in her mind. "It was … everywhere. In the desk. Around it."

"Have you been getting enough sleep?" Frank asked, tilting his head and taking in Augusta's trembling hands and bloodshot eyes. In that second, Augusta would have believed that he somehow knew something, but was holding it back—about last night, Philips in the archives, everything. That was quite obviously impossible.

When she didn't answer, Frank continued. "I'll look into it. Philips is out of vacation days at any rate," he said with a sigh. He suddenly looked his age. Was that a slight tremor in the hands she saw? Frank folded his hands. "I'll have to send a memo out about that. Can't have people squandering their three days of vacation, then trying to steal company time, like a client-company. I trust you can see yourself out?"

"But, sir," Augusta began. Her tongue felt heavy.

"Thank you, Ms. Derleth. That will be all." Frank's eyes went back to his computer screen, and his fingers tapped out a dirge on the keyboard as Augusta slunk from his office to her car.

Augusta didn't go back to her desk. Something was wrong, something disrupted her steps, made them arrhythmic.

She clocked out. She saw the timestamp: 4:59 PM.

She ignored it.

She found Philips, finally. In the parking lot.

He was sitting in a distant corner; he would have been invisible if Augusta hadn't accidentally flicked on her high beams on her way to the exit.

Augusta stopped her car and looked from the rounded, comforting interior shell.

He seemed somehow incomplete.

Philips was sitting cross-legged, his head severed and placed in his open palms. His hands were bloody and scraped raw. In the horrible clarity brought on by adrenaline, Augusta thought she saw a few chips of stucco under the fingernails.

His mouth was open in a scream.

Augusta, without knowing why, thought of Tindalos. Of the hounds and collectors and blue tongues and the foulness from corners that Phillips had shrieked about.

The possibility of synonyms flicked through her forebrain—she ignored it.

When Augusta inched closer to Phillips, she saw that he glowed a faint blue.

Augusta hit the gas. The squeal of tires drowned out her initial shriek.

Augusta broke the barrier that held the cars in the lot without a second thought, ignored the spider-webs that spread through her windshield. Her heart was doing overtime, sweat choking her vision. She blitzed through red lights like an errant lightning bolt. She took the curves too fast, once skidding onto a shoulder, heart pounding.

But she made it. Back to Old Prognosticator Parson's place, the one black mark on Tindalos Inc's collection record, at a guess, until he swallowed a revolver years ago.

Of course, she had to call it in. Philips' body. It had to be a murder. Most people didn't cut their own heads off as a sartorial statement. Her hand reached for the phone in her jacket pocket, only to find it empty as she opened the car door outside her home.

She'd left it on her desk. Back at Tindalos. Something about even thinking that name made her throat dry. There was a smell of putrefying eggs, of carcasses too long in the sun.

A flicker of blue, unattached to matter, in the angle of the open door.

Augusta saw a tendril of smoke forming in the hinges of her car door. The tendril became a cloud, and her nose rebelled at the stench just as Augusta's hands mutinied and refused to obey her command to slam the door shut.

A blue tongue and lean hateful shape squeezed from the angle of the car door like puss from a wound. It didn't look anything like a dog, or anything that drew breath.

Jaws and blue ichor swallowed Augusta's screams. The collectors, the hounds, had come.

MEMORANDUM:

FROM: Management
TO: All Tindalos, Inc. Staff
RE: Mission Statement

At Tindalos, Inc. we strive to cleave to our mission statement: productivity and accountability over passivity. It's why we dominate the market. Unspeakable Enterprises and Ithaqua Ltd. are second fiddle because they don't prioritize promptness and precision.

It seems that some of you need a reminder that work is work—get in on time, leave on time. In light of recent events at the Old Parson place, access to or discussion of archival records before 2001 now requires the written permission of upper management. Additionally, we will be institutionalizing a "collectors sent" per-day quota for our client companies—no better way to encourage excellence!

Have a productive and focused day.
FRANK LONG, Supervisor, TINDALOS, INC.

CLEAN UP AISLE FOUR

by Josh Storey

Tear the roof off of any Circle-Mart department store and you find over an acre and a half of pristine consumer paradise, divvied up into smaller fiefdoms organized by purpose: Electronics, Toys, Tire and Battery, Farm-Mart (a mediocre grocery department), and even a café that serves trumped-up coffee drinks and slices of cheesecake.

I left my apron behind the café counter and went to clock out. At the border of every department, I dropped little pouches full of consecrated salt, chicken bones, and other bits of juju I'd rather not think about. Then I kicked the bags under displays, hiding them out of the way.

Of all the things I expected to find when I walked into the back room, Darren driving the business end of a Scherl & Jackson Potting Trowel through the pudgy chest of our store manager Phil was not one of them.

But there you had it.

"Hattie, don't just stand there!" Darren yelled while he buried the trowel deeper into Phil. "Gimme the salt!"

If my life were a television show, this would be the cold open. You know cold opens? They're the first five minutes before the theme song kicks in. TV writers use them to grab your attention, tossing you *in medias res*, and forcing you to watch a beloved side-character's imminent demise. They're a real kick in the pathos.

Of course the scene always cuts to black before the final moment, and next thing you know "THREE DAYS EARLIER" appears in all caps in the middle of the screen.

Dark blood frothed out of the hole in Phil's chest. His eyes went all buggy, and by that I mean they turned into actual bugs.

Squirming brown beetles.

"The salt, woman!" Darren said. "Now!"

I really hate cold opens.

THREE DAYS EARLIER

In the infernal codex of soulless corporations, Circle-Mart ranked somewhere below Amazon but well above Monsanto. The Kingfisher Club across town paid thirty cents more per hour, but my friend Milo had worked there in high school, and he told me they had corporate-mandated "Praise Meetings" before every shift. A girl's gotta have standards when she's selling her soul to big corporate, and anyway after three months I'd get health care.

I was about a week into my career as a café harpy when Assistant Manager Darren asked me to help with some inventory.

"Sure," said Meghan, the café manager. "Take the new girl and short-shift me. I don't mind."

The post-school rush peaked at four thirty in the afternoon. We had a line seven deep, full of tweens looking for their coffee fix.

"Safety regulations require two employees to operate any free-standing ladder." Darren didn't look up from his clipboard. "So unless you want to help me count adult diapers...."

Meghan waved her hand at me. "You're losing your smoke break."

Anything that got me away from the mob of millennials. I didn't smoke anyway.

Darren led me to the health care aisle. Circle-Mart went for a kind of warehouse club vibe, so the shelves were high and filled with overstock. He pointed to a metal ladder. "I read the UPC number, you check the tags and give me a count."

I hated heights, but it was too early to become That Girl. Up I went, and so did my store-issued polo, exposing my midriff and my birthmark.

"You know," Darren said. "Store policy says tattoos must

be covered at all times." He didn't look like he belonged in retail. He looked like he should be in a courtroom, arguing the
case for baby ducks in the hinterlands or something. Close
cropped blonde beard. Chiseled cheek bones. Eyes like green
emeralds. Milo would love this guy, and I was pretty sure Darren was gay too.

I tugged at the back of my shirt. "Then don't make the
short girl check the high shelves," I said. "Besides, it's not a tattoo."

Darren gave me The Look™. I'm used to The Look™. No
one believes me when I tell them about my birthmark. The
black keyhole-shaped patch of skin on my lower back is way too
neat and way too centered to be natural.

"Then you'll definitely want to keep it covered," Darren
said. He looked left and right before lowering his voice. "Especially here," he whispered and gave me this weird wink. "The
stars tell trouble when the long night falls. The Knight Shift's
watch is eternal."

"How the hell did you hear the 'K'?" Milo said through my
headset. On my screen, his sorcerer grabbed aggro on a trash
mob and died like the pathetic clothy he was.

"It was the way he said it." CTRL+3 and I resurrected him
with 50% health. "Like, with gravitas. I dunno, it's hard to explain."

"He likes the D, you say?" In real life, Milo was built like a
really tall Mexican dwarf. Not, like, a little person. Like Tolkien
dwarf. With axes. He was also back at school, finishing up his
capstone project and applying to graduate programs. Like I
should have been.

"Is he single?" Milo asked. "Is he hot?"

I typed /SLAP and on screen my paladin smacked Milo's
sorcerer with a fish.

"What?" Milo protested. "I'm not allowed to have a sex drive?"

"Seriously," I said. "I think Darren's—"

"A member of the Big Box Illuminati?"

"Mentally unbalanced."

"Isn't that what Human Resources is for?"

"Sure. Great way to make an impression." We circled around the dungeon. " 'Hi, yeah, I know I haven't even gotten my first paycheck yet, but I think my assistant manager is cray-cray. Why? Oh, because I heard him pronounce a silent K when he was lecturing me on store dress code.' "

Three more levels down in the dungeon, we ran into High Demon Lord Who's-His-Face. A cyclopean terror conjured from the depths of some digital netherverse.

CTRL+1 and my paladin charged into battle, sword raised, war cry ululating.

"I need this job, Milo."

"I know, Hattie." He sighed. On screen his wizard rolled his shoulders and waved his arms as he conjured a cloud of acidic gas around the boss' feet. "How's your dad?"

A calendar filled with doctors' appointments. Pill bottles lined the bathroom sink.

"Tired, mostly." Demon Lord Who's-His-Face put up a good fight, but we out-leveled him by, like, a lot. When we eventually logged out, I stayed connected to the voice chat. "Tell me you're coming to visit for spring break. I will literally kill someone if I'm left alone here."

"In the interest of keeping you out of jail and grammatically correct, you have my word." I could hear the smirk in his voice through my headset. "On the condition you introduce me to crazy Knight Manager."

The next day, Meghan scheduled me to close the coffee shop. By myself. The little Circle-Mart café wasn't exactly high traffic in the afternoons, but come four thirty and the coffee shop exploded with middle schoolers. I love a fancy coffee drink as much as the next college student, but these kids put craft brew hipsters to shame with their orders.

Extra hot double shot hazelnut mochas. Double blended frappes with whipped almond soy cream. Cinnamon chai lattes in mugs, not cups. Coffee. Coffee. Coffee. And cheesecakes. Cookies. Bars of chocolate. Screaming their orders. Screaming at each other. Screaming into their phones.

I was never gonna mock education majors ever again.

Darren was scarce my whole shift, but I hadn't figured out how to hook him up with Milo anyway. Honestly, I wasn't even 100% certain Darren liked guys, and how did I broach that subject without getting sued? I still didn't know the answer at the end of the night, when I went to go count out my register drawer.

The money room was in the back, between the employee bathroom and Phil's office. It had a big security door made of metal and a lock that required both a combination and a key. I knocked softly, register drawer tucked between my arm and hip. There was a beep, a metal whirr, and then a tidal wave of hostile noise.

"...DON'T CARE HOW YOU FIX IT." I jumped out of the way as Phil barreled out of the money room. The store manager was an enraged silverback gorilla yelling into a cell phone. "YOUR NUMBERS ARE TANKING, AND MS. SATURNINA IS BREATHING DOWN MY NECK. YOU DO *NOT* WANT CORPORATE TO CATCH YOU SLACKING! COMPRENDE?"

Phil stormed his way into his office, slammed the door, and pulled the blinds like a police chief in an action movie.

Darren waved me into the money room. It was the size of a handicapped bathroom stall. There was a single desk built into the wall, a safe, a security monitor, one of those automatic money counters, and stacks of empty register tills.

"What was all that?" I took the empty seat and began counting my drawer, separating the sweaty bills into piles of ones, fives, and twenties.

"Meghan," Darren said. "The café's profits are bleeding out all over the place."

Circle-Mart's in-store café was one of the first establishments to sell espressos to the ageing yuppies in town. I remembered back in high school, before the big box stores took over this area, you could either pop into Circle-Mart for your latte or drive thirty more minutes into the city.

Nowadays, there are four Seattle Gold stand-alone stores within spitting distance. And they have drive-throughs. Even with our afternoon rush, we couldn't compete.

I say as much and Darren agrees, even laughs as he double-checks my till.

Maybe I made up the silent "K". God knows I'd look for any excuse to make this dumb job interesting.

Small talk would redeem me. I'm charming as fuck when I talk small. So I said, "How's our little sub-par café supposed to compete?"

And he said, "I see you're overflowing with company pride."

And I thought, *Yeah, this is going well.* All I had to do was bring the conversation around to Milo. Slip Darren his number. Bam. Best friend achievement unlocked.

But then Darren said, "I'm not talking about those kinds of profits, though." And I knew, I *knew* I should let that comment slide.

But instead I said, "Huh?"

"Prophets. The barista priests." Darren leaned in close. "They're at war with each other. If Circle-Mart loses any more meta-ground on the coffee front, corporate could lose the entire store to a rival faction, and then where will we be?"

"Damned if I know," I said under my breath.

"Exactly!" Darren said.

In the parking lot, after lock up, with everyone gone and the windows dark, a quiet kind of calm settled over the shopping plaza. During the day, this place was a battlefield. Whoever designed the roads around here had a head for neither aesthetics nor logistics. Traffic jams were frequent, and the paths between stores were vertigo-inducing loops. It only got worse over the years as the big boxes spread out, flattening hills to make room for more super stores.

But at that moment in the middle of March, for two whole seconds, the place seemed sorta … indescribably perfect. Maybe I was just fried after my shift, but when I closed my eyes, I could hear a low humming buzz of energy coursing across the blacktop.

It was pushing midnight, and I was losing an argument with my dad's old sedan. The only things holding the car together were rust and crusted bird shit.

Darren rapped on my window. "Problem?"

He wore a light sports coat and a long scarf. Like he'd stepped out of a BBC drama. Milo would fall so hard for this guy if he saw him standing out there in the wind and moody parking lot lights.

Don't worry, Milo, I thought to myself as I opened the door and got out of the car. *Crazy or not, momma's still gonna get that for you.*

But before I could start into my wingman spiel, I spotted Meghan and three other Circle-Mart baristas tromping down the center of the parking lot. They made a beeline for a clump of Seattle Gold employees on the other side of the plaza.

"The heck?" I said, and moved around to the front of the car for a better look. "When did things go all West Side Story?"

Meghan and her gang stopped about fifteen feet away from the Seattle Gold crew. Then she threw a punch at the open air, but still POW. On the other side of the lot, one of the rival baristas went down.

She must have thrown a rock. Maybe one of those tiny little espresso mugs, a demitasse.

Whatever. With one man down, it was an all out brawl.

You couldn't blame me for wanting to laugh. I mean, a bunch of coffee nerds having some sort of slap fight turf war?

One of the Circle-Mart barista's fell back from the group. He was a skinny kid with long hair and a peach fuzz goatee. Jeremy, maybe? I hadn't learned everyone's name yet. Anyway, Maybe Jeremy takes this stance that I vaguely I recognized: feet spread, hips angled, arms and shoulders rolling in opposite directions.

At first I thought he was channeling some sorta Keanu Reeves "I know kung fu" shit, but then the air crackled and spit. Just like Milo's—no, couldn't be.

Writhing tentacles of purple/green electricity erupted out of Maybe Jeremy's back, shot down his arms, and tore through the Seattle Gold crew.

This kid was a fucking DPS wizard.

"The fucking fuck!?" I ducked behind the front bumper. The sharp smell of ozone stabbed at my nose. "Are you kidding me?"

The parking lot trembled beneath me, rumbling as Meghan raised her hands to the sky. She drew the night around her as a wave of screeching bats swooped down, screaming and clawing at everything in their path.

Darren threw himself behind the bumper with me. Between the localized earthquake and the flock of flying rats, the noise consumed my world.

"FUCK?!" Years of philosophy courses taught me to squeeze every ounce of connotation from short pithy phrases.

"Told you!" Darren yelled over the noise. A few bolts of conjured lightning streaked across the lot. Neo-hippies and aging hipsters were tossed left and right by tentacled limbs. "The barista priests are getting desperate. This is their last chance to regain lost ground."

"But," I stammered. "Magic? All that stuff you were saying earlier. It's all ... real?"

"Of course it's real." Darren looked confused and then horrified. "You must have thought I was a lunatic."

I sat in the lunatic's apartment. If a one-room, ten-by-ten box could be called such a thing without a serious application of air quotes.

The walls were bare save for some computer printouts tacked up above the bed. A few cardboard boxes served as end tables. There were thick leather tomes that looked like they came off the set of *Buffy the Vampire Slayer*, and about twenty or thirty photocopied applications to retail stores stuck between the pages.

The only place to sit was his mattress, so we were close. He smelled like sweat and aftershave.

"You don't know anything about The Struggle?" He pulled up his sleeve and showed me his bicep. He had a keyhole tattoo, eerily similar to my birthmark: deep cobalt blue with intricate scroll work along the edges.

It had only been thirty minutes since the showdown in the parking lot, and my head was still swimming with tentacle-summoning coffee slingers. "Pretend I walked into the movie halfway through. Explain me the plot?"

Darren frowned, probably trying to judge if I was playing dumb or, you know, just dumb. Eventually he pulled down a satellite photo from the wall. I'd never bothered googling Circle-Mart's shopping plaza before. From above, the roads looped and crossed one another in patterns ripped from a magical girl anime. It looked like a giant magical seal, and the keystone in the center of the whole thing: good old Circle-Mart.

"Thumbnail summary?" Darren said. "Ley lines cover the globe, connecting nodes of magical power. Outsiders, demons if you want, try to take advantage of the places where these lines cross." He looked at me. "Back in the old days, shaman watched over these spots, but they're all gone now, so we make do with what we have."

"And what do we have?" I asked, looking at the photo. "Shopping malls? They're what, protective talismans?"

"They're the epitome of consumer culture," Darren said. "They're horrible blights on the environment. But malls are better than hordes of tentacled demon beasts crawling up out of the ass-crack of creation."

I pulled out my phone and started browsing.

"You're not tweeting this are you?" Darren asked.

"I'm looking for a new job."

"Even if you're not a Knight," he said, a hint of desperation in his voice, "you can't just walk away from all this."

"At-will employee," I said, pointing to myself. "Means I can quit any time I want. As cool as it would look on a resume, guarding the world against cosmic horrors is not worth $7.25 an hour. Besides, you've got the coffee bean wizards."

"No," Darren said. "It's just us."

He moved across the room to his mini-fridge and started deboning a chicken. There were little glass vials in the fridge full of powders and liquids I couldn't identify.

"The Priests are no more benevolent than any of the other factions, but their war keeps The Managers of Ephriel distracted, and that means The Managers don't notice the Hidden Lifters, who keep the supplies of arcane detritus low. There are hundreds of different sects and schisms, all vying for control of the Circle-Mart's node. The Knight Shift, we keep the balance. Make sure no one group gets the upper hand."

"You're not even trying to win?"

"I'm trying to keep everything from falling apart. It's … it's a battle to maintain normalcy."

Maintaining normalcy? I thought of the pill bottles lined up along dad's sink. I needed a job, and a two-week black mark would not help me get another one.

"Meghan lost half her coven in that brawl in the parking lot," Darren said. "Corporate's ready to insert Ephriel agents into the staff. If that happens, we'll be overwhelmed by regional managers without anyone to offset their dark rituals."

"How do you know I'm not one of these corporate double agents?"

"At this point, I don't have a choice but to trust you," Darren said. "Please, Hattie. I need your help."

After Darren's apartment, I sat in my car (which still wouldn't start) and watched delivery truck drivers smoke cigars as they waited for the early morning stock crews. What faction did these guys belong to? The Fraternal Order of Hermes? The Esoteric Congress of the Open Road?

When Mom heard I had dropped out of college to take care of Dad, she'd sent me a text, the first one in years: He's not your responsibility.

I stared at that message as the sun rose. Responsibility. This "Struggle" Darren talked about, it wasn't my responsibility. Wasn't my fight.

A battle to maintain normalcy.

My phone's screen displayed a flashing red battery. Less than five percent left.

I scrolled through my contacts and tapped Milo's icon.

"*This* is your life and death favor?" Milo said from behind the Circle-Mart Café counter. He'd hauled his ass across the state overnight to don the blue apron of a Circle-Mart barista.

"You're the only coffee snob I could trust. Besides," I said, glancing over my shoulder. "He thinks you're cute."

"Really?" Milo had a full beard and was almost old enough to rent cars, but when his face lit up, he looked like a twinkie teenager.

Darren was down near the front of the store, arguing with Phil. Probably over Milo's credentials.

With Meghan in traction, Darren became the de facto café manager. He'd slipped Milo into the Circle-Mart computer system this morning, before Phil could veto anything.

The store manager stormed off towards the back and Darren pulled me aside, leaving Milo to grind a bag of coffee and set out the pastries.

"Your friend bought us a day or two," Darren said. "Phil's got a mountain of paperwork now."

"In the meanwhile, we what?"

Darren passed me box of salt and a blue plastic shopping bag full of juju pouches. "Strengthen the wards," he said. "The Managers of Ephriel will align the merchandise in an anti-Cartesian pattern. To counter that, we need to prepare dimensional syncs and draw out the ambient energies."

"You said some words there." I shook the box of salt. "I'm pretty sure they made sense to one of us."

"I wrote out instructions." He handed me a diagram.

"Shui the Feng," I said. "Got it."

"You're sure he can handle this?"

"Relax," I told Darren. "Milo and I have been taking down big bads for years. We know what we're doing."

Darren looked at Milo and give him a nod. Milo promptly dropped the bag of beans he was grinding, scattering raw coffee across the floor. He almost slipped on the slick little legumes when he went for a broom.

I caught Milo's attention, pointed at Darren, and gave him a thumbs-up.

Darren checked his watch. "Don't forget to clock in."

NOW

Phil erupted from his spot on the floor, shooting upward in a swarm of cockroaches. The bugs buzzed and whirred. They coalesced into a man. A bug man. A huge hulk, lumbering towards me.

I fumbled with the box of salt and ended up tossing the whole thing at Phil.

It bounced off the bug body and spilled a meager line at the manager's feet. There was some slight sizzling as he stepped on the sodium, but not enough to keep him away from me.

This wasn't part of the plan. Being attacked by a manager-turned-bug demon wasn't even on the same continent as the plan. We were just going to delay. Keep the wards fresh and tie Phil's hands with paperwork while we recruited our own people into the café.

Phil rammed into me. You wouldn't think a swarm of bugs would have much mass behind them.

You'd be wrong.

He wrapped his beefy arms around my waist and squeezed the air out of my lungs.

The buzzing took on a hypnotic quality, like listening to a white noise machine. It could have just been a lack of oxygen, but I thought I heard voices between the bug noises: sharp chanting, over and over.

Ms. Saturnina is coming for a surprise inspection. Ms. Saturnina is coming for a surprise inspection. Inspection. Inspection. She comes. SHE ARRIVES!

The bugs that made up Phil's head drew back, parting like a velvet curtain of chitin. I swear to you, between the curtains, I could see a woman walking down a long twisting tunnel.

Her legs were too long. Her fingers too many. One moment she had a tail. The next wings. The next as many mouths as there were insects crawling over my skin. Ms. Saturnina, the district manager.

Yes, all of this was happening inside Phil's head. Like physically inside his cranium. Some sort of transdimensional, cross-realm bullshit. I don't know. I just started working here last week.

Phil squeezed me again and the last of my breath left my body. I was suffocating. Passing out, too. Probably (hopefully) hallucinating.

Ms. Saturnina stopped halfway down the head-tunnel. She was small enough to fit in there, but I got the feeling she was actually very, very large. As it was, she looked like a squat woman in an off-the-rack pantsuit. All around her, the tunnel twisted, warping into tubes of flesh with eyes and mouths.

When Saturnina looked at me, her eyes became serpents. Scaly black anacondas, digesting someone's dog.

"Harriet Daniels," Saturnina said my name, and for two heartbeats that stretched across eternity, I panicked. How did she know my name? How did this thing that can walk in the spaces between worlds know I existed?

"Span of employment 1.5 weeks. Position, store associate. Education history: high school diploma, partial bachelors of arts degree in philosophy. Previous employment history: summer camp counselor, 2.5 months."

She … it … whatever was reading from some extra-dimensional employee file.

"Family medical history includes numerous instances of cancer of the thyroid, lymph nodes, breasts, and ovaries." So much for doctor-patient confidentiality. "Most likely due to bloodline connection to the Keystone. Prognostication: employed with Circle-Mart for 2.5 years before termination."

WHAT?!

"Of employment."

Oh.

She looked at me with those unblinking anaconda eyes. "Open the way, gatekeeper."

This was the part where the demon offered me power in exchange for my soul. Maybe even a cure for my dad. And that's when I got it: This was what it meant to be a member of the Knight Shift. We stood on the threshold and spat in the face of dark gods.

Hell, I wasn't standing on the threshold. I *was* the fucking threshold!

"No," Saturnina said in a voice like dead leaves. "No offers. No exchanges. Open the door."

"Or what?"

"Or you're fired."

Just like that.

Saturnina's voice was so flat and deadpan that I could tell she didn't give two shits about my newly discovered status as humanity's last line of defense. She was the personification of an indifferent corporate entity. She had a goal and she'd achieve it; how was just a constantly shifting variable in her massive calculations of profit and loss.

I wasn't a threshold to her. I was a decimal point.

"Fine," I said. A draft started to emanate from my lower back. I don't know how I summoned the portal (I was operating on dream-logic here). To Saturnina, I was just cog. "Welcome to Circle-Mart. How may we help you?"

"You LET her in?!?" Darren was tangling with a cornucopia of tentacles. They wrapped around his midsection, thrashing him about the back room. He hacked through them with a Scherl & Jackson campfire axe.

"I have a plan!" I said, ducking a gash in reality full of sharp teeth.

A chunk of tentacle the size of a small child splurched onto the floor in front of me, cut from its core by Darren's axe. The Knight Shifter dropped down after it, covered in extradimensional muck. "Your plan was to invite that thing into our world?"

I groaned, grabbed hold of Darren's belt loops, and

dragged him into the money room. With the door slammed shut and the electronic locks in place, it was practically a fallout shelter.

"Gimme your phone," I said, holding out my hand.

Darren passed his over. "Why?"

"Because I left mine charging behind the café counter." I sent off a text.

Milo replied almost instantly: You're sure?!?! (@_@)

I replied: YES. >:|

Moments later, Milo's voice came over the store intercom. "Ms. Saturnina, you're needed at the café. Ms. Saturnina, you're needed at the café." And then he hung up with an audible clatter-click that echoed across the store.

"What good will—"

I fluttered my hand and stuck my fingers into Darren's mouth, shutting him up.

From outside, the sounds of a thrashing outer god slowed, then stopped. There was a whooshing noise as air filled empty space. We watched on the security camera as Ms. Saturnina shrank from an ever-expanding tentacled horror into a stocky corporate middle manager. Until the cult of Ephriel had complete control of the Circle-Mart node, Ms. Saturnina was a manager first and an elder goddess second.

She left the back room a disaster zone. Gallon bottles of floor cleaner dripped down the walls. Broken mops and overturned tables lay strewn about like picnic tables in Tornado Alley. There was even a single broken cash register spinning on one corner. It wobbled, then tipped over with a solid crash.

Darren mumbled something into my fingers.

I ignored him, picked up the store phone, and dialed 9-0 for the intercom system. "Attention, Circle-Mart shoppers. For the next fifteen minutes, super double mocha brownie frappes are buy one get one in the café."

To Darren, I said, "It's four thirty."

SIXTEEN MINUTES LATER

Ms. Saturnina used her transdimensional insubstantiality to curled herself into an impossibly tight ball underneath the Circle-Mart coffee bar. Fat globs of frappé mix dripped from every inch of her pantsuit, and her hair had become a rat king of stirring straws and demitasse spoons. On the other side of the counter, hordes of gibbering twelve-year-olds clamored for blended ice coffees. They were all fresh out of school and jonesing for a sugary caffeine fix.

"Nice work," Darren admitted as he placed a series of votive candles from housewares in a circle around Saturnina.

"Doubleskinnylightwhip," Ms. Saturnina chanted to herself. Over and over. The snakes that lived in her eyes had returned, but they churned and shivered as if in shock. "Doubleskinnylightwhip."

Suddenly Saturnina grabbed Darren by the shoulders. *"What in the nine hells is a mochachino?!"*

Darren gently pushed her hands away and recited some Latin to banish the outer manager back to whence she came.

Meanwhile, Milo and I dealt with the drink orders. I handed over a dripping frappé to a screaming kid in a private school uniform.

"Is every day like this?" Milo asked. He gave the last customer his change, but spared a glance beneath the bar to watch Saturnina wink out of our existence. Darren's eyes met Milo's and they lingered on each other for a few moments. They shared a shy smile between them.

Achievement Unlocked: Wingman Hookup.

Darren stood. "You should be here for Black Friday," he said.

I laughed.

Milo laughed.

Darren didn't.

"No, seriously," he said. "You're both on the schedule."

FORCED LABOR

by Peter Rawlik

Toussaint Delapore sat in the chairman's office and looked out over Delapore Chemical and the city of Bolton, Massachusetts beyond. The factory was his now, he had spent most of the afternoon with lawyers and board members making sure of that. He had signed his name to every piece of paper that they put in front of him; he had signed his name until his hand had begun to cramp. Now it was all over, and everything he could see outside his window belonged to him. Suddenly he was no longer the second-rate houngan of the Bayou d'Ys south of New Orleans, now he was a rich industrialist like Rockefeller or Ford. Well, maybe not *that* rich, but there was money in the bank, a house on the hill, and the factory that was stretched out below him. It had been meant to go to his cousin, but Alfred had died in the Great War, and the old man who had created all this had died in a British madhouse. Toussaint had been the only living heir, even if his complexion was a bit darker than the board and their lawyers would have liked.

There had been looks, of course, and whispers too, mostly between a number of floor managers who weren't as skilled at hiding their bigotry as their superiors. It made Toussaint's blood boil, as had his introduction to the factory staff. It wasn't just that every face he looked at was white, but that there were so many children as well, and so little safety equipment. The managers all walked around with rubberized gloves and aprons, and goggles, but the workers only had their own clothes and rags to protect them. The conditions were deplorable and they all knew it. There was a national movement to change such things, a constitutional amendment barring industrial labor by children had been written, but too few states had acted to ratify it, and it was languishing in limbo. Child labor was just too profitable. It would take a serious change in the psyche of America to keep children out of the factories, and that just wasn't in the cards right now. But while he couldn't change what the rest of America did, he could change what happened in his own factory. He would start tomorrow. There would be complaints about the loss of profits for sure. Change, even for the better, was never easy. Tomorrow would be a good day. He mumbled a prayer to Dhamballah, a sing-song mantra that always brought him comfort, packed up his things and left his new office, heading to the first night in his new home.

As he entered the hallway he saw that he wasn't alone. "Grandmother," he said to the woman who was pushing a mop back and forth across the wooden floor. She was an ancient thing; her brown skin had grown thin and still bore the thick black scars that told Toussaint that she had frequently felt the lash of a slave master. Hers was the first familiarly shaded face that he had seen in days. "Grandmother, aren't you too old to be cleaning? Shouldn't you be at home taking care of your grandchildren?"

She looked up and smiled a gap-toothed smile. Her eyes were sunken, but even so Toussaint could see the pale shadows that hinted at cataracts. There were scars on her face too, but not from the whip, from a branding iron. "I've no grandchildren to take care of, and no children no more neither." Her accent placed her origin someplace in Mississippi.

"I'm sorry," he touched her hand, in an attempt to comfort her. "Was it the flood?"

The old woman shook her head in the highly exaggerated manner. "No sir. The '27 Flood took all we had, but my daughter Chloe and her husband Birmingham both lived through the rising waters. We came north looking for work. And we found it, Chloe at the laundry, and Birmingham worked nights at the steam plant down by the river. It was good work too, we found a room to rent and a shop that sold good food at fair prices, tripe, and greens, and pigs feet. We had a good life and Chloe and Birmingham started talking 'bout having a baby." She paused and wiped her eyes. "But six months ago Birmingham didn't come home and the men at the plant didn't know where he was, all they knew was that he owed money at the company store. Sure enough his name was there in the ledger. Birmingham had charged more than two hundred dollars. Chloe and I didn't have enough to pay it back, and then they offered Chloe work, Birmingham's job, and she had no choice but to take it." She paused, tears welling up in those big puffy eyes. "Then one morning last month Chloe don't come home either. I go down to the factory and they tell me Chloe hadn't shown up for work that night. They tell me Birmingham's debt is gone, Chloe done paid it off, and ifin I want to I can come work at the steam plant. They offered me good wages too. Too good for an old woman like me. Old Tata can't read, but she ain't dumb. Nossir. I don't work at the plant, I work here. I do honest work, cleaning. And I stay far away from the steam plant."

"Surely the police," but Toussaint never finished that sentence.

"The police!" She said the word with emphasis on the first syllable—POE-lease. "They's all ex-Pinks, strikebreakers. They ain't here to protect the workers, they here to make sure to protect the bosses and the factories. They don't give no care to factory workers, least of all an old black woman and her kin."

Toussaint sighed in frustration. It wasn't the first time he had heard such things. A priest, regardless of faith, often becomes a sounding board for the miseries of those that he ministered to, and in his role as houngan he had heard his fair share. Old Tata was just another victim of a system that let wealthy industrialists hire private security forces or even the police to enforce their will. What men couldn't do through negotiation or fair compensation, they achieved through the liberal application of muscle. It didn't surprise him, not one bit, it was the way of the world—but here, in Bolton, he was no longer powerless to act against it.

He took her hand and tried to comfort. "I am new here Grandmother, I know neither the city nor its players. I can't promise you any results, but I assure you I will personally investigate what has happened to your daughter and her husband." The old woman's dull eyes sparkled as best they could, but she said nothing and tried her best to get back to work as her new employer left the building with a strange determination. He was reciting a poem as he went.

Old Tata didn't recognize the lines of verse, but they still gave her chills down her spine. She crossed herself and whispered a little prayer to the Black Madonna asking for protection.

They stole little Bridget
For seven years long;
When she came down again
Her friends were all gone.
They took her lightly back,
Between the night and morrow,
They thought that she was fast asleep,
But she was dead with sorrow.

Out on the streets of Bolton the winds blew dry leaves into rustling spirals. The roads were long deserted and the street lamps crackled as electric current waxed and waned along uncertain cables. A fat moon hung in a cloudless sky illuminating the dozens of smokestacks that rose up from the city like spires burning offerings to the new god of industry and labor. Those towers were silent now, the belching hiss of smoke and ash had ceased for the day, and would remain so until a new shift began at dawn. Only a single chimney still poured forth a discharge, and this Toussaint knew to be not smoke or chemical ash, but rather water vapor used to turn the great steam engine that supplied power and light to the factories and streets that made up the vast labyrinth that was the city of Bolton. The steam plume rose into the sky dissipating into the night, but where the one chimney was the source of an unending stream of gaseous vapor, its twin, the chimney that handled the smoke from the burning of coal and other combustibles, that smokestack had no discharge, and that alone would have drawn his attention. How could the factory be making steam without burning something?

Perplexed, perhaps by the conundrum of steam without heat, but also by the tale that Old Tata had told, and the promise he had made, Toussaint turned off the road that would take him to his new home, and instead meandered purposefully toward the steam plant. He walked down a street built into a sloping hill, something that was not common in the bayous or New Orleans. He made his way past alleyways and doors, gates and roundabouts that looked as old as anything he had seen in St. Augustine or Havana, but he knew that all of that was illusion. The city had been built in the eighteenth century; the rapid state of decay and premature age had been brought about by overuse, disrepair, and the perpetual ash fall that regularly blanketed the tiny metropolis. Bolton wasn't old, it was merely abused, like a fresh woman in a house of ill repute.

The walk took longer than he expected, but soon he was wandering the streets in the shadows of the immense complex and the towering stacks. There was an audible drone in the air, an intense hum that made his teeth ache. It was more intense at one end of the building than the other, and Toussaint linked it to the action of the giant pumps that drew water in from the river to feed the steam engine.

"No one ever comes out." Toussaint was startled. He turned his gaze away from the twelve-foot-tall cast iron fence that encircled the property and toward the source of the voice. There was an old man sitting on the wall that ran along a portion of the river. He had a fishing rod in his hand. He spoke in a matter of fact manner. He didn't even bother to look at Toussaint, he just kept staring out at the black river as it rolled by.

"I beg your pardon?"

The old man finally turned to look at the newly minted businessman. "I come here every day. Weeks now. Ever since they let me out of the hospital. I live with my son; he has a house over on Elm Street. Used to work as a bookkeeper for the Shattuck's, now he's a scheduler for a chemical plant." He paused and sighed. "Doesn't seem like a proper job for a working man. I worked in the mill until my accident, and now I fish. I may not be able to run a cotton picker anymore, but I can still put food on the table." He began reeling his line in.

"You said that nobody ever comes out. What did you mean?"

"The steam plant. I come here every day. Nobody ever comes out. Nobody ever goes in. Look at the gates. Chained shut, with garbage accumulated all around the bottom. They ain't been swung open in weeks." He coughed a little. "It's a queer thing, a place like that with nobody going in to take care of it."

He stumbled to his feet, grasping his tackle in the crook of his arm and revealing that his left hand was a mangled bit of broken flesh. He tottered from the bank of the river to just a few feet from Toussaint. "They promised us a new age of industry. Great machines to do what hundreds of men couldn't. They never bothered to mention that eventually the machines wouldn't need men at all!" The curmudgeon never bothered to wait for an answer, he just turned and limped down the street muttering to himself about the unfairness of it all. "Men need to work," Toussaint heard him say. "They needs to be part of something, to feel like they matter." The night streets swallowed him up, but Toussaint could still hear him, his voice a faint whisper, but in a moment even that was gone, lost in the darkness.

There was a queer splashing coming from where the man had been sitting and Toussaint took a step and cast an eye over the embankment. There was a quick and sudden movement, and something dark and slick slipped from the mud and into the saffron-shaded foam that floated at the edge, clinging to the banks. It was too cold for turtles or frogs, and surely the old man hadn't left a fish behind. He thought back to the Allingham poem he had been reciting earlier. This time the lines made him shudder.

Down along the rocky shore
Some make their home,
They live on crispy pancakes
Of yellow tide-foam.

He walked around the steam plant property twice, looking for an easy way in, but the fence was in good repair and the gates were all sealed with heavy chains and oversized locks. It wasn't that he was averse to doing a little work to get in—on the contrary, in his youth he had been rather skilled at second-story work—but it helped, when things went wrong, to know the layout, the escape routes and the obstacles in the way of your retreat. And in his experience, things went sideways more often than not.

He found a tree with branches that overhung a supporting wall and with a bit of a run he was up the trunk and over the fence with only a muffled thump to give himself away. It was only after he was sure that his entrance had gone unobserved that he let his breathing resume. But even this made him uncomfortable. The place was damned odd. Locked up tight and obviously up to something, but not a single watchman patrolling the grounds. If the steam plant was holding people against their will, they were very confident in their security.

Inside the fence, the vibration was stronger, and if he held still he could see the leaves scattered across the lawn were vibrating, but it wasn't a constant drone as he had suspected, there was a rhythm to it. It was fast, but you could see the gathered detritus shudder. He placed a hand to the cold earth and let the tempo travel up his arm. It was so fast, as if a small bird's heart was beating, trapped down there in the grasp of some titanic loa, perhaps Ti Malice. Driven on he darted forward and into the shadows of the building. He skulked along the wall like a rat, low, fast, and skittish. Inching his way through shadows and then darting through the irregular patches of cool light, he slowly and carefully made his way to a door. Not the main door, but a side door, one that might have gone unnoticed, or if forced would not be immediately reported.

With a cautious grip he turned the handle and was pleasantly surprised when the latch turned and the door popped free of its frame. His pleasure rapidly turned to disgust as a hot, fetid odor assaulted his senses. It was a sickening smell, like the bayou at low tide, and an abattoir at the end of a summer day, and the cesspool in the basement of his aunt's house outside Havana. All these long-buried memories and images and feelings welled up out of the depths of his psyche and flooded his mind. He gagged. He felt something well up from his stomach and he swallowed it back down, but the acid lingered and burned in the back of his throat. He could even see the light of the moon waver in the miasma that leaked out of the gap.

With the stench and heat came a sound. A deep throaty rumble as if Agou L'Ephant—the Elephant loa—was breathing. It took him a few seconds to realize that the breathing was in time with the vibrations that were shaking the very earth itself. As repulsed as he was, Toussaint was overcome by his desire to investigate. He checked his coat and found the secret pocket that held the small Remington Derringer that was concealed there. It was small, cold, and heavy, and that felt good in his hand. It didn't have much range, but up close and personal it was deadly. Toussaint had used it more than once, to devastating effect. With his other hand he removed a large perfumed handkerchief and tied it over his mouth and nose. It not only served to conceal his identity, but the lavender scent helped mask the odor. With gun in one hand and his face concealed he stepped out of the shadows, through the great steel door, and into the bowels of Hell itself.

The cloth barely worked to ameliorate the stink, and of course the heat and humidity was nearly intolerable. Sweat began almost immediately, running down his back and collecting along the bulge of his shirt just above his belt. The thrumming beat filled his ears and made his teeth hurt even more than they had outside. He could feel it in his joints and in the long bones, and in the hollow of his chest. He moved quickly down a narrow corridor dimly lit by periodically spaced bulbs whose glow waxed and waned in time with the pneumatic pulse. He had thought that he was entering a labyrinth, but that was not the case. The hallway had no doors, no turns, nor any intersections at all. It was simply a straight, almost tunnel-like construct that sloped ever so slightly down. The comparison to a tunnel grew as he transitioned from stacked brick to rock and then finally to simply the rough-hewn earth itself. He traveled further than he thought possible, and wondered how it was that he had not yet reached the riverbank. It was only when he cast a backward glance that he realized the tunnel was not straight at all, but rather possessed a gentle, almost imperceptible dextral curve. He was spiraling down, slowly but surely, as if he was inside a titanic conch whose tenant had long since been extracted.

Down he went, down deeper into the twilight darkness. The gun led the way, even if it did tremble in his hand. With each cautious step the stink and heat grew ever greater, and that great throbbing drum beating ever louder. Everything he had ever been taught by his parents, by his brothers, by the old houngan who had taken him in, told him to turn and run. He had no responsibility here, no matter what he had promised the old woman at his office. And yet still he moved forward, drawn on by something greater than curiosity. He was a moth circling a candle, fully aware of the danger he was in as each spiral took him ever closer to the burning flame.

Without warning he burst forth from the clay-lined tunnel and into a vast chamber. He had thought he would see hordes of missing men and women enslaved to some electro-mechanical monstrosity. He had expected to see men with whips and guns on catwalks like grey-skinned Morlocks standing above enslaved

Eloi who toiled, one way or another, to produce the steam that bellowed from the towers above. But there was none of that, the tableau that presented itself below him was not the result of any anthropogenic action, but the horror was greater than anything that he had ever seen before, and he spat out a quick prayer to Ghede Doubye for protection.

The chamber before him was huge, and how such a thing could have been carved out beneath the city of Bolton without collapsing the streets or surrounding factories he could not comprehend. Dozens of electric lights, larger than Toussaint had ever seen, had been strung from the ceiling and dangled like immense fireflies caught in a spider's web of cables. Their light was dazzling, hypnotic even, and if it weren't for the terrible spectacle below he might have been lost in the lights themselves.

But the thing below, the thing that sat in a great lake of river water that rushed into the chamber through a Promethean pipe in the upper wall, that thing pulsed and throbbed like an immense bloated maggot. Its translucent skin showed the vast organs and musculature that dwelt beneath it, including the network of tubules that seemed to draw water up out of the pool, through its body, and then out of the array of tubules that stood like titanic fins on its back, but belched forth immeasurable gouts of steam. The steam drifted upward through gaps cut into the ceiling, and from his vantage point Toussaint could see the electrical turbines as they turned above. A collection of cables ran down to a small makeshift set of controls. The vents in the ceiling could be closed or opened, and there were other controls as well. Wheels and levers to open and close the inflows, and the outflow as well, a massive sluice gate that was open just a few inches.

All around the pulsating juggernaut dozens upon dozens of men and women waded in the chest-deep water, their hands massaging the skin of the cyclopean thing. And it was truly cyclopean in both senses of the word, for in the center of its scabrous head was a single carmine eye that seemed like a great lens to follow the tiny things that passed before it, tending to its every possible need. There were people rubbing lotion into its skin, others fed fruits and vegetables into its maw while yet more men cleared away a steady stream of waste from the far end. And all of them, regardless of task, seemed to have the same look on their face. These people were all enraptured. He had seen a similar look when his parishioners were being ridden by loa. They were in divine ecstasy, they were in service to their god and there could be no greater joy.

But it was not joy that Toussaint Delapore sensed in that cavernous room. No matter how joyous these people were, the overwhelming sensation, the palpable emotion that flooded his soul, was despair. He could feel it. It hung in the air like a broken heart, like the pall that falls over a church during the funeral of a child. It was a terrible thing to suffer, and not understand the source of the suffering. He flexed his hand around the gun, and once more he fell back on the poetry of Allingham.

They have kept her ever since
Deep within the lake,
On a bed of fig-leaves,
Watching till she wake.

"She's hurting," he muttered out loud to no one in particular, and as soon as he said it, he knew it to be true.

"It's the heat," a woman had come up to meet him. Toussaint was startled, but did his best to hide any reaction. She was pretty in a rustic sort of way, but bedraggled as well. Her clothes were soaked and worn, her hair unkempt, her skin was blotched red. "The water helps keep her cool, but it's not enough. We do what we can to ease her pain, but she is so much greater than we few. We're glad you've come to help us serve her."

There were tears in his eyes. He stared down at the bloated grub-like thing that floundered in the rushing waters. "What is she?" It was less of a question and more of a plea.

"Her kind are ancient, they inhabited the seas before the

whales, before even the ichthyosaurs ruled the coastal shallows. They are cryptic things, rarely rising from the abyssal ocean, and even then as you can see she would be hard to discern. Her skin is nearly translucent; it makes her almost invisible amongst the dark, rolling surf. Only when they are gravid do the females come up out of the depths and make their way up the ancient rivers to spawn their young." She paused and placed a hand on his shoulder. "She needs you, she needs us all. As the young grow they produce a terrible heat within her. That's why we built this place around her, to keep her cool, to ease her pain."

"Built it around her? But that must mean she's been here for decades." Toussaint's eyes swept around the enormity of the place. "Longer than that, perhaps."

The strange woman smiled and Toussaint could see that many of her teeth were missing. "The first colonist to settle the area found her already here and being tended by natives. They called her The River Mother; she needs no other name. She only needs to be tended to, to be kept cool while her children grow."

She was right; Toussaint could feel the need to serve clawing at the deepest recesses of his brain, like a loa coming in to mount. But there was something wrong in the feel of the spirit. It felt strange. Over the years he had been ridden by both gods and goddesses, and this one, the one clamoring to be let in, was decidedly male. "You've got it all wrong," he muttered to his strange hostess. "She doesn't need to be kept cool."

"What are you saying?" There was panic in her voice.

"It's not *her* that wants the heat!" Suddenly it all made sense, and Toussaint was sprinting down into the pool. He dropped the gun, he didn't even care, it wasn't important. He plowed through the water, splashing through the attendants, pushing them out of the way. He was making for the controls. No one tried to stop him. He doubted that any of the enraptured even knew what they were for. As he drew closer he could see that almost all of the wheels and levers were, in one way or another, corroded or in disrepair.

The equipment hadn't been used in years; it hadn't even

been properly maintained. As he put his hands on the chains a few of the links groaned as they rust that mired them broke free. It took a good amount of his weight to set the chain in motion around the pulleys, but as soon as he got them moving the grates above his head swung shut. Almost immediately he could see the great clouds of steam begin to accumulate in the ceiling. Next he turned to the wheel that controlled the water source. It too was connected to its mechanism by a great chain, which was likewise encrusted with rust. The gear creaked as he pushed against it, but with each arc of gain the water flowing into the cavern lessened until finally it became little more than a trickle.

It was when the flow of water ceased that the enraptured began to react. At first it was just a moaning, but that quickly grew to a shrill panic and then finally a scream of abject terror. They stood there in the pool screaming as the water level slowly dropped and the steam began to work its way down from above. With a swift kick Toussaint knocked the other mechanism into motion. The sluice gates opened wide, and with a rushing sound the pool began to drain. That appeared to be the last straw, and the dozens of servants of the River Mother moved forward towards Toussaint's position.

The time for being delicate was over, and Toussaint needed to make sure that what he had done was not undone. With more force than was prudent, he wrenched each of the corrupted wheels to the furthest they could be turned. Then he wrenched them some more, making sure they were jammed. The approaching horde shuffling through the draining waters grew ever closer, oblivious to the impact the falling waters were having on their vermiform Madonna.

The great beast was changing colors, from a pale translucence to a violent, almost explosive red. Her limbs, dozens of flipper-like things, were flailing about uselessly. On her back the spouts ceased to belch forth steam and instead began to wilt to either side. There was a terrible tearing sound, like fabric ripping apart, but it was so tremendously loud that the source itself must have been of immense size. The bulk of the thing shuddered and trembled, there was a terrible keening cry that hurt his ears, but what was exactly happening was blocked by the hordes of her servants.

He slowly backed away, leading his pursuers further and further from the receding pool. They were marching forward, pressing ever closer to their quarry, and to themselves. They were like ants, crawling over each other, jostling each other, not as dozens of individuals, but as a single organism, with a single-minded purpose. They came closer and closer and were within an arm's length of him when the tearing noise ceased, and the twittering began. And with that, the slaves of the River Mother collapsed.

It was over their convulsing bodies that Toussaint watched the children of the River Mother explode forth from her pulsating womb. They were crab-like things, armored and clawed, but the size of dogs. They swarmed out by the dozens, skittering across the body of their mother, their claws clacking against each other as they scrambled toward the pool, toward the water that was now rushing out of the chamber. In his mind Toussaint could only hear a single phrase being screamed over and over again.

Get out. Get out. Get out. Get OUT!

The others could hear it too, for they rose to their feet and began running for the tunnel that had brought Toussaint down into the chamber. They ran one way and their slavers, the cancerous children of the River Mother, ran the other. As one group ran up, the other followed the pipes down. Toussaint helped a few of the slaves to their feet and sent them on their way, then joined them himself. Like Lot, he cast a single glance backward, and saw the logjam of creatures swarming the sluice gate, struggling against each other to find an exit. And then their mother rose up, free from the mass of them, free from their enslavement. She wavered there in the air, towering over them like a titanic snake, and then she fell. Her bulk cracked the gate wide open and she slithered through into the chasm below. In her wake she left dozens of her own children as shattered corpses. Toussaint could feel the very earth shake as she burrowed through it, and all around him masonry and equipment began to tumble free from the walls.

The lights in the tunnel flickered as cables stretched and snapped. Toussaint screamed at those in front of him to run, but there was only so much room. The tunnel was simply too narrow for the masses to move any quicker through. No matter how fast they ran, it wasn't fast enough, and the tunnel began to collapse around them. He clawed his way forward, desperate to survive, but he could gain little ground. The crowd surged forward, and he was like a boat tossed on a human wave. When he suddenly popped free and tumbled to the ground, the moon shining above him, he began to laugh in joy. The others—those others that had survived—merely stared at him and thought him mad.

In the weeks that followed, investigators found more than a dozen corpses amongst the rubble of the collapsed buildings. Most of the bodies were easily identified as foremen and shift supervisors. They had all been older men, unaccustomed to manual labor. They'd died of exhaustion, worked to death it seemed, and their bodies had been left where they'd fallen. It made no sense to the investigators, but it made perfect sense to Toussaint Delapore: The River Mother and her children were nearly immortal, they had no concept of old age or death, and no concept of human decency either.

Which is, he supposed, what had started the whole thing to begin with. Somebody ages ago coming across the River Mother and helping her, being enslaved by some kind of empathic charm. Perhaps at first, it had been the River Mother, but some time along the ages the children took over. The children reached out and enslaved people—it must have been hundreds of thousands over the centuries—to keep their mother cool, to keep her from giving birth, to keep them comfortable inside her womb, and safe from the outside world. It was a terrible thing to force somebody to work against their will, but infants are like that, and Toussaint wasn't sure who was the greater victim, the people or the River Mother herself.

As for Old Tata, Toussaint never saw her again. He did go by the address listed in her employment file, but the landlord said she had vanished in the middle of the night to avoid paying the rent. Toussaint paid her delinquent bills and left it at that. He thought it was over.

About a year later he received a small envelope with no return address, but bearing the postmark of Perfection, Nevada. Inside there was no letter, only a photograph of a couple and their newborn child. Behind them stood an old black woman that Toussaint thought looked like Old Tata. The words "The Brown Family" were written on the back.

Toussaint thought they looked happy.

THE SHADOWS LENGTHEN
IN THE CLOSE

by Ethan Gibney

The coffee was mediocre. This is not to say it was bad. It was perfectly functional. It was not the greatest coffee I'd ever had; that was made by Tish, the woman who agreed to make me her wife. Nor was it the worst; at least it came from a new machine.

Prior to the new machine, my employer only supplied a coffee pot that sat on a single burner which ran too hot. The thing smelled like burned rubber (even when we weren't using it), and tasted like the grounds had been steeped in diesel. We tried using new blends, we ran boiling vinegar through, tried "industry standard" cleaners, and one of our number even attempted to outright destroy the machine, but we stopped him—if it were killed, there was no guarantee the company would buy a new one. Hideous coffee was better than none. Arguably.

Then, the changeover occurred: after much hemming and hawing from the owner, our company was bought out. In only a few weeks, the logos on the walls had changed, and the name outside the manager's office changed to *Mr. Thomas Chambers.* Instead of working for S-Tech, we now worked for Stellar Technologies, wholly owned subsidiary of Haste Industries.

Our new boss was introduced to us by way of a meeting in the break room. All twelve employees gathered. I don't know that any of us noticed that the old coffee pot was gone.

The new boss entered, escorted by Mr. Regis, our contact with the new owners. Mr. Regis wore a black three-piece suit of fine material, with a yellow damask tie. He introduced Mr. Chambers, a round white man with a salesman's smile that never seemed to be far from his lips. He dressed comfortably—not

like a "boss" boss, but like an approachable leader. Rather than
a clean suit, he wore a nice (but not too nice) button shirt, and
kept his tie (yellow, like Mr. Regis's) pulled slightly away from
his neck. Before he spoke a word, a ripple of applause moved
through the whole room, though I can't recall any particular
reason for it.

"Thank you," he said, with a voice that sounded like its res-
onance came from deep in the stomach. "I'm excited to work
with you. I could give you my work history but, frankly, that's
boring, and I'm much more interested in each of you. What I'd
like to do now is go around the room and really get to know
each of you, one-on-one. It may take a while, and that's alright."
There were murmurs here—such a statement from the prior
manager would have been considered sacrilege. The idea that
something other than productivity could be emphasized was a
cosmic concept, simply unknowable.

"First, though," he said, and moved over to where the old
coffee pot had been. In its place was a tall structure, draped
with golden cloth that shimmered, just slightly, when it shifted.
He grabbed the cloth. "I want to make it clear that while I'm
here, my goal is to make us all happier, so that we can all work
really well together. So, I give you all, a new breath of life!"

In one motion, he revealed the new coffee machine. It was
a tall model, the kind that mixed hot water with a coffee concentrate, so that the coffee would be just about instant. I don't
think it was a brand-new model. It was well-cared-for, certainly,
but the way it stood, and a slight beating about the edges,
seemed to show that we were by no means the machine's first
customers. Not that anybody cared. Even used, the machine
earned a round of cheers.

"There are three roasts," he said, "A full city roast, an Italian one, and our unique 'King's Choice' blend, which is my personal favorite. I hope you like it. Plus, decaf options for all
three."

We flocked eagerly, and the rest of the work day was given
over to meeting with the new management staff. There were

jokes, and games, and introductions, and long conversations. At one point, my friend Aria snuck out to get some work done, but was found by Mr. Regis, who escorted her back to the ersatz party.

I had questions. I always have questions, it's what I do. But I had extra questions that day. We'd heard almost nothing about Haste Industries. Even when we were first officially told of the takeover, all we were told was that they were "an up-and-coming European conglomerate".

"Can you tell me about Haste?" I asked Mr. Regis. "I mean, I'd never heard of the company before the takeover."

"Ah," he said, fidgeting with the bottom of his yellow tie. --He wasn't nervous, but he seemed anxious to get to some other business. His answer was spoken like it was being read from an encyclopedia. "Haste Industries was formed in 1895, in England, by a businessman who wanted to increase the popularity of coffee in his home country."

"So the company came from the coffee, rather than the other way around?"

"Yes. He settled on a blend that created a uniquely golden color in the coffee. Because of the cost of producing the blend, it remains relatively small in market, but we are able to provide it to our employees, *gratis*."

I looked at the coffee cup in my hand. This dull brew was good enough to found a corporate empire? Yet further evidence that (as my barista wife has often told me) I didn't have a professional understanding of the stuff. Now that he mentioned it, though, the coffee did have a unique color, like the normal black of the coffee had a yellow hue, despite having no milk in it.

I looked up to ask Mr. Regis more questions, but he had slipped away while I looked at the coffee. I shrugged, and went to try the cake that was brought in.

The event lasted longer than expected. The normal end of the work day was five o'clock, but the break room was an inner area without windows, and it wasn't until eight o'clock that somebody checked the time, realized the hour, and left, prompting the party to break up. Tish was going to be worried about me. It was my fault, I left my phone on my desk and didn't think to check it. When I did, there were a few texts and one voicemail from her, asking me to check in. I gave her a call, promised to be home soon, and went for the door. Before I left, though, Mr. Chambers caught me, with a hand on my shoulder.

"Rosemary," he said, then quickly removed his hand when I recoiled. He looked at the hand, then me, with a smile. "Sorry, I hope that wasn't inappropriate, I just wanted to catch you before you left. Mr. Regis and I have been going over the numbers here, and I find that you're one of the top performers."

"Well," I said, "if you say so, I guess." Our former boss had never really gone over numbers with us. If you weren't doing well, you heard about it, but other than that, no news was the best news.

"Oh, no modesty, Rosemary. I don't know you well enough to lie about this."

I smiled without looking at him. I've never been good with confronting my success.

"Look, I just want you to know, I care about my people. If you ever need anything, come to me. And don't be surprised if good things start coming your way."

I thanked him and left.

Outside, the late-October sky was giving up the last of its gold light, but our part of town, The Close (as in "nearby") was already cast in dark by the wall of tall buildings that surrounds it. It's an area of half-occupied low buildings, shops and homes, within the larger city. A single tower, the Ducard building, stands at the heart of the Close. You can see it from just about everywhere.

The drive home felt different, like I was more aware of the city. I drove the same route every day, but that evening I noticed things I had never seen. I had always thought our part of the Close was at least okay. Not nice, exactly, but better than many neighborhoods. But that night, I felt a weight as I drove.

The windows were dark and the streetlights seemed to throw no light. Clouds hid the moon once the sun set, so only my headlights showed the way. It's a strange thing, but I got the impression that the buildings were sick, decaying somehow. There were more broken windows than I realized, doors ajar or at odd angles. Waste bins were disturbed. The occasional parked cars all seemed incomplete—missing tires, broken windows.

I didn't earn much at S-Tech, and Tish worked part-time as barista and spent her nights painting. This is to say, our home was not a historic Victorian. Instead, we lived in a squat brick square with one storey and a flat roof.

I got home, and prepared to meet with Tish's anger.

As I got out of the car, I looked to the Ducard, a ten-storey tower home to S-Tech and nothing else (and we only took up one of the ten floors). The previous owners had bought it for a song and moved us to the top floor. Not that "top floor" means much when that's the only floor where people work, but the view was relatively nice.

That night, the lights were still on in the Ducard.

I went inside the house expecting to meet anger, but what I found was concern: Tish grabbed me, kissed me, held me close for several seconds before finally saying, "I was so worried. A little late is one thing, three hours is a lot." She ran through her list of fears while I rubbed her back. Later, we made dinner and fell asleep together on couch.

When I woke, Tish was already at work. Through the window, the Ducard stood over the Close, golden sun reflecting in its windows. Some days, it looked like a guard, watching over us. Today, though, I found myself thinking of it as a beacon, as if the Ducard were reaching for the sky, instead of laying low to the ground like us mortals.

I realized, driving to work, that I was excited. For the first time in a very long while, I was excited to get in, write code, and sit on the top floor of a titanic building in the middle of a sea of brick hovels, each no more than a memory of a city that, only a few decades ago, had been a guiding light for the country. Tish, who included theatre among her creative endeavors, once said, "From guiding light to a ghost light; somebody turned the lights out, but nobody told us to go home."

I parked, which was easy. The parking was meant for hundreds of employees, so the twelve of us had plenty of options. Sadly, public transportation had been cut out here, so not-driving wasn't an option, except for Aria. She only lived a block away, and we all fake-hated her for it.

The first surprise of the new day: the elevator was working. It was an old elevator, a small room of steel enclosed in arms of brass with gold trimmings. Inside, sodium lights flickered on the walls and floor. The elevator hadn't worked in two years, and tradition dictated that everyone arrive an hour prior to the start time to guarantee time to climb the stairs. The resulting daily workout maintains a figure which Tish has never been shy about appreciating.

I almost took the stairs again, purely out of confusion. But the elevator was fully functional, apart from creaking as it moved. This concern, though, I dismissed. This elevator was decades old, and could be forgiven for having some tired joints.

On the top floor, the lights were on, and three or four of my comrades-in-code were already working in their cubicles. This was when I noticed the second surprise.

"It's warm," I said, loudly. I'm not sure if it was a statement or a question.

"They got the heat working!" said Darryl. He stood, gave me a smile, and lifted a coffee mug that wore the Haste Industries logo, a yellow ankh with a small crown. He moved it forward, as if toasting.

"You're always late," I said. Since starting, Darryl had never beaten anyone to the office.

"I know, right?" he said with a wider smile. "I was just really excited to get to work today. Get in, do some coding, drink some coffee, repeat!"

I smiled back without thinking, then went to my own cubicle. My chair had been replaced. A flash of apprehension washed over me, tinted with a slight feeling of (admittedly irrational) anger: why would they switch out chairs without letting us know? It seemed like a small enough thing that it could have waited until Haste realized we weren't worth the money; plus, the chairs were comfortable enough before.

Then I recalled that this was patently false: this new chair appeared to have no metal whatsits that were going to poke my hide for the next eight hours.

"They must have had people working all night," I said as I sat, not really expecting anyone to respond.

"We did!" boomed a voice. Mr. Chambers.

I jumped. Hearing a full voice come from the manager's office, before I'd had a second cup of coffee even, was nerve-shattering. "I'm sorry," he said, lowering his volume. "I should really learn to handle my voice. You're Rosemary, as I recall?" He lifted a diner-style coffee mug and drank from it.

"Yes, sorry, yes. I'm Rosemary."

"Would you mind terribly ... having a quick chat in here?"

The obvious question: how was I already in trouble? But I agreed and joined Mr. Chambers in his corner office. The walls were cream-colored, without decoration, and the desk lacked anything but his coffee, a pen, and a computer. The platonic office ideal.

"Rosemary Matraxia," he smiled, sitting. "Is that Italian?"

"Greek. But born in Detroit, raised all over the state, and moved to the Close a couple of years ago. It's been a century since the family was Greek." I smiled, trying not to show that I didn't care to talk about my family history. This wasn't what I wanted from a new boss, no matter how encouraging he had been on the first day. Luckily, he changed gears quickly.

"Rosemary, what is it you want?"

"What do you mean?"

"In life. Why are you here? What's your dream job?"

I started to answer, but stopped. I had to think about this. To be directly confronted with the question of "what do you want" is a profoundly disjointing experience. I had been raised by extremely capitalist parents, so the idea of "dream" had always been "make money, propagate, retire." I had already disappointed my parents once by not wanting kids, then again by marrying (a) a woman, one who (b) also did not want kids.

That train of thought brought the question into sharp focus, and I realized that I knew exactly what I wanted out of life. Pretty simple, actually.

"I want my wife to be happy," I said. "I want her to not worry."

"Noble." He smiled. He always seemed to be smiling, but when he *actively* smiled, it was like he was smiling ... I don't know, *more*. "So why are you working here?"

"I'm not sure what you mean."

"Your former employer paid you thirty percent less than the national average for a programmer of your work history."

I knew this. It was something Tish and I had discussed on occasion. The problem was that to earn more money would require moving somewhere else. Which would require money. Which required a better paying job. And so on, in a dismal capitalist loop. Money wasn't the only thing I was interested in, but being stuck in the cycle of needing more to earn more was a situation that could ruin your week if you thought too hard about it.

I explained this to Mr. Chambers. He nodded sympathetically before responding.

"Yes, I've seen that often before. Rosemary, I want to fix it. My employers believe very strongly in this company, and this city, and very strongly in you in particular. So, first, I'm going to bump your pay by enough to close the wage gap. After that, I'm going to increase your earnings by ninety-seven percent."

This was too much. If I'd been drinking King's Choice, I would have spit it out.

"Why?" I was firm with the question. No such thing as free money.

"Rosemary, every study under the sun has shown that treating your employees well means better results. I won't pretend it's anything other than numbers." As he spoke, his words seemed distant to me. I was losing my focus, staring at the patterns of his yellow tie. "I'm not going to be sentimental and call the office my family. You aren't my family, but you *are* my people, and I can show you dozens of charts that tell me that if I increase your pay by exactly that amount, you'll become the optimal employee."

I appreciated the man's candor. This was about numbers, nothing else. I could understand numbers.

"You said the company was interested in me in particular. Why?"

"Because you're good at what you do."

"You said that yesterday, but 'good' is a bit vague for my understanding."

He slid a folder, filled with papers, from his desk drawer. He went through the papers as he spoke. This pulled me away from staring at his tie.

"Before the takeover, we did an in-depth vetting of every employee. Their work history, their time here, their willingness to work with the team. That's why your former manager was booted from the start. He was a self-important monster with nothing but himself on his mind. Drugs, drinking, whatever. Do you know what he did in his office all day?"

"Drank, smoked, and played online poker."

"Yes. Never once did he ever give you a performance review, am I right?" He pulled a paper from the pile.

"We all just assumed that if we're not getting yelled at, we're doing fine."

"In eight years at this company, no project you've ever worked on has received a single complaint or bug report from any tester or end-user."

My eyes widened slightly.

"That's not fine," he intoned, his face saturnine, "that's staggering."

I looked at the report that he slid across the table. I didn't take the time to read it in detail, but the facts were there.

"Rosemary, all I want you to do, right now, is go back to being an excellent performer. Things are going to be changing in the Close." He dropped his voice to a low whisper. "The company will be making this place a priority. And I want you here while it happens."

"Why? I mean, honestly, why? Okay, I'm a good programmer, but I still don't understand what makes me special."

Without pausing, he said, "I've been around a long time, Rosemary. I'm much older than I seem. So trust me when I say that the people who don't think they're special are the best around." He sat back up. "So, what do you say? Are you in it with Haste?"

I smiled, confused, excited, staggered. I finally nodded and said, "Yes."

"Good!" He stood, shook my hand, and walked me to the office door. "And have some of that coffee!" he said as I walked away.

I did. I don't know if it was my mood, or the coffee itself, but it tasted better that day.

After twelve months, the face of the Close had begun to change, and the Ducard building had become a major business hub. Our department was moved down a floor, not because we were being demoted, but because the scale changed. The top floor became dedicated exclusively to Haste management and was locked off. You couldn't get there by elevator without a special ID card.

I confess to being a bit creeped out by the folks on the top floor. The elevator never seemed to move past us to get to the top, and we never heard voices from up there. We heard foot-steps, though, and the light stayed on all through the night, visi-ble all throughout the Close.

Rumors spread that ghosts had moved in. These started as a joke, but there seemed to be something quietly strange about the top floor. One night, I was working late (this time I called Tish in advance) when footsteps above began walking toward my location. They stopped directly above me, and didn't move for an hour. When I got up to go home, they walked away from me.

With the new money, I encouraged Tish to drop the barista job and focus on her painting. She was hesitant, didn't want to be a freeloader, but I managed to convince her and she was be-yond grateful. She even sold a few paintings, after a gallery opened at the Ducard. One of Haste's other subsidiaries, the gallery was run by a small twig-like man who loved Tish's work. The first one went to Mr. Chambers, in fact. Tish called the painting *These, Our Placid Stars*. It showed a beautiful star field, viewed from the sewers. I didn't expect it to sell, since it was a somewhat squalid (though not unrealistic) painting. Mr. Cham-bers said it reminded him of the work of Richard Upton. He had a third name, but Mr. Chambers couldn't remember it. Tish and I couldn't find anything about Upton online, but Mr. Chambers described him as "a distant family friend" so we didn't search too hard.

It wasn't until after that first year that things started turning. For a while, there was that new-car love, where everything seems beautiful and nobody could detect a flaw. But the closer you looked, the more the whole thing seemed odd. Mr. Cham-bers spent most of his time out of the office, on the top floor. When he *did* come back to our floor, he was often accompanied by a new employee. The problem was, Stellar didn't have room for new employees, so every hire appeared just a few days after someone else quit. I don't know if there was some reason we were kept at twelve employees, but that's where we sat.

Nobody was ever fired, but they quit. The first two seemed

unrelated, but it only takes three to make a pattern and Darryl made three. They'd be tired, not eat enough. Lose weight, not change their clothes. All of these things were fairly familiar to all of us that had studied computer science in school, but in the workplace it was more than a little strange, and it happened far too quickly. After less than a week of deteriorating habits, the person would disappear, and we'd get the notice that they had quit.

My attention was drawn because these weren't just anonymous drones, I knew everyone that worked there. One of my best friends, Aria, was one of them. She said she was having bad dreams, missed work, and then just disappeared, moved to another city. The others went radio silent, not responding to messages or calls. Soon I was the last of the pre-Haste group.

Another curiosity. This one is a small thing, but it was something I noticed. The employees all wore yellow. Not full outfits, but small flourishes: neckties, ascots. One woman wore a fake yellow lily.

It wasn't just at work. The people of the Close took on a strange light. No more block parties or picnics (not that there were ever many), and instead of people moving *into* the Close because of the new industries there, people fled. Before Haste, maybe half of the homes there were full. After that first year? Maybe a tenth. And without the people to keep them up, houses decayed, clean stone turning yellow with grime, caution signs appearing to warn of condemned homes. Yet more people kept coming to work in the Ducard.

And, in the end, came the dreams.

In the first, I was in the Ducard's lobby. The floor plan was the same, but instead of a receptionist's desk and waiting chairs, the whole floor had turned into a grand lobby, like you'd see in a nice theatre. Soft carpet, velvet ropes, coat check. The elevator was replaced by a grand staircase.

I heard a noise, like a chime or bell, which called me forward. The small part of my mind that was awake told me not to go, but I went anyway, my feet carrying me smoothly, as if I were floating on a cloud. I ascended a set of stairs. They twisted around themselves, up to the top of the building. The stairs twisted outside of the building, and I saw the Close. It was barren, abandoned. No buildings save the Ducard, and from the top floor of the building poured a gleaming golden light.

I followed the stairs and was engulfed by the light.

At which point I woke. When I did, I was more confused than frightened, but I found myself unable to get back to sleep. When Tish woke, I told her about the dream. We talked through it, making sure I remembered the details, then I went on to work. I assumed this would be the end of it, but of course, things are never that easy.

The next night, I dreamed again of that lobby, and of my ascent, in my pajamas. But now, when I reached the top of the stairs, I was in an enormous theatre, clearly meant to host hundreds of people. There was a main floor, a balcony, and several boxes for seats. But instead of dozens of rows of seats, there was a single wooden chair. It seemed to be cobbled together of mismatched wooden pieces and creaked under the weight of a very thin man, who wore an alabaster mask and a tuxedo that seemed woven of starlight. I can't describe it in any more detail, yet the certainty of dream-logic tells me that this was the case: it was woven of starlight.

I asked a question, though I couldn't hear myself. The man turned to face me, and I saw that his mask was of a perfectly neutral face. The emotion was in his true eyes, beneath the mask, which must have been irritated, as they were a sharp red.

"Do you have your ticket?" asked a voice behind me. I turned to find a woman, also in a suit, apparently an usher. The woman also wore a mask, and it made a slight echo in her voice. She wore a yellow choker.

I recall fumbling for a ticket, but couldn't find a pocket. My clothing had changed: I was in a tremendous golden gown, like a princess in a fairy tale. And, like all the great fairy tale dresses, the thing had no pockets.

The usher pointed to my hand. I looked, and found that I

was holding a handbag. I opened it and found a single ticket inside. It seemed to be hand-made, rather than printed. The usher snatched it away, and I only just managed to see the title—*The King in Yellow*—before she looked at it.

"Ah, but your ticket is for two, miss. Come back when you have your second."

I woke again, this time gasping for air. My mind raced with possibilities and fears. I shook in bed, and Tish had to hold me for some time to help me calm down; rubbed my back, held my hand. She even sang to me for a while (she hates her voice; I love her voice). I told her the dream. She said she remembered hearing about a play called *The King in Yellow*, but didn't remember much about it. I clearly had to do something about the dreams, but how do you avoid sleep? I spent all day worrying about going to bed that night. I drank cup after cup of King's Choice.

Aria wasn't far from my mind. She had never described her dreams to me, but she left Haste only a few days after they started.

Fear of your own dreams can be a strange motivator, and I resolved not to sleep if I could help it. I came to relish the flavor of King's Choice, with its uniquely balanced spices. I went home, kissed Tish goodnight, and set up shop in the home office, planning to work on any little puzzle I could set myself to.

You've probably guessed it already, but I immediately fell asleep. In my defense, I didn't yet realize the gravity of things. That night, mercifully, was a completely dreamless sleep. I woke up well rested, despite a crick in my neck brought about choosing to sleep in an office chair, slumped over a keyboard.

I stretched my arms, my legs, took some ibuprofen for my neck, began to do morning things. Breakfast in the toaster.

Then Tish started screaming my name.

I ran to the bedroom, found her holding something that looked like a white credit card and shouting my name. I ran to her side.

"Tish, what is it?" I asked, taking her hands. She stopped

shouting for me, but didn't answer, her wide eyes, staring at the thing in her hands.

As I sat beside her, I saw that it was a rectangle of heavy paper. I had thought it was a credit card because of the size, but that wasn't it. The paper was high quality, with a perforated line along one side. Tish's grip had crumpled it.

On the face was writing. Elegant calligraphy, right in the middle-quality where it could have been either computer-printed or hand-printed. It read:

"The King in Yellow"
A Reward, in Two Acts
One Night Only
This Saturday, 8:00 pm • Ducard Building, Top Floor
Dress as You Like • Admit 2

She had found the ticket in her hand when she woke. Once she calmed down, I took the thing and slipped it into my pocket, out of her sight. She had managed to calm down, but I was nowhere near calm. Tish went to take a shower, saying something quietly. It wasn't clear, but I heard the words *King* and *Yellow*. I sat on the bed and shook with rage and fear.

The time it took, only two days of dreams, and then this? It seemed like insanity. If Tish hadn't been the one to find it, I would have assumed the ticket was a hallucination, or a prank. But sitting, shaking and staring at the thing, I realized that it was real. Whatever happened in my dream was real. And it had to be connected to Haste. The connection between "King's Choice" coffee and the title of the play? The company logo, the yellow accessories that mark employees, the decay in the Close, these couldn't be products of chance.

I had to know. I had to find something about it. The internet provided a few small hints, but they all led off to websites in foreign languages that the computer wouldn't translate. I elected not to go down that road, and started looking at the books we had in the house. Tish had several theatre books, so I started skimming their indices, looking for something. I didn't know what I would find, but I found it in a thin paperback with a glossy cover.

The book was a compendium of passages from plays that had been lost to history, and the "Author Unknown" section held a single page dedicated to *The King in Yellow*.

THE KING IN YELLOW (c. 1895)

This play, first published about 1895, is a curious volume. It seems to have come from nowhere, sweeping across Europe around the turn of the century. Paris banned the script and its translations, rounding them up and setting them ablaze. This has, perhaps inevitably, created a litany of myths and rumors. Does the second act truly drive people mad? Did the author truly kill himself? Is it true that the play has never been performed? These questions, and many more, are yours to ponder, reader. Meanwhile, enjoy one of the few fragments that are confirmed to have come from the play.

What followed was a very short exchange, only five lines of dialogue. The interaction, between two characters ("Stranger" and "Camilla") was about a mask. Camilla urged the other to remove their mask, and was staggered when she found out that the Stranger's face wasn't a mask.

I've watched a lot of horror movies, so those few lines didn't move me much. It probably had more punch when you were watching with living people a century ago.

Tish urged me to stay home. It was a Friday, we could make it a three-day weekend. I made a farce of saying no, playing at refusing. But the appearance of the ticket had shaken me deeply. If it had only been the dream, I could dismiss it. It would take some effort, probably, but I could dismiss it. Even the name of the play. Perhaps I'd heard it mentioned somewhere, which would plant it into the dream.

But the ticket.

I called in sick and we spent Friday doing our best to enjoy each other's company, staying at the house with our hands never far from each other's bodies. I was more relaxed by the end of the day than I had been in a long while. I sat in the corner and watched Tish paint for a while. She managed to put the whole thing out of her mind, but I couldn't. Every few minutes, my thoughts would turn to the crumpled paper in my pajama pocket.

That night, I dreamed again of that theatre. There were no other patrons this time. I was alone, wearing my usual work outfit: slacks, a button-up, vest, and my hair tied back. The ochre curtain was down, waving slightly. I found myself lost in the cracks on the walls and in the floor. The plaster had ripped away in many places, revealing boards behind. Sometimes, amid those boards, were deeper gaps, black recesses from which I could sense a gaze I could not shake.

The curtain lifted. Beyond it was the unique darkness of the theatre. An artificial one, poised to be dispelled. Above me, old circuits clicked into life and the lights began to flare. My eyes adjusted, revealing a set, figures, and—

I awoke to a phone call from work. I rubbed my eyes, saw the number, and disentangled myself from Tish's arms.

I went to the living room and answered, standing in front of the window in my pajamas, looking across the Close to the Ducard. It was barely sunrise. The pollution of the city beyond was mixed with the sun, making the sky a curtain of tarnished gold. On the other side of the curtain stood the Ducard, a dark monolith against the early yellow light, the top three floors lit for workers.

"Hello," I said, though I knew exactly who it would be. I closed my eyes when Mr. Chambers responded.

"Hello! Rosemary, I wonder if you might do me a favor." There was a note of urgency in his voice, poorly hidden behind his usual Santa-like cheer.

"It's Saturday."

"I know, and it's tremendously unfair to call on a Saturday. You've every right to tell me to go jump in a dirty yellow river."

"But?" Don't think I didn't notice that he didn't ask how I was feeling after yesterday's sick call.

"There's a great opportunity for you to help yourself, as well as *my*self, at the office tonight. Our fair CEO of Haste Industries will be there to give an address to some management."

I waited.

"But, you see, I failed to realize it was *today*, and I'm about to board a flight out of town." There was something odd, a little hook in his voice. I thought he might be lying, but I wasn't sure exactly which part was untrue.

"Why me?"

"Well, I need to send *someone* from Stellar, and you're the only old hat there. The most experienced, and certainly the one I trust the most! It's less of a formal engagement and more of a social one, really just a chance to hobnob with corporate royalty. The CEO will say a few words, thank everyone for their hard work, and there will be a performance of some kind. A touring play, I believe. I don't know the title." Again, that little hook in his voice. An odd affectation. "You could bring your wife, if you like, to help feel more comfortable. I'm afraid it will be a lot of strange faces for you."

I stood there, my eyes closed. I ran fingers through my hair, rubbed my neck, thought of the dream, the ticket. Held the ticket, still in the pocket of my sleep sweats. There was no reason for me to say yes. I was happy, Tish was happy.

But, damn it, I needed to know what I would find.

"Alright," I whispered. "I'll be coming alone."

"Great!" he shouted, jumping on my answer. "I'm sure there will be more seats if you change your mind about that. Eight o'clock, dress however you'd like. Although do remember you're meeting a CEO of a major conglomerate."

I ended the call. Behind me, Tish spoke.

"This is about that ticket, isn't it."

She was walking toward me, face contoured with concern. I nodded, searching for words to ease her worries.

"Have I told you when I realized I love you?" Tish asked.

"After I was mugged?"

She nodded. "We were barely even a couple, we'd been dating less than two weeks. I found you knocking on my door, drenched with rain. Shaking like a wounded puppy." She wrapped her arms around my waist. "My heart broke, seeing you so scared. I was supposed to have a meeting with a gallery owner that afternoon, my first shot at getting my paintings hung. I cancelled it."

"I didn't know that."

"I cancelled because I realized I cared more about you being safe than anything else. Nothing was as important as being with you, helping you feel better. So I sat with you all day, and I've never questioned that choice. Right now, Button, I see you scared again. I know I'll never convince you not to go, so I want to come with you. Whatever you find, I want to be with you."

She was right: she would never convince me not to go, and I would never convince her not to come. And, honestly, I was glad there would be someone with me. To share in whatever we found, despite the danger. To hold my hand.

I kissed her cheek. We stood there a while, feeling each other's warmth.

That evening, the sun seemed to hold on longer than usual, sitting just above the towers beyond the Close and casting long autumn shadows along the streets. Dust on my windshield made the illusion of a double-sun that, as we drove to the Ducard, sank behind the city. Long shadows grew longer, casting the Close into a twilight of gold.

We laughed. We talked. We were wrapped in the fears of the day, both of us feeling the ice of terror in our veins. At work, I deal with cause and effect, yes and no. Everything I held dear said that the most likely outcome of this would be nothing more than a chat with a boring but well-connected CEO. Perhaps it would lead to promotion, likely not.

But that ice in my veins said none of that was even in the same ballpark as what was going to happen.

When we reached the building, we both got quiet. We walked in without a word.

Inside, braided yellow cords linked stanchions together, forming a path from the door to the elevator. The card reader which granted access to the top floor now had a small sign hanging above it, reading "TICKET". The ticket still appeared to be only paper, but I held it to the pad and the elevator shuddered to life, old mechanisms creaking above us.

The doors opened at the top floor. More signs, this time with arrows, led us to a large conference room. Chairs had been set out in rows facing the doors, away from the windows. There were eleven cars down below, but many more people than that. I didn't recognize one of them. Some wore tees and jeans, other work clothes. One man wore a tuxedo; I wondered if he was the man from my dream. A table was loaded with cold cuts and a samovar of King's Choice.

Tish and I introduced ourselves, made painful small talk. We split up to hunt for information, but the only thing we learned was that the others had all dreamed of the theatre, and the play, as well.

The rest of the evening seemed to pass in only a few instants.

The sky outside had gone dark, but at exactly eight o'clock, there was a flash of light that spread across everything in sight. We guests turned and looked at the windows. I took Tish's hand. The windows were giving off some kind of light that seemed to illuminate nothing. Yellow, inevitably.

While we watched the window, the door clicked open.

We all turned and, when I saw the King in Yellow, I went mad.

Madness is not illness, and illness is not madness.

Illness is anxiety, depression, paranoia. You might say that uncertainty is an illness.

Madness is a certainty. Knowledge on a higher level. Not the temperature at which water boils, but the *reason* the water boils. Not the dance of the stars and worlds, but seeing the face of the one who decided: "These worlds are thus."

Some attain madness and are destroyed by it. Some attain it and are ascended.

I have only fleeting recollections of the moments that followed the unfolding of my awareness.

Beneath the King's robes were truths that destroyed the minds of some of us. There was screaming, but the screams weren't mine, nor Tish's. We learned the facts of the King, and we learned what Haste Industries wants.

I was offered a deal. In truth, I don't even know who offered it. But I know that I gained security in exchange for serving the King. I don't know what others gained, or what they exchanged for it, but I gained certainty. I work for Haste. I dedicate everything to the company. I rise through the ranks, I write software, I manage teams, I shape policy, all to satisfy Him. I had always resisted the company colors, but now I wear them gladly: an enamel pin over my heart, bearing the yellow ankh and crown.

And when all is done, when Haste's mission is complete, then I will see Tish again.

All those people that quit, that disappeared? They were weak. They wouldn't serve, they wouldn't fight for what they wanted. All you need to do is join. Work *for* the corporation, not against it. I have signed my life to Haste Industries, so that in death I may have my great wish.

At nights, now, I feel the cold bed beside me, and sometimes want to cry. But then I remember. I remember where she

is. She sings in the King's court now, and paints for Him, and
dances for Him. She is happy, and safe, and dreams of me, just
as I dream of her. She waits for me where the twin suns sink
and black stars rise.

   She waits for me.

      In Carcosa.

IT CAME FROM I.T.

by Gordon Linzner

It may strain one's credulity, in the first quarter of the twenty-first century, to learn that the exact details of the initial meeting between the board of directors of Starbright Enterprises and the enigmatic Dexter Charles are nowhere to be found. After all, each of the company's boardrooms, as well as every public and semi-public space within Starbright's Providence headquarters, is equipped with closed circuit cameras. Every member of the board, indeed every Starbright employee, possesses a phone capable of recording sound (and video, as needed), in addition to the occasional hand-written note.

Yet, in spite of all this technology, the most reliable record of that presentation are the notes taken by company stenographer Walter Abbott, who has worked for Starbright over forty years, and whose presence at these meetings has, since the turn of the century, been required more out of habit than necessity. And even his meticulous penmanship occasionally drifted into incomprehensible scrawls.

The highly localized storm which engulfed the building during that hour may have played a part in the disruption of those electronic devices. Lights in the room flickered from time to time. At key points of the meeting, the main illumination was provided by a flash of lightning just outside the floor-to-ceiling windows; lightning accompanied not by a roar of thunder but a vague buzzing, as of a distant swarm of hornets.

Yet at no point during Mr. Charles' presentation was the video feed from the laptop to the projector affected.

The small New England manufacturing company known as Starbright Enterprises was founded in the late 1940s, as the country recovered from World War II. They specialized in producing souvenirs and trinkets distributed primarily to small shops in Providence and the Massachusetts Bay area. The company's big breakthrough came with the offer of an exclusive contract with the Miskatonic University bookshop.

Initially this project involved creating and manufacturing such items as Squids' soccer team sweatshirts, coffee mugs with the school insignia, prints of Richard Upton Pickman paintings (which oddly sold better in Rhode Island than in Pickman's native Boston), and a key ring self-referentially shaped like a silver key. In the late 1970s the school became more welcoming to female students, and Starbright broadened their range of products. The Hound amulet, for example, could now be purchased as either a pendant, a brooch, or a lapel pin. The University soon became their largest client, to the point where today they barely manufacture anything not related to the school's history or curriculum. They even have exclusive e-book rights to Miskatonic's library of arcane books, including perennial best-sellers *Unaussprechlichen Kulten* and the *Necronomicon* (numerous public domain versions exist, but none of those are as complete or well-annotated).

Still, there remained one item Starbright was particularly anxious to add to their catalogue of replicas, an item for which they received a steady stream of requests from collectors but for which they possessed neither access to the original nor a useable description for replication.

Until that special board meeting in early June.

Relying on Mr. Abbott's incomplete notes, and the often contradictory memories of the board members, the best, or at least most likely, reconstruction of events leading to the tragedy is as follows.

In addition to the six members of the Starbright Enterprises board, including the newly promoted Thomas Scott, for whom this was his initial meeting, and stenographer Walter Abbott, two more figures attended the presentation that afternoon.

Dexter Charles sat off to one side, a few feet from the long conference table that dominated the center of the room. He was a thin, dark (but not dark-skinned) man with a long chin and tightly curled hair. A dull black suit gave his gaunt frame an even more skeletal appearance. According to most board members' accounts, Charles was of average or slightly below average height, yet gave the impression of looming over the executives, even while seated.

At the far end of the table sat Whitney Washio Waller. He was the youngest person in the room, and the mainstay of Starbright's IT department. Waller had recently saved the company tens of thousands of dollars by devising a program to customize and personalize most of their articles of jewelry through the use of 3D printing technology. The twenty-seven year old technician rarely strayed from his workspace on a lower floor. As a concession to the meeting's formality, Waller wore a light blue blazer over his Miskatonic Squids t-shirt. The fingers of his left hand idly drummed the tabletop until an older board member glanced at him in irritation; then he switched to repeatedly smoothing his pencil-thin moustache. He'd not been told the purpose of the meeting, save that it involved a possible new product, and his input would be vital. No one in the room save the Director, and of course Charles Dexter, knew much more than that.

Waller was uncomfortable with the lack of advance knowledge. It was a personal rule of his, almost an obsession, to have as much information as possible at his disposal before proceeding with any project.

The meeting was called to order by an uncharacteristically excited Director Harvey Bellinger, who briefly recapped the company's decades of frustrating attempts to reconstruct a replica of the Shining Trapezohedron retrieved from the tomb of Pharoah Nephren-Ka by Professor Enoch Bowen in 1843. Bowen later quit academia to found the sinister, now-defunct, Church of the Starry Wisdom. The Trapezohedron itself had been lost in Narragansett Bay in the 1930s; based on the only visual documentation, some hastily drawn yellowed sketches, and part of a photographic print, it was impossible to tell even how many angles and sides made up the object, let alone its dimensions.

Waller squirmed in his seat. Early in his employment, he'd spent weeks trying to fill in the blanks on just this topic. His efforts had proven as productive as an all-day session of computer solitaire.

Bellinger continued. Two days earlier, he'd received a letter from one Dexter Charles (he indicated the stranger in the room with a brief nod), who identified himself as proprietor of a small antiquities shop just outside of Providence. The missive told how, while examining the contents of a recently acquired nineteenth century trunk, the origin of which Charles was not at liberty to divulge, he discovered, individually wrapped in layers of fine cotton, two dozen glass photographic plates. Charles only needed to examine a couple of these to realize they had once been the property of an anonymous apprentice of Matthew Brady, a young man who'd been hired by that notorious aforementioned Church to document their most valued artifact during the Civil War period, as various threats of sabotage aimed at munitions manufacturers in the city by the Confederacy posed a small but palpable danger to its safety.

The original prints of those photos, which had been kept in the church's archives, were, along with various other items, destroyed by an angry Irish mob in 1869 after one mysterious disappearance too many connected to the Starry Wisdom cult. Only a fragment of one survived, now in possession of Miskatonic University. The original glass negatives were assumed to have also been destroyed.

Bellinger then formally introduced Mr. Charles, who rose to explain that he had not brought the actual glass negatives with him this day; they were too fragile to transport more than necessary, and he had already promised to donate them to the University's library. However, as one who was fascinated with older technology himself, particularly in regard to the art of photography, Charles had first made a complete set of prints. He followed that announcement by moving toward the conference table, where he settled into an empty seat in front of a nondescript laptop. A pale yellow video cable ran from one port of the computer to a projector facing the whiteboard behind Director Bellinger, who shifted slightly aside. Abbott then turned down the lights.

Charles opened the laptop, waking the machine from its slumber. The USB thumb drive in its left port flickered.

Waller leaned forward eagerly, as if poised to clamber onto the table for a better view.

As the skies outside grew more ominous, the slideshow began.

The first image greatly resembled the partial photograph of which Starbright had a copy in their archives, with one important difference. Whereas the object in that fragment appeared partially in shadow, the one projected onto the whiteboard facing the conference table was brightly illuminated from all sides, clearly showing each facet of the Trapezohedron, revealing more angles than seemed possible for a single object to possess.

"My god," Waller gasped.

Every board member recalled the technician's exclamation.

None of the executives could recall who among them had muttered, in response, "Someone's, anyway."

The second image, at a slightly different angle, was equally sharp and clear. As was the third, and the fourth, and each one following. There were even a few stereo views, made with twin lenses.

After each individual slide had been viewed, Mr. Charles begged the indulgence of the board and uploaded one more file—a stop-motion video created by combining all the images. The resulting impression was of the Shining Trapezohedron spinning in place, like a planet in an alien solar system being observed from outside its orbit.

"Whitney," Ballinger called out, when Charles' presentation concluded. "You see now why I insisted you be here today. Is there enough information in these images for you to create a passable copy?"

Waller could barely speak. "Yes. No. I.... Yes. I can do this. I need to do this. When can I start? Now?"

"How long do you think it will take?"

"With traditional subtractive manufacturing techniques, months. However, by using the additive method of the company's 3D printer ... first I'll have to create a viable CAD program. That will take the most time. Just analyzing this wealth of information will consume most of a week. Maybe ... ten days? Minimum."

"That seems reasonable. Gentlemen, we shall reconvene a week from next Wednesday, assuming the prototype is ready."

"One moment, Bellinger." Emmet Jordan raised a gnarled hand. The white-haired octogenarian was the oldest member of the board, as well as one of the most influential governors of Miskatonic University. "This seems a bit hasty. Shouldn't we take a vote before proceeding?"

Bellinger waved a hand in deprecation. "This meeting is intended merely as a presentation, Emmet. There's no point in our voting on how to continue until we know if duplication is even feasible."

Jordan harumphed. "I'm old enough to remember my grandfather's stories about this Trapezohedron. For most people who encountered it, things did not end well. Suicides. Madness. Vanishings."

"Your concern is noted, Emmet. I would, however, point out that many such stories are connected with the originals of most of the items we've manufactured for your school, including the e-books. Yet no one who's purchased a Hound amulet, for example, has been attacked by a ghostly canine, as far as we know. Besides, based on our limited information, the original Trapezohedron was created from materials not found on earth. We couldn't replicate the thing perfectly if even we wanted to, and I would honestly have your same doubts if we attempted more than a facsimile."

"In simply attempting to duplicate something this complex," Waller chipped in, "the knowledge I, we, can gain from working out the program would be enough justification to proceed."

The remainder of the board nodded. Jordan sat back in defeat.

Dexter Charles switched off the laptop, removed the USB thumb drive, and passed it to Waller. "I have a backup," he explained. Addressing the others in the room, he added, "With the board's permission, I should like to be able to call on this young man from time to time, so I might follow his progress. Merely to satisfy my own curiosity, you understand." He met Waller's eyes. "I doubt I'll have a clue what you're doing."

"If you've time now, Mr. Charles," Waller replied, "you can join me in my workspace. I'll be happy to explain the basics of 3D printing to you."

"I should very much like that."

"We could hardly deny you access, Mr. Charles," Bellinger agreed. "I'll arrange for a pass from security."

Even Jordan grudgingly acceded to that.

"Gentlemen," the Director concluded. "In a fortnight we shall hopefully take the first steps toward adding the Shining Trapezohedron to our catalogue. If there are no further questions...?"

Thomas Scott hesitantly raised a hand. This was his first meeting. He didn't want to seem pushy, nor did he want to look like an idiot with an inappropriate comment, but what was the point of being on the board if he didn't give some input?

"Yes, Tommy?" Bellinger asked, with a slight hint of condescension.

"Well, sir, sirs, the Shining Trapezohedron is quite a mouthful. Is it possible to shorten the name?"

A few heads inclined in agreement.

"Perhaps. Any suggestions?"

Scott nervously plucked at his left eyebrow as all eyes turned to him. The Zoe? Too much like an app. The Shining?

That just sounded off.

"HA!" he exclaimed. "How about … the Trap!"

"The Trap." Bellinger pondered the name as he scanned other board members' reactions. "Yes. A paperweight to keep those essential documents from escaping? I see the potential. I'll talk to advertising and R&D."

In retrospect, the name was a bit too much on the nose.

Waller threw himself into the project, spending long nights hunched over his computer both at work and home. Eventually he set up a cot in his office workspace to save on commuting time. At first the young technician tried to pace himself, but the deeper he got into the program the more obsessed he became. His overactive brain began inducing headaches if he took a break for more than a few minutes, and only by continuing to work could he dull the pain.

On Friday night of the week following the presentation, long after working hours, Dexter Charles arrived at Starbright Enterprises. Waller met him in the lobby. The only other personnel in the building were cleaning staff and a security guard.

"Thank you for coming, Mr. Charles," Waller said, leading the visitor to his workspace. "I know it's rather late."

"Thank you for calling me, Mr. Waller," Charles returned. "Are you all right? You look exhausted."

"It's a happy exhaustion. Mostly. I've been working long hours every night, developing my CAD. Computer Aided Design. Not spending much time at home. Oscar keeps me company."

"Oscar?"

"My tortoise." Waller indicated a terrarium tank on the floor along one wall. "I brought him from my apartment. Gives me someone to talk to. Non-judgmental. And he needs to be fed from time to time, providing an occasional much-needed distraction. But here's what I called you about." He led Charles to his work desk and pushed aside a stack of fast food containers. "I started the print this morning. There you have it. The legendary Shining Trapezohedron. It finished about an hour ago. That's when I called you. There are faster, less wasteful methods, but those printers are prohibitively expensive even for Starbright. I'll show this to Mr. Bellinger first thing Monday morning, but I felt you deserved the first look. After all, it was your discovery that made this possible."

Charles nodded. His face remained impassive.

Waller sighed. "You see it, too. Or, rather, you don't. Something's wrong. I don't know what. The proportions are exact. I checked and rechecked. I may not have replicated the exact size of the original, since there were no other objects in the photographs to compare it to, but based on written documents I can't be more than a few centimeters off."

"The color is off," Charles declared.

Waller blinked. "The color? How can you possibly know that? The photographs were black and white."

"And shades of gray, each representing a slightly different color, if you have the eye to interpret. The restoration of old photographs, remember, is a hobby of mine. Given enough practice, one can study pictures from the Civil War and tell a Union Army uniform from a Confederate one."

Waller frowned. "I suppose it's possible, but...."

"I suspected this might be a problem when you first described the process of replication, the slow extruding of liquid plastic layers through a heated nozzle."

"Fused deposition modeling," Waller interjected. He was too used to technical jargon to refrain from clarifying.

"Exactly. That plastic you told me about, ASB—"

"ABS," Waller corrected. "Acrylonitrile butadiene styrene. The stuff they use for LEGOs. That's its natural color, a kind of whitish-yellow."

"My point exactly. The difference between the real thing and that copy in front of us is subtle; easy to observe, hard to

define. As an analogy, you would likely know whether your pet
in that glass case is alive or dead just by looking at him. You
wouldn't necessarily know *how* you knew."

"Leave Oscar out of this." Waller folded his arms across his
chest. Lack of sleep was making him defensive. He took a deep
breath before speaking again. "It sounds like you've had more
time to consider this than I have. Any suggestions?"

"Better than a suggestion. A probable solution. Remember,
the original Trapezohedron is an alien artifact. What you need is
a pigment that hints at those origins. A color out of space, so to
speak." He reached into a side pocket of his jacket and took out
a small jar of yellowish-red powder. "I stopped by Jerry's art
supply store earlier this week, in anticipation of your call. This
shade is, I believe, the nearest match to my interpretation of the
images."

Waller accepted the jar, turning it over in his hands. He
frowned again. This was beginning to seem too convenient.

Of course, in science, done correctly, sometimes things really did just fall into place. In rare instances. Very rare.

"That was thoughtful of you, Mr. Charles."

"Dexter is fine."

"Dexter. I need to examine this powder first, of course, for
compatibility with the ABS, and run a few basic tests. Might
have to adjust the temperature a few degrees to obtain the best
mix."

"You're the expert."

Waller placed the jar of powdered pigment next to the
Trapezohedron replica, then led Charles to the break room for
coffee to continue their talk. The caffeine accomplished little;
his brain was still exhausted from lack of sleep. After Waller
nearly nodded off for the third time, Charles graciously said
good night, offering to see himself to the elevators as Waller
again apologized.

Alone once more, Waller returned to his work station,
picked up the pigment jar, studied it again, and placed it in a
drawer. He dropped a fresh lettuce leaf into Oscar's terrarium,

then settled onto his cot.

"Fresh eye in the morning, eh, Oscar?"

Suddenly, for reasons he could not articulate, the image evoked of a single alert eye made Waller shiver. He definitely needed more sleep.

A chill in the air woke Waller sometime before dawn, and a dull, persistent thumping kept him from falling back asleep. At first the technician thought the noise was the night guard making his rounds, but after several minutes, with the origin point unchanging, he rose to investigate. A quick glance at the terrarium showed Oscar stretching his neck; the tortoise, too, heard the sound.

It came from the 3D printer room.

Waller made his way there and opened the door. There was no need to turn on the light. In the machine's glow, another Trapezohedron clearly took shape, slowly but steadily, layer by layer, the extrusion nozzle shifting back and forth. To judge by the state of near-completion, Waller guessed the machine had been in operation several hours.

Had he accidentally left it in sleep mode instead of shutting it down completely? Maybe he'd unconsciously hit print twice, and just not noticed the long gap between the two jobs? Neither scenario seemed likely. He was certain the ABS supply had been too low to fully form a second object. On the other hand, his mind had been operating almost on fumes the past day or two.

Waller moved toward the printer, hand outstretched to shut it down. There was no need to waste money on an identical prototype.

Then he froze.

The object on the movable printer platform should have been an exact duplicate of the one he'd already created. It almost was. Almost. It took a moment for the one slight difference to register in his mind.

The heart of the new Trapezohedron glowed a faint, unearthly red.

Waller stared at it for what felt like a long minute, but in reality was nearer half an hour, judging by the increased size of the object when he finally tore himself away. His vision blurred. Walls seemed to buckle inward. The air was almost too thick to breathe.

He returned to his desk, pulled open the top drawer, and removed the jar of pigment. It was still sealed.

His fingers felt stiff. He dropped the jar on the desk. The room felt colder now, deeply so, close to freezing.

Oscar! This was not a safe environment for a reptile.

"Oscar?"

Waller bent over the terrarium. The tortoise appeared to be sleeping again, having withdrawn head and limbs. Waller gingerly tapped the shell, and noticed with relief a slight movement at the left rear as a foot began to protrude.

No. Not a foot. A tentacle.

Waller staggered back. His first instinct, for reasons he could not have explained, was to race back to the printer room. Covering his eyes to avoid being distracted again, he fumbled for the off switch. There! In a few seconds, the whole thing should power down....

Another layer completed extruding. The machine showed no sign of stopping.

He crouched behind it and hit the breaker switch on the wall.

Moments later, he heard yet another layer being put down.

He pulled the plug.

When that too failed, Waller decided to head downstairs to the basement fuse box. As he rose to stand, however, he instinctively glanced at the printing bed to assess the replica's progress.

The glow absorbed the last of his free will, holding him entranced, unable to move of his own accord, save to inch slowly, ever so slowly, closer to the Trapezohedron, eyes glazed, fixed on that central throbbing patch of red.

Saturday morning, the early shift security man discovered the night guard face down at his desk, unconscious, having apparently suffered a stroke. An ambulance was immediately summoned. The guard lay in a coma for three days before passing on.

Waller's clothes lay in a pile on the floor beside the 3D printer, which stood silent and empty. A single yellow-white replica of a shining Trapezohedron sat on the technician's desk; in the corner of the room, a terrarium contained only a wilted piece of lettuce. Close examination of the printer nozzle indicated fragments of contaminant in the ABS which, after being sent to an outside laboratory, turned out to be meteorite dust.

The USB thumb drive containing the photographic slide show of the original Trapezohedron was nowhere to be found. Fortunately, Waller had uploaded his CAD program to the Cloud. Starbright was able to reproduce the object on the desk. Sales were solid though not spectacular. Starbright Enterprises could never quite match the awe inspired by the photos, but Miskatonic's students were content.

Dexter Charles' antiquity shop was found to be shuttered and, when police finally entered, completely empty, and had obviously been so for years.

The governors at Miskatonic University claimed they never received any donation of glass photographic negatives, nor, with the exception of Emmet Jordan, had they even heard of Dexter Charles.

Whitney Washio Waller was never seen again, save for one possible incident a year later, when Jordan claimed, on his way to a Governors' meeting at the college, to have glimpsed the mustached young man from a distance, briefly, near the main parking lot. But Jordan himself would be first to admit the figure could have been anyone.

RETRACTION

by Marie Michaels

Physici – The Journal of Natural Sciences
Vol. XVII, Summer Issue
Letters to the Editor

For years, *Physici* has been a last bastion of science. No clickbait here, no infotainment generated for audiences of attention deficit children unable to entertain a single serious thought. *Physici* exposed me to the cutting edge science that shapes our world. *Physici*, almost alone, kept true to its legacy of learning when other once-proud publications have been reduced to splashy headlines and listicles.

But now it has finally succumbed. I've no doubt that future issues will hold breathless reports of pet psychics, Mexican goat suckers, and lizard people manipulating the gold standard. And the hold of the brainless on today's world will grow stronger.

The reason I am writing is, of course, *Physici*'s publication of "At the Gate of the Burning Bush" by Dr. R. Nasser. The melodramatic title delivers on its promise of befuddled science and unprofessional hyperbole. The conclusion is more fitting for a cultish screed than a serious scientific publication.

———

Can you guys be serious? "At the Gate of the Burning Bush" is the worst article I've ever seen in this journal. I've seen more intelligent arguments in chain emails that begin FW: FW: FW: and end with half a dozen exclamation points. There isn't enough room in the whole issue to go through everything that's wrong and ridiculous about this.

I had to laugh at the list of instruments used by the supposed doctor. A Geiger counter or spectroscope alone is one thing, but taken together with manometers, ion meters, and some nonsense about Corellian measurements and infrasound, it's borderline incoherent. I think I saw the same inventory on an episode of *Ghost Hunters*.

And then there's the equipment he needed for the descent itself. It reads like an inventory of Evel Knievel's estate sale: custom made heat reflective suits, a Kevlar climbing harness, and a SCUBA apparatus designed to withstand gouts of flames.

———

What I want to know is how this work of fantasy got approved by your editorial staff. Will *Physici* publish anybody who pays their reading fee? Frankly, your publication comes off even worse than Dr. Nasser himself. He may be a victim of a sincere delusion. But you are either cynical or simply indifferent to the quality of this publication. I remember when you were considered an innovator among serious scientific publications.

True, there really is a so-called "Door to Hell" that exists in the Turkmen desert, a mining crater of fire that has been burning for decades. Beyond that, though, I can't help wondering whether a single word of this article, beyond the opening paragraph, is true.

I could barely get through his travelogue of an opening, documenting his hardships in reaching the village of Derweze. I think it was two flights, a half-day layover, another day in customs, and an interminable bumpy drive in an old Soviet vehicle. All this, mind you, following sixteen months of planning and endless bureaucratic wrangling with the Turkmen government, not to mention abstruse analyses of Turkmen media clips impossible to find in the West.

Soon enough, Nasser gives up all pretenses at scientific analysis. How can anyone take seriously his proposition that sentient creatures—not simple extremophile bacteria—can live inside the fires of the Door to Hell? No, not merely survive inside the pit of flame, but actually call other hapless beings into their fiery embrace.

Physici – The Journal of Natural Sciences
Vol. XVIII, Autumn Issue
Corrections, Changes, and Comments

It is with a heavy heart that I, your faithful Editor in Chief, and the entire editorial staff of *Physici*, the Journal of Natural Sciences, issue the following retraction regarding an article that appeared in the pages of Vol. XVI, Spring Issue, entitled "At the Gate of the Burning Bush" by Dr. R. Nasser.

Here at *Physici*, we pride ourselves on publishing the highest caliber articles for you, our audience of inquisitive, intelligent persons of science. Each article undergoes a rigorous peer review process, and, as the Editor in Chief, I personally evaluate every piece that appears in our journal to ensure that it addresses salient questions of utmost concern in today's world, contributes materially to the betterment and enlightenment of humankind, and meets our stringent quality standards.

Immediately after publication of this article, the journal received Letters to the Editor expressing numerous concerns about the article and its publication in the pages of our humble journal. As is the journal's practice, several of these letters were printed in the subsequent Summer Issue. The full text of the aforesaid letters are available in full on our website.

No response was received from Dr. Nasser after publication of these letters. Due to the many concerns raised by the letters, I endeavored to communicate the concerns of our esteemed readers to Dr. Nasser and to review with my own eyes the data underlying the article.

My staff and I worked thoroughly to contact Dr. Nasser. We reached out by all telephone numbers, physical addresses, and email addresses provided by the author but received no response. Telephone numbers were found to be out of service, mail was returned to our office with unintelligible markings, and electronic messages were automatically bounced back with the notation that the addresses did not exist. I have called and emailed Dr. Nasser's affiliated Universities and Foundations but have to date received no answers.

Upon my inquiry, peer readers repeated their confidence in the article and the data and methods underlying the author's conclusions, radical and controversial though they are. While I and the entire staff of *Physici* remain dedicated to exposing our readers to all rigorous articles of science, no matter how radical or controversial, we must conclude that there is legitimate cause for concern. Ultimately, the author has not made himself available to this journal to respond to the many concerns of our readers, nor has he provided his raw data to me or any member of the editorial staff for further review. For these reasons we at *Physici* must retract the aforesaid article and repeat to our readers our promise of rigorous peer review and the highest standards for scientific merit and the improvement of the human condition. I offer my deepest apologies to all readers who were offended by the article.

Physici – The Journal of Natural Sciences
Vol. XIX, Winter Issue
Corrections, Changes, and Comments

It is with most sincere regret that I, your devoted Editor in Chief, issue the following counter-retraction regarding a retraction appearing the pages of Vol. XVIII, Autumn Issue, regarding an article entitled "At the Gate of the Burning Bush" by Dr. R. Nasser.

I will not repeat the entire history of the article, which is of course well known to our readers. Suffice to say, I retracted the article following the receipt of many Letters to the Editor expressing the deepest concern regarding the nature of the studies and the quality of the data from which the author drew the radical conclusions set forth in the article, as well as the inability of myself and the other editors to contact Dr. Nasser to discuss these several legitimate concerns.

Earlier tonight, I received the most extraordinary visit from Dr. R. Nasser himself, accompanied by a graduate student assistant and three of the individuals who participated in the peer review for the article. The peer reviewers have requested anonymity at this time. Dr. Nasser and these persons each wheeled a handcart containing the instruments discussed in the article into my office. At this time I was permitted to examine the Geiger counters, spectroscopes, ion meters, and various other devices and take readings to confirm their accuracy. Hard drives were produced containing the original raw data gathered by the apparatuses. I must confess that I do not have the technological savvy of my eleven-year-old niece, but as far as I understood the read-outs, they appeared to conform with Dr. Nasser's descriptions in the article.

Recordings of interviews with individuals residing in the local village of Derweze, also known as Darvasa depending upon one's preferred Cyrillic transliteration, were played. I was able to confirm Dr. Nasser's translation of these interviews and various media reports with the help of a certain intern at *Physici*. This intern's willingness to advance the cause of objective, unbiased science and to stay at the office after she missed the day's last commuter train is to be commended. This intern has requested anonymity at this time.

I am now convinced of the following information. Since the natural gas in the mining pit was first ignited several decades ago, residents of Derweze have observed swarms of crawling insects and spiders approaching and falling into the flames. Beginning approximately eighteen months before Dr. Nasser's investigation, larger animals began throwing themselves into the fires—sporadically at first, reaching a peak frequency of a dozen per day. Villagers likened the movements of the animals drawn to the pit to inexpertly handled puppets. Within six months, livestock and the small, stout ponies kept by the Teke tribe went missing from areas within one hundred kilometers from the pit. Villagers likened the movements of the animals drawn to the pit with increasing frequency to inexpertly handled puppets. The disappearances incited armed confrontations between the residents of Derweze and their neighbors as ranchers and farmers noticed the depletion of their herds. These clashes were quelled only when the aggressors viewed the spectacle with their own eyes.

Dr. Nasser proffered videos documenting his descent into the "Door to Hell" as well as amateur smartphone photographs and videos. Though dark and blurry, the events taking place are unmistakable. Animals totter toward the pit, sway at the edge of the flames, and leap inside. No human casualties have been reported, no doubt thanks to the vigilance of the Derweze villagers. But without their intervention ... I shudder away from thinking too closely on it. One video showed a very dangerous rescue of a human being—dear readers, a child no older than my niece—from the brink of the crater by one of Dr. Nasser's graduate student assistants. But even this was not the most disturbing thing I witnessed.

Until one year before Dr. Nasser's investigation, sporadic news articles referred to livestock disappearances and an increase in visitor interest in the Door to Hell. One farmer published a letter in a regional newspaper calling on the administration to mobilize troops, although to what end he never made clear. The man claimed to have followed his entire goat herd to the pit and watched with horror as they threw themselves in, one by one destroying his livelihood. Yet all these reports ceased altogether after the publication of this letter in that local newspaper, and online archives could not retrieve them.

What chilled me, friends, were the follow-up visits Dr. Nasser and his companions made to each of the subjects they interviewed and each of the authors of news articles he could trace to addresses. Their apartment rooms and modest little houses were empty. Food moldered in pantries, and dust had just started to film over surfaces. Text messages and emails bounced back although messages had arrived from those sources only weeks prior. I observed videos of extremely perplexed neighbors who could not recall the last time they saw the individuals, and at times could hardly recall the individuals at all.

Dr. Nasser begged my indulgence and the indulgence of our readers for his failure to respond promptly to the Letters to the Editor and the retraction published in our recent issues. When we first attempted to contact him, he was undergoing medical treatment for attacks of acute anxiety, idiopathic peripheral neuropathy, and prolonged fugue states that plagued him after he returned from Derweze. Dr. Nasser has requested secrecy at this time as to the identity of his treating physicians but permitted me to review the medical records. In spite of his treatments, I observed that he continues to suffer from a moderate intermittent palsy, and if not for his evident exhaustion and anxiety I would not have permitted him to chain smoke throughout our interview.

In my opinion, these materials adequately support each statement and conclusion set forth in the article. In fact, I will venture that the article presented a conservative perspective on certain implications that must necessarily arise from measurements taken by Dr. Nasser's instruments. And I shall never forget those videos of the strange enchantment that appeared to possess so many hapless creatures—and the even stranger enchantment that fogged the brains of dozens of human subjects. As the Editor in Chief and the sole member of the editorial staff working at the late hour of Dr. Nasser's visit, I have exercised my discretion to print this counter-retraction without the approval of my fellow editors.

I gave my word that I would not divulge the current location of Dr. Nasser or his assistants, but I wish to reassure our readers that Dr. Nasser has at all times acted according to the loftiest virtues of science and true courage. I conclude this counter-retraction with joy and no little anxiety at the upheaval that may result from certain proofs that I have seen. More information, including the raw data and further analysis, will be published in the following issues of this humble journal and may in the future be available on our website.

Physici – The Journal of Natural Sciences
Vol. XX, Spring Issue
Corrections, Changes, and Comments

There are things I cannot explain, dear readers.

It is with a growing sense of dread that I issue the following retraction regarding a counter-retraction that appeared in Vol. XIX, Winter Issue, in turn regarding a retraction appearing the pages of Vol. XVIII, Autumn Issue, pertaining to an article that first appeared in Vol. XVI , Spring Issue, entitled "At the Gate of the Burning Bush" by Dr. R. Nasser. I deeply regret the mounting confusion surrounding the publication of this article, which has provoked more response than any other article in the history of this proud journal.

I do not recall inserting the counter-retraction. Perhaps you, dear readers, you inquisitive persons of science, may illuminate some portion of what occurred the night of November 15. I remember reviewing final drafts of prospective articles until ap-proximately 8:50 p.m., when an intern, who has requested ano-nymity at this time, left the office and wished me a pleasant evening. Meta-data extracted from Corel WordPerfect support this recollection. After the intern's departure, our offices were empty, and the night custodial staff had not yet appeared. In-formation from our web hosted email server shows that the counter-retraction was inserted thirteen minutes after submis-sion of Vol. XIX, Winter Issue to our printer, Antwerp Consol-idated Publishing Group. Each member of our editorial staff received an email from Ms. Mischa Smullin at Antwerp Consol-idated, informing us that she was exceedingly annoyed by the last minute changes to Vol. XIX, Winter Issue. No one viewed the message until the following morning. I have been assured that our firewalls are reasonably secure, and an inspection of our security measures has yielded no evidence of tampering or breach by outside or inside forces.

Video cameras of the lobby experienced a malfunction one hour and twenty-six minutes before the email was sent to Ms. Smullin. The cameras experienced the same malfunction seven minutes after the timestamp of the email from my account inserting the counter-retraction. Another of our graduate student interns has timed the duration of her trip between the revolving door of our lobby and my office on the fourteenth floor of the Linnehein Building. She took eighteen measurements of the trip at various times during the day, with a majority of those trips occurring during times known to building security to be lulls in traffic. The average trip lasted six minutes and twenty-six seconds. The median of the eighteen trips is six minutes and twenty-four seconds. The standard deviation is .72078.

Finally, readers, there is one final piece to the puzzle of the counter-retraction. The Linnehein Building has a strict no-smoking policy, and we at *Physici* have of course known for many decades of the deleterious effects of tobacco use on human health. Yet, when I returned to my office on Thursday morning, I discovered a note from my administrative assistant, which he found on his desk. The note was hand-written on a blank phone message pad, from a member of the custodial staff of the Linnehein Building, scolding us for leaving a thick haze of cigarette smoke in the office. She asked us, and particularly myself, to be more considerate in the future because she has asthma. At my request, my assistant then retrieved the original manuscript of "At the Gate of the Burning Bush" that we received from Dr. R. Nasser, which was smudged in several of the upper right-hand corners with ash. Testing has not yet revealed whether it is cigarette ash.

In conclusion, readers, I must repeat that we have at this time no evidence to support the controversial claims of Dr. R.

Nasser contained in the article and regretfully re-issue a retraction of the article.

Physici Online – The Blog of Natural Sciences
At the Burning Solstice
The Unspoken The Unspeakable

The editorial staff are all fools.

Yet I know it is I who am the fool, for I had hoped that these men and women of science would prove stronger of mind than those poor Turkmen villagers. But again I reveal my own weakness and bias, for now I see that these fools are burdened by conventional cynicism, ignorant in their own way to that which exceeds the petty strictures of what we call science. Science! A half-baked shibboleth cobbled together with arithmetical mewlings.

Are there not more things in heaven and on earth than are dreamt of in our philosophies? Is this not true in our philosophy above all, the veneration of Science as all All-Mother, Destroyer and Creator and Succubus?

Readers, the fire. My burning heart.

I speak of nothing less than the power of Life itself: that enduring, that mindless, that chaotic struggle to conquer death for fleeting moments of frenzied spawning. We have catalogued a handful of creatures visible to our eyes and our clumsy instruments, and worship ourselves as gods. We believe that we understand the world since we have seen it. When one of us is so foolish as to draw back the veil of our paltry senses, he sets in his motion his own ultimate Doom. Only a man of the most dogged powers of persistence may reach this point. I envy the whimpering and brain-deadened majority of the human race that does not possess the necessary levels of spiritual fortitude.

It hurts, readers. How does it burn? How do the flames call

across the seas? The smell of burning bone coats the back of my throat.

Once or twice over the span of many generations, a man succeeds in rending an infinitesimal stitch of that shroud that safeguards the ignorance of our gibbering race. And when he does, he cannot help but strive to sow the seeds of understanding that he has destroyed his life to nurture. Such knowledge is all to him: faith, hope, charity, family, warmth, food and drink. So much has he sacrificed in pursuit of this knowledge that he forgets all he has learned in books and all that his forbearers have learned at the flaming ends of torches. There is but one inevitable reaction of the sniveling human animal to notions that upset the rattletrap edifices of superstition or tottering reason that structure his puny, obscure existence.

The damned windows open but a few inches! The air is chill but it is not enough. My breath, readers. My breath is fire.

Therefore how fitting that I speak of torches, I who have descended into the Door to Hell. I faced the unquenchable flames that have roared for thousands of nights. I emerged from that place not unscathed, a scarred Prometheus bearing perilous knowledge.

Therefore I—not your Editor in Chief but one who pities the poor fool, wherever he has gone—issue the following retraction. All that this journal has printed throughout the feeble history of our publication is inanity and idiot scribbles, amounting to nothing but the foul breath of a putrescent people. Yet with the article I have penned, I howl into the glittering void that surrounds and bewilders our eyes. If I believed in the existence of a benevolent creator, I would plead until my throat rasped with blood for a crumb of understanding to fall into man's collective anima. But now I can harbor no such fantasies, either of the innate beneficence of the universe or of the decrepit mind of man. Not after I have lost yet more men and women to the Force or Intelligence or pure Malignance that dogs me.

Thus do I damn you all. Thus do I damn myself.

I fear, readers. I burn. My only salvation is a hotter flame yet, where I may forget. Where all I am and have been and could be may burn for eternity.

Physici – The Journal of Natural Sciences
Vol. XXII, Autumn Issue
Announcements!

It is with great excitement that I, your new Editor in Chief, announce that the recent Editor in Chief and editorial board have, effective as of this Vol. XXII, Autumn Issue, elected to take early retirement with the generous severance package offered by *Physici*'s parent holdings company. The families of several of the editors expressed their long-held dreams to live out their remaining years in monasteries in secret green mountains where no word has passed human lips in decades. I have been told that the former Editor in Chief is undergoing treatments for a touch of exhaustion—no surprise when we consider the many hours he has put into making *Physici* the most reliable source for science in our modern world. I am also given to understand that he is working diligently to secure a visa to various exotic locales, and I and the new editorial board wish him the very best wherever his travels may lead him! He joins me in thanking our readers for their vigorous dedication to this journal that was communicated to all our staff after we were unfortunately unable to produce our regular summer issue.

I am also thrilled to announce the beginning of a new semester of interns at the Journal of Natural Sciences! One of our former class of interns is pursuing new and exciting opportunities with a securities firm she regrets she cannot name pursuant to a non-disclosure agreement. Good luck to all of this past semester's interns, and I would like to give a special shout-out to one in particular who has been expressly requested by a certain former Soviet socialist republic to join their science ministry. We cannot name the lucky student until she passes all the applicable background checks, but a preliminary "pozdravleniya" to you! Our new crop of interns brings us all the fire and glow of youth with a passion for scientific analysis and cutting edge questions. We are fortunate to have them on our team!

Observant readers may notice that certain articles and "Comments, Changes, and Corrections" are currently unavailable in the archives of *Physici*. Rest assured that we have contacted our web host and will surely have the missing files restored shortly. Readers with concerns about recent issues of *Physici* may contact me personally at the email address below, as many of you already have, and I will be happy to answer any and all questions. But I hope that, at the beginning of my tenure as Editor in Chief and with the help of my newly hired editorial stff, all of us can lay the past and any oddities therein to rest and move forward into a bright, rational, and reasonable future.

I would like to respectfully point prospective submitters to the recently revised Submission Guidelines, reflecting certain subjects that my colleagues and I believe have been overexposed in today's busy and bustling scientific community. As always, the editorial board reserves the right to reject any submission that fails to conform to the Guidelines in any respect.

Finally, and I hope to phrase this delicately so as not to rehash old business, but I would like to issue a formal apology to all persons who have had their fair homes defamed by certain miscreant authors.

I have been encouraged, and have no hesitation, to invite all of our readers to consider visiting these natural wonders of our modern world, to marvel at the surprises Nature continues to hold for us. If you are anything like me, readers, you cannot help but be changed by what you will see. So let me propose a toast to new cycles and new life—in this hallowed institution and in the most unexpected of places.

FACILITIES MANAGEMENT AT DAGOCORP HQ

by L Chan

Name: Douglas Finklehorn
Department: Accounting
Room: 4-10
Ticket Number: 103
Issue: Color of walls
I'm still not satisfied with the color of the paint used. I specified that it had to be purplish-green of unearthly hue, shifting when stared at directly. Get someone up here to redo it.
Ticket Response:
For the last time, the color out of space is NOT a color. I've given you purple. I've given you green. We've looked at the color wheel for hours. If you can't give me a Pantone number, we're not repainting your office. Seven times is enough.

Name: Quincy Primavera
Department: Strategic Planning
Room: 10-13
Ticket Number: 107
Issue: Office humidity
Hi guys,
Is there an issue with the vents? There's a lot of condensation in the office. It's too wet here. I've got water running down my laptop screen. The network connection seems to be shot too. Do you guys do that?

Ticket Response:
Dear Ms. Primavera
The humidity in the building is carefully controlled for the comfort of all occupants. I've forwarded your connectivity issues to Technical Support and will close this ticket.

Name: Eliza Burlington
Department: Customer Service
Room: 08-54
Ticket Number: 109
Issue: New hires
I saw a couple of fresh faces on the orientation tour earlier today. Look, I love ethnic food as much as anybody, but there are too damn many Egyptians, Orientals, and other dark-skinned folks around the office. I prefer the company the way it used to be.
Ticket Response:
Eliza,
For the twentieth time, this isn't Human Resources. We don't take these complaints at Facilities Management and I've got half a mind to report this breach of our diversity policy.

Name: Brandon Carter
Department: Sales
Room: 02-02
Ticket Number: 113
Issue: Lost pass
Hi
I'm just wondering if there's a chance that someone turned in a security pass to Facilities? I can't find mine anywhere.

Ticket Response:
Sir

I don't mean to be forward, but any lost pass with Vice President clearance and above needs to be reported to Security quickly. You know what kind of access you have.

Issue: Re: Lost pass
Look here, I come to you with a problem and now it's your problem. I mean to have it solved.

Ticket Response #2:
OK sir, I'll remind all the cleaning staff to be on the lookout. I really suggest you alert Security to disable your pass. You do know that Vice President passes have both RFID chips as well as a Silver Key for Dreamland access, right? It's more than my job's worth to rat on you, but you need to watch yourself.

Ticket Response #3:
Dave, we're gonna need a cleanup in 02-02. Bring Bob and the industrial bleach. I tried to tell him, I really did. The thing about Silver Keys is that the doors unlock both ways. It's not just for management to get in.

Better bring along some of the top-shelf pesticide as well. I hope it didn't lay any eggs.

Name: Quincy Primavera
Department: Strategic Planning
Room: 10-13
Ticket Number: 127
Issue: Trapdoor?

Did Facilities install a large trapdoor under my desk? I can't work. It's drafty and even colder than the ventilation. I've already brought a blanket for my legs but this is too much.

p.s. Did you forward my last ticket to Tech Support? Connectivity is still wonky.

Ticket Response:

Dear Ms. Primavera

Tech Support assures me that there's nothing wrong with your network port on their end.

It's not a trap door. The thing that you see is just the false floor access panel. We need the false floor for all the wiring. Under no circumstances are you to open the trapdoor to trace your network wire. God knows we've already lost two staff that way.

I'm closing this ticket.

Name: Rashid al Haroun
Department: Warehouse Management
Room: 03-13
Ticket Number: 131
Issue: Lift does not stop on the eleventh and twelfth floors
As above
Ticket Response:
You don't work on the eleventh or twelfth floor. Stop pressing the buttons.

Name: Undefined
Department: Undefined
Room: Undefined
Ticket Number: 137
Issue: Safety violations
Jim,

I was down in the basement the other day and noticed that the shoggoths were working WITHOUT the wet floor sign again. Need I remind you that we already have two pending compensation cases because of people slipping on shoggoth slime? The stuff is damn near frictionless.

I am still waiting for you to submit your investigation report as to who coated my doorknob with shoggoth slime. I was trapped in my office for two days. TWO DAYS.

Ticket Response:

Dear Director,

Pardon the delayed response. I have spoken to all the staff concerned and reminded them of the seriousness with which management views health and safety. The security camera system is still a bit problematic, and I hope to view the relevant footage and present you with my report within the week.

Name: Quincy Primavera
Department: Strategic Planning
Room: 10-13
Ticket Number: 139
Issue: Trapdoor?

Hi

There's something weird with the trapdoor. I took a peek to see if I could find where the draft is coming from. I swear that the false floor under the trapdoor goes uphill in all directions. But the floor above it doesn't go up, what gives? I know you said the ventilation and humidity was set based on company policy but it's strangely rhythmic. Are you sure there isn't anything wrong?

Ticket Response:

Dear Ms. Primavera

I have to reiterate that there will be no more meddling with the false floor under your desk. The angle of the floor is just a trick of the light.

Name: Eva García Molina
Department: Archives
Room: B1-11
Ticket Number: 149
Issue: Damn cat

Hey

I'm working down in the basement with the archive records, next to the Skye Room? There's a cat that found its way into the archives. It's making a racket and I can't begin to stress how much trouble we'll all be in if it pees on anything. How'd it get here?

Ticket Response:

We don't have any cats in the complex, and strays avoid us at street level. I sent Bob down after hours to take a look, and Bob found a half-eaten tuna sandwich in the bin. I've requisitioned a covered bin for the archives if you must insist on taking lunch at your desk.

Issue: Re: Damn cat

The covered bin didn't help. Now there are five cats in the room. How are they getting in? I chase them round the corners and they vanish into dead ends and under shelves into walls! When they purr, the walls shake and they meow together like the heartbeat of the world.

Ticket Response #2:

Look I'll send Bob around again, leave your door open, shoggoths aren't so good with doorknobs and I'd rather not replace another one.

Ticket Response #3:

Hi Dave, do me a favor and bust out the big dredging hook. Been meaning to send Bob down to deal with that recurring cat problem, but I've been putting it off for a bit and the cats got another archivist. Honestly, I think management feels it's cheaper to hire new archivists than to approve my requests to bring in professional help for dream cats. Anyway, I've got to tell Human Resources about this, so you're going have to hook Ms. García Molina's remains out of Bob. Bob's a solid worker, but we really have to talk to him about just sucking stuff off the floor. He's like a seven foot tall gelatinous Roomba.

Anyway, last time Bob wandered around with a skeleton in him, we all got yelled at by the bosses, so get on it quick.

Name: Burt Jones
Department: Sales
Room: 02-04
Ticket Number: 151
Issue: Angles of the walls

My office just got refurbished. I specifically requested for each of the four corners to be exactly seventy-seven degrees. Not regular ninety degrees. What do we even pay you for?

Ticket Response:

You have to take that up with the fellow in your department who put up the budget for refurbishment. Our contractors only do standard geometry. Non-Euclidean is chargeable at star rates. Did you get the budget for that? I don't think so.

Name: Joe Bonetti
Department: Security
Room: 01-04
Ticket Number: 157
Issue: CCTV problems

Hey, it's Joe from security. We've been having some problems with the security cameras. We're getting recordings of a tall, dark figure ambling through the corridors on the screens. It doesn't sync with any of the door records. Could you get the vendor to come down and take a look at the system?

Ticket Response:

Hey Joe, sorry it took me a while. The security systems guys will be down next Monday. They'll update me after that. We missed you at the weekly poker game, you down for Friday?

Ticket Response #2:

Surveillance company got back to me. They've checked all the cameras and the door systems. They're working fine. Company boys can't replicate the anomaly. Have you considered that maybe the black figure isn't in the corridors, but on the screen in the room with you?

Ticket Response #3:

Hey Joe, I'm going to need your acknowledgement to close the ticket. By the way, if you don't reply about Friday poker, I'm giving your slot to Dave.

Ticket Response #4:

Joe?

Name: Quincy Primavera
Department: Strategic Planning
Room: 10-13
Ticket Number: 163
Issue: Trapdoor?

Hi

I know you told me not to fool around with the false floor and I really didn't, I swear. But the other day I knocked my Brita over and half of it went down the trapdoor. I stole the industrial roll of toilet paper from the bathroom and went to soak the water up but the water was flowing away from the trapdoor.

Uphill.

What the hell is wrong with this building? I got down into the trapdoor to try and dry some of that shit up but it all disappeared by the time I got down. Was the trapdoor always this big? The vent's as loud as ever down there. Sounds a lot like breathing. I swear it called my name.

Ticket Response:

Noted on the spillage issue. I'll send someone to replace the toilet paper. Thanks for informing me.

Name: Eliza Burlington
Department: Customer Service
Room: 08-54
Ticket Number: 167
Issue: Half-eaten food in the break room

This has gone on long enough. Brown Jenkins is scuttering around. I hear him in the walls. He eats my food. I see his tiny teeth marks all over my sandwiches. I see his handprints on the cake.

Ticket Response:

For the last time, this isn't the Human Resources email address.

This is also the last warning about your borderline racist tirades. There are two Jenkins in the building, Hank and Leroy. I guess you're talking about Hank. For the love of god, man, you don't just refer to him by his skin color. Anyway, he's not brown, he's just very tanned.

Name: Sam Ward
Department: Strategic Planning
Room: 10-17
Ticket Number: NA
Issue: Statue in the foyer

Hi

You know there was a Bring Your Family to Work Day last week? What's the cost of repairing one of the green stone statues in the foyer if, say, an employee's son had jumped the queue poles and broken off one of the mouth tentacles? I'm asking for a friend.

Ticket Response:

Dear Sam

First, I've already checked the security camera recordings and I know it wasn't your kid, it was you and your bunch of frat boy buffoons in an after-hours party.

Second, management is very protective of the statues. Had them shipped from overseas at no small expense. You can't get that green soapstone hereabouts. So, we never had this interaction, and if anything ever comes back to me on this, I will write you up for paranoia and hallucinations.

Go get your ass down to a toy store. Get two tubs of playdough. Green and black. Now you mix them until you get the right color. Mix a big batch. You mould yourself a mouth tentacle and you come by every week to adjust it while the original grows back.

Also, if you still have the piece of statue, go home and bury it. Seven or eight feet deep to be safe. Don't worry about wild animals digging it up, they'll stay away. Anything under six feet and the damn thing will dig its own way out.

By the way, the cleaner's welfare fund thanks you for your generous donation. PayPal is fine.

Name: Quincy Primavera
Department: Strategic Planning
Room: 10-13
Ticket Number: 173
Issue: Trapdoor?

The trapdoor still calls my name. I need to go. I'm working with it open now. The cool air comforts me. I can fit in. I know I can.

Ticket Response:
I'm going to forward this to Human Resources. You've clearly been working too hard.

Name: Janet Peabody
Department: Sales
Room: 02-15
Ticket Number: 179
Issue: Noise from the floor above

There's some infernal music coming from floor above after hours. The beating of the drums! The shrill shrieks of infernal flutes! The nefarious thud of footsteps! The chanting! Iä! Iä! Shub-Niggurath!

Ticket Response:
That's the fourth complaint this month about Mrs. Henderson's Zumba class. We never had this problem before she started using dubstep music. Thanks for bringing it to my attention, I'll take it up with her.

Name: Quincy Primavera
Department: Strategic Planning
Room: 10-13
Ticket Number: 181
Issue: Trapdoor?

There are such sights beyond the eleventh floor. You were foolish to dissuade me. There is an ocean in the building. Fathoms deep, I would have drowned, had I not seen the Great

Ones hold court in the sea between eleventh and twelfth. They
allowed me to bear witness to the court, to imbibe of the womb
fluid of their world. Nobody comes back unchanged.

You're the only one who's fully human in the building, you
know that right? I can hear your breath from all the way up
here. You may be locked up all nice and secure in the basement,
but you can't wait forever. You have to eat. You have family. I'll
be waiting, you'll never leave this building.

Ticket Response:

Dear Ms. Primavera

I see you have ignored my well-meaning advice and gone
ahead to explore your office environment. I also assume that
you were responsible for the banging at my door earlier. Don't
bother, it's reinforced steel and more than adequate for any
fresh changeling.

You're right. I am the only full human in the building. I have
a wife and kids and this job pays just fine. You think the aco-
lytes of Dagon know how to run a contract? Fix a window?
Paint a wall? Sure, you beasties with the gills and the bugged out
eyes can work Human Resources and Tech Support, the transi-
tion to Windows 10 is surprisingly easy for your kind. But contract management? Please. The Great Old Ones know this and
I'm very well compensated.

You've been complaining about the humidity in your office
for ages. I've taken the liberty of turning up the dehumidifier.
While you've been sitting there reading this email, that slight
dryness you feel in your neck? It's your new gills drying out.
Don't be alarmed, death comes slowly and painfully. But not for
you. You're just going to lie there gasping for breath while security moves you to your new cubicle. A word to the wise, do not
struggle against the shoggoths. A changeling will survive the
loss of a limb or two but the carpet just got shampooed last
week and calling them in early costs extra. Human Resources
will be along with your second orientation pack over the next
few days.

The shoggoths will clear out your desk for you. I'm told that changelings forsake all memories of the flesh, but your personal effects will be kept for a month before disposal in case you still want them. We'll have a new hire at your desk come Monday. Welcome to Dagocorp.

NO DOVES COME FROM RAVEN EGGS

by Mark Oxbrow

"Winter follows fall. Night falls when day is done. My father told me: 'No doves come out of raven eggs.' It's real. All of it is real. I don't want to believe it anymore. But it's real and I have to."
Katla G.

BBC News:
Fears Mounting for Missing Crew of Stricken Iceland Rig
9 confirmed dead, 7 missing after explosions destroy Iceland Deepwater Oil Rig.

Marine rescue experts say they will continue to search for the seven crew members still missing from the Myrká Deepwater Oil Rig nearly twenty-four hours after a series of massive explosions tore through the drilling platform.

The Myrká Oil Rig lies 350 km northeast of mainland Iceland in the frigid Norwegian Sea. One man was successfully rescued by helicopter from rough seas. Rescuers managed to retrieve nine bodies overnight before stormy conditions forced them to abandon further rescue attempts.

Haelhaf Nordson, a spokesperson for Kongshavn Deepwater Oil, operators of the stricken Myrká Rig, read from a prepared statement: "At this time, I cannot share any details about the survivor and I have no more information regarding our missing men. I do want to say that these were highly experienced, dedicated men. Professionals. Kongshavn Energy is a family. We have lost part of our family tonight. And I want to extend my condolences to the families of the men that are confirmed lost."

Nordson continued: "This tragedy is unspeakable. But now is not the time to seek reasons, now we join in prayers for the safety of the seven men that are missing."

Chief Executive Nord Halstrom of Kongshavn Energy, the parent company of Kongshavn Deepwater Oil, was unavailable for comment overnight. He is expected to hold a press conference later today. Kongshavn stock has taken a sharp downturn since trading opened a little over an hour ago.

Email dated 21 October, 23:09
Robert Atwood wrote
To | Katla Gunnarsdóttir
Cc |
Hæ Katla

You never told me they eat pony in Iceland. I mean I know there's a lot of Icelandic ponies but I wasn't expecting to be offered pony steak at dinner last night. But hey, I guess we eat kangaroo. Still remember the look on your face when you saw the menu at the Australian Hotel in the Rocks. Crocodile pizza.

I never saw the Northern Lights before. It's like the sky is on fire. Hard to imagine anything so magical can be real. I lived in cities nearly all my life. Barely seen stars in the sky and now it's lit up like Christmas in red and green and orange and silver.

It's like the world's turned upside down. The sky's bright and the sea's dark. I thought I saw something earlier, far out beyond the cliffs, out in the deep. Thought I saw a flickering flame. Maybe a light from the Myrká Rig. Don't think I'd see the fire from this far. It's massive, thousands of gallons of oil sending sheets of flame up into the sky, but it's got to be too far out. Nothing could get all the way here from out there.

I'm staying on Grimsey Island tonight. I visited your parents' graves this morning. I took your mother flowers like you wanted. I remember you said she loved sunflowers, but there are no sunflowers so I took her an orchid. I got your father a bottle of twenty-five-year-old Glenmorangie Scotch. I left the photo of you at Redleaf Beach.

The owner of the guesthouse remembers you playing with her daughter. You were a little girl. She remembers you crying because you spilt black ink on your dress. She said you looked for the hidden people, the huldufólk, with her daughter and your sister. She says you were scared of skrimsli—monsters that came out of the sea.

Tomorrow I fly back to the mainland. I meet your sister in Vopnafjörður in two days. I think I've figured it all out—Kongshavn, Rahn, the book, the key, all of it. I decoded your father's letters. I'll give everything to your sister.

I miss you. Miss you this day and every day. – Rob

Australian Museum Special Archives Item: AMS1890/20
Idol, Southern Pacific
Added to Australian Museum collection: April, 1925.
Donated by Gustaf Johansen, sailor, yacht *Alert*.
Notes: This curious carved stone idol was donated to curator of ethnology, Professor Edward Rookwood, by able seaman Gustaf Johansen, lately of the steam yacht *Alert* which was found disabled off the coast near The Gap and towed into Sydney Harbor. Other members of yacht's crew all lost.
Description of item: Hand-carved sculpture of unidentified deity or mythical creature. Does not correspond to any known Polynesian god. Base is marked with unknown form of hieroglyphs. Hunched figure. Head most closely resembles cuttlefish. Body and wings of a dragon.

Robert Atwood | LinkedIn profile
Games producer - Digital technologist
Invisible Inc. | Shiny Evil Games | Academy of Interactive Entertainment
Sydney, Australia
I love stories and I love games. Games that make you think and stories that mess with your mind. I'm into virtual reality gaming, augmented reality experiences, tabletop strategy, first-person shooters, 8-bit retro game consoles, and Redfish's Pad Thai.

You'll find me in the library, at the arcade, on the beach, but mostly sitting in Suzie Q Coffee & Records, Surry Hills, with a breakfast bowl, a cup of single origin coffee, and my MacBook Pro.

Transcript of audio file on Robert Atwood's phone:
So the archivist at the Australian Museum finally agreed to let me see the idol. I showed her your father's letter—the one with the sketch. She'd read your father's paper on the 1997 U.S. Navy's deep ocean noise. Think she was intrigued. The idol looks almost identical to the sketch.

Which doesn't explain how a carving on a Viking runestone can look like some unexplained stone idol from the South Pacific?

Deep Ocean Noise International Symposium: Speaker Biographies
Prof. Gunnar Sigurdsson is a Senior Scientist at Kongshavn Deepwater Oil, a subsidiary of Kongshavn Energy.

Emeritus Professor at the World Maritime University (WMU) in Malmö, Sweden, and Visiting Professor at the Institute of Ocean Sciences, Uni. Zurich (Switzerland). He holds degrees in oceanography (University of Iceland) and physics (Miskatonic University), and a PhD in seabed acoustics (University of Cambridge).

Prof. Sigurdsson will present his paper, "Ultra-low-frequency underwater sounds in the Drekasvæðið Area, Iceland."

Email dated 22 October, 15:56
Mr. Deacon wrote
To | Haelhaf Nordson, Sóley Gunnarsdóttir, Aalt De Jong
Cc |
Haelhaf, Sóley, Aalt
I have just had word that a major oil spill from Myrká is heading for the mainland coast.

I expect your team on the ground to manage the media response immediately. Get Sóley out in front—she's young and pretty enough to distract the bastards.

We are bringing in Aibne McCabe—consultant from Dexter Crisis Management Planning. He will lead on reputation damage control. Sóley—I think you attended their Crisis Response course?

I will keep Nord out of the way. If anyone asks directly: obfuscate. CEO Nord Halstrom is too distressed / unavailable / whatever. Ignore questions about any of his previous gaffes.
Deacon
Vice President | Kongshavn Energy

Email dated 22 October, 18:12
Robert Atwood wrote

To | Katla Gunnarsdóttir
Cc |
Hæ Katla
I found the Thule Society's copy of the book. Hess didn't keep it. Obersturmführer Otto Rahn had it. Rahn was part writer, part adventurer, like a Nazi Indiana Jones. He believed the Cathar heretics had the Holy Grail at Montségur Castle. Rahn was also a member of Himmler's SS.

Rahn gave the book to a friend he made before the war. I tracked down the daughter of Rahn's old Nazi pal, Wilhelm Karl Heinrich. He'd talked about helping Rahn tend his flower garden in Dachau. You were right about the book. It's not the 1839 edition. Rahn had a copy of the 1909 Golden Goblin Press edition from New York. Heinrich's daughter sold me Rahn's copy.

Rahn annotated the book when he visited Iceland for the SS in 1936. I can barely make sense of his indecipherable scribbles and notes. He sailed with twenty men but says he feels utterly alone. Rahn spent Midsummer night at Reykholt. He stayed at a hotel by Lake Laugarvatn listening to jazz records on the gramophone. But he didn't find what he was looking for.

Rahn's copy of *Nameless Cults* is riddled with mistakes. The NY edition mistranslates the German on pretty much every page and it cuts whole sections of the Black Book. Otto sailed all the way to Iceland but he never had a chance—he was looking in the wrong places. He travelled to Vik but couldn't find any trace of the town—because he was on the wrong side of Iceland!

The NY edition is terrible—total hack job. Rahn would have been better off using a bloody Ouija board.

A rare book dealer near Rindermarkt in München managed to track down a copy of the 1839 first edition *Unaussprechlichen Kulten*. I didn't ask how. It cost more than our first car. I got it translated.

The 1839 *Unaussprechlichen Kulten* has a chapter on an earlier incarnation of the Starry Wisdom Cult—decades before Bowen founded his sect in Providence. The cultists didn't build a town near Vik like Otto's Black Book said—their town was at "the hill at the bay"—at a place called Haedvik.

I found Haedvik. It's in Vopnafjörður, near the black sand beach at the bay. The lost town only ever appeared on one map. It is so weird that I'll finally be there tomorrow. We talked about it for so long and you never got to see it. Feel alone. You should be here with me. But I never did get anything I wanted.

Love you – Rob

Reuters Newswire: for immediate release

Witness statement (translated) from Sóley Gunnarsdóttir, Public Relations department. Kongshavn Energy.

Egil Hagen, sole survivor of Myrká Deepwater Oil Rig tragedy, has recovered consciousness and has made the following statement about the incident:

"I was below making coffee. I heard an alarm. The whole rig ripped apart. There was barely any warning. Nothing we could do.

"I've never heard a sound like it and the fire as the rec room just sort of buckled, crumpled, like paper. I couldn't see nothing for the smoke. Felt it burn my lungs. Someone was screaming without end. I don't know who grabbed me. They dragged and pushed me out into the air.

"That was when I saw. Half the rig was gone. It was all gutted. Nothing but metal black bones. The sea was on fire. Black oil and water sprayed up everywhere.

"I saw some men. Couldn't recognize them. They were black with oil. The fire had them cornered. I saw them throw themselves into the sea."

Mr. Hagen was caught up in an explosion and was rescued, unconscious, by helicopter from the accident site.

Guardian News:
Missing Oil Rig Crew Raised Safety Concerns

Two days after the Myrká Deepwater Oil Rig off Iceland was lost, the cause of the fire and explosions that devastated the multimillion-dollar rig remain a mystery.

The Myrká Deepwater Oil Rig was carrying out exploratory drilling in the Drekasvæðið Area, a barely-tapped region of the Norwegian Sea that was opened to oil companies for exploration less than a decade ago.

Kongshavn Energy CEO Nord Halstrom took to Twitter to angrily deny that there are any safety issues on any of Kongshavn's seven international oil rigs. He has so far refused to talk directly to the media.

Safety Fears

Marine experts are speculating that reported safety breaches over the past year on the Myrká Oil Rig may be responsible for the catastrophic explosion.

"Six months ago I called for an independent inquiry after the death of Alexander Johannessen," says marine safety expert, Virginia Gallagher. "We are still waiting for the authorities to fully investigate the circumstances surrounding Alexander's death. Johannessen's children deserve the truth about the loss of their father."

The cause of the Myrká tragedy is still unknown.

Email dated 22 October, 23:02
Robert Atwood wrote
To | Katla Gunnarsdóttir
Cc |
Hæ Katla

I found this newspaper cutting in the box of things you left behind:

Nordstjernan News Sweden:
One Year On, University Professor Still Missing
Wednesday marks the anniversary of the disappearance of Emeritus Professor Gunnar Sigurdsson of Malmö's World Maritime University (WMU).

Professor Sigurdsson was a familiar face around the campus and a popular lecturer, well loved by academic staff and students.

Sigurdsson's cutting edge work on deep sea sound analysis in the 1980s and 90s earned him a global reputation as an innovator in the field. In particular, Professor Sigurdsson's wide spectral studies of the 1997 southern Pacific anomaly recorded by the U.S. Navy were hailed as groundbreaking.

In recent years, Professor Sigurdsson made many trips back to his native Iceland to study anomalous deep sea sounds recorded in the Dreki "Dragon" Area.

I know your father's grave is empty. But I think he'd have appreciated the bottle of whisky I took him. I asked the police in Malmö if they were any closer to making an arrest or finding him. Nothing. They've learning nothing in the years he's been missing.

I visited the Viking runestone that started this whole mess. Still don't know if I believe that the runestone, the idol, the Midnight Zone noise, the skrimsli, and the cult at Haedvik are all connected. It was always you that believed six impossible things before breakfast. Never will be anyone else. Not now.

The key your father mailed you opened a safe deposit box in Zurich. I say safe deposit box but it was more like a shelf in Fort Knox. It was in the special high security vault at Degussa.

The key unlocked box number 1405. Fourteen zero five—14 May, your birthday.

Your father left you two 500 g Degussa gold ingots and six 1 kg Lunar Dragon Silver Coins. There was a small card with the numbers 47-9 - 126-43 written on it. He also locked a bundle of letters in the vault box. The pages were handwritten and encrypted. I recognized the code from your research.

I've started to decrypt the letters. I'll give everything to your sister. She'll know what to do with it.

Miss you – Rob

Letter addressed to Bishop of Reykjavik, 1887
To the Reverend Bishop Magnússon
Diocese of Reykjavik
29th of November, 1887

Princes and priests were the murderers of Christ. This is the truth, as is all I tell you here. And I tell you in truth that you must act without mercy nor pity to destroy the evil that has taken root in these lands.

Not more than five years ago a small number of sailors settled at the border of my parish. From the papers I have seen, their origins lie in Massachusetts, but they say that they are come home.

God has told us that there can be no salvation, save the name of Jesus alone. He "who, by that sacrifice which He did once offer upon the cross, hath sanctified for ever those that shall inherit the kingdom promised." (Hebrews 10:12-13)

But others have come. They have rebuilt a damnable village. Others that do not seek salvation, that do not acknowledge Christ nor God. I have witnessed with my own eyes their idolatry.

You did tell me once at Hólar that it is against God's ordinance that idolaters, murderers, false teachers, and blasphemers shall be exempted from punishment. I call on you to act as the pitiless hand of God. Do not forsake us. The Westminster Larger Catechism notes that the second commandment requires us to act by "disapproving, detesting, opposing, all false worship; and according to each one's place and calling, removing it, and all monuments of idolatry." Do not let the heresy I saw in the village of Haedvik grow unbounded.

I never thought to see an obscene graven idol raised on a holy altar, nor the worship of heathen gods in this age. Blasphemous rites are practiced in their chapel built deep in the water. Its walls are black as the sand on the shore. These are enemies of Christ that delight in Godless acts and the blasphemous preaching of deceitful spirits. They will know no redemption.

Nebuchadnezzar, the king of Babylon, served as God's instrument of judgment upon Judah. He destroyed Jerusalem and cast Judah into slavery for their idolatry, their disobedience, and their lack of faith. But still you do nothing. I call on you, Bishop Magnússon, to become the wrath of God upon Haedvik.

Your servant,
Rev Ástvald Grímsson
Parish of Vopnafjörður

Note by Robert Atwood:
The 1887 map with Haedvik was hand-drawn on the back of the priest's letter. The archivist at the bishop's library knew about the priest and told me this story:

The priest, Ástvald Grímsson, vanished two weeks after he sent the letter with the map to the Bishop of Reykjavik.

It was winter, so no one thought too much of people lost in the snow. Some said that the priest had a sweetheart on the far side of the river and he would simply be cut off and snowbound with her.

The following year, the priest's sweetheart told a strange

story. She said that he had made arrangements to meet her so they could be married in secret. When the day came the priest arrived on horseback and the girl climbed up on the horse behind him. He didn't say a word. They rode off towards the church at Myrká. Still the priest said nothing.

The girl noticed that he had the collar of his greatcoat pulled up and he wore his hat low. She'd thought nothing of it as there was an icy wind that day, but now she reached out one hand and took off the priest's hat. Under the hat, where his hair and his skin should have been, she saw the priest's white skull.

The priest tugged the reins and the horse veered into Myrká's graveyard. The girl saw an open grave and she threw herself to the ground. The corpse priest jumped down from his horse and dragged the girl screaming towards his grave. She kicked and clawed at the dirt, fighting to get away. She broke his fingers and she ran from the churchyard, never looking back.

With the spring thaws they found the priest's body facedown in the waters of the River Myrká. It was horribly mutilated. The people that found him said it looked like he had been savaged by wolves.

The oil rig, the one that just exploded, it was called The Myrká. The people at Kongshavn Deepwater Oil named it after the river.

Transcript of video on Robert Atwood's iPhone:

Haedvik is a lost town. It never made it onto the government maps. I found it on the priest's map. He wrote to the bishop of his diocese complaining about the "Godless acts" committed by the townsfolk of Haedvik. I learned they were fishermen. They sailed out from the bay over there, catching herring for the town markets. The priest claims that they had built a "graven idol" that they worshipped in their "chapel built deep in the water."

The priest denounced their blasphemies and complained that his bishop did nothing to stand against the fishermen's heresy.

The priest drew his own map showing the location of Haedvik and their chapel in the water. And now, after searching for about a year, I'm finally going to visit Haedvik.

Email dated 23 October, 13:07
Robert Atwood wrote
To | Katla Gunnarsdóttir
Cc |
Hæ Katla

Barely anything remains of Haedvik. It's like the black beach just swallowed the village whole.

I found some foundation stones buried under the black sand—corners of houses. There were old broken glass bottles worn smooth. I found a button.

It's hard to believe this is where it all began.

I found out more about the Cult and their connections to Kongshavn. The 1839 *Unaussprechlichen Kulten* talks about the Cult forming after a "dragon slid from the sea on its belly. It walked tall, scorching the rocks, bringing death to Vopnafjörður as its shadow fell across the mountains."

On Midwinter night the founder of the Cult, a woman named Garún, summoned the thing from the sea. It's remembered as a dragon—the Icelanders even named an area of sea northeast of the mainland Drekasvæðið—"The Dragon Region"—after the dragon that walked through Vopnafjörður.

In January 2009 Iceland's National Energy Authority, Orkustofnun, started licensing Drekasvæðið, to oil companies for hydrocarbon exploration and production.

And guess who was waiting at the head of the line for a license? Kongshavn Deepwater Oil.

They built the Myrká Deepwater Oil Rig there two years ago, and a couple of days ago it was lost in an explosion. The sea is on fire. The papers think the lost men are probably dead. I saw the pictures. I don't think anyone is coming back from that fire.

The ruins of Haedvik are half-drowned by the sea and half-buried under black sand. It was never more than a scattered handful of stone houses from what I can see. The stone's been mostly robbed out for walls, but I could still make out the edges of the houses here and there. And I found the abandoned chapel.

I thought it was nothing more than a spike of rock in the water at first, black against the sky. But when I got closer I saw dressed stone and tool marks and masons' secret signs cut in the rock. But there was something else carved in stone. Some kind of effigy. Some lost, nameless thing worn by the waves. I couldn't make out its shape. But I saw a sign above it: a triangle cut deep into the stone within a circle.

I saw that sign drawn in Otto Rahn's book. It was the sign of the Church of Starry Wisdom. The New York edition of the Black Book of Nameless Cults says the faithful fled when their church was burned in New England. They scattered to the winds and washed up on far shores, planting the poison seeds of their heresy.

They were here. In Iceland, at Haedvik, on this black sand beach staring out into this pitch-black sea.

One of their children rose to lead the congregation out of Haedvik. They took their gods with them. And the fishermen hid in the cities and the towns and took over a whaling company. And you've pieced together the story after that.

The whaling company that gutted humpbacks and blue whales for the whale oil that lit the lamps in Reykjavik grew, and bought its way into mining and shipyards and sold slaves in the Belgian Congo. And then, as the world buried the dead of World War One, it became the Kongshavn Petroleum Company, later Kongshavn Deepwater Oil.

But it never left the hands of the old Haedvik families. A hundred years later, the same incestuous half-dozen families are still the inner circle of Kongshavn Energy.

I still have the note you wrote for Deacon: *"Ég skal sýna þér í tvo heimana*—I will show you the two worlds."

Almost there now. I figured so much out. I should feel something, shouldn't I? Thought it might mend the hurt.

I love you – Rob

Kongshavn Energy press release

It's about family. Kongshavn Energy started out small. Our founders sat around a kitchen table with a shared vision: they would make a difference to ordinary people's lives; they would make life better for everyone, for families just like theirs.

Today, Kongshavn Energy is one of the world's largest energy giants, but we are still a family company at heart. We care about our workers and we care about your family.

For more than fifty years, Kongshavn Energy has been at the forefront of deepwater oil exploration. We grew from mining and petroleum, but we saw the need to protect the planet for the future. Kongshavn Energy is now the world's fastest-growing green-energy multinational.

Over the last decade we have invested millions of dollars to harness the limitless natural geothermal energy of Iceland's volcanoes. We are constructing offshore windfarms on three continents and funding breakthrough research into wave power and biofuel technologies.

Kongshavn Energy is now proud to announce the next revolution in natural energy: deep sea geothermal. Life itself may have begun at the hydrothermal vents in the depths of our oceans. Kongshavn Energy will harness the infinite geothermal power of the ocean-floor.

Media contact: Sóley Gunnarsdóttir

Transcript of audio file on Robert Atwood's iPhone:

"Hæ Katla—I just read Kongshavn's media release. Still remember what your father told you: "No doves come from raven eggs." Jesus, they just killed those men on the Myrká Rig and now they want us to believe they're flower children. And everyone will believe their lies because they want to. But your father knew. Nothing good is ever born from evil.""

Intercepted encrypted phone call, deciphered by Anonymous:

Deacon (Vice President of Kongshavn Energy): Halstrom will be found dead tomorrow…. Yes, fell from his yacht in the Caribbean and drowned. Yes. Drink and drugs. Always. Our project at Myrká has exceeded all expectations. It was perfect. Yes. We will proceed with exploration at Site B. I gave orders this morning to commence drilling.

Transcript of video on Robert Atwood's iPhone:

Do you hear that? I don't think you can see this. It's too dark. Can barely see my hand in front of my face.

I'm at Haedvik. The oil spill reached the black sand beach this evening. Dead seabirds. Harp seals. Everywhere.

It's about … I don't know … about 2 AM, I think. Christ, I don't know what that noise is.

Do you hear it? The beach is thick with oil. Oil from the Myrká. It made it all the way here. There's something on the beach. Something in the oil spill. Jesus. I can barely stand up in this stuff.

The noise. What is that? Something … oh Jesus. There's a whale. It's beached. That sound. It's a whale. It's drowning in oil.

I can't tell what … what the … there's something under its skin. Something alive, writhing, under the whale's skin. Christ, it's eating its way out. Skrimsli. Oh God.

No. It's impossible. Do you see that? There's someone out there. Someone by the chapel. Walking out of the oil, out of the water…. The sky is burning. Please, God no. It's burning. Ph'nglui mglw'nafh … R'lyeh wgah'nagl.…

Email dated 26 October, 05:01
Sóley Gunnarsdóttir wrote
To | Guardian News; Reuters; Associated Press; London Times; Washington Post; The Independent; New York Times; BBC News; Los Angeles Times; Chicago Tribune; Toronto Star; Globe and Mail; Le Journal de Montréal; Bild; Die Welt; Der Spiegel; Svenska Dagblade; Morgunbladið; Fréttabladið; 24 stundir
Cc | Sydney Morning Herald; Channel 4 News; CNN; Time Magazine; Huffington Post; BuzzFeed

Nord Halstrom, Chief Executive of Kongshavn Energy, was murdered on his yacht on the orders of Vice President Deacon. In the attached audio file you will hear VP Deacon detail the planned killing.

The official witness statement of Egil Hagen, the only survivor of Myrká Deepwater Oil Rig disaster, was heavily redacted by the senior leaders of Kongshavn Deepwater Oil, including Vice President Deacon.

I kept a copy of the original unedited transcription. This part was cut:

"I saw some men. Couldn't recognize them. They were black with oil. Burning *i helvete*. The fire had them cornered. I saw them throw themselves into the sea.

"But it wasn't just the sea down there. I saw something in the black water. Some *jævla* thing was moving, under the water, waiting. They lie about monsters.

"I didn't jump. Couldn't. Not after I saw it. Saw that. Saw what it did. Tore them all apart. If I had to die, I would burn. But the fire caught something. A fireball hit me. Threw me out high and down into the water. And I saw that thing burning but it didn't care.

"And I remember knowing that I'd die then, and I closed my eyes."

Statement of Sóley Gunnarsdóttir:

My name is Sóley Gunnarsdóttir. My father was Professor Gunnar Sigurdsson. My sister was Katla Gunnarsdóttir. For the last seven years I have worked for Kongshavn Energy.

I work in their public relations department. Three years ago I trained in disaster mitigation to minimize reputational damage in the event of major oil spills, accidental deaths, or industrial disasters.

I spent almost a third of my life working for Kongshavn and now I am a whistleblower.

They thought my father was a true believer. One of them. But they were wrong. For years he worked for Kongshavn, studying underwater sounds from the Southern Pacific to the Arctic Circle but all the while he was gathering evidence of their wrongdoing. Never let an expert in sound recording into your headquarters. My father set up a series of sophisticated listening devices. He taped meetings of Kongshavn's inner circle.

He transcribed and encrypted the conversations he recorded. In the end he locked away all the files in letters in a safe deposit box in Zurich. Two days before he disappeared he sent my sister Katla the safe deposit key and a scribbled note she could never decode.

Kongshavn made my father disappear. Towards the end he was deeply paranoid, suffering from anxiety. He barely left his apartment. The last time I called him he raved about the sounds he'd recorded near the Myrká Oil Rig. He told me they were identical to the noises recorded by the United States Navy in 1997 in the south Pacific Ocean. "They heard it 5000 fathoms deep," he said, "something alive in the Midnight Zone. Down beneath the world's bloody heart."

That noise has been studied by academics from around the world. Most dismiss it now as ice grinding on the rocky seabed. But my father heard the noise again in the Drekasvæðið, the Dragon Region, 350 km off Iceland.

After my father's vanishing, my little sister Katla looked for him. She investigated Kongshavn, dug up the dirt. She met Robert in Sydney two years ago. She never thought she'd fall in love. But I knew she would someday. She started to publicly campaign against Kongshavn. She made a noise until they noticed her.

CEO Nord Halstrom and VP Deacon don't like it when their secrets are shared online with the whole world.

I know they killed my sister. They made it look like suicide, but Katla would never have taken her own life. No, they took her to cliffs at The Gap in Sydney and they killed her.

Robert never gave up. He knew they murdered Katla. And he knew the truth about Kongshavn Energy was hidden at Haedvik. He found it there, found the last survivors of the Cult of Starry Wisdom. He pieced it together. The sect that rose from the ashes half a world away. A tiny village at the black sand beach. Vopnafjörður, the dragon from the deep they summoned. The Dragon Area. Skrimsli. The monsters Katla always feared in the sea.

They hunted for the sound, and my father found it for them. Kongshavn was never really looking for oil on the Myrká Rig. They were looking for something else. And I think they found it.

And now Robert is dead. I saw the pieces of his body taken from the black sand beach.

I found his notes. I took his iPhone. And now I've uploaded all of Kongshavn's secrets. I know they will look for me. But they will never find me. Not ever. I've dug myself down too deep. I spent a lifetime hiding who I was, and they never knew I wasn't really one of them.

Robert used the safe deposit key and found Haedvik. And he deciphered both the note my father sent and the numbers he left in the locked box.

They are details of Kongshavn's Site B.

Site B is a specific place that my father studied in the southern Pacific Ocean. He believed the anomalous noises recorded there, thousands of nautical miles from anywhere, were made by something alive. Kongshavn's Vice President Deacon is sending a deep water oil rig to Site B to drill down into the depths at 47°9'S 126°43'W.

Site B, my father wrote, is somewhere called R'lyeh.

APOTHEOSIS

by Darren Todd

The details of Blake's plan spun through his mind on endless loop, so when the direct line rang in his private tent, he welcomed the distraction.

"Captain Blake," he said into the receiver. The phone aped the landline models from his childhood, though only for effect. In the field, no cord snaked behind the tan-colored plastic. Its signal came from satellite, not from cables atop phone poles. At least they'd stopped using such technology by the time the monsters came, since the beasts toppled power and phone lines alike in their rampages.

"What's your last name, Captain?" asked the cool, male voice on the other end, surely from somewhere safe behind one of the barricades built to keep the monsters at bay. The smooth tone, a blend of aplomb and even mild amusement, presented a diametric opposite to Blake's own feelings, which teetered between panic and certainty as quickly as a flipped coin changed between heads and tails.

"Blake *is* my last name, sir." He didn't offer his first name, though Blake had no doubt the man behind that voice could learn it and everything else about him in seconds.

"I see," said the silky tone. "So how are we doing?"

We. Ha. Probably learned that trick in some corporate retreat where they did trust falls and high ropes courses to team-build. Put your subordinates at ease by coupling yourself with them, as if a CEO a hundred miles from danger could align with his battle-worn troops using a collective pronoun alone.

What little remained of Blake's platoons needed no harmless challenges to cement their kinship. He'd hand-picked most of his leadership from past skirmishes. Men and women he'd seen in combat, little as it had mattered against the monsters.

"We're good," Blake said, deadpan.

"No complaints?"

"None that would matter," Blake said.

The man laughed, which—despite the mediocre connection—sounded authentic.

"You understand what awaits you?"

"Of course," Blake said. "A class three, landlocked brawler, with—"

"No, no. Not the monster. I mean what comes after. What glory awaits if your plan succeeds."

Blake had refused to indulge any thoughts of what came next. "We'll see" was all he said.

"I'll be watching," the silk voice intoned. "You've put your faith in me. Now I hang mine on you, Captain. Through cunning and craft."

"Through cunning and craft," Blake echoed and hung up.

The same words were embroidered on the back of the flak vest he shrugged into, just beneath the GenTek logo. It had been the catch-phrase of GenTek, Inc. for years prior to the monsters' arrival—even before corporate armies took the place of the federal forces. The Apple Army was five times the size of GenTek's outfit, but still only half the size of the Google Knights. In this case, GenTek's smaller troop size proved a benefit, since the larger armies would never consider letting a lowly captain attempt such a Hail Mary.

As Blake slowly donned his thirty pounds of tactical gear over several long minutes, the buzz outside swelled. All that lay between his low-lit space and the outside was a double layer of canvas. Such were the luxuries of his field promotion: a few more square feet and an extra barrier no better at keeping out the incessant mooing of the cattle herd than the fevered, anxious chatter of his troops.

He stepped out of his tent for what he gave even odds was the last time. Instantly, a handful of people assailed him, as if they'd been pacing outside his tent flap for the last hour.

Several were GenTek Public Relations prats, their GoPro helmet-mounted videocameras filming his every move, large shotgun mics recording each word and sigh. Three at once asked for a statement, fumbling over the others' scripted lines.

Blake stood straighter, panned the field of troops and cattle alike as if inspecting a formation of soldiers. "Today's the day our GenTek family fights for what is ours." He had more prepared, but couldn't bring himself to keep going. "Through cunning and craft," he bellowed, and several troops passing by turned to shout back the phrase.

His shoulders slumped, his face fell, and he stared down the PR team. "Now fuck off."

The camera crew drew back, and others filled their place.

"Sir," came one of his three lieutenants, named Fisher. She'd been weeks away from receiving her PhD in Economics before the war broke out, and now focused solely on the economy of battle.

Blake held a hand up to silence the others and turned to Fisher. "Yes?"

"Chutes five and three ran out of plastic two-thirds of the way through their payload, so—"

"Then they go to battle with two-thirds the bait. I'm not waiting half a day for more plastic. Wouldn't have time to set it up anyway, and we can't risk a single piece of cargo falling to the enemy."

Fisher saluted, turned, and left without a word. To the others, her silent acquiescence might have seemed sulky, but Blake had learned different during the six months they'd served together. If she needed nothing more to do her job, she would not waste a single syllable on talk.

Next came a sergeant from a security detail he'd mobilized a week ago—a stocky, mustached man named O'Malley, a transfer to GenTek from the Microsoft forces. He probably thought joining a smaller corporation's army would mean hanging back and letting the big dogs fight and die. Someone at Microsoft must have despised him to send the guy to this detail.

"Captain. I understand about ten percent of what's going on here, but I can't put my guys in these vests. We're just as ready to lay down our lives, but—"

"The vests are non-negotiable." He knew nothing else to say. Before monsters wiped out a few million people, he wouldn't have put one on, either. Their arrival changed everything.

"They won't have it," the sergeant said, chopping the air.

"Then cut loose the ones who refuse. You know the blowback. Surrender of all stock options, life and health insurance bennies gone. No more food vouchers or housing."

"But it's suicide," the sergeant said, teeth clamped together. "If they get within a mile of the payload—"

"They won't be, Sergeant. I'm gonna put your guys on the MK-19s and fifty-cals. Mobile Infantry's got a dozen humvees on standby. You'll be on the lip of the bowl with the rest of us. You fire what I need when I need it, and your troops will be just fine."

"Yessir." O'Malley turned and left, shoulders rolled more forward in acceptance than back in defiance.

That left only the drafted "gamekeeper," a farmer who'd handled the hundred cattle attached to the contingent for the last two stinking weeks. The man smelled like his cows, and with as little shame. Mud spattered his tan coveralls, and he continued working the fingers of his leather gloves onto his hands as he'd done while waiting for the captain.

"Mr. Spinnel?" Blake asked.

"The vests ain't the problem."

Blake looked over the old farmer's shoulder to find custom harnesses on each cow, the bulk of them already covered in mud and manure. "Good to hear." But something obviously *was* the problem, as the cows were mooing loud and long, echoing one another in waves. Steam billowed thick above them from their own body heat and their heavy breaths in the bitter air.

"It's the feel of the camp."

"Okay."

The farmer smiled, but his eyebrows turned up, making it the saddest grin Blake had ever seen.

"It ain't like they know what's comin', but they can tell something ain't right. The men know it, so the cows feed off that."

"What's this mean for the mission?" Blake asked.

"Probably nothin'. But they're gonna be hell to load into the chutes, that's for sure. If I could get a few volunteers to help with the blindfolds, and maybe an extra pair of hands for gettin' em outta the trucks."

"You!" Blake barked to a man walking by with a jerry can. "Gather ten guys not outfitted and help this man with the cows. You have five minutes."

"Yessir." The troop dropped the jerry can to the sandy ground and sprinted toward one of the tents.

"Shouldn't feel any different than usual," Spinnel said.

"Sorry?"

He turned to look at his herd. "Been takin' cattle to slaughter since before you was born. Don't know why this time's any different."

Blake put a hand on the farmer's dusty shoulder, and the man pivoted back to face him. "It *is* different. This time, they get to die for more than hamburgers."

The farmer laughed, and Blake offered a sympathetic smile.

From Fisher, a simple "ready" over his radio signaled the beginning, and a series of pre-packaged orders flew from Blake's mouth. His troops knew the routine; they'd been over it a hundred times on a shared video feed and then several dry runs leading up to today.

He put on his vest with shaking hands. He'd pulled the pin on a hundred grenades, had clicked off claymores and buried land mines; not that any of those had done a thing to the monsters. But somehow dealing with plastic explosives rattled his already edgy nerves. His lungs pulled in air only when he ordered them to do so, as if breathing were no longer involuntary.

Hooking the blasting caps up to his heart monitor took a half-dozen attempts. His fingertips felt like lumps of ice—clumsy and with no tactile feedback.

He climbed into his Jeep and signaled his driver, a sprightly three-striper named Easy, to move. She turned and looked at him, then jerked her head to the rear. Two of the Public Relations crew fumbled over the side of the Jeep and into the bucket seats. Along with their GoPro helmets, they lugged tripods, a sound recorder the size of a desktop computer, and a camera drone.

"Are you kidding me? Get out!" Blake said.

"Corporate's orders, Captain. Sorry." This from the small woman who looked no sorrier than her cameraman, though *he* had the decency to keep his eyes trained down.

Blake spun in his seat and hit the dash several times. He took a deep breath and said, "Roll on."

Easy slammed her foot on the gas before he'd gotten to the second word, jostling the camera crew and soliciting several curses from the backseat.

She drove them up onto a small plateau overlooking the bowl. The moment they crested the rocks and shrubs, the camera crew stood up in the back and panned the landscape. The woman wove trite, off-the-cuff commentary about the juxtaposition of beauty and danger. Any other day, the sight would have inspired Blake, or at least conjured awe. But today, when he stood, blithely blocking the cameraman's shot, nature paled compared to the visual oddity playing out before them.

The monster stood about a hundred feet tall, though it was hard to tell, since it moved hunched over and in a canter that resembled an ape walking on his knuckles. Only *this* ape bore phosphorescent green accents along dark green armored skin, similar to the others. The accents lit up whenever a monster took damage, in a kind of built-in healing mechanism. Nothing short of a direct hit with a nuke had felled a single monster in the last ten months. Despite the tremendous loss of life, no corporation had yet to greenlight dropping nukes as standard protocol. Even with the Boeing Air Forces' superb navigation technology, they'd struck out more often than not, failing to kill four of the six monsters they'd bombed. A nuke can wipe out humans miles away, but a monster all but had to eat the thing for it to kill him.

Him, her. Whatever. *It.*

And these "its" had decimated the human population the world over and done as much damage to the other animals, which they devoured ceaselessly.

Now, looking like a cross between Mighty Joe Young and Godzilla, Blake's monster was following the four remaining helicopters into the bowl. Blake had no nuke at his disposal, only a hypothesis with a very costly test.

"It's gotta be in range now, Captain," came a voice over the radio. "You can take it from here. I need to call my choppers off 'fore that bastard downs another."

This from the Wal-Mart Cavalry colonel who'd loaned the choppers to GenTek at God knows what price.

Blake dropped back into the Jeep's passenger seat and yanked the radio away from Easy. "Negative, Colonel. I need it all the way in. At least so my artillery on the far side of the bowl can lay down fire."

"Goddamn it, son. We've already lost eight choppers on this horseshit plan. In a real army, we take our losses seriously. You wanna piss away the rest of their lives? Is that it? If this were *my* operation…."

The bitch about radios: no interrupting. Blake listened with pursed lips and the mic gripped in white fingers until the colonel finished.

"The orders stand, Colonel," he responded, trying to keep his voice level, without a hint of haughtiness or attitude. "Past the opening, and then they can break away."

He wanted to say sorry, but didn't dare. If the choppers could have tempted the monster any other way than flying in and out of its face while pelting it with M-60 fire, he would never have risked so many lives. But Blake had fought the monsters enough to know that anything less than buzzing the thing like gnats would leave the beast disinterested and they'd lose their chance.

"You and I are gonna have a talk when this is over, son," the colonel said. "And you'll be lucky to clean the head in any army *if* you even survive."

Blake again stood and stared through binoculars into the crater. The cattle spilled from the backs of cargo trucks into their chutes, the reluctant ones prodded with heated pokers. No electric prods today, not considering their payload. They looked as small as beetles from his vantage, and the monsters weren't known for having excellent eyesight. The cargo trucks sped off after unloading, bound for a rendezvous at a low point in the crater wall, where the troops could ascend and rejoin the others on the rim.

"Payload ready," came Fisher's terse monotone.

All around the crater, his troops waited, pegging their lives to the machinations of a field-promoted captain who'd logged more hours playing video games than serving in the military.

"Gimme the tablet," he called down to Easy. She handed him a two-by-one foot tablet computer showing all of his assets in green and the monster in red. An AWACS radar jet circled above and dozens of drones hovered nearby to paint this picture, to link him to his forces. He laughed, now thinking perhaps those thousands of video game hours might pay off more than military training after all.

"Another quarter mile," he said.

"Yessir," came Easy's reply. Her fingers hovered over the radio channel selector.

He looked up in time to see another chopper fall, its tail end ripped off with a flick of the monster's gargantuan paw. The other three choppers continued their buzzing, the crew showing bravery Blake could only dream of.

The ape monster took another, lumbering step into the bowl, and Blake's stomach dropped.

"Choppers away," he all but whispered.

Easy's fingers flew, radioing the evac order before Blake had time to take a breath.

He stared at the tablet. "Engage Thunder Three and Four," he said, and again Easy's fingers danced and her voice followed, sharp and steady.

"Gimme the quad fifty."

As soon as he'd spoken, the thump-thump-thump of the fifty-cals began, a line of tracers punctuating the stream of lead. They locked in on the monster's center mass, though the rounds only annoyed it.

The whistle of incoming mortar fire gave way to deafening explosions that seemed to shake the canyon itself, and great fountains of earth flew skyward preceding each boom.

"Artillery...." He checked his tablet. Already, the connection between his brain and his vocal chords was short-circuiting. "Engage fire teams alpha and bravo," he said, and Easy parroted his command with a surfeit of syllables so fast he barely understood it as English.

The artillery cannons made the fifty-cals sound positively quiet. How on earth someone could be near the source of such a sound and not have their brains turned to sludge at the concussion amazed him.

What began as the monster annoyed and distracted turned into its trademark rage. It let out a horrible wail, one that scientists had thought at first called on other beasts, but which they now understood as nothing more than a primal display of anger and intimidation.

It charged at the artillery first, as if knowing by instinct what was causing it the most harm. From Blake's own encounters and from watching countless hours of footage of monster attacks, he now believed they lacked the intelligence to triage threats or attack with anything bordering on strategy. And why would they, at the rate they regenerated?

Blake's heart picked up its pace as the monster drew closer to the artillery nests. He held his breath for another half-dozen of the monster's enormous strides.

He dipped his head down to the tablet. "Open chute seven," he ordered. "And cease fire."

Easy's echoed orders flew out, and all noise ceased for several glorious seconds. And then came the amplified mooing of cattle from below. The handful of cows from chute seven called out, their moos boosted by the Public Address system attached to the enclosure. Each cow wore a blindfold, but they shared a collective horror. In the haze, they scrambled over one another in a primeval attempt to escape what must have seemed like imminent death—and in that, they were correct.

The monster swung its meaty, scaly arms at the air, though the artillery had stopped. For long seconds, it stared toward the artillery nests, camouflaged though they were.

"Come on," Blake spat.

"Take it, you motherfucker," said Easy, without apology. Who knows who she'd lost in the last year. Everyone there knew someone who'd fallen to the beasts.

Finally, the monster turned toward the sound of the cattle. It scanned the desert floor, which had grown coated in dust during the barrage.

After a protracted minute, the monster seemed to lose interest, and Blake pulled in a breath. Finally, just a few hundred yards from leaving the bowl entirely, the dust settled enough so that—despite the monster's poor eyesight—it'd have to be blind to miss them.

The moment the monster sprang after the cattle, Blake's held breath left him and he nearly broke down at the physical relief that flooded him.

"It's going for it," he said. He consulted his tablet. "On my command."

The monster launched into an all out sprint now, using his ape-like arms to propel him along. Half-mile.

"Steady."

Quarter mile.

"Steady."

At a hundred yards, he said: "Fire."

The reporter screamed, "It's too soon. It won't—"

Though the monster was a good fifty yards from the cattle when their plastic explosive vests detonated, it reeled from the concussion, releasing an ear-splitting roar. Instead of bits of carnage flying skyward, the plastic literally vaporized the animals, leaving nothing behind but a red stain on the desert floor.

"You missed," the reporter yelled, the sound more like a cry than speech.

Blake wheeled on her. "It wasn't a miss. Shut up and point the camera."

Back to the tablet. "Scrap the mortar teams. I can't have a smokescreen mucking this up. Put them on artillery support. Or arm them with goddamn pistols for all I care. Give me MK-19 rounds on that bastard from mobile infantry. Humvees six through ten."

The boom of war commenced. A string of high explosive rounds pelted the monster from its flank. For a moment, it only stared at the earth. Where once stood a handful of cows lay only a swell of blood the size of a swimming pool.

The beast shrieked in anger and began its deadly canter toward the humvees.

"Chute three," Blake said, and the process began anew. Cease fire, cows' confused and scared calls amplified by the PA. The monster again forgot about the danger once the firing stopped, and responded only to the meal that called out to him. He ran for it, but again Blake ordered the cattle blown to a horrible red mist a second before the monster could feed.

Five more times this went like clockwork, seven of the ten payloads spent, and the monster kept coming. Each time, Blake called for fire on the opposite side of the bowl, an enormous, insane version of keep-away.

For most, the end game loomed out of sight, despite the success of the rope-a-dope. To the handful of CEOs, including his own, no doubt watching via satellite feed halfway across the world, there was little to substantiate the tremendous resources required to take such a gambit.

But a small smile formed on Blake's lips. He tried to force it back, to give the situation the somber face it deserved, but he saw something on that surreal battlefield, even if no one else could. The monster was wearing down.

Which was the very moment chute nine's PA failed to broadcast.

The cows lay exposed on the floor of the bowl, clear even from where Blake stood farther away than the monster.

"I don't hear the cows," the reporter said. "Captain Blake, I can't hear—"

"I know," he snapped.

Despite the cease fire, the beast continued heading toward the rim with no tempting meal to lure it away. If it drew too close, even the camouflage might fail to hide Blake's forces.

He pointed down at Easy. "Open chute...." He checked his tablet. The only remaining chutes were both near the monster and lay close to the rim on that side. Not ideal, but better than nothing. "Eight," he finished.

She relayed his command, and soon the PA system above chute eight came to life with the mooing of its payload, but too late. The monster's brain was primitive, but it at least remembered the last thing to fire on it, an artillery pit close by. As it charged, ignoring the broadcast mooing, Blake said, "Pull bravo gun crew. Have them fall back a hundred yards."

But before Easy transmitted the message, a shell erupted from the battery and struck the monster dead on: successful hit if facing any other foe. The beast recoiled from the explosion, but quickly recovered and headed for the crew, its hide illuminated with healing green light.

"Cease fire and pull the hell back," Blake screamed. But now all he could do was watch. The monster dragged a long, terrible arm up from the ground and swiped at the artillery crew behind a wall of fake leaves and brush. The blow didn't have to be pinpoint accurate, not when the beast's meaty arms could clear a strip of forest in a casual swat.

"Did they get—" the journalist asked, before a series of

concussions answered her question. Like horrible fireworks, the soldiers from the crew first flew out from the camo netting and into the open air above the canyon, and then detonated. Some struck the ground before exploding.

The creature showed first confusion and then anger, as yet another prey turned to pink mist instead of a meal.

Still, the sight of this carnage produced only one effect, yet another consequence Blake had not considered. Everyone opened up on the monster. Even the mortar teams recommenced their assault after a full minute of tracer rounds and explosive shells had pelted the creature.

"Cease fire, cease fire," Blake ordered, but no matter how many times Easy relayed his order, the barrage continued.

It looked like the creature was being beaten. It wobbled on unsteady limbs several times during the attack. It stumbled and fell, despite the neon green telegraphing its arcane healing process in action.

Maybe it was working, this terrible version of his plan.

And then it rose and shot out in a dead sprint like a runner from a track block. Only the gunfire could trace it, but that might as well have been a guiding light for the beast to follow. It stormed after a quad fifty with a three-person crew, and a second later a trio of successive booms sounded. Still another machine gun pit kept firing, perhaps in some desperate hope that their few hundred rounds of ammunition would do what the previous million rounds had failed to. Another four booms.

Over the radio, transmissions poured in, despite standing orders for radio silence. The consensus sounded like a full-on retreat, complete with screams and curses and yelled requests for extraction or a rendezvous point.

Blake closed his eyes in a blink that he seemed unable to end, as if his eyelids had sealed shut.

The monster proceeded to tear at the lip of the bowl with mighty swipes of its arms. Equipment and small explosions peppered this enraged display, but nothing as pronounced as before, where soldiers met a grisly end via their explosive vests.

That, it seemed, was over. But so was the mission. Whatever ideas Blake had harbored, the countless conversations he'd had with scientists, the stacks of papers he'd read to come to this conclusion—all lost.

"It looks," the reporter said, her voice mirroring Blake's despair. Then her tone shifted. "It looks… bored."

"What?" Blake asked.

"The monster. After all that, it looks bored. Like it's ready for a nap or something."

Blake almost laughed at the absurdity of it, but something about her words snagged in his mind. He had learned to listen to his inner voice as the religious would the word of their god; the gut—he'd found—was incapable of deceit. If something seemed off, it was.

He looked up to see that the monster indeed appeared languid and spent, as if its rage had exhausted it, or like the whole war had left it as tired of killing humans as they were of dying.

But something had changed, in the gait, perhaps, or its posture.

"Not a scratch on him," the cameraman said.

"Shut up," Easy snapped at him. "Like you did shit about it."

"As you were, Easy," Blake said. "I don't give a damn about scratches."

"Then what the hell were we fighting for?" the cameraman asked. He pulled off his GoPro helmet, no longer concerned with posterity, it seemed. "What were you expecting to happen?"

Blake thought for a few seconds. Sure, he'd played the scene over in his mind a thousand times—what it might look like when a monster fell without taking a twenty-square mile radius with it and without risking nuclear winter. He watched the monster lumbering toward the opening in the bowl and then laughed to himself. "Well… that, I guess." He laughed some more and turned to Easy. "Open the last chute."

"Sir?"

"Do it. If I'm wrong, it won't matter anyway."

Easy gave the order, getting a prompt response and making it apparent that Fisher hadn't abandoned her post like so many others.

The chute opened well behind the monster, near the rim but a good mile from where the creature ambled along. The broadcast sound, near deafening now in the eerie silence of the canyon on the heels of full-on assault, caused the monster to pivot. It heaved its massive shoulders several times, and then turned back for the source of the sound.

It made it another hundred yards before collapsing.

"Jesus," Easy called, her bearing forgotten. "What just happened?"

"It worked, Easy. Bastard just ran out of calories." Blake laughed and held his hands up to the sky as if asking for rain.

"Do I call the crews back?" Easy asked.

"No, get them out of that gear and pull them in. Even if that fucker lives another hour, it's spent. Might as well call in air support and let them have their way with it."

Easy complied, a broad smile on her face as she worked. In between her out-going messages, celebratory snippets broke through. Amid the radio chatter, hoots and hollering brought an unconscious smile to Blake's lips.

The reporter's cell phone rang. No one was even supposed to have them, both to exercise tight intelligence, and—most notably—to minimize the chance a signal might trigger their explosive vests.

Blake unplugged his heart monitor and took off his vest, signaling Easy to do so as well. He turned to tell the camera crew the same, but he all but bumped into the woman.

She held out the phone and shook it in his face, her smile apoplectic. "It's the president."

"The president? The president of the United States is calling me?" he asked and chuckled. "Why?" The commander-in-chief had become little more than a running joke in the last decade, the figurehead of a powerless bureaucracy as beholden to corporations as the average citizen.

Her smile vanished. "No, *our* president. Of GenTek. The CEO."

"Oh, right. I'll take it," Blake said.

As if knowing the moment Blake put the receiver to his ear, that smooth voice spoke before Blake offered a greeting.

"I knew you could do it, Captain," the silky words poured over the connection. "We're a world away from where we were just an hour ago, and it's all because of you."

"I lost troops," Blake said. "Men and women who trusted me."

"And their trust was well placed," the voice drolled. "You took a major malfunction and reshaped it into a strategic success. What is a great leader but that?"

Blake's momentary elation faded. The call was meant as the proverbial cherry on top, but it somehow grounded the otherwise surreal experience.

"I guess so," he managed.

"I'd like you to come in," the voice said. A shift from the smooth, rehearsed tone betrayed that the CEO had gone offscript.

"What's that, Mr. President?"

"When you can. No hurry. I'd like you to come in to GenTek headquarters to see me. I have something for you, and I won't keep you long."

An odd warmth settled into Blake's stomach, though. At that moment, he gave no more than a damn what any CEO thought of their work.

"Yessir," he answered, and then handed the phone off to the reporter.

Nine days later, Blake passed through the multiple layers of security that waited on the danger-side of the mighty wall around

Manhattan. Most of the smooth, metal facade rose sharply into the dense, fall fog like a cliff face, as uninviting as a skull and crossbones. The southern entrance, however, offered a complete contrast. At least a thousand people milled about the boundaries of the security detail. Some petitioned for entry in one of the many processing lines, and others set up shop to cater to the desperate masses stuck on danger-side.

Through the throngs of people stood an interlocking line of security personnel, complemented by raised heavy gun pits behind cement barriers and concertina wire.

He approached the front line private, whose black, Exxon armband looked more at home at a twentieth century funeral than on a military uniform.

"Captain Blake to GenTek Headquarters. I have an appointment."

Without a word, the tall young private raised a phone and snapped Blake's photo. His thumb danced over the screen and his eyes remained on the glass until a soft ding sounded. He pocketed the phone and stepped aside. "Your escort will meet you just on the other side of the wall. Go nowhere without her. Drones maintain facial recognition for all residents every few seconds, and yours will only work while you're in proximity to your escort. Otherwise, you'll be flagged as hostile and apprehended or worse."

"I understand," Blake said. He looked behind him to the hoi polloi vying for a spot inside and wondered how many like them had suffered the "or worse" option over the last year.

A loud clunk rang out and the doors swung inward. Farther along the zig-zagging entranceway, a guard summoned him onward with a crisp gesture resembling a salute.

His escort's name was Mede, a second lieutenant also with Exxon. Her uniform not only bore the standard, crisp creases on the sleeve and down the front of the trousers, but along the back and down the shoulder blades. It completed an almost wooden look alongside her chiseled features and perfect make-up.

They walked a short distance to a tram, Blake moving uncomfortably close to her without meaning to, in case the pletho-
ra of drones overhead considered his proximity too loose.

"Don't worry about the drones," she told him. "The actual
distance you can wander is classified, but let's just say that if you
can hear me talking, you're safe."

He nodded and backed off slightly.

Predictably, GenTek CEO Stephen Hall's office lay on the
100th floor, in the penthouse. Once there, Mede stood by the
elevator door at parade rest.

"You're not coming?" Blake asked her. "Won't that—"

"Perfectly safe in here, Captain," she said. "I'll be waiting
for you."

A suited man buttoning the front of his jacket walked out from
behind an oak door twice as tall as he. The man's features held
none of Mede's precise, fabricated perfection, but echoed a
warm, genuine bonhomie.

"Captain Blake," the man said and held out his hand. "Stephen Hall." The corner of his mouth curled into a smile as authentic as his appearance. Blake felt like a brother coming for a
visit after years apart. The voice rang familiar, though the radio
did no justice to the bass-lined lull of Hall's words.

Blake took the hand and shrank inside the strong but soft
grip, though the men stood equal in height.

Without another word, Hall gestured back through the
door, inviting Blake into his sanctum sanctorum.

The office's vaulted ceilings bore dark, driftwood beams.
Two-way glass in the line of bay windows let in the pale autumn
sun, while white light from hidden bulbs banked off a lip
around the walls. Blake walked to one of the two leather chairs
opposite a desk twice the size of his war room table at base
camp. Atop lay only a cigar box and a white envelope near the

high-backed wooden chair on the far side.

The men took their seats. Hall continued his warm smile and cracked the cigar box. He spun it around and Blake straightened his back to look inside.

"Cubans," the man said. "Some of the final batch. God knows why the monsters sacked the island, but there won't be another cigar coming out of that place for a few generations."

Without asking, Hall pulled out and snipped two cigars, lit one, and summoned Blake over.

Blake rounded the table, took the cigar, and bent to the golden lighter Hall fired to light the stogie. The tobacco tasted of leather, with something nutty on the back. Blake hadn't scored more than a pack of cigarettes since the war began, capping his missions with whatever scrap the supply guys put together that resembled tobacco, ditto for the homemade hooch that sufficed for brew. The Cuban produced a near-instant heady sensation that had him gripping the desk for support.

He smiled, held up the cigar in salute, and returned to his chair. Before he could even consider where to tip his ashes, Hall slid over a crystal ashtray as neatly as a shuffleboard champion, the heavy glass coming to rest not a foot from Blake's side of the table.

"Again," Hall said, "I offer my thanks and congratulations. We couldn't have done this without you."

"And what *have* we done?" Blake asked. The cigar had left him distant from his body and loosened his usual filters.

Hall laughed. "A fair question. We have created a packageable, patentable process for killing the monsters without nukes. And on record, no less, albeit with a bit of editing to protect our intellectual property."

Blake's lightheadedness faded and a rock formed in his stomach. "You're keeping it secret?"

Hall waved his hand back and forth. "No, no. That would be," he wrinkled his face, "inhumane. The process, the idea let's say, is public knowledge now. We've spread the word to every corporation on Earth."

"So why the patent? Why *any* secrecy?"

Hall drew deeply from his cigar, looking at the ceiling. He blew out a heavy cloud and pointed to Blake with the stogie dancing between his fingers. "As you may know, Jonas Salk pioneered a working Polio vaccine with money from the University of Pittsburgh and what we now call the March of Dimes. But come time to replicate the results and push it out to the masses, they needed a pharmaceutical giant to handle the job. If Salk's lab was the oracle, GlaxoSmithKline was their Hermes."

"But they never patented the vaccine," Blake said.

Hall slapped the table and laughed again. "A learned man. I knew I had the right tool for the job the moment I read your proposal."

Blake winced at the odd compliment.

"That's right. They didn't patent it. Salk assured the reporters that the vaccine belonged to the people. And they spread the kitchen science to every country that would listen, even Cold War enemies in Soviet Russia and China. You bet. But while underfunded labs tried to replicate Salk's work, where do you think they had to turn to solve their immediate problems? To save their kids right now instead of *years* from now?"

"Big pharma."

"Right again, Captain. And that's us. Sure, we'll tell you the good news: the monsters gotta eat too, and if you can starve them out, it beats nuking your own backyard. But in the meantime…"

"We'll do it for you," Blake said. "For a price."

"That's the hat trick, Captain, and you got it. They don't have *you*. Well, you and your plans, which are *our* plans."

Blake took another drag, but the tobacco tasted off now. He ejected the smoke as soon as he pulled it. "I could train people. Get them to do what we did in the desert. Probably better."

"No time," Hall said, his smile fading.

"When you called me here, you said—"

"I knew you'd come when you were ready," Hall said. "No

point rushing you until you'd wrapped your head around it. But now, the die is cast. You're scheduled in Tehran in two days. Bejing in five. Los Angeles in a week. To repeat your good work at the crater."

"That's not possible."

"With GenTek's coffers, maybe not. But with the endless resources of every corporation at your disposal… you'll do fine."

"I lost men. I need to refine the process, smooth corners—"

"A hundred people have perished since we began this conversation. For every puff of your cigar, a dozen men, women, and children become food for the monsters."

"We got lucky."

"There is no luck, Major Blake," Hall said, and slid over the white envelope with the same practiced grace as he had the ashtray.

Blake put a trembling hand atop the thick paper, propped the cigar in the ashtray, and pulled the envelope from the glass-like tabletop.

From inside, he removed a tri-folded sheet of paper with a GenTek logo in gold at the bottom.

"I'm a major now," Blake said, reading.

"That's right," Hall said.

Blake pulled another piece of paper from the envelope, its watermark evident in the light pouring in from behind Hall. The check was for a million dollars. Even after the hyper-inflation and crashing markets that followed the monster invasion, the amount sent a chill over him.

The envelope still weighed heavy in his hands, and he held it up to the light. The gray outline of a key shone against the milky white of the paper. He shook the metal into his open palm.

"Right here in Manhattan," Hall said, answering Blake's unasked question. "Room for a family—"

"I have no family," Blake said.

"Then make one."

Blake set the contents of the envelope onto the desk. "I want Easy. And Fisher and Finnel."

"You got it."

"All my troops. And no goddamn film crew following me around. And lifetime pay for the dependents of those who fall in battle."

"It's all yours."

"I still don't get it," Blake said.

"What's that?"

"You backed the endgame. Now everyone else knows how to bring them down. Or close to it. Even if you did nothing now, we'd beat the monsters eventually. Why the whole mercenary thing? I get the money angle, but could it be that much?"

Hall shook his head and set his own cigar into a twin crystal ashtray. "You want to know why we're doing this? It's because we owe you. All of you. A few thousand years ago, men worshiped fire or the moon or the sun. Then they worshiped gods. They'd sacrifice their own lives for them. Then it was nations. Now corporations command more money and resources than any government, and without all the red tape and bureaucratic nonsense."

"So what? *You're* the gods now?"

Hall shrugged, but a smile crept to his lips. "Something like that. But we're only as powerful as your faith in us. And no matter why these big bastards are here, we can't sell widgets so long as they are. You get me?"

Blake gathered up the key, the check, and his promotion papers, and stuffed them back into the envelope. He stood and snubbed out the cigar. "I think so, sir."

Hall rose as well. He pulled in a deep breath. "Through cunning and craft."

Blake nodded. "Through cunning and craft." He shook the envelope. "And a few more of these."

Hall laughed, gestured to the door, and turned toward the bay windows to stare out over his domain.

ABOUT THE AUTHORS

Charlie Allison is a writer based in West Philadelphia, where he works as a storyteller and swimming instructor. When he isn't scrubbing chlorine from his body or the antics of his role-playing group from his forebrain, he can be found re-learning how to cook, standing on his head, and perfecting his Nahuatl suffixes. His first novel is forthcoming and involves the transnational nature of worship, inter-planar rail-lines, murder and of course, spiders that infiltrate the subconscious. Charlie Allison recently received his MFA from Arcadia University's creative writing program. His work has previously appeared in *Podcastle, Ellipsis Zine, Stonecoast Review, Devilfish Review* and *Bride of Chaos*. He runs a forum for writers at http://fitsofprint.proboards.com, and he can be found on Twitter @cballison421.

Justin Bailey holds a Master's degree in Writing Popular Fiction from Seton Hill University under the mentorship of novelist Tim Waggoner. He has previously been published in *Nightmare Magazine, Blood in the Rain 2*, and *Old Scratch and Owl Hoots: A Collection of Utah Horror.*

John M. Campbell is an engineer who spent thirty-five years in the aerospace industry. He has a master's degree in electrical engineering and led engineering teams building computer systems for the government. Now, he speculates on the worlds currently unknown to us that modern physics may unlock. He is compelled by the promise technology offers to address many of the issues facing human survival. He is fascinated by the prospect of extraterrestrial life in our solar system in Mars and the outer planets. He is intrigued by the likelihood that machine intelligence will likely surpass man's ability to control it in this century. He hopes sanity prevails on this planet, and humans live to see this future. The Loponine Exploitation is his fourth published short story. He lives with his wife in Denver, Colorado.

L Chan hails from Singapore, where he alternates being walked by his dog and writing speculative fiction after work. His work has appeared in places like *Liminal Stories, Metaphorosis Magazine,* and *Arsenika*. He tweets occasionally @lchanwrites.

Jeff Deck is a fiction ghostwriter and editor whose writing has been featured on the Today Show. He lives in Maine with his wife, Jane, and their silly dog, Burleigh. Deck writes science fiction, fantasy, horror, dark fantasy, and other speculative fiction, as well as helping other authors tell their stories. Deck's latest book is the supernatural thriller novel *The Pseudo-Chronicles of Mark Huntley*. His previous book is the sci-fi gaming adventure novel *Player Choice*. Deck is also the author, with Benjamin D. Herson, of the nonfiction book *The Great Typo Hunt: Two Friends Changing the World, One Correction at a Time* (Crown/Random House). He has a story in the anthology *Murder Ink 2: Sixteen More Tales of New England Newsroom Crime* (Plaidswede). Get a **FREE** book when you subscribe to Deck's e-mail updates. Just go to: www.jeffdeck.com.

By day, **Evan Dicken** studies old Japanese maps and crunches data for all manner of fascinating medical research at the Ohio State University. By night, he does neither of these things. His short fiction has most recently appeared in: *Apex, Beneath Ceaseless Skies,* and *Tales to Terrify,* and he has stories forthcoming from publishers such as Chaosium and *Analog*. Feel free to visit him at evandicken.com, where he wastes both his time and yours.

Todd H. C. Fischer is a graduate of York University in Canada, with a double honors BA in English and Creative Writing, where he studied many different forms of literature and poetry. He has had work appear in several publications around the world and has published almost two dozen books though his own publishing house (Stonebunny Press). Mr. Fischer has had work recently appear in (or is slated to appear in): *The Compleat Anachronist* (a medievalist journal), *Helios Quarterly, NonBinary Review,* and *The Healing Muse.* You can read more about Todd H. C. Fischer on his website: http://todd-fischer.com.

Ethan Gibney is easiest understood if you know that the two pieces of media that most informed his aesthetic were the Sherlock Holmes stories and The Addams Family. His Gomez is John Astin, his Bond is Timothy Dalton, his Holmes is Jeremy Brett and his Doctor is Peter Davison. He drinks his cider brewed with chai spices. His affection for the King in Yellow may be because he's also a theatre person, but it's also possible he just likes yellow cloaks and pallid masks. Who doesn't? Check out his website at www.ethanmgibney.com.

Marcus Johnston grew up a navy brat, so after moving many times in his childhood, he was infected with a permanent wanderlust. He's traveled the world working in international schools, before finding himself in the corporate world, becoming a mercenary teacher who travels the US selling his training to the highest bidder. Through his travels, Marcus often finds himself between worlds, so its not surprising that his characters do as well. When he does get home to Phoenix, Arizona, he comes home to his wife and two kids, who don't bother to read his stories, so he shares them with those who will.

Gordon Linzner is editor emeritus of *Space and Time Magazine*, and the author of three published novels and dozens of short stories that have seen print in numerous magazines and anthologies, including *The Magazine of Fantasy and Science Fiction* and *Rod Serling's Twilight Zone Magazine*.

Adrian Ludens is the author of *Ant Farm Necropolis* (A Murder of Storytellers LLC), and is a member of the Horror Writers Association with Active status. Recent and favorite publication appearances include *DOA 3* (Blood Bound Books), *HWA Poetry Showcase IV*, *Blood in the Rain 3* (Cwtch Press), and *Zippered Flesh 3* (Smart Rhino Publications). Adrian is a radio announcer and a fan of hockey, reading and writing horror fiction, swimming, and exploring abandoned buildings. Visit him at www.adrianludens.com.

Marie Michaels is a lawyer and nerd living in Portland, Oregon. Her short stories have appeared in anthologies including *Visions V: Milky Way*, *Tell Me a Fable*, and *Rejected*, and the webzines *Fiction Vortex* and *Devolution Z*. Upcoming stories will appear in *Keeping Pace with Eternity* and *New Legends: Mercenary, Engineer, Captain v. 2*. She tweets about science fiction, fantasy, writing and feminism at @lavidanerdy and can be found on Facebook.

Adam Millard is the author of thirteen novels and more than a hundred short stories, which can be found in various collections and anthologies. Probably best known for his post-apocalyptic fiction, Adam also writes fantasy/horror for children. He created the character Peter Crombie, Teenage Zombie just so he had something decent to read to his son at bedtime. Adam also writes Bizarro fiction for several publishers, who enjoy his tales of flesh-eating clown-beetles and rabies-infected derrieres so much that they keep printing them. His "Dead" series has been the filling in a Stephen King/Bram

Stoker sandwich on Amazon's bestsellers chart, and the translation rights have recently sold to German publisher, Voodoo Press. Adam also writes for *This Is Horror*, whose columnists include Shaun Hutson, Simon Bestwick and Simon Marshall-Jones. Adam lives in the post-apocalyptic landscape known as Wolverhampton, England, with his wife, Zoe, and son, Phoenix.

Nicholas Nacario is an author and award-winning graphic designer living in the beautiful Pacific Northwest. His work can be found in *Destroy All Robots* (Dunhams Manor Press), *Ill-Considered Expeditions* (April Moon Books), shoggoth.net, microphonesofmadness.wordpress.com, *The Chabot Review*, and in the forthcoming anthology *Puncture Wounds* (Stygian Fox Publishing). He splits his time between designing books for the respective Call of Cthulhu and Fiction product lines for Chaosium Inc. and dreaming about living on a Polynesian-style outrigger canoe in the Pacific Ocean.

Harry Pauff writes science fiction, fantasy, and horror and lives in Maryland with his wife and two cats. He tries to write as much as possible, but when not writing he's reading, playing basketball, traveling, or making blood sacrifices to this thing that lives in his house and meows at him all day. Follow him on Twitter @HarryNotGood.

Pete Rawlik is the author of more than fifty short stories, the novels *Reanimators*, *The Weird Company*, and *Reanimatrix*, and *The Peaslee Papers*, a chronicle of the distant past, the present, and the far future. As editor he has produced *The Legacy of the Reanimator* and the forthcoming *Chromatic Court*. His short story *Revenge of the Reanimator* was nominated for a New Pulp Award. He is a regular member of the *Lovecraft Ezine Podcast* which in 2016 won the *This is Hor-*

ror Non-Fiction Podcast of the year award. He is a frequent contributor to the *New York Review of Science Fiction*.

Sam Rent grew up and lives in New Orleans, Louisiana. He was working behind a register while writing this story.

Andrew Scott writes fantasy, horror, science fiction, alt-history and myth in prose and comics. His most recent work appeared in an anthology about Salmiakki, reportedly the most disgusting sweet in the world.

Max D. Stanton is an academic and a student of the weird who lives in Philadelphia. His literary heroes include Cormac McCarthy, H.P. Lovecraft, Charles Portis, and R.A. Wilson. He is outnumbered by his animals, and increasingly fears that they are conspiring against him. Max has published fiction in magazines including *Hinnom*, *Lovecraftiana*, and *Sanitarium*. He has new stories forthcoming in the anthologies *Pickman's Gallery*, *Year's Best Transhuman Sci-Fi*, and *Death's Garden*. Feel free to contact him via the Book of Faces or Twitter (@max_d_stanton).

Edward Stasheff is wanted in thirteen states for armchair anarchy, contributing to the delinquency of everyone, and criminally bad jokes. Despite his growing notoriety and infamy, he remains a big nerd. He has a short story appearing in Elm Books' steampunk mystery anthology *Death and the Age of Steam* coming soon in 2018. *Corporate Cthulhu* is his first time organizing and editing an anthology, but hopefully not his last.

In his life, **Josh Storey** has only ever had three career ambitions: astronaut, Superman, and writer. Since he's no good at math and (as far as his parents will admit) not from Krypton, he's going with option three. A reformed pantser and proud

Shimmer badger, Josh occasionally blathers about writing, comic books, and other geekery on twitter @soless. You can find his other stories at www.phantasypunk.com.

David Tallerman is the author of the YA fantasy series *The Black River Chronicles*, which began in late 2016 with *Level One* and continues in 2017 with *The Ursvaal Exchange*, the *Tales of Easie Damasco* series, and the Tor.com novella *Patchwerk*. His comics work includes the absurdist steampunk graphic novel *Endangered Weapon B: Mechanimal Science* and the Rosarium miniseries *C21st Gods*. David's short stories have appeared in around eighty markets, including *Clarkesworld*, *Nightmare*, *Alfred Hitchcock Mystery Magazine* and *Beneath Ceaseless Skies*. A number of his best dark fantasy and horror stories were gathered together in his debut collection *The Sign in the Moonlight and Other Stories*. He can be found online at davidtallerman.co.uk.

John Taloni has been reading SF/F since he was eight and stumbled across a copy of Alexei Panshin's *Rite of Passage*. His major influences include Anne McCaffrey and Larry Niven. His interest in horror stems from Neil Gaiman's *Sandman* series. Taloni is a long-time attendee at SF conventions, and he met his wife while dressed as a Pernese dragon rider. Their daughter asked at the age of four if they could watch more of the show with "the robots that say 'exterminate' ", and the entire family has happily watched *Doctor Who* together ever since.

Darren Todd writes short fiction full time, along with freelance book editing for Evolved Publications and narrating the occasional audiobook for Audible, Inc. His short fiction has appeared in twenty-four publications over the last eleven years. He has had four plays produced and a non-fiction book published. While many of his works fall under the literary umbrella, he often returns to horror. His style and reading preferences tend toward the psychological, as he enjoys stories that linger in the imagination long after he's closed the book on them. He lives in Scottsdale, Arizona with his wife and son and does his best work in coffee shops on a dated word processor. Find more at darrentodd.net.

DJ Tyrer is the person behind Atlantean Publishing and has been widely published in anthologies and magazines around the world, such as *Chilling Horror Short Stories* (Flame Tree), *Cthulhu Haiku and Other Mythos Madness* (Popcorn Press), *Sorcery & Sanctity: A Homage to Arthur Machen* (Hieroglyphics Press), *Tales of the Black Arts* (Hazardous Press), *Ill-considered Expeditions* (April Moon Books), *Cosmic Horror* (Dark Hall Press), and *Steampunk Cthulhu* (Chaosium), as well as having a Yellow Mythos novella available in paperback and on the Kindle, *The Yellow House* (Dunhams Manor). Check out his website at djtyrer.blogspot.co.uk, or follow him on Twitter @djtyrer.

Wile E. Young is an author of the bizarre, horrific, and fantastical. When not fleeing from angry mobs or tormenting members of various schools and universities, he can be found running, playing a video game of some sort, stitching someone up on the side of the road, or hanging out with his friends. No matter what, he will always be writing when the day ends.

81398912R00231

Made in the USA
Lexington, KY
16 February 2018